A PROPHET WITHOUT HONOR... TO SAY THE LEAST!

Many questions arose after Tananius-Ofo, God of the Universe, selected Evander Harold McMurtrey to deliver a startling celestial message. Certainly McMurtrey, of the small planet D'Urth, was no religious leader to rival Hoddha, Zillaster, Krassos or Isammed. He was merely the self-proclaimed Grand Exalted Rooster of "ICCC," the Interplanetary Church of Cosmic Chickenhood. Never before in history had God spoken through such a droll personage...

The Race for God

Praise For Brian Herbert's <u>Prisoners of Arionn:</u>

"A fresh approach to one of science fiction's classic themes."
—*New York Times*

"Vividly imagined...Every time you round a corner in this novel, bright bits and ideas surprise you!"   —*Fantasy Review*

"Filled with wit and action...featuring a cast of the quirkiest individuals science fiction has seen in a long time."
—Paul Preuss

"A great story...a great new talent!"   —A.E. Van Vogt

"A bewitching book...fascinating!"   —Roger Zelazny

Other Books by Brian Herbert

MEMORYMAKERS (with Marie Landis)
THE NOTEBOOKS OF DUNE (Editor)
PRISONERS OF ARIONN
MAN OF TWO WORLDS (with Frank Herbert)
SUDANNA, SUDANNA
THE GARBAGE CHRONICLES
SIDNEY'S COMET
INCREDIBLE INSURANCE CLAIMS
CLASSIC COMEBACKS

THE RACE FOR GOD

BRIAN HERBERT

ACE BOOKS, NEW YORK

This book is an Ace original edition,
and has never been previously published.

THE RACE FOR GOD

An Ace Book / published by arrangement with
the author

PRINTING HISTORY
Ace edition / August 1990

All rights reserved.
Copyright © 1990 by Brian Herbert.
Cover art by Joe Burleson.
This book may not be reproduced in whole or in part,
by mimeograph or any other means, without permission.
For information address: The Berkley Publishing Group,
200 Madison Avenue, New York, New York 10016.

ISBN: 0-441-70283-X

Ace Books are published by The Berkley Publishing Group,
200 Madison Avenue, New York, New York 10016.
The name "ACE" and the "A" logo
are trademarks belonging to Charter Communications, Inc.

PRINTED IN THE UNITED STATES OF AMERICA

10 9 8 7 6 5 4 3 2 1

For Darel Jenkins and Audrey Alande

Prologue

Many questions arose after Tananius-Ofo, God of the Universe, selected Evander Harold McMurtrey to deliver a startling celestial message. Certainly McMurtrey, of the small planet D'Urth, was no religious leader to rival Hoddha, Zillaster, Krassos or Isammed. He was merely the self-proclaimed Grand Exalted Rooster of "ICCC," the Interplanetary Church of Cosmic Chickenhood.

Never before in history had God spoken through such a droll personage.

It was a crazy time anyway, even before the Holy Event. One escaped Tenusian dissident termed it "an age of peculiar turmoil, of war mania without evidence of war." According to government propaganda, the terraformed planets Tenusia, Maros, and Ercu were allied with D'Urth in the "Inner Planet League," opposing a like "Outer Planet Confederacy" comprising the rest of the solar system. Inner Planet dissidents were hunted down routinely by Bureau of Loyalty agents and executed without trial. Often the executions became public spectacles with bizarre means of death, scenes that had chilling and predictable effects upon the populace.

No one acquainted with McMurtrey knew where the war zones were, if they existed at all, and he didn't pursue the topic. Rumors favored Saturus or the larger moons of Ranus.

McMurtrey, like every other Inner Planet citizen, had to take annual loyalty oaths, and the Bureau assigned him a "Loyalty Quotient." It was like the old IQ number except it was called "LQ" and had other connotations beyond being smart enough not to oppose the system. McMurtrey didn't have any idea what his own LQ number was, but he knew braggarts who professed to have high numbers.

1

He didn't care much about any of that, except to the extent that he tried to stay out of trouble.

He had been fairly successful in that regard for a number of years, but he sensed the old ways would never work for him again. . . .

One

In the vast majority of religions, the really nasty practices and beliefs aren't documented in sacred texts. These have become matters of practice, of oral tradition or simply of interpretation. Nowhere is it written, for example, that women, blacks and physically handicapped persons cannot be priests in the Church of Modern Day Believers. But this is the way of the organization. For this and allied reasons I say to you: Dismantle every religion.

—General Commentary,
Autobiography of Tananius-Ofo

"Don't waste my time," the little man at the cluttered desk said. "We don't print rubbish in the *Crier*!"

With two thick pillows on his chair, he still sat lower than McMurtrey. This was James Robbins, the cantankerous managing editor of the St. Charles Beach *Crier*, a man whose reputation held he never smiled. He was young, with pale gray eyes.

"Every word is the truth!" McMurtrey heard his voice crack, looked away. *I can't sound anxious*, he thought. *But I've got to get the message out*!

It was a musty, paper-cluttered postage stamp of an office, with only one other desk and no one at it. Muffled voices and sounds of machinery came from the other side of a wall to the rear.

"I know about you," Robbins said. "The Grand Exalted Rooster . . . the wacko who goes around with a chicken on his shoulder." His tone became smooth, an irritating whine: "Where is your little pet this morning?"

"I didn't have to come to your flea-bitten office. Any big city press would—"

The editor sneered, motioned toward a computer terminal by his desk. "We're all on NewsData. They could find out about you in seconds—unless you used a phony name. But you wouldn't dare do that, would you?"

Against Bureau rules, McMurtrey thought. *Presumption of disloyalty.*

"It happens that I've known about you for quite a while, McMurtrey—everyone in these parts does. Is that rumor true? Did your feisty chicken really peck a man's eyes out in the last town you lived in?"

McMurtrey didn't know where the rumor of his pet's ferocity came from, had never protested it.

"And that mantra of yours, how does it go?"

"Listen, you—"

"It's coming back to me. 'O Chubby Mother, let me rubba your belly . . . let me rubba your belly.' " He waggled the thumb and forefinger of one hand in the beaklike ritual of McMurtrey's organization.

"You're a rude little twerp."

The editor's eyes flashed. "You wanna start calling names, fella? I could burn your ears, but lucky for you I'm in a good mood today. Speaking of names, what is it you call that chicken? No Name, right?"

McMurtrey sighed, didn't recall telling anyone about that. Nervously, he rubbed one finger against a broken wooden edge on his chair.

"Your chicken has green plumes and you can walk around with it on one of your big wide shoulders. What is it, a mutant parrot?"

"I had it checked by an expert once," McMurtrey replied. "He said it was a light Rahma, but a most unusual one, with unique plumage."

"I see."

"Aren't you going to enter that in the data base?"

"Later, maybe. Does it ever defecate on your shoulder?"

McMurtrey shook his head, felt a vein throbbing in his temple. "We get along fine. Look, I don't have to defend myself. This is the biggest scoop of your squalid little life. It's exactly like I told you. I was lying in bed this morning, just waking up, and God spoke to me. He told me where He is, gave me the exact astronomical coordinates!"

"Yeah, yeah. At the break of dawn. You said His first words were 'Seeker, who says religion is the way to God?' What the hell is that supposed to be—some kind of trumped-up justification for your offbeat society? Is this a publicity stunt?"

"No! The ICCC is a religion, too!"

"Don't try to kid me. I think you're up to something."

"You're impossible!"

"Why were you chosen, of all people?"

"I don't know!"

"How did you say it went? Words were floating in the airspace above you . . . little flashes of voice-accompanied white light on glimmering wavetops—as if the bedroom air were ocean water and you were above the surface looking down on it—a surface that hung over you, defying gravity."

"That's close."

"You're damn right it's close. That's my business. I don't misquote. And I don't print lies."

McMurtrey sighed, stared at the ceiling. It was a sprayed-on rough texture, off-white with a brown scrape mark near one wall.

When God's voice had come to him, it made him feel insignificant and dominated, but in retrospect he didn't think it had been a complete, all-consuming domination. The voice had been urgent and curiously plaintive, not the expected commanding tone. It gave McMurtrey the feeling he could have refused to deliver God's message.

How could he feel this way, that a request from on high was not an edict?

Of course he didn't oppose it, for God had selected him from all others for a momentous occasion, an unheard-of occasion. McMurtrey couldn't wait to discover more. Since childhood, he'd felt a deep longing to know God, a longing that hadn't waned with the formation of his farcical Interplanetary Church of Cosmic Chickenhood. Now he had the opportunity to fulfill the penultimate dream of anyone's life, from a package of information thrust conveniently on his lap. But first he had to get past fools like this.

McMurtrey lowered his gaze. The editor was bent over

the computer screen, an amber-lit unit, reading Mc-
Murtrey's dossier.

"I've never printed a word about you," Robbins said,
without turning his head. "People know you're a fraud,
and I have my own reputation to consider."

"So you refuse to run the story?"

"I haven't decided."

"Well, I have." McMurtrey lunged his big frame up and
made for the door to the street. He was ready to slam the
door through the jamb, when the editor spoke.

"Come back and sit down. I'll see what we can use."

McMurtrey looked over his shoulder, and they locked
gazes.

Robbins shook his head. "Credibility you ain't got. I
don't know why I'm doing this." He turned back to the
computer, began tapping keys.

McMurtrey resumed his seat, watched black letters appear on the screen as the managing editor wrote about the
visitation.

Robbins paused. "NewsData says there are around nine
thousand church members in your I Triple C. Do those
members know it's a scam? Are they in for the fun of it?
With an acronym pronounced 'ICK' they'd have to suspect
something. I'm sorry, but a lot of details keep bothering
me."

"I'm not here to discuss that," McMurtrey said. "There
is a more important matter." From the correspondence he
received, it was clear that most of his members believed
the drivel he'd made up about D'Urth being "an egg of
the Great Mother Chicken, the originator of all life in the
universe." A few recognized the ICCC as a spoof, to their
great amusement.

"Just a couple of details before we proceed," the editor
insisted. "I've got to make you sound credible. With a
message from God, that's critical, I'd say."

McMurtrey sighed. "All right."

"You started this organization out with ads—almost
twenty years ago, after you dropped out of college. Rumor
has it you didn't expect any response, that you'd been
freebasing sparkle. And *voilà*! Checks started pouring in!"

"I wasn't on drugs!" *Not when I ran the ads, anyway*.

McMurtrey stared at his hands, recalled crawling around

on the floor of his college dormitory room several months before he ran the ads, looking for spilled bits of Anian sparkle. He and three buddies came up with the chicken church that uproarious night, and before the evening was over they carried the concept to preposterous extremes. Afterward, his buddies promptly forgot about it.

But McMurtrey didn't forget.

"You're not making this easy," Robbins said. "Your grandmother invented pickpocket-proof trousers, and I see you're wearing a pair. She made a bundle, left you with a trust fund. Are you still living off it or do you need publicity?"

"What's the matter?" McMurtrey asked. "Don't you have all the answers in your precious NewsData?"

An uncomfortable pause. Then: "Okay, we'll stick to the visitation, and I'll try to make it sound plausible."

McMurtrey repeated his tale, and presently he was outside with an unseasonably warm winter breeze on his face. The air was clean, a contrast to the mustiness of the office. He walked home through the hilly seaside town, thinking about one of God's more curious comments.

"Seeker, who says religion is the way to God?"

This had rattled McMurtrey to the core when he heard it—so much so that for agonizing moments as God continued to speak, McMurtrey couldn't think of a thing to say. He was turned sideways in bed, staring at a pearly, many-chambered nautilus shell that had fallen from the dresser to the carpeted floor months before. He hadn't bothered to pick it up, had hardly noticed it before the "visitation." Frequently he didn't get around to housekeeping anyway.

But as the Leader of the Universe spoke, McMurtrey found himself staring at the shell as if he had never seen it before. The chambers displayed were so exquisitely detailed, coiling to the core where the tiny animal once lived. In its utter perfection, the design brought to mind leaf patterns, spider webs, honeycombs and the flawless rippling wavelets caused by a stone dropped in a pond.

Recalling this, McMurtrey crossed a sandy field of ice plants, heading toward his modest bungalow on the other side, a tiny driftwood gray structure several houses up from the beach.

There had been something else too, something he hadn't told the editor. One statement of God's, in a voice that pulsed weak and strong, was especially provocative: "Cosmic Chickenhood is not everything. It might amount to nothing, along with everything else."

McMurtrey chewed at one side of his upper lip.

What did that mean? "might amount to nothing . . ." *Might.* The Interplanetary Church of Cosmic Chickenhood might amount to something then, something important if it deserved God's special attention.

And the voice—mellifluous at times, barely audible at others—like a distant, struggling radio signal. It was not as McMurtrey imagined the God soundtrack should be, but in the marrow of his bones he sensed authenticity.

It scared the hell out of him.

Beyond the rooftops of town, along the horizon between the broad Bluepac Ocean and the cerulean sky, dark clouds were forming. McMurtrey picked up his pace.

Late that afternoon, McMurtrey touched his Wriskron to deactivate the alarm system on his pickpocket-proof trousers, opened three sequential pocket zippers that were keyed to his metabolism so that they could be undone only by him. He removed two sorneys, dropped the coins into the newspaper vending machine, and they clicked into place. The glass front of the machine slid open, and a scoop on a mechanical arm thrust a newspaper into McMurtrey's hands.

He rezipped his pockets, set the alarm system on his trousers.

It was late afternoon, overcast, and as McMurtrey opened the newspaper a few raindrops spattered dark little splotches on the pages. He located the article on a back page, and it was headed: "STARTLING ANNOUNCEMENT BY CHICKEN MAN."

He flew into an instant rage.

Chicken man! How he hated that appellation! The implications were obvious.

He read on:

"ST. CHARLES BEACH, Wessornia of D'Urth— Some of you who are familiar with Evander Harold

McMurtrey have never taken his words seriously. How does one take this man seriously? After all, his religious ritual involves waggling a thumb and forefinger together as if they were upper and lower beaks, while uttering this mantra:

'O Chubby Mother,
Let me rubba your belly...
Let me rubba your belly.'

There is more which good taste prohibits describing, and for manifest reasons we in his home town have never before published anything by him or about him. But this unbearded holy man told our managing editor today in an eery, strangely convincing fashion that God revealed His location to him at dawn in some sort of an oral visitation, that God is domiciled on the planet Tananius-Ofo in the barely discernible galaxy 722C12009. This planet, according to Mr. McMurtrey, is at the origin of the universe, and is stationary. You-Know-Who lives there, and He's waiting to be visited by man. The Big Guy has, it seems, invited us to tea.

There is the slight problem of several trillion parsecs between us and 722C12009, but Mr. McMurtrey indicates that this poses no obstacle, for God is at this moment preparing the means by which we can narrow the gap. 'Devices' (unexplained term) will be made available soon. 'Tomorrow or the day after,' McMurtrey said. 'I didn't hear that part clearly.'

As to how his own pseudoreligion of Cosmic Chickenhood ties in, the Grand Exalted Rooster did not seem to know.

Tune in tomorrow, or the next day."

A heavy vehicle rattled across a speed bump, and McMurtrey looked up from where he stood by the vending machine. The county bookmobile pulled into its usual spot in the parking lot.

He rolled the newspaper in one hand, and when the bookmobile door swung open, he boarded behind an elderly man who was carrying an armload of book-tapes.

The vehicle shook with each step that McMurtrey took, for his corpulence registered in excess of 150 kilos.

The librarian, an effeminate young man with closely cropped blond hair, stood behind a desk at the rear. He was new, had a trembling lower lip that McMurtrey tried not to look at.

A short while after his period of drug abuse, McMurtrey developed a severe problem in which he couldn't help noticing a person's mannerisms: He became distracted to the point of speechlessness by little tics. He'd been to innumerable doctors during his life, but none of them, not even the most expensive psychoformers, had been of any assistance.

McMurtrey's gaze flitted involuntarily back to the librarian, to the still-quivering lip. The librarian removed foil from a plate of cookies and placed the plate to one side of the counter, apparently for patrons.

McMurtrey cleared his throat, spoke with an absence of difficulty that surprised him. He asked for a read-along cassette of Savnoy's *Critique On Scholastic Theology*, requested the week before.

This guy has a bad tic, McMurtrey thought. He stared at the quivering lip, felt unaffected, and breathed a tentative sigh of relief. It had been a most disquieting problem, and he wondered now if God's visitation that very morning might have something to do with the improvement. Maybe it was intended as proof, a small-scale miracle. In any event, McMurtrey hoped it would last.

The librarian searched through two stacks of book-tapes behind him.

A black fly buzzed irritatingly in McMurtrey's face and landed on his nose. McMurtrey shook his head, swatted at the insect, and it circled his head, relanded on an ear. McMurtrey swatted the insect away, but within moments it was back once more upon his nose, as if it had landing rights there.

McMurtrey had been through this before. St. Charles Beach flies were tenacious, worse than he had seen in any other climate or locale. The creatures weren't content to crawl along windows or counter tops. They didn't look for ways out of rooms, didn't even seem to care much about morsels of unattended food. They hovered in people's faces.

McMurtrey shook his head briskly and used the rolled newspaper this time, making wild passes through the air. The fly disappeared from view, may have lodged itself in his hair. He didn't feel it, gave up the effort.

"Oh, there you are, Savnoy," the librarian said, locating a cassette that had been lying on its edge behind one pile. He held the book-tape up so that McMurtrey could read the title on its spine. It looked like one of the old-fashioned books still sold in specialty shops, but this was thinner than most of them, with a single cassette inside the cover.

For as long as he could remember, McMurtrey had been intrigued by the different facets of religion, all the major faiths. But the more he learned, the more utterly confused about God he became. He had always been convinced of God's existence and longed to know God, but none of the doctrinal categories formed by other men seemed acceptable to him.

When the checkout procedure was completed, the librarian chirped, "Have a nice day, sir." His lip stopped quivering, and he presented a warmed-over, unimpassioned smile, the sort everyone who stepped up to this counter probably received.

"Do something about the flies in this place," McMurtrey said. "And don't give me any of that 'nice day' crap, you phony functionary!"

"All right," came the response, with hardly a missed beat. "Fuck you, sir. Are you happy now?" These words were in the identical "Have a nice day" tone, with the same smile.

McMurtrey felt his jaw drop, and his eyes opened so wide in surprise that they ached.

The irritating fellow held his expression and gazed off insipidly into the distance, civil-servant fashion. He showed no appearance of hostility.

McMurtrey whirled and left without another word, carrying the newspaper and book-tape.

Someday I'll use my God pipeline to take care of guys like that, McMurtrey thought.

He cast an anxious gaze at the gray sky over the Bluepac Ocean, half expecting fiery thunder to lash him for the impropriety of what he'd been thinking. It did begin to rain harder, but maybe it would have done so anyway. Nervously, McMurtrey hurried home.

Two evenings later, in Rimil, Wessornia of D'Urth...
Johnny Orbust let the fingers of his left hand dangle at his side and stared into the big red electronic eye mounted on one wall of his apartment. A digital counter beneath the eye ticked off thousandths of a second in reverse, and beneath that, a computer-selected scriptural reference was displayed, in black on amber letters: "Omanus 5:12."

When the counter reached zero, the eye turned green.

Orbust's hand darted across his body to a shoulder holster concealed beneath his sportscoat, making a soft, rapid slap of leather. Almost instantly he had a black Babul open in both hands, and Omanus 5:12 was beneath one forefinger.

The counter showed his time: 3.414 seconds. Not his best performance, but not bad, either. Orbust practiced constantly, keeping himself in shape for the religious arguments he had a habit of getting into.

He patted an .85 caliber elephant pistol on his hip, smiled at the thought of adversaries who stammered and perspired whenever he unclipped the holster flap. He could never shoot a human, and only once, with an obstinate MDB missionary, had he even drawn the piece. Orbust had toyed with the ammo clip while the terrified missionary glanced around for avenues of escape.

Supposedly military-issue, the gun was part of a miniaturized weapons and demolition kit he picked up cheap from a door-to-door Bureau of Loyalty-sanctioned armaments salesman. It was a 100 percent prepayment deal, where Orbust received part of the kit on the spot and the rest was supposed to be shipped to him. Secreted cleverly in the holster and the belt were a chemstrip and an array of kill-stun-disable-destroy devices, not all of which worked as represented. Orbust never did receive the additional items in the mail. He had tested what he had on a bunch of old factory-closeout androids and mechanized taxidermy animals that another salesman had unloaded on him earlier, and only half of the devices in the kit worked at all. Some, like the GI Randy Handy Dandy Automatic

Lasso, were out and out duds. But the salesman had left him with no address or telephone number, and there were no brand names on anything to contact manufacturers.

Despite all this, the kit was easily worth its price. The pistol worked admirably, blowing a running droidman in half with surprisingly little recoil. Also, the chemstrip was, in Orbust's words: "neat." A long white strip of plazymer-like material with a built-in microprocessor, it was activated when a user spoke into it, explaining a particular chemical need. The strip then metamorphosed into what looked like a butterfly, and flew off.

Within a few minutes it would return, carrying a white plazymer bag suspended from a harness arrangement under its "body." After setting down, the strip would again become a strip, absorbing the butterfly and the bag and revealing the bag's contents—sometimes pellets, sometimes Plexiglas-like pump sprayers, sometimes vials of liquid or powder. Orbust had employed the device for rat killer, spot remover, and even a miraculous concoction that when sprayed over the fence onto a next door neighbor's unruly pet harbor seal prevented the animal from barking for four weeks, without apparent permanent harm.

Orbust hadn't yet ordered food with the chemstrip, fearing it might malfunction and poison him. He wondered where it obtained raw materials, hoped it was from the natural environment and not from a private party. But the device was BOL-sanctioned, so he didn't have to worry about that. The chemstrip became like a light switch to him, activated when needed without too much thought about its workings.

The weapons kit and quick-draw Babul weren't all Johnny Orbust had in his arsenal-for-God.

In a sheath strapped to one calf he kept his Snapcard, the ultimate verbal combat weapon, the photon bomb of debating.

He didn't use it all the time, because he feared atrophy of the brain, worried about over-reliance on the card. Something could happen to it, and if he lost it where would he be? Nonetheless he had grown more dependent on it than he would have liked.

The Snapcard was, for all intents and purposes, irre-
placeable.

Orbust was, according to his wife Karin, a "money-
squandering gadget freak," and the devices he had all over
the house were a constant source of arguments.

He hadn't made his high-school debating team. Then in
college he vaulted onto the first team, with the help of this
card, a crib card, really. Another salesman had been his
salvation with this baby, an elderly Floriental gentleman
who showed up early one Monday morning and spoke of
recent cataract and back surgery as much as he did of his
wares, apparently to elicit sympathy.

But Orbust hadn't liked anything the man showed him
on the first go-around. A perennial sucker for sales pitches,
Orbust had been a solicitor himself for a time, marketing
advertising novelties . . . and an old saying held that the
easiest person to sell was another salesman. But on this
occasion Orbust was slow to buy. It was early, he felt tired
from not having slept well, and he asked the man to leave.

The salesman requested a glass of water, a familiar stall-
ing technique.

Orbust motioned toward the kitchen. "In there."

Presently the man had a glass of water in hand, and
stood in the kitchen doorway, sipping slowly from the
glass.

"Look," the salesman said. "I was a merchant on Maros,
and we had a tradition there I still follow. You're the first
customer of the week and I have to make a sale or my
whole week is ruined."

"All right, all right. Whattaya have for under five javits?"

The man shook his head, and his epicanthic eyes narrowed. "No, it must be a real sale. Something valuable."

"But you don't have anything I want or need. I'd like
to help you out, but I'm tired and—"

"I have just the thing," the salesman said, smiling in a
strange way that revealed the gums of his teeth.

He set the glass on a table, reached down and lifted one
pant leg. From a calf-strapped sheath he removed a slender
silver metallic card.

"This is ver-r-r-y special," he said.

The card was about the size of a credit card, and he said

there weren't very many of them in existence. The salesman hesitated for a moment, as if deciding whether or not he wanted to go through with what he was about to say.

"What is it?" Orbust asked.

"With this Snapcard in hand, I could sell you anything. It would tell me precisely how to win any argument with you on any subject. I use it—on occasion—but never for the first sale of the week. That wouldn't be right. Even when most desperate, I've never offered it to another customer. But you . . . for some reason . . ."

"If it's so valuable, why sell it to me?"

He considered this for a moment. Then: "I'm getting older, nearing retirement age, and I don't have any children. You seem like a nice young fellow."

The salesman held the card in the upturned palm of one hand and squeezed each end of the card slightly, bending it into a gentle arc.

Orbust stared transfixed at the card. It sparkled with tiny golden lights against silver, lights that danced and spun. A while later he was to recall that looking at the lights had made his eyelids heavy. Now thinking back on this years later, Orbust believed he had been hypnotized by the card, which suggested an explanation of how it worked. But the capabilities of the card went far beyond that. They touched one or more ESP wavelengths and tapped into storehouses of information that were too vast to be confined within any one brain.

He tossed such recollections aside for the moment, became aware of a noise behind him. An organizing robot entered the room, carrying a heap of family pictures. The boxy, simulated-oak robot had shelves and trays all over its body, made accessible by its long flexible arms.

"Is this everything?" the robot asked, in a very sophisticated voice.

Orbust shrugged. "I dunno. I guess."

The robot's eyes flashed green, indicating message received, and it stood to one side, scanning the photographs for chronology and sliding them into compartments. Orbust didn't know how it figured out dates, only knew what he'd heard when he bought it, that it always worked.

Orbust's wife hated the robot, despite the fact that she

was a messy person, one who should have welcomed the device, or so it seemed to him.

She used bad language as well, and Orbust couldn't abide that.

Orbust flipped on the televid and strolled into the kitchen. He opened the upright-freezer door, felt a blast of coolness, and stared without enthusiasm at a leftover plazymer bowl of pastawax he could reheat for dinner.

A news program blared from the televid in the other room, but only bits of information entered his consciousness. He was thinking about his wife, lamenting the problems he had with her.

Karin, his wife of six years, was at a coffeehouse poetry session near the university. Orbust hated those readings, found them boring. Karin was the only money earner in the household, and as a consequence she went where she pleased, whenever she pleased. This had been another source of friction in their lives, and religion was yet another. Orbust had given up trying to discuss religion with his wife, and for nearly a year he had gone off to church without her. He was a Reborn Krassee, one of the recently formed fundamentalist Krassian denominations.

He had the bowl of pastawax in his hands, and as he turned toward the microwave he realized the news announcer had been talking about God.

The oval televid screen was visible through the doorway, and Orbust beheld a most peculiar individual on the screen—an immense man with scraggly hair and what looked like a green-plumed chicken on his shoulder. *Green plumes?* The woman reporter interviewing the man was keeping her distance, because the bird was snapping and hissing and spitting menacingly. Orbust realized in a rush who the man was, from wire-service stories that had been carrying his incredible message across the solar system.

This was the lunatic who said he knew where God was.

"Is it true that the Bureau of Loyalty has approved your spaceships for takeoff, Mr. McMurtrey?" the reporter queried, extending a microphone cautiously.

"Well, I haven't actually been in touch with any BOL people," McMurtrey said, uneasily, "but a reliable intermediary informed me today that the Bureau is staying out of this."

The reporter shook her head, smiled. "I've counted half a dozen red and gold Bureau guncopters in the area, every one of 'em undoubtedly brimming with electronic gizmos. You can bet undercover agents are crawling all over this place."

McMurtrey shifted on his feet. He appeared uncomfortable at the reporter's candor.

In the background, Orbust saw an almost uniform fleet of spaceships, described in recent news accounts. They extended far into the distance in a most unusual straight line, with some perched precariously on frameworks over building tops or straddling streets, as if the whole bunch had been set down indiscriminately from above. They were fat ships of nearly the same size and shape, like big ripe pomegranates with nubby points on top. Some were bright and shiny red, others glistened varying shades of yellow and orange, and others were white. There appeared to have been some consideration for the town beneath the ships, for wherever a building top, fence, or other structure lay beneath, the underside of the craft had been custom-fitted with a shiny metal landing platform that straddled the structure without touching it, so that the weight of the ship actually rested on the ground.

"For those who tuned in late," the reporter said, "tell everyone again where you're going with these ships. I'm still having a hard time believing this."

"We're going to see God!" McMurtrey responded ebulliently.

The reporter faced the camera, and it zoomed in for a close-up of her face. "There you have it, Inner Planet citizens," she said. "Shortly after Mr. McMurtrey's historical announcement of God's location, a fleet of ships appeared in his town from out of nowhere, apparently ready to go. Who will fly them? The Grand Exalted Rooster does not know. Only God, it seems, has this information. No explanation has been tendered as to how the ships got here, but the fact remains that they are here. I have touched their outsides, and they are not apparitions. Something very unusual is occurring here on the Wessornian coast."

Orbust focused on the nearest ship visible, a white craft behind the reporter, and as the picture changed he held the image of the ship in his mind. It looked familiar, inexplicably so, and he felt particularly drawn to it. Despite its apparent similarity to the other ships, there remained something materially different about this one, something intriguing and magnetic.

He had to touch it.

Within an hour, Orbust was on his way to St. Charles Beach by airbus, having exchanged his wife's stash of household money for a note.

TWO

The concept of my memory machine "Mnemo" came to me in a dream that provided a complete vision of the device, its name and its operation. For a long while before, I had postulated a collective genetic memory in mankind, going back to antiquity—one that fired electrochemical impulses along imprinted brain routes, causing people to war repeatedly in the same tragic ways. My theory explained *déjà-vu* and the instantaneous love or hatred people felt for one another, for old emotions never died. I longed to prove that each human life created an overlay of events in the collective brain, a track over old tracks, and that with each new tracking old incidents slipped further into an individual's subconscious. Ancient events were just beneath the surface, and I needed to find them. The miracle of my dream revealed how! A subject connected to my mnemonic machine could carry us back in his memory to the earliest twitchings of all life. Inevitably that had to lead to the Creator Himself, if He existed, and to the singularity of explosion whence the universe began.

—Notes of Professor Nathan Pelter,
League Penitentiary System Archives

A short distance inland from St. Charles Beach, a shiny-black truck-trailer with no chrome or markings slithered along the winding road to Santa Quininas Federal Penitentiary. It was shortly past sunrise, and the rig's tinted windows reflected the day's first rays of sun. The rig came to a stop outside the main gate, hissed its brakes.

A guard in magenta and brown armor stepped from his

booth and waved a transmitter baton at the heavy iron alloy gate. The gate swung open toward the interior of the compound, and the truck went through.

Harley Gutan parked the Dispatch Unit in the same spot as always, by the heavy alloy door that led to Death Row. Wondering how many prisoners would be dispatched this time, he activated the electronic clip pad on the seat by him and noted twenty-nine names.

He felt cold pain in an airspace where a severed little finger once had been, before a childhood tricycling accident. Sometimes he moved the missing finger as if it were in an unseen dimension, even touched it with his other hand and felt it. Now he tucked the affected hand between his flank and the seat cushion, to keep the finger warm.

Why did it get so cold?

In the Inner Planet League, prison authorities no longer executed people with gas, electricity, hanging, lethal injections or Damoclean body crushers. Not since Professor Nathan Pelter left his machine to the Inner Planet League when he died. It wasn't designed as a killing machine, so the story went, but it worked admirably to that purpose, dispatching prisoners on a fantastic journey as they died.

Gutan was a Dispatcher, a euphemistic title selected for public relations purposes.

Pelter had died in his own machine, and rumor held that he went out with a broad smile on his face. An accidental death, some said, but there were other theories extrapolated from rumored personal problems. It was said that his unusual machine could not be opened for servicing or adjustment without destroying it and all of its secrets, and that it couldn't be 'rayed to see its mysterious inner workings. It was one-of-a-kind, and had to be moved between numerous truck-trailer rigs like the one Gutan was in.

So far, to Gutan's knowledge, the machine had required no servicing by the prison system. And it had been used extensively in the half century since Pelter's death, with inmates brought from all over the solar system to facilities accessible by the truck-trailers. There was an order out that the prison system was not to risk flying the machine, based upon statistics proving that these special trucks were the safest means of transport.

None of the criminals that Gutan "dispatched" died with

a smile, although some entered the machine that way. A standard tough con's sneer, usually. Gutan had seen it often. But there was nothing standard in the way they died. Always they screamed before it was over, with death masks twisted into nightmare hideousness.

If Pelter went out with a smile, Gutan thought as the cab door slid open, *he must have been one tough son of a bitch. Either that or he hypnotized himself.*

"What's new and exciting, Harl?" a guard of about Gutan's height asked, coming around the outside of the truck.

Gutan stepped down from the cab and grunted a barely civil and purposefully unintelligible acknowledgment. He touched a button on his Wriskron, locking the truck and setting the vehicular alarm system. With a second press of the button, a light on the time dial flashed pink, indicating the alarms were operational.

The air was cool, with the ground still in shadow and early rays of sunlight glistening from the highest points of the guard towers.

The magenta and brown of the guard's armor matched the prison-system shirt and trousers Gutan wore. The guard's armor was thin but sturdy, of a new and arcane alloy that light artillery projectiles could not penetrate, not even those How-How-tipped, exploding microparticle shells. There were matching helmets, but guards refused to wear them because of razzing from prisoners. It was an act of perceived manhood to go around without a helmet, and it struck Gutan that guards and prisoners were to a great extent of one ilk. He didn't trust any of them.

"Show me the new batch," Gutan said, staring at the door to Death Row. "My schedule is tight, and I want the dispatchees ready when the system goes on-line at seven A.M."

St. Charles Beach was a low-lying town just off the old Bluepac Highway that skirted Wessornia's coast in those days. The town attracted its share of vacationers, mostly in-staters from big cities to the north and south. Its swimming beach was privately owned by one family, the Domingos, and they also owned the general store, the gas pump, and a recreational vehicle campground (Domingo's Reef) that stretched north of town along the dunes.

"No parking" signs were everywhere, as if the place were a breeding ground for them, and they were posted in eclectic unfriendliness by the Domingos and almost everyone else who owned property. One sign that stuck in McMurtrey's memory like a bad song depicted a ferocious, red-bearded cartoon character holding a hogleg handgun. The caption: DON'T EVEN THINK ABOUT PARKING HERE.

It cost twenty javits to get into the swimming beach, seventy-five javits a night for the RV facility, and a visitor couldn't even leave a car in the store parking lot to take a half-hour walk. Tow trucks lurked in alleyways and shadows like hulking muggers, waiting for opportunities. One Domingo son-in-law held the towing concession. He was also the sheriff, a one-man town council, and the local judge, so towing abuses couldn't be appealed.

"A cutthroat town," McMurtrey called it. But he had grown accustomed to the place, even liked it now during the winter off-season. Winters on the Wessornian coast hadn't been cold since earlier in the century when three of the continent's biggest volcanoes went off. The locals got their town back to a great extent at this time of the year . . . except for the parking situation, which irked most everyone at one time or another. At least the locals didn't have to deal with surly, chiseling old Mr. Domingo for supplies, because Faberville was only a couple of miles inland. Prices were better there, and there weren't any "no parking" signs.

As McMurtrey looked out of his living room window, he saw the multicolored pomegranate-shaped flying ships assembled in a long, straight line from the northernmost tip of Domingo's Reef right through the center of town, across building tops, in iceplant-covered yards, and in streets. Throngs of people milled around the ships, waiting to see what would happen next.

They looked like movie extras at an employment hall, so diverse was their raiment. Most were men, some in traditional white or pastel robes, with the long beards and sandals or shaven heads of ascetics. Others resembled ferocious warriors, with sharply cut beards and weapons that hung at angles from their hips—swords, pulverizers, guns, knives and stunbows. Still other men resembled royalty, with gold-trimmed, jewel-encrusted robes, long coats and tiers of jewelry. There were numerous turbans, in a panoply of folds and colors.

The women were nearly as impressive in range, including nuns in plain white or black cotton habits alongside weapon-toting musclefems in flak-resistant jumpsuits. There were even those who could easily have passed for princesses or queens, bedecked as they were in exquisite long gowns with high, swirled coiffures. Some women came to town in elegant landaus, drawn by robotic horses, while others had come long distances on foot.

Life insurance robots worked in the midst of all this, selling flight insurance to people who thought they were going on the journey.

Thus far no one had been able to open a ship's hatch, and despite entreaties from some that he try, McMurtrey hadn't done so. He had a feeling that he could get into any one of them if he wanted to, and that others . . . only certain people with certain ships, the ones they . . . It wasn't clear.

McMurtrey occupied a special position, and realized for the first time as he gazed out on the town that he was one of the few that God had ever selected to deliver messages to mankind.

I am a messenger of God, he thought. *A prophet?*

Several of the ships were white, and one that stood nearest to his bungalow held his attention most often. Sometimes he caught himself staring into its whiteness hypnotically, and when this happened he couldn't recall how long he had been so engrossed. He felt curiously soothed when he finished looking at it, and coming to consciousness was not unlike awakening from a good sleep.

McMurtrey assumed that these were ships, despite their rather unaerodynamic, pudgy shapes. Each vessel had a nubby pointed tip at the top, exhaustlike vents at the bottom, an exterior hatch, and flight-deck-type windshields way up near the top. The ships were too high for a person on a lift truck or ladder truck to see inside the windshields, and thus far McMurtrey had only seen Bureau of Loyalty guncopters and hoverplanes near the ships at that height. The Bureau knew something, and it disturbed McMurtrey that he hadn't heard anything directly from them.

How did the fleet of ships get to St. Charles Beach, and were they really going to transport people to God? A number of people theorized they were full of aliens or Outer Planet warriors, prepared to leap out and carry humans off into subjugation. Some felt the ships ran automatically, with computer-controlled drive systems or robopilots. Others subscribed to none of this: The ships had no controls, no crews, no robots, and were there simply because God willed it so. The last theory seemed easiest for McMurtrey to accept, although paradoxically it was the most illogical and difficult to explain.

Not even Old Man Jacoby, a stargazer and the most nocturnal person in town, had seen or heard the ships arrive. They were just there for everyone to see and marvel at when the sun came up one day. Reportedly, Jacoby only shrugged his shoulders when asked how it could have happened.

Old men doze off, McMurtrey thought. *Or their minds wander. He must have missed something. . . . What an understatement!*

McMurtrey recalled a game he and a friend used to play as children in Ciscola, when they walked over cars instead of around them, denting car tops in the process. They were thoughtless acts, recalled to mind by these ships, the way they had set down wherever they pleased—atop buildings, yards, vehicles, spanning streets. But the ships had platforms that prevented damage to anything. Even Domingo's Video Palace with its high marquee was straddled without damage. This suggested a degree of courtesy as well as flexibility, and phenomenally rapid construction technology.

Look at all the parking violators, McMurtrey thought, scratching the back of his head. *And not a tow truck in sight*.

It amused him to think of the insidious Domingos and their vulture trucks, with no way of hauling off spaceships. No doubt the Domingos were in touch with their lawyers, ready to ticket God if they dared.

McMurtrey's pulse quickened.

He gazed upon the throngs of people and life insurance robots knotted around each ship, and a sensation rushed through his brain. He closed his eyes momentarily, and when he reopened them he squinted and was able to distinguish the pious from the onlookers and hangers-on, for he detected a slight, barely discernible pale yellow aura around some, those he sensed were the pious. A sensation of Great Wordless Truth enveloped him, and he barely got an angle on it. He tried to concentrate, felt the concept slipping away.

He knew those with auras were the pious, the ones who truly belonged here. Some of them wore white, black, saffron or other raiment of various religious orders, and others wore common everyday clothing, as anyone on any street might wear. These pious comprised only a small proportion of those present, but in the distance, on the road winding down the rocky hillside to town, he saw more approaching on foot—the followers of many religions. Their bodies glowed slightly, a pale yellow, and McMurtrey felt like a man wearing infraglasses, seeing things that others could not or should not see.

Three deer watched from a safe distance on a hillside, then scurried up the hill and disappeared into a cluster of sycamore trees.

The dunes and flatlands around Domingo's Reef were covered with tents, and locals were beginning to call that area "Tent City." Only a few recreational vehicles were visible.

McMurtrey knew he would have to face the multitude sooner or later, explaining God's message to the extent that he could. One answer was awakening in his mind as he stood looking out on the town, and he was beginning to feel that he could explain why everything was here, in St. Charles Beach.

It's because I'm here, he thought. *The white ship—something special about it for me. Why?*

Tremendous energy had been channeled through his mind in recent days, from the aura people. Strangely, despite knowing this viscerally, he felt no fatigue. Adrenalin pumped through his veins, kept him charged. But he felt rising trepidation, an onrushing fear that people would laugh at him.

He had been going around in public with a chicken on his shoulder for years, letting people think him odd, letting them talk as they wished about him. None of it bothered him before, because it had all been a great big private joke. He didn't think he cared what anyone thought. Now it seemed to matter, and he wished he hadn't appeared on televid with No Name.

He should go before the public now and make them take him seriously. It had to be that way, almost by definition, for he was carrying a momentous holy message.

He had asked God about that, if religion was supposed to be serious, and the response hadn't really answered the question. God asked if religion were the way to reach Him, and He phrased it rhetorically, as if it weren't the way.

God had chosen *him*, dammit! People wouldn't dare laugh at him, not with the evidence of God's power all around, not with the auras, even if only McMurtrey could see them. These were good people, and . . . but some carried weapons.

It was another problem of definition. Religious people had auras, or at least it was said the holiest did, the saints and prophets. The aura concept seemed almost hackneyed to McMurtrey, too pat, and this was troublesome. Didn't people only see auras in imagination, in strange visions?

With so many theological representatives appearing at his doorstep, McMurtrey feared some were there to show him up, to prove him an infamous fraud. He might go out and bluff his way through for a while, taking full credit for the fleet and asserting that this miracle was an affirmation of the Interplanetary Church of Cosmic Chickenhood. But this façade wouldn't last long if God intervened.

On the other hand, maybe God would want him to have fun with it for a while. What was the Leader of the Universe really like?

McMurtrey agonized over this for a long time, focusing his energies inwardly so intensely that his vision fogged over. Presently he shook his head, and again gazed upon the town.

Best to be humble, he decided. *I'll go out with No Name and admit everything.*

The man slipped into the seclusion of a thick oak grove, and upon the ground he placed a sheet of white plazymer, which he stepped upon. With two fingers he rubbed the back of one hand until it was hot and a blister formed there.

From the forefinger of the other hand, a slender blade of blue bone pierced the fingertip bloodlessly, forming a cutting tool. With that blade he sliced around the sides of the blister, releasing an ooze of water and leaving it attached to the back of his hand with only a flap of epidermis. The blue bone blade receded into the fingertip, disappeared from view.

He lifted the flap of skin, and at a thought-impulse, a lance of red light emerged from one eye, passing through the epidermal flap and touching one of his black leather shoes. The shoe shriveled into a tiny dark flake which dropped on the plazymer. Then the thin white sock on that foot shriveled and fell as a white flake. This exposed the bare skin of the foot, and the skin was not affected by the light.

Quickly he repeated this procedure with the other shoe and sock, resulting in four flakes on the plazymer sheet. His coat, shirt, trousers and underclothes followed in like manner, and in short order he stood entirely in the buff, with a number of tiny flakes beneath him on the plazymer.

Then he remembered his cap, removed it and reduced it, relegating it to the micro-collection.

From his other eye a lance of violet light emerged, melding with the red light as both passed through the epidermal flap. They formed a spectrum of color on the other side of the flap, and a spectral light-bath covered the plazymer and the tiny flakes upon it.

He stepped from the plazymer onto moist soil, and as he did so the edges of the plazymer shrank and wrapped around the flakes, enclosing them in a neat little white packet.

The packet, no more than a quarter the width of his smallest fingernail and only a little bit thicker, rose on the spectral beam. He focused the beam on his now-exposed bellybutton at the center of a round and protruding belly, and the packet tucked itself neatly into the orifice, disappearing from view.

'*Loyalty to the Bureau,*' he thought. '*The Bureau of Loyalty.*'

With the fingers of one hand, he smoothed the epidermal

flap back onto the back of the other hand and sealed the bloodless wound, leaving no visible evidence of incision.

Cool, smooth currents of electricity traversed the superconductors of his artificial brain. He was pleased with this assignment, for he had been programmed to feel this way.

The happiest government employees were not human.

Jin understood full well that he wasn't human, but felt no remorse at this. His cyberoo parts didn't wear out easily, and theoretically he could go on forever with only minimal self-maintenance. He had been programmed to troubleshoot his own parts, a nearly fail-safe method that encompassed backups on top of backups. Every part in his body and every power system had twelvefold redundancy.

This C-Unit 7891 was nearly invincible. Anyone attempting to destroy it would have to accomplish annihilation in one quick, efficient act. Short of that, one of the biogenerating redundancies would remain functional, from which Jin could reconstruct himself in a matter of seconds, using the raw material of his body and nearby materials of virtually any kind.

His last backup system represented self-preservation, a priority in this series exceeded only by Jin's obligations to the Bureau.

Anyone attempting to destroy Jin had another obstacle to overcome, which Jin displayed now as part of his testing procedure. He touched his nose, and in a nanosecond little gunports opened around his body, revealing a panoply of mini-cannons. Some were on his face, with one on each cheek, one on his forehead and one in the center of his chin. Even his sexual organ had been converted to a baby howitzer.

He tested his guns, using silencers and blank cartridges. None misfired.

Now where did I put that damned broom? he thought.

His eyes continued to project beams of red and violet, but in parallel.

With an unadulterated fingernail, he dug into his bellybutton, pulling out the white packet and dozens of others, in varying colors. He settled on a brown one, replaced the other packets. The beams of eye-light re-merged, and he narrowed the spectral force, passing the tip of it over the packet. The packet unfolded in his hands, revealing a pile of light and dark flakes.

He heard and then felt a slight wind, sheltered the flakes to prevent scattering.

He nudged them around with a forefinger, found the one he wanted, which was distinguishable to his field of vision by its shape and hue.

The red light receded into one eye, leaving only violet, which touched only the selected flake. On the end of the light beam, he lifted the flake and watched it enlarge, into a rough straw broom on a long bamboo handle.

Momentarily he held the broom in midair on the beam, then let the broom thump to the ground.

Presently the brown packet had been replaced in his body cavity, and he was ready for the assignment. Now he was Jin the Plarnjarn, a holy man of uncommon excellence.

Stark naked and brushing the ground before each step, Jin emerged from the oak grove and merged slowly with the crowd approaching St. Charles Beach.

Don't step on the tiniest insect, he thought. *Not while anyone's looking*.

The forty-foot van trailer behind the truck was a fully contained execution and cryogenic body-freezing facility—automated, but not to the extent it might have been. Gutan had no say in how it was set up, but nevertheless it seemed just right to him. He savored personal involvement, enjoyed hitting toggles, pushing buttons, sliding electronic switches.

It was mid-afternoon, and he'd labored nonstop since arriving early that morning. Only one more inmate to go, a woman whose corpse he had been looking forward to. He felt little fatigue, despite having traveled straight through from Oenix, where he had dispatched eighty-seven in two days.

Holding a lit opium pipe, he stood by the pentahedral-shaped mnemonic memory machine, watching while a robotic helper removed the last Death Row inmate from the onboard holding cell.

The pipe, which held black chunks of opium in an oval

bowl, had a built-in rechargeable electric coil inside double
walls of the bowl. This heated the opium and made it
smokable. The smoke was black and acrid.

Mnemo was on, glowing yellow in neutral mode, and it
emitted a faint, characteristic whine. The sound, unlike
any Gutan had ever heard elsewhere, always brought to
mind images of spinning orange and lilac Mobius strips.
Today as always they were strips of every conceivable
Mobius shape, from those approaching standard geometri-
cal configurations to others that Gutan couldn't categorize.
Simultaneously they all stretched into perfectly round
cylinders, and then spun away into a white void. They
were seen to him internally with the sound of the machine,
and he saw them whether his eyes were closed or open,
through a separate viewing channel. Nothing in Gutan's
training instructed him about this sensory phenomenon,
but from his understanding of the machine he assumed
that the whirl into whiteness carried the memory of anyone
inside the machine to incredible reaches of the past.
Mnemo had a screen that projected the mental images of
subjects, but Gutan had never seen the spinning Mobius
colors on that screen.

With the sound off, he couldn't bring even the simplest
shapes forth in memory, though he had vague images of
fields of shapes, and though he made the attempt innumerable times. This frightened him, for he had been taught
that Mnemo carried its subject back through alternate
paths of memory, and always they died in the machine. It
seemed to him that his own alternate memory paths were
being touched by the sound and perhaps by more, essentially priming him without carrying him back.

He was afraid to ask about this, for someone might think
him particularly susceptible and decide that he would be
a good subject for experimentation. This wasn't simply a
killing machine after all; it hadn't been designed for that.
And there were intriguing clues Gutan had seen, suggesting that he and the machine were engaged in a clandestine
scientific experiment.

Curiously he had developed a longing to travel those
mysterious paths, to enter the machine himself and EX-
PERIENCE. It was perhaps a death wish or entropy, or
alternately a longing for another plane of existence where

he might live in a different, unfamiliar form. Gutan didn't
fear death, but he didn't want to lose the perks of his life:
opium and fresh cadavers.

Things could be done with fresh cadavers.

Sometimes he estimated survival odds. Every person
known to have entered the machine had died within it.
But Gutan's chance, it seemed to him, lay in the stories
concerning Professor Pelter, that the professor didn't have
killing in mind when he designed the thing. Purportedly
it was for a different, more important purpose, and the
promise of discovering that purpose sometimes bolstered
Gutan's courage. Maybe with just the right settings . . .

The thought of a "more important purpose" amused
Gutan. How deliciously ironic it would be if he of all people
discovered something significant, something *really* significant.

The robotic helper was a PYA1200, with exponential
strength. It could lift a medium-sized building if called
upon to do so, and had the added feature of storage com-
pactability. Now through black wisps of opium smoke Gutan saw it as a rolling Erector-set-man more than two
meters high, that in an instant, at an operator's command,
could compress itself into a neat little box no larger than
a toaster oven. Gutan called it "Fork" because of the stiff-
armed forklift-like manner in which it loaded and unloaded
dispatchees from Mnemo.

Fork had pincers on the ends of his arms, which he was
using to hold a huge naked woman. The van floor flexed
as Fork rolled toward Gutan, passing the cryogenic body-
chambers that were on one side.

The robot was like a good hunting dog with a prize for
its master, but before the kill. The designers of Fork hadn't
bothered with much of a face—just a few rivets where
features belonged, on a paper-thin alloy surface. Most
modern robots had faces, apparently by popular demand,
and even this unit had one, despite the premium of utility
and compactness. Fork's tightly riveted expression was entirely neutral—two parallel straight lines for the mouth,
two rectangles for eyes, a circle for the nose. But now, in
a drug-induced hallucination, Gutan thought he detected
the glimmerings of a smile around the edges of the rivets
comprising the mouth.

The woman in Fork's grasp rivaled small planet mass, and in her naked, prone position her great pendulous breasts hung halfway to the floor. She didn't struggle, although five of the twenty-eight already dispatched this day had struggled ferociously and paid for it. Fork wasn't programmed to show patience or compassion, so he gave them pincer shots to the kidneys.

According to the death docket on the electronic clip pad, this woman was a "war criminal," which probably meant she was a dissident involved in the peace movement, sentenced to death by the Bureau of Loyalty. A keloid scar spanned her face, and by her calm expression Gutan guessed she was either playing possum or in acceptance of her fate.

Gutan wished he were on commission, or better yet that he owned all this equipment. Just think what he could earn with a cushy government dispatch contract!

He tugged at the pipe, felt soothing smoke permeate his body.

In the reflection of a mirrored partition to his left he saw himself. A short man nearing sixty, he had curly black hair, black eyes and a close-cropped beard flecked with gray. He had a rather simian appearance, with a protruding forehead and high cheekbones. His head had a forward thrust to it, and as he stood by the memory machine he leaned forward involuntarily, his posture having long before been sacrificed through inattention. The stoop made him appear shorter than he actually was, but none of the cadavers he made love to ever complained. His arms and hands were long and apelike, with slender graceful fingers that dangled below his knees. His mother used to say he might have been a pianist with those fingers, if he hadn't lost one in the tricycling accident.

Mnemo was regularly moved between truck-trailer rigs, and the rigs needed maintenance—so someone undoubtedly had a ripe government contract there for the picking. At appointed stops, workers in lime-green rubber coveralls moved Mnemo between truck transporters with strange-looking extruders. At these stops, Dispatchers and rigs changed.

There were four Dispatchers including Gutan, and the general routine was one month on duty and two months off, with allowances for sick pay. Most of the time Gutan ended up flying home to Ciscola from all over the country, then flying to meet the mnemonic machine wherever it ended up two months later.

Gutan's first work experience had been as an embalming technician in his father's mortuary. After Gutan spent fifteen years there, a scandal over gold and silver fillings that were missing from cadavers forced the firm into bankruptcy. There were also rumors of corneas and other body parts sold illegally to hospitals, but all of it, while true, went unproven by authorities.

A long period of blacklisting and destitution ensued, in which Gutan bounced between a variety of minimum-wage jobs. Finally he landed a worthwhile position with the government in the Body Disposal Corps. Through a series of staff and management shakeups this led him to the Dispatch Division of the League Penitentiary System.

Initially Gutan worked with what the prison system called "Damoclean boxes," giant one-to-a-prisoner cages, with a ten-ton weight suspended from the ceiling of each cage. Through remarkable gearing and engineering, the weight was held by but a single cut-away strand of the prisoner's own hair. It remained but for the Dispatcher to slice the hair, a simple task. When the Mnemo position became available, Gutan took a skills test and was selected as one of the elite crew to operate the machine.

For this assignment Gutan was trained differently, through a job computer chip implanted in his brain. As a consequence, Gutan wondered why any testing had been necessary, unless the job chip worked from a platform of skills already present in the individual.

The opium permitted Gutan to look at himself objectively, as from afar, and in one facet of this he could study the implanted chip as if he were an outside observer, without having to remove it and subject it to electronic analysis. He perused it occasionally for diversion, and found within the chip some of the documentation left by the professor.

Anytime Gutan wanted to do so, he could call internally upon all the data in the chip for review. It was a conscious/subconscious experience, since with the extent and method of training he didn't need to think about his tasks. He

wondered if he was learning unauthorized information in
this process.

The laboratory-type control methods utilized in the executions, for example, became very apparent upon analysis—the way each condemned prisoner was dispatched
with different machine settings, with data fed constantly
into an adjacent and sealed government-installed computer.

Gutan watched Fork place the big woman in the mnemonic machine and strap her into the seat.

Working with uncharacteristic slowness, Fork unhooked
a spray unit from a bracket on an inside wall, pointed the
unit at the woman and pulled a long trigger. Clear electropulmonary gel inundated her naked body, covering
even her mouth and nose. The stuff gave her body a sweaty
sheen and blocked her breathing, causing her face to turn
red for several seconds. It made her eyes red as well, and
as Gutan had been taught, temporarily distorted vision
without permanent harm. As if it mattered.

A strawberry odor from the gel filled his nostrils, excited
him. He used the substance left on bodies as a sexual
lubricant.

Fork clamped a strand of red plazymer tubing from the
machine to a gel-covered spot on her neck, and she resumed breathing. Her coloration returned to near normal,
but she couldn't conceal agitation, manifested in little mus-
cular twitches all over her body.

After a few seconds, convex bubbles formed in front of
her eyes, giving her face an alien cast. These bubbles were
as clear as those of eyeglass lenses, enabling the dispatchee
and the Dispatcher to look at one another.

Fear had set into her eyes, and this intrigued Gutan. He
always enjoyed watching the eyes.

Soon the woman would scream and her face would become horribly distorted, like all the other dispatchees.
Then she would be Gutan's for a time, to have his way
with her.

Someone was assimilating data from Mnemo, correlat-
ing the different settings with variations in the dispatchees'
vital signs and in the times of death. The subjects were
being wrenched back in their memories to prior lives, according to Gutan's implanted job chip. He had seen in-

credible images flash across the LCD screen, scenes resembling those in history books, with images that focused only briefly and sometimes not at all, then blurred and provided glimpses of still earlier times, in various societies. As the images spun into antiquity, they were like a film on uncontrolled rewind, skipping onto prior films, separate films. It shouldn't have been possible.

At times with the mnemonic equipment Gutan thought he might be close to observing the whole history of mankind—in a mind-boggling amalgam one life might become every life, focusing ultimately in the distant, nearly erased past to explain the reason for everything.

Had Professor Pelter discovered what he had been looking for, the culmination of all his efforts? Did each inmate at death discover this priceless information, whatever it was? And if so, was that data transferrable to living persons? It seemed obvious to Gutan that the government didn't have all the answers, that dispatchings were conducted with Mnemo to learn more.

Professor Pelter went out with a head full of secrets.

Gutan didn't know how many variables there were in machine settings, and this had to be factored in with the variables in human subjects. The possibilities had to be calculator-boggling. With just the right settings and just the right subject, maybe the memory trail, as it rocketed back, wouldn't kill the subject.

He suspected with this thought that the monitors couldn't control the speed of memory recapture, that the subjects needed more time to adjust to each setting before going back, before traversing lives. They were being overwhelmed.

Was one life every life?

Gutan had to laugh at these thoughts. An opium-saturated ex-mortician thinking about philosophy, about the meaning of life? If not for a couple of turns of fate, he might still be working in his family's funeral parlor, just as so many Gutans had done for more than two centuries.

It seemed like only a short while ago that he had worked with his family, but it had been nearly three decades. What had happened to his life? When the family business slipped beneath the waves he felt a shock to his system, a shock to the chain of his bloodline, and in all the time since then he had not recovered.

He felt guilt for something he'd never discussed with his family or with those few friends he'd had over the years, friends who inevitably came no closer to him than acquaintances. Barriers. He always kept them up. Barriers protected him from discovery.

It was this terrible personal truth that kept him from wanting to see anyone in his family. He had a sister, two brothers, nephews and cousins somewhere, but would never see any of them again. Maybe they didn't want to see him, anyway. Maybe they knew what went on in the shadows.

The opium helped Gutan deal with this, and thus far he hadn't experienced the usual sleepiness or other adverse side effects. It wasn't ordinary somniferous opium, according to the mail-order literature that came with it. Gutan had noticed a need for ever-increasing doses, however, in order to achieve the desired state of euphoria.

When Gutan was off duty he thought about being on duty, couldn't wait to get back to work. Despite his shame, this work intrigued him, and he wanted to learn more about Mnemo than the iceberg tip he had seen so far.

He harbored no doubts that this project was big, far greater than a traveling execution machine. He sensed glimmerings of that truth and of a greater one beyond, like the glimmerings of the smile he thought he saw at times on Fork's sheet-metal face.

McMurtrey hadn't considered for an instant the possibility that he might freeze in front of a crowd. Never before had he spoken to large gatherings, but it occurred to him that a crowd might be easier to handle in one sense than an individual. With individuals he had this chronic, nagging tendency to be distracted by mannerisms. With a crowd, he assured himself, he wouldn't focus on any individual. It would be a sea of sameness, and his thoughts would remain in line.

So with his chicken on his shoulder that sunny afternoon, McMurtrey went to the podium on the makeshift stage and faced the multitude.

They stood shoulder to shoulder and belly to backside

as far as he could see—on the beaches, on the roads, on the rocky hillsides. Big black speakers had been placed everywhere so that all might hear.

The ocean was a cool pale blue, lapping relentlessly in shimmering wave armies at the shoreline, wearing the land away little by little, imperceptibly. McMurtrey, as he stood there listening to the waves and watching them, thought he heard the subtle raspings of shoreline erosion, and in his mind's eye he tried to envision the great storms of history at this place—as if all were occurring at once in a tremendous blast of water, wind and sound.

Then the storms subsided and the people grew quiet, with the exception of a stooped woman in the front who waggled her fingers in the chicken beak ritual and sang out loudly:

> "O Chubby Mother,
> Let me rubba your belly . . .
> Let me rubba your belly."

One of my followers, McMurtrey thought. *God, she's one of the stupid zealots!*

McMurtrey touched his lips, asking for quiet.

He stood in afternoon sunlight telling the people he was a fraud. He told them everything, and it gushed forth in a torrent of phrases he hadn't known he would use.

The woman in the front moaned that she didn't believe it, and other solitary cries rang from the throng. It saddened McMurtrey that his words were like knives in the hearts of some, but he knew this had to be done, that ultimately it would be for the best.

When he had said everything, it seemed natural, comfortable, a confessional. He had purged his conscience, bared his tainted soul before all. He stood naked before them.

He saw tears in the audience among those of all denominations, most evidently among the pious, whom he could see glowing softly yellow when he squinted. Nowhere, not even among those who bore swords and other weapons on their hips, did he detect even the flickering of a sneer or any sort of unkind expression. This despite the fact that he stood before them with a fat chicken on his shoulder.

It should have been a mockery; they should have been hurling vegetables and fruit at him.

As they waited for him to speak further, he looked beyond the people on the highest hillside, to the sky. A small cloud was chasing a puffy fat one, and they traveled on a high wind. He heard the wind beyond the sea noise, beyond the whisperings of the crowd.

He looked back at them, and raised his voice to be heard above all the sounds crashing in his ears. His words boomed through the speakers:

"I've told you of my life, that I've wasted years, that I've been a charlatan, a liar. Now, like the boy who cried wolf, I'm asking you to believe me when I tell you that God has spoken to me."

"Verily, it is so!" came a shout from the crowd. It was a man's voice, deep and resonant.

"We believe you!" a teenage girl exclaimed. "Praise the Lord! Our ships have come!" She had a shiny, bronze-colored stunbow strapped to her back.

"'Is anything too difficult for the Lord?'" a man called out, from just in front of the podium. He held an open Babul, and an electronic concordance pendant dangling from his neck flashed the scriptural reference in orange: NESI 18:14.

A bearded man in a black caftan stepped forward, holding his Kooraq high. It was a brown leather tome, with elegant, flowing script inscribed on the cover. The man's lips barely moved, and a voice seemed to come not from him, but rather, as in the case of a ventriloquist, from the volume itself: "WE BELIEVE IN ALLAH, AND IN THAT WHICH HAS BEEN SENT DOWN ON US. . . . TO HIM WE SURRENDER!"

Then a Floriental man in a Wessornian business suit stepped forth with a long rolled scroll, identified himself as an Ota, and said, in a very high, clear voice: "'THE WISE MAN NEVER STRIVES HIMSELF FOR THE GREAT, AND THEREBY THE GREAT IS ACHIEVED!' WE DIDN'T CALL FOR THE SHIPS! WE DID NOT BUILD THEM! HAD WE SOUGHT THESE SHIPS, WE COULD NOT ENTER THEM, FOR THEY WOULD NOT EXIST."

"I think he's saying it's okay to go," a woman said, within earshot of McMurtrey.

"Who cares what he says?" a man said.

A few in the crowd chuckled, a rolling, gentle sound.

Then other holy men and women stepped forward and spoke, with each giving reasons from their sacred scriptures why people should travel by ship to God's domain far across the universe. No one spoke against the ships, not even a number of atheists who made their presence known. All agreed that it would be a great adventure, and that someone should embark upon it, although all present did not want to make the journey.

Generally, McMurtrey was impressed with the respect that each religion displayed for others. There were a few rude individuals in the gathering, but their choppy words of criticism toward other faiths fell as stones into a pit—unanswered—and these outcasts fell silent.

After waiting more patiently than he might have, McMurtrey wanted to continue his address. He asked the various representatives to yield to him.

They did so graciously, and McMurtrey spoke for a while longer.

Then he paused, and a current of assent swept all around, building to a crescendo of chanting: "PRAISE GOD AND McMURTREY! PRAISE GOD AND McMURTREY!"

McMurtrey saw the faces of many in the audience uplifted toward him, as if people were beholding divine light. To them, his words were God's words.

McMurtrey spread his arms wide, gazed reverently at the sky.

But a solitary male voice rose from the multitude, to McMurtrey's right. It cut through sanctified air like a razor on flesh, making McMurtrey shiver. But he was not cold.

"Why you, Rooster?" the voice asked. "Why in the name of all that's holy did God select you as His messenger?" As the man spoke, he pushed his way through the crowd. People let him past, and soon he stood on the bottom step of the stage, staring up defiantly at McMurtrey.

"He has a gun!" someone shouted.

McMurtrey saw it even as he heard the warning, but he didn't flinch.

An elephant pistol was holstered on the man's hip, but he wasn't making a move for the weapon. He wore a green sportscoat and was tall, with thinning brown hair combed straight back through untamable cowlicks. The eyes were the pale blue of the sea, looking through people, looking through this fraud, Evander McMurtrey.

McMurtrey was glad he hadn't lied, for men such as this would have seen the truth and exposed him. McMurtrey's knees quivered, threatening to fold on him and send him crashing to the floor of the stage.

He noticed that this man had a lot of nervous tics, the sort that invariably had distracted McMurtrey in the past, flooding his brain with images that blocked the thought patterns required for conversation. One of the man's eyelids twitched occasionally, he tapped one foot on the step importunately, and his trigger finger, like an insect leg, rubbed the adjacent thumb.

Inexplicably, McMurtrey didn't feel his thoughts muddling. He felt strong, at the crest of a momentous event. This was a purposeful strength, and it seemed capable of carrying him a long way.

McMurtrey took a deep breath and met the man's gaze. "Your name?" McMurtrey asked.

"Johnny Orbust. I'm a Reborn Krassee, here to debate the Lord's word and way with you, Rooster."

"I always like to know who I'm talking to," McMurtrey said. He squinted, detected no aura around the man. Then as he looked out upon the crowd in this fashion, McMurtrey no longer saw any auras, not even around individuals he had seen glowing before.

"Sun bothering you?" Orbust queried.

"No . . . it's . . . You want to know why the Lord didn't select a great leader for this task? Why not a person of grand stature, a person capable of engendering the admiration of millions? Why a man who goes around with a chicken on his shoulder?"

Orbust smiled sardonically.

"I'm not here to sell myself to anyone," McMurtrey said, smoothing the green plumage on No Name's backside. "Far from it. I've denigrated myself before you, exposed my life for the utter farce that it's been. But the fact remains that God did speak to me and He did produce these marvelous ships. He communicated with many of you as well, or you wouldn't be here. Perhaps not as He spoke to me, revealing His location, but differently. I sense the truth of this. As I look upon your face, Orbust, and upon the countenances of so many here, I know this is fact."

Orbust's jaw dropped. He took a step back, off the staircase and onto the ground. He bent over and lifted a pant leg, revealing a small sheath strapped to his calf.

A weapon, McMurtrey thought, preparing to duck behind the lectern. *Why not the cannon on his hip?* McMurtrey didn't see anyone moving toward Orbust to stop him, felt alone and abandoned.

Orbust seemed to have a second thought and paused. He let his pant leg down without pulling forth whatever the sheath held, and straightened.

"What did God say to you?" McMurtrey asked, staring so intensely at Orbust that he forced the man to look away.

"It wasn't . . . words. . . ." Orbust said. "I felt . . . compelled to come here."

"You came here concerning a ship? A particular ship that will carry you to Heaven?"

Orbust looked at the ground, like a child being reprimanded. "Y-yes. I saw it on televid." He pointed. "That white one!"

It was the same ship McMurtrey had selected for himself, likewise for no reason he could form into words.

"Others are here to board that ship as well," McMurtrey said. "It will hold many passengers. When God's location was announced and we had no way to go there, many of us formed visions of how we would voyage to God. These ships are from our imaginations, from transmitted thought waves. I didn't fully realize it myself until scant seconds ago, as I gazed out upon you and absorbed your energies. It wasn't the first time I had known these energies, and they were familiar to me."

The crowd grew exceedingly quiet.

McMurtrey felt an adrenalin surge, and the ensuing words came with a rush: "In days past, your thoughts and mine were channeled through me with such force that they materialized into objects. These ships are not mirages.

While I sense what has happened, I don't fully understand how. But it is something I cannot question, and I sense many of you believe this with me."

By the hush in the crowd and the trusting, childlike faces that stared at him, McMurtrey saw he had struck a responsive chord. They were hanging on his every word.

"THESE ARE OUR CREATIONS!" McMurtrey shouted. "ENTER THEM!"

Orbust's impertinent question didn't require an answer. Not in words. Ironically, God had selected the lowliest prophet in the history of mankind for the most important assignment, a pilgrimage to the Master of Masters.

Gutan took a puff on his opium pipe, watched the subject. She had her eyes closed, awaiting the inevitable that would be brought on when Gutan made the prescribed machine settings and adjustments.

He heard Fork rolling back, the harsh whirrings and squeakings Gutan didn't always notice.

If this was an elaborate, veiled experiment, it now occurred to Gutan that it had to go beyond the data pouring into the computer system. And theft protection had to be more extensive than the satellite tracking system that his implanted chip said watched the truck-trailer rigs at all times. There had to be eyes everywhere *inside*, something or someone watching Mnemo at all times. Might it be Fork? Or Gutan himself, transmitting via the chip to headquarters, made complacent by the opium that had appeared too conveniently in his life?

Could Gutan destroy the memory machine if he decided he wanted to? Or did the job chip contain within it a governor that prevented such acts? If the opium was part of the conspiracy, part of the veil, how could he have the thoughts he was experiencing now?

He didn't want to destroy the machine, couldn't envision doing anything like that.

He studied his pipe, the graceful curvatures of the dark wood stem that circulated the narcotic through his body. A special variety of opium, part of the conspiracy?

He wanted to dash the pipe to the floor and stomp the addiction mechanism to pieces. Then he recalled something he had heard, about drugs inducing paranoia in certain people.

With one hand he slammed shut the door of the mnemonic machine, and through the dark yellow-tinted glass of the door saw the subject's expression change from serenity to terror.

Gutan glanced at the electric clip pad on the countertop to his left, noted the subject's name, Anna Salazar, and the required machine settings. He began to make the settings.

Mnemo's wide instrument console had a thousand tiny dials, half as many miniature toggles and levers, and ninety-three buttons so small they had to be pressed with a metal pick that was kept on a narrow, lipped shelf. All controls were numbered without explanation as to function, but the job chip implanted in Gutan's cerebrum gave a smattering of information. The dial he was turning now, Number 271, was a sensory deprivator, tied in with the gelatin on Salazar's body and designed to free the logjam of current events that was suppressing old memories. Sensory stimulation would follow.

The gelatin covering Salazar's body glowed pale red for an instant, indicating Sensory Deprivation engaged.

Professor Pelter referred to the gelatin as a "Variable Texture Suit," an electrically conductive surface that could make a subject believe he was wearing any manner of clothing, touching any surface, tasting any type of food ever created, smelling any smell. Pelter had refined and identified more than 600,000 different smells, nearly 100,000 different sounds, thousands more textures, temperatures and tastes. His remarkable machine could simulate any of these sensory enhancers in infinite variety, carrying a subject back in his memory to lives long forgotten.

Gutan knew from his own experiences before this job that senses triggered memory, and his smell-induced memories were legion. Sometimes as an adult he picked up the pungent aroma of shrubbery that was reminiscent of a yard he used to pass on the way to elementary school. Prison-system cooking aromas were like those of school cafeterias, and embalming fluid odors brought back days spent in the family funeral home. So Mnemo's capabilities hadn't surprised Gutan that much.

He lifted a small blue lever in a vertical channel on the console, until it reached the numeral "1." A brief blue glow in the gelatin indicated Sensory Stimulation engaged, a phase-one injection They were starting her out slowly, getting her used to the machine. It had to be easier on the body that way, and to this extent she seemed lucky. Automatic testing would follow, for dream images and recent memories, with subtle suggestions from the machine based upon information programmed into it about the subject's life history.

When the government computer beeped twice, as it would in a few minutes, Gutan would set the stimulator lever on "2," and so on. Then to other controls, bringing more power, and back the subject would go. In a sense, Gutan and the Feds monitoring the equipment went along for the ride. Even Pelter went along, for his one-of-a-kind machine still lived.

Another dial, Number 140, was a Climate Control setting, and this Gutan set on zero to begin, neutral. He wouldn't have to reset it for this subject, since Mnemo's built-in computer would take over when things really got rolling. If a subject was experiencing a life in ancient Afsornia, for example (as in the recent case of a dispatchee at San Felipe Penitentiary), the computer would set temperature, humidity and air components according to known historical data and probabilities—thus enhancing the odds of stimulating more memories. All the foods, ancient and modern, were in other automatic mechanisms that Gutan didn't have to fool with.

Some of the settings involved the injection of memory-enhancing nutrients, such as lecithin, phosphatidylcholine, arginine vasopressin and thiamine. Varying combinations of these and other neurotransmitters softened neuron membranes, produced acetylcholine in the tissues, improved synaptic connections and made further structural and chemical renovations, thus maximizing the ability of the brain to accept sensory stimulators.

Gutan stepped back, saw his own reflection clearly in the tinted mnemonic machine door, with Salazar visible beyond.

Like a camera lens adjusting focal length, he focused on Salazar, then back on his own reflection and then to the entire mnemonic machine itself. The machine was taller than Gutan and pentahedral front and back, but not at the sides. The flat surfaces circumnavigating the sides gave it the appearance of a big wheel that needed further refinement by its inventor before it would roll. It was pale yellow alloy, of indeterminate composition, with a darker yellow-tint oblong door taking up most of the front and an oblong LCD screen on top. The wide console was separate, on the side of the door, and linked to the machine via the entrance platform, which apparently had cables concealed within it.

On schedule, Gutan threw on the red master power switch. Salazar's body jerked, and the LCD screen projected an explosion of orange followed by a wild array of other colors. A landscape came into focus: high arched streetlight in the foreground with a long driveway beyond, leading to a barn-shaped house. Colors faded to black and white, then contrast darkened and the screen became black.

Salazar jerked again, hideously, and a "pop" sound issued from the machine. Six faces of men and women appeared side by side, then drew back, revealing frumpy-clothed forms. The clothing fell away, reappeared and fell away again.

A whirl of faces, landscapes, buildings and colors filled the screen. Cars, homes and household articles appeared, from centuries past. They were going fast, piling on top of one another. The ferocious, hate-crazed image of a man came into focus, and suddenly the image folded in upon itself, turned inside out. Salazar screamed, the most awful, gut-wrenching sound in all of creation. Her arms ripped free of their restraint straps, flailed wildly, and her face was a picture of hideous terror, features distorted beyond recognition.

For an instant Gutan saw his own reflection in the glass: His eyes were feral, satanic.

Salazar's body went limp, the screen grew dark and all became silent except for Gutan's labored breathing. It always ended like this, with overwhelming images that stopped everything.

Mnemo's life-support systems couldn't keep subjects alive when they went into trauma, and this seemed to be a great failing of the machine. Perhaps Professor Pelter should have worked in close or closer collaboration with medical technicians. Maybe he relied too much on his own knowledge, tried to do too much himself.

These thoughts took but an instant, as in a dream. Gutan had experienced them previously, and more rapidly each time, perfecting them it seemed, honing them and getting them out of his way.

He became frenzied, and beyond his own reflection saw what he wanted. He threw open Mnemo's door, and in a superhuman effort freed Salazar's massive cadaver from the seat and dragged it out.

Twenty minutes later she was quick-chilled and lay in bed beneath Gutan. He used the slippery electropulmonary gel still on her to perform the sexual act, but rationalized that he wasn't a complete degenerate. . . . He didn't do this with children, and with a man only once—an act of desperation.

Only after the passion subsided did his recurring worry about surveillance surface, those Federal eyes he suspected were everywhere. Why didn't they put him under arrest? They had to know! The airspace once occupied by his severed finger throbbed from the cold, and he thrust the entire hand between his thighs, seeking warmth.

The sleeping compartment was permeated with the strawberry odor of gel, and Gutan felt unclean.

A wave of guilt struck him and he thought: *I'm an ungodly son of a bitch if there ever was one! Why do I do these terrible things?*

He felt helpless to change. *Why bother? When a life has as many debits as mine, nothing I do now can change the balance. Perhaps if I had started to change earlier, if I'd tried to overcome . . . But now my acts are heaped around me and I can't get past them. It's easier to continue. . . .*

He sat up despondently, sank his face into his upturned hands. They reeked of gel.

I've always taken the easiest path. The choices I've made have not been thought out.

Fear, always just beneath the surface of every other emotion he felt, flooded away the guilt and inundated it in a terrible wash of terror. His terror grew with each infraction, and beneath these torrents that threatened to drown him, he heard the rapid drumbeat of his heart, increasing in tempo with each passing moment.

Sweat dripped into his eyes, stung them. Pain from his missing finger ran up his arm into his brain. It was nearly unbearable.

In the dark, Gutan crawled over the mountainous form and stumbled out of bed, groping toward the bedstand for his opium pipe.

Three

All is never as it seems.

—Ancient Saying

_____

It wasn't quite the way McMurtrey had envisioned it. He thought that only those who had mentally projected these ships could enter them. But several days later, when two local boys figured out the complex puzzle-lock latch systems on every vessel and the townspeople got aboard, McMurtrey had to rethink the situation.

Not only were the vessels accessible to everyone, they were extraordinary inside. Most of them had what appeared to be flight decks, and these ships had been fitted with compact fold-down beds that came out of the walls, something like old-style Murphy sleepers. The beds were operated by control panels that seemed to have identity scanners in them, so only certain people could operate them. Screens could be dropped around each bed, thus forming individual cabins. Only a few people on McMurtrey's ship had located their cabins; McMurtrey hadn't taken the time to find his, for he was vexed that God hadn't given him much information—just that initial, somewhat cryptic communication, the appearance of the fleet and the brief perception of auras. He wished God would clarify matters.

None of the "flight decks" contained instrumentation, and no control surfaces were apparent on the exteriors of the ships. An engineer that McMurtrey spoke with thought the vessels appeared spaceworthy from their components and shapes; but this man and a number of other experts were baffled for the most part.

It seemed particularly bizarre to these engineers and to most everyone else that some of the vessels appeared more

48

appropriately to be vessels of a different definition—that is to say, they had the look of massive containers for holding things. These had no flight decks or sleeping facilities. Inside the one straddling the main road to Domingo's Reef there was a small, living conifer forest on fifteen deck levels, with a remarkable mirror-activated moisture-transfer mechanism that fed sunlight and rainwater to the ecosystem. Another vessel contained deck after deck of simple prayer rugs and bare praying platforms—with here and there religious statues and sacramental articles. Hoddhists, Nandus, Plarnjarns, and others of the Eassornian philosophies congregated in these structures soon after they were opened, but they didn't pray in them. An air of hesitancy predominated, as people were afraid to assert themselves, afraid to proceed without clear-cut approval and instruction.

Three weeks passed with little occurring. Many visitors grew impatient and left town. Property owners began to speak of having everything demolished and hauled off, and one of the Domingos told the St. Charles Beach *Crier* that he could secure heavy cables to the vessels and topple them onto flatbed trailers, by which they could be hauled off.

The biggest problem seemed to be the ships that straddled houses and roads. It wasn't known how heavy the vessels were, because no one could figure out what they were made of. An alloy, it was believed, and the town council sent for experts to figure that out and to determine if big helicopters could lift everything away. Some people talked about using cutting torches. Insurance companies were going nuts, and their agents were getting in the way of the plans of the property owners, citing exclusions that would or could apply if anyone caused damage by bumping things around.

The more that occurred along these lines, the more McMurtrey faded into the background. Increasingly, people said unkind things to him on the streets, or pixtelled him, or pounded upon his door, and he couldn't come up with much to say in return. He stopped answering his pixtel or the door, and began sending a neighbor boy to the store for supplies. Letters piled up for him at the mail station.

Isolation wasn't new to Evander McMurtrey. He hadn't ever cared much for socializing anyway.

One evening when he was sitting in his darkened living room mulling events over, he heard clunking footsteps on the porch and a sharp series of raps at the door. He didn't move, heard No Name rustle around in a specially built birdcage.

There were more raps upon the door, louder.

A man called out: "Open up, Rooster! We know you're in there!" Something familiar and unpleasant in that voice.

McMurtrey didn't move. Why should he? Undoubtedly they wanted answers, and he had run out.

The door handle rattled, followed by voices, low and urgent.

A splintering crash shook the house, and McMurtrey jumped to his feet. The front door was kicked in, with the doorway full of silhouetted figures, their shapes outlined by backlight from the street.

"There he is," one of the intruders said, the same one who had called from outside.

McMurtrey choked out a response: "Get off my property!"

Someone heat-activated the light switch by the door, and half a dozen men filed in. They were led by a man in a sports jacket who toted a big pistol on his hip, and as this one moved into the light, McMurtrey recognized Johnny Orbust. The familiar voice.

Orbust's coat was green, with a lump under one arm that might have been another gun. And McMurtrey recalled the sheath strapped to one calf under the trousers. The visible firearm was in its holster, flap unsnapped. Orbust glanced around nervously, like a cat on unfamiliar ground.

His companions were a mixed lot: a priest in black, but with an unusual red collar; just behind the priest a disheveled man long of beard and hair whom McMurtrey had noticed panhandling in town; then two very tall, thin men who looked enough alike to be brothers, both with angular birdlike features; and off to one side a fat little man with a stubble of beard and a girth that nearly equaled his height. All looked tough and hard.

"Let's go!" Orbust barked. His eyelid twitched nervously, and he gestured with one hand, beckoning McMurtrey.

McMurtrey felt no fogging of his brain induced by nervous tics, hadn't suffered that debility since God spoke to him.

"Go where?" McMurtrey asked. "What are you talking about?"

"Those ships, Rooster," the fat man snarled. He wore a long peacoat.

"Ships in a row and nowhere to go?" one of the tall men said. Then he said something in a low tone to the fat man, calling him "Tully."

"Don't bug me about the ships," McMurtrey said. "I've told everything I know about them."

"The power that brought those ships is able to get 'em off the ground," Orbust said. "Just one's all we need. The white one you've been admiring yourself."

Orbust was directly in front of McMurtrey now. Orbust's pale blue gaze followed McMurtrey's line of sight to the pistol. Then their gazes met, and Orbust's expression seemed to say, "Go ahead and try for it, if you dare."

McMurtrey tried to relax, took a deep breath. He looked everywhere except at the gun.

With a soft, rapid slap of sound, Orbust drew a Babul from inside his coat, and began reading scripture aloud. McMurtrey didn't pay attention to the words, so surprised and intrigued had he been by the maneuver. When Orbust replaced the Babul, McMurtrey saw that it went into a shoulder holster.

Then Orbust grabbed McMurtrey by an arm, and Tully took the other. They jerked him toward the door. The disheveled man was quoting more scripture and making commentary, something about the prophesies of Divan.

"I can't do what you want," McMurtrey said. "Whatever power I had is gone."

"We're gonna wind your little battery up," Tully said.

The chicken rustled in its cage, hopped through the open cage door and fluttered ungracefully to the floor. It hopped toward Tully.

"Keep that thing away from me," Tully rasped, "or I'll—"

The chicken squawked.

McMurtrey stepped toward the bird, felt the men release their grasps on him. With a wave of his hand, McMurtrey ordered No Name back to its cage.

With a tremendous commotion of wings, it complied.

"What kinda fuckin' chicken izzat?" Tully asked, scowling.

"There's no need for language like that," Orbust said.

A pen and a small notebook fell from one of Tully's pockets. The notebook lay open on the floor, revealing Babulical passages written in calligraphy. This rough little man appeared to have a talent.

"I say what I want when I want," Tully retorted. He leaned over and retrieved his belongings. They went into a pocket of his peacoat.

Angrily, Orbust turned toward his associate, and the fingers of his gun hand twitched near the holstered weapon. Then he took a deep breath and looked away.

"Izzat a rooster or a hen?" Tully asked.

"Hen," McMurtrey said.

"What are you, some kinda chicken-fucker?"

"Enough of this," Orbust said. He pulled McMurtrey through the doorway and outside.

Tully again took hold of one of McMurtrey's arms when they reached the street, and McMurtrey held back a little, exerting just enough reverse inertia to provide him with precious additional seconds to think. The night air was cool, with a breeze blowing in from the ocean.

Orbust had a flashlight, and he played its powerful beam ahead of them, illuminating hazardous areas of broken sidewalk that the town's antiquated street lamps failed to reveal.

They were going toward the nearest white ship, the one McMurtrey favored. It stood as a plump monolith in lights from the town, and beyond it were the stars of God's firmament. One star that might have been a bright planet caught McMurtrey's attention. It was high in the eastern sky, clean and sharp against an inky background. McMurtrey wondered if a force could be riveting his attention to it, and if so to what purpose.

It struck him that everything, even the tiniest, seemingly insignificant incident or object, had a purpose. They were threads in a heavenly tapestry.

He felt a sharp pain in the arm that Tully held, and someone pushed him rudely from behind with the admonition, "Quit dragging your heels." It was one of the tall men. McMurtrey couldn't tell which, and didn't look back.

A street light popped and fizzled with static electricity, went dark and then came back on slowly, producing a sickly yellow glow.

When they reached the ship, Orbust played the flashlight beam on it. A coarse-surfaced metal ramp led to the entrance hatch, and it was open, its puzzle-lock having been released. The men boarded.

Inside it smelled pungently of urine and feces, and McMurtrey began breathing through his mouth. When the flashlight played against the walls he noted graffiti that hadn't been there several weeks before.

Orbust and Tully let go of him. The arm on Tully's side throbbed.

"Yeesh what a stench," the priest said. He flipped on a powerful little incandescent lamp that McMurtrey hadn't noticed he had, kicked several beer cans aside and set the lamp down in the middle of the cabin. This was the principal compartment of the ship, a tubular-shaped room, and overhead were a dozen or more mezzanines, stacked atop one another in circling, doughnut-shaped tiers. Hundreds of compact fold-down beds lined the walls of the mezzanines, some open and some concealed inside the walls.

"Kids have been partying in here," Orbust said. "This fleet has no management, no guards, and it's deteriorating." He turned off his flashlight, set it on the deck beside the lamp.

"Don't blame me," McMurtrey said. "There's nothing I can do about it."

"Hocus-pocus," the disheveled man said. "Do a little magic."

"We Krassians have to get to God first," Tully said. "So get with it."

"Get with what?"

"I don't know," said Tully. "Talk to the ship, plead with it, whatever it takes. It don't listen to us. Hell, bless it. Try everything. You're the mover and shaker here, and nothing's been happening with you hiding at your place."

"I think a blessing would be a capital idea," the priest

said, stroking the front of his red collar. The way light was hitting him, he looked like a man whose throat had been slashed. His nose hooked downward. "I'm Kundo Smith, Mr. McMurtrey. I live in this shire, so you might have heard of me."

McMurtrey shook his head.

Smith appeared displeased at this.

I'd rather refer to you as Redneck, McMurtrey thought.

Someone nudged McMurtrey from behind, hissed: "The blessing!"

"I know one that seems appropriate," McMurtrey said. "A cousin taught it to me when I was young."

"Is it Krassian?" Orbust asked.

"I'm not sure, but it isn't offensive."

"Go ahead," Orbust said hesitantly.

McMurtrey cleared his throat, and his voice echoed through the high mezzanines:

> " 'When we hoist the silver goblets
> To toast the men who've dared
> May the goblets all be filled
> And the good times they be shared.
>
> For the empty cup it's known
> Is the one who ne'er came back
> From a far off distant land
> Where he's a lyin' on his back.
>
> To avert that from occurrin',
> In the lives of those we love
> A blessing do we offer
> With some guidance from above:
>
> 'May the men who go to space
> Toward a far-off distant land
> Be a circlin' in the palm
> Of the Lord's magnif'cent hand.' "

McMurtrey paused, and the ship was silent, without a creak or a whir. His nostrils were more comfortable, and the odor was either diminishing or he had become accustomed to it.

"Nothing," Orbust said presently. He didn't seem to notice what McMurtrey's nose had detected.

Then McMurtrey saw the graffiti fade from the walls, so that they were again creamy white, and the beer cans disappeared into the deck, all soundlessly.

"Now we're getting somewhere," Smith said. "You only know one, Rooster?"

McMurtrey grunted. "I wish you wouldn't call me that," he said.

"Whatever you say, Big Mac," came the response.

The Krassians guffawed.

McMurtrey showed no reaction.

"You expected maybe a takeoff?" a voice said in an odd, clipped accent. It came from no particular direction.

The incandescent lamp flicked off with a little *pop*, leaving them in blackness. The men cursed and stumbled around. Smith fumbled with the lamp, couldn't get it to work. He said the flashlight wouldn't go on either.

A hand slapped into something, and against the open hatchway McMurtrey saw Orbust silhouetted against town lights, his Babul drawn. Orbust moved out of the doorway, became a dark and amorphous shape against one wall.

He didn't pull the gun, McMurtrey thought. *What is it, a prop*?

"No G-harnesses secured," the voice said, sounding ubiquitous and of an ethnicity McMurtrey hadn't yet placed. "All of you just standing around ready to take off. How nice. And how fortunate for fools that it's not so easy as that. You've assumed that food is on board?"

"We've got energy bars in our pockets," Tully said.

"McMurtrey doesn't have anything," the voice said. "You were planning to jettison him?"

McMurtrey felt his heart skip a beat.

"Naw, we'da shared," Tully said.

"What is the duration of the trip? Do you have any idea how much food is required?"

No one answered.

McMurtrey felt like scurrying out the hatch, hesitated.

The walls and deck flashed on, as frosty amber light panels. This revealed Orbust crouching off to one side against a bulkhead, his Babul clutched tightly in his hands.

The incandescent lamp and flashlight were on, and Smith switched them off.

Orbust stood up and asked of the voice, "Are you God?"

"Are you nuts? I'm just a biocomputer! You want I should be God? You want God should answer every silly poem?"

"I'd like to know what's going on here," McMurtrey snapped. "God contacted me, got me into this mess. The least He could do is—"

"All right, call me God if it'll make you feel better." A long pause, then: "Forget it. That name's already taken, as the Boss just told me by comlink. God says call me Appy instead, short for 'apprentice.' On previous missions no one has ever suggested I should have a name. I guess it's time."

Orbust opened his Babul.

"God says to call the ship Shusher," Appy said. "Does anyone want to know why?"

"Tell us why," Orbust said, accommodatingly. He flipped through the scriptures.

"This ship likes to travel quietly, and it has effective methods of enforcing its wishes. Fortunately it cannot hear everything, or travel with it would be unbearable. The ship, you see, is a separate personality from the biocomputer. I have a private connection to Shusher on his hearing frequency—a comlink I can open and close at will. Shusher probably won't hear any of you, unless the line happens to be open while one of you is near an entry point, making commotion. Those entry points are on the highest mezzanines, where I have posted off-limits signs, warning you away."

"Sounds pretty strange," Orbust said.

"We are the hierarchy here," Appy said. "God, me and Shusher—sort of a triumvirate. I must inform you, however, that Shusher isn't the brightest of sentients. Occasionally God and I must make up for his blunders."

Appy droned on for minutes that seemed like hours, with a plethora of information about the extreme age of the ship, its prior missions to distant galaxies, and its pedigree, which apparently wasn't all that impressive by Appy's standards. This monologue opened up a lot of questions that McMurtrey wanted to ask. But the computer spoke so rapidly and disseminated such an incredible flow of data that McMurtrey couldn't find an opening.

Appy's accent was the most inconsistent McMurtrey had ever heard, a mannerism in and of itself of good syntax that didn't sound like good syntax, so ornately weighted were some of the words and phrases. But while McMurtrey noticed this, he did so only because it was impossible to overlook, and he didn't feel mentally derailed for it.

I'm beating it! McMurtrey thought, recalling all the times in his life when odd habits had distracted him to the point of mental paralysis.

"Another thing," Appy said. "On this trip in rather confined quarters we want you should consider the similarities between religions. Fasting, for example is a common practice among the pious of purportedly different persuasions: the Middist's Day of Atonement, the Isammedan's month-long Kamad, the KothoLu's Lent. Hoddhists eat nothing between noon and dawn. Some ascetics, particularly the Nandubhagas, travel the land as sadhus, searching for the truth of God while eating nothing but forest berries and cow dung. There are those in all religions who have renounced worldly goods. Some Isammedans feel there is an even greater jihad than the killing of infidels, and that is the conquering of human desires, of human passion.

"There is a nudist aboard, I see, a Plarnjarn. On other ships are other nudists of varying faiths. There is a Krassian sect, for example, dating to pre-Eassornian Ussia that believes nudity is the purest state, and that burning material possessions is the way to salvation. Unfortunately they burn other people's things, and have an extensive arson record. Be thankful they aren't among your ship's company."

Appy laughed wildly, then continued: "You will observe one another in prayer and in the cleansing processes therewith, and you will be startled at the reflections of yourselves that you see. The only true church of God on Earth? What does that really mean, and by whose authority is it asserted by so many different groups?"

"Are you saying that God sent prophets to several cultures?" McMurtrey asked. "That He sent Dosek to the

Middists, Krassos to the Krassians, Isammed to the Arabs, Hoddha to the—"

"There were no Krassians before Mark Krassos," Appy said, his tone scornful.

"You know what I mean," McMurtrey said. "Different prophets for different cultures? All with similar messages, suited to particular locales, particular ways of life? I mean, God couldn't send a Caucasian Krassos into Florentia or a guy dressed in a parka into the desert."

Appy chortled. "You're extrapolating," he said. "If I wanted to tell you that, I would have come right out and said it."

"Aren't you?"

"You weren't listening carefully, McMurtrey. I was quite specific."

McMurtrey grumbled to himself, shifted on his feet.

"Consider it from a different perspective," Appy said. "Envision a Wessornian doctor relying on only one medical method, the technologically immersed Wessornian way. I want you should know, this may not provide enough knowledge to cure a patient. Just as there might be more than one path to God, so too might there be more than one path to perfect healing. The path to healing might employ technology, acupiercing, faith remedies, even holistic sessions. . . ."

McMurtrey scratched the side of his head.

"Exclusive Revelation," Appy said. "So many people claiming to have the one and only way to God. Fascinating! Let the subject of holiness spin, so that we should study its facets. Does one facet shine above all others?"

"You're playing with words," Orbust said.

"Am I?" Appy countered.

"Krassos said 'I am the way, the truth, and the life,'" Orbust said. "Further, He said, 'I am *He*.' So Krassos was not only *the* way, He was God."

McMurtrey saw a shiny silver card in Orbust's hand. It looked like a credit card, and he held it so that it bent slightly. Light reflected from its surface.

"Does that preclude other ways?" McMurtrey queried, his voice timid. This Orbust seemed nearly fanatical, and that gun on his hip bothered McMurtrey. "I mean, couldn't the way of Krassos be correct, along with the way of Hod-dha?"

Orbust glared at him, trembled with anger. "'He that believeth not is condemned already, because he hath not believed in the name of the only begotten Son of God.' Did you hear that? The only begotten Son of God!"

McMurtrey shrugged.

"Come now, Mr. McMurtrey," Appy said. "Don't let Orbust's Snapcard intimidate you. That little card in his hand allows him to debate far above his ability."

Orbust scowled, slipped the card into his coat pocket. "I don't need this," he said.

Appy laughed, a screwball guffaw. "Then reply to this: What if Mr. McMurtrey should ask if there were other ways of producing sons than begetting them? And what if he should ask why God's other prophets had to be sons? Couldn't they have equal merit if they were daughters? And what if Mr. McMurtrey should ask if people couldn't accept Krassos *and* accept alternative paths to God?"

"I'll ask my own questions, thank you," McMurtrey said.

"Heresy!" Orbust exclaimed.

"Just by suggesting questions that might be asked?" Appy queried. "I made no statements, mind you. How can non-statements be heresy?"

"You're tricky with words," Orbust said. "That's the sign of a false prophet."

"I've never claimed to be a prophet! I'm merely an apprentice."

"You're an apprentice to God," Smith said. "An apprentice to God! Has anyone focused on what that means? It means that this computer bastard claims it's *in training to become God*! That's blasphemy! God isn't a fancy computer, one that has to put other computers through apprenticeship programs. This is ludicrous! Computers competing to become the next God?"

"Appy said *biocomputer*," McMurtrey pointed out. "Whatever that is." It bothered McMurtrey that he couldn't see the entity.

Appy laughed loudly, and longer this time. It was a crazy ejaculation, the sort one might expect to hear in an insane asylum. "I'm an apprentice, yes. But I didn't say *what* I was in training for."

"Then you don't claim to be in training to become God?" Smith asked.

"I didn't say that," Appy said. "Never assume anything, gentlemen. That's one of the greatest problems of this universe . . . assumptions."

Orbust had his hand in the pocket containing the Snapcard. "Krassos said, 'I am *the* way,'" he said, "*The* way. Not *a* way."

"Johan, Chapter Fourteen, Verse Six," Appy said. "That's the report of Johan, a mortal. Mortals, *unlike computers*, make mistakes. What if Johan took it down wrong? What if, in fact, Krassos said, 'I am *a* way'? What if Johan was distracted by something at that moment? Maybe someone's sheep got loose, causing him to get a single key word wrong. What if someone translating the Babul over the centuries made a mistake? What if something was lost in translation?"

"You're so smart, Appy," Smith interjected, "you tell us. You should know all the answers. Don't toy with us, you mother—"

Smith caught Orbust's disapproving gaze, didn't complete the imprecation.

"Most religions believe in some form of life after death and the immortality of the soul," Appy said. "Why do you suppose that is?"

Silence permeated the passenger compartment.

"Think of me as a guide," Appy said. "I suggest certain lines of inquiry, direct you along certain paths. Always remember that God gave man Free Will, and with Free Will he gave man a mind. He wants man to use that mind, to figure things out for himself."

"But aren't you prejudicing our pursuit of knowledge by suggesting certain things?" McMurtrey asked. "If we follow your suggestions, aren't we succumbing to your particular bias, whatever that is?"

"You're intimating that God might be biased?" Appy said, in a tone so loud and ferocious it sent a chill down McMurtrey's spine.

"I'm thinking," McMurtrey said. "Isn't that what you want us to do?"

"Of course," Appy said. He snickered a little, added: "You aren't using a Snapcard on me, are you?"

"Certainly not," McMurtrey responded. He didn't understand how Orbust's Snapcard worked, was intrigued by it.

Orbust had his hand in the pocket with the card.

Appy's voice, pedantically: "Ask yourselves as you journey across the universe if the benefits of organized religion are confined to particular belief systems. Consider a woman I heard of recently, for example. She embraced no formal religion for many years. But then, when she was deathly ill, she accepted the Blue Presby faith, and later credited it with pulling her through. Might this have been *any* religion? Can a belief in *any* greater power help people survive such dire straits?"

"This guy sounds like an instrument of Satan," Orbust said.

McMurtrey recalled God's words, from the morning of the visitation: "*Seeker, who says religion is the way to God?*"

McMurtrey said nothing of this, for the words, while rhetorical, remained unclear.

"Mr. Orbust," Appy continued, "you are an enthusiast of a particular brand of organized religion. What are the benefits and liabilities of such systems? The benefits are legion, but I suggest to you the liabilities are legion as well. Viewed as an entire system, with interlocking religious parts, what is the balance? Which way does it tip?"

"Toward the evil side," Orbust said. "Because there are so many nonbelievers."

"Many would agree with the tilt toward evil," Appy said, "but not with your particular interpretation. The tilt, if it exists, may be caused by competing belief systems, by communication failures, by cussed stubbornness and narrow-mindedness. In short, the difficulties may be attributed to cells of little minds. Every religion has certain laudable ideals upon which it was established, from The Twelve Commandments to the Multifold Path. In practice, many of these ideals hold force, but many do not. Consider the terrible holy wars, for example. Certainly Krassos and Isammed would not have condoned the savage acts performed in their names."

"Isammed would have approved," Orbust said.

"Perhaps not," Appy said. "If you study the Kooraq carefully and keep an open mind, you will see much of an ethical nature that is very similar to your own value systems. I suggest to you that it is more fair to attack religions than it is to attack the prophets of those religions. They are not one and the same, you see. Krassos did not found Krassianism. His disciples did that, based upon His teachings and perhaps upon certain mystical beliefs prevalent at the time, such as reincarnation and dual resurrection. Attack Krassianism but not Krassos; attack Isammedanism but not Isammed; attack Hoddhism but not Hoddha. Attack what those organizations became under mortal guidance and interpretation, not the ideals upon which they were founded. Search fairly for similarities in belief systems, gentlemen, and you may discover that the differences aren't worth arguing about. Stretch interpretations to find areas of agreement. Wouldn't that be better than going to war in the name of religion?"

"I agree with McMurtrey," Orbust said. "You are biased, Appy."

"I would suggest that you keep an open mind," Appy said. "It helps in the weathering of strange seas."

"I already know what's right and what's wrong," Orbust said. "Everything that's worth knowing is in the Babul." He held up the book.

"Do you know what's wrong with religion today?" Appy asked. "Too many people are practicing it and not enough people are good at it." He guffawed like a lunatic, letting the laughter go with such uncontrolled enthusiasm that it frightened McMurtrey.

Orbust, Smith and Tully exchanged nervous glances.

McMurtrey felt out of balance. These weren't events he could have expected or planned for, and he felt uncomfortable in unpredictable situations. Was this computer creature mentally ill? Might it close the hatches and asphyxiate everyone? It didn't sound crazy when it spoke, and it did speak of love and tolerance. But its laughter was decidedly demented, not normal by any stretch of the imagination.

"Dear me," Appy said. "I'm being too loquacious. I'm an ethnic unit, you know, and ethnics—Oh, why be vague—I'll tell you. I'm supposed to be of the Middist bioethnicity, and some say that's why I'm so talkative. Dear me, why did I say that, casting aspersions on my own kind?"

McMurtrey heard a programming whir all around, a noise that didn't sound quite right.

After a few seconds, Appy came back: "God informs me that talkativeness is not confined to one race or culture. He informs me that my ethnicity was programmed incorrectly and irreparably in the rush and press of events. Most particularly my accent is flawed; the Boss describes it as like that of a second-rate actor. I wish He hadn't used the phrase 'second-rate,' and in your hands, gentlemen, this shouldn't be taken out of context, shouldn't be made into something it isn't. I perform my job well, thank you, as evidenced by numerous holy kudos in my memory banks. I speak only the truth, even about myself."

Orbust shook his head, slipped his Babul into its holster.

"Above all," Appy said, "I'm a big-deal machine—a little rough around the edges, but God tolerates me."

"What do you mean 'the rush and press of events'?" Smith asked. "We've been waiting around this paltry burg for three weeks waiting to get off the ground!"

"Three weeks is nothing. You should know Time! In the circles I travel, we spell Time with a capital T!"

"I'd like some answers myself," McMurtrey said. "Why was I left wondering what to do next? It's been very unpleasant."

"You have a brain, don't you?" Appy said. "You want God should force-feed you?"

McMurtrey felt blood rush to his face.

"If you want to travel with me," Appy said, "you must get used to caustic comments. I can't abide stupidity, and as far as reprogramming me goes, get any ideas like that out of your heads. My type of computer only gets programmed once, and then most of the rest of it is up to me. I have as much Free Will as you do. Oh, I've got a hot line to God; you've seen that, and I get a lot of orders. But I am what I am. Computers, ships, any kinda mechanism working for God has to have a personality, see? It goes with the job, and everything is always in a rush."

"Well, rush us to your Boss," Orbust demanded.

"Take us to your leader?" Appy asked. No laughter this time.

After a pause, Appy said: "Your definition of rush is different from ours."

"Exactly where are you," McMurtrey asked, "inside the walls, on the flight deck?"

"You don't need to know. Ho hum, tweedledee-dum, such an empty head!" This came in singsong.

Then, in a normal tone of voice, Appy said, "I could fill your cerebral cavities to bursting. You gotta coupla million years to listen? You want I should tell you how I dust my microcircuitry, too? There's no time! Now I must take my leave and check all ship's systems! God wants you to go out and bless the other ships while I'm occupied. Leave me for a while!"

"When should we come back?" Smith asked.

"You'll know when to return," Appy said. "And you'll know *who* should return."

McMurtrey felt like a child being sent from the room. He held his temper, asked, "You're in instantaneous communication with God?"

"I'd have to explain different time frames to fully answer that. Weeks are as nothing to God, but a second can be a very long time. When you use the word 'instantaneous,' understand that we are not on any spectrum you would understand. Instantaneous to you might seem very slow to God, or exceedingly fast, depending upon circumstance. I'm on a thirty-eight D'Urthsecond delay to Him now. In the past it's been slower and quicker, and under certain circumstances I've actually felt like I'm Him, the thoughts are so meshed with my own."

Appy paused, then: "Look, stop diverting me with chit-chat. You know how I like to talk, but there's a mission here and this is the primary ship, the one McMurtrey is to travel in. How intuitive of you to know that and appear here, McMurtrey. But be somewhere else for a while, okay?"

"That sounds silly, blessing all the ships," McMurtrey said, unwisely.

"A hacking cough upon you!" Appy roared. "Do as I say!"

So McMurtrey went off in the night to bless the balance

of the fleet, carrying Orbust's flashlight. The men accompanied McMurtrey for a short distance. Presently Orbust said something to Tully, and Orbust dropped back around a corner by himself while the others went on.

With a wind from the ocean picking up, Johnny Orbust slid stealthily to one side of a ship just south of Shusher. There, in low illumination from a porch light across the street he took off his holster and belt and removed the chemstrip from a pocket inside the belt. He spoke to the chemstrip: "Something highly concentrated that will metastasize in minutes, dissolving the metal of these ships."

Suddenly Orbust remembered Appy's comment that Shusher had a personality of its own, and wondered if this ship had a personality and a name. Were there listening devices on the skins of every ship in God's fleet, detecting every word? It was too late to think of that now. He waited with bated breath.

For a moment the chemstrip remained in the upturned palms of Orbust's hands Then without changing shape it jerked into the air, and like a flying leech it attached itself to the ship. Orbust heard a scraping sound followed by hissing, as from meat on a griddle. Presently the chemstrip metamorphosed into its butterfly form and flew off.

Within ten minutes, Orbust had a hand-held pumper, and he sprayed a landing strut of the nameless ship. He leaned close to the strut, couldn't see its surface clearly. But he heard a corrosive, hissing sound. The chemical was doing its work!

He ran to rejoin McMurtrey and the others.

Orbust saw the flashlight beam two ships ahead, and the amorphous shapes of the small group of men. Sheltering himself from the wind, he sprayed another ship while hurrying by it—just a little liquid on a strut as he had done before.

McMurtrey and his Krassian escort were on a platform above the flat roof of a private garage, where another ship happened to set down. Orbust scaled a metal staircase that came with the platform, joined the others.

McMurtrey, standing with his head bowed and hair

whipping in the breeze, was nearly finished with the same blessing he had administered to Shusher.

A dog barked from the yard next door, and on the lighted rear porch of that house a man and woman stood watching.

When McMurtrey finished, Orbust shot two sprays on the ship, with this comment: "Anointing fluid."

Thinking this strange, McMurtrey nonetheless nodded his head in assent. There seemed to be no point in arguing either with this motley bunch or with Appy. He felt pressed from all sides, and as he descended the steps he felt the sudden onslaught of a ferocious, hammering headache.

Dogs were barking all over town, in a drumlike, message-laden cacophony. House lights flashed on, and in the distance around Domingo's Reef, Tent City was lighting up.

Orbust led the way between the rest of the vessels in the fleet. At each, McMurtrey invoked the blessing, and Orbust followed with a misting of anointing fluid.

"You still need to spray Shusher," the long-bearded, disheveled Krassian said to Orbust. They were on the way back to town, from the tip of Domingo's Reef where the farthest vessel had been.

"Already did," Orbust growled.

The wind whistled, roared and surged through the streets of town, rattling fence boards and pieces of roofing metal. These noises, combined with the incessant wave action, prevented anyone except Orbust from noticing low, hissing sounds that came from ships the men passed on their way back to Shusher. Orbust smiled to himself at the surprise he had prepared for so many heathens and infidels.

He thought as well of the people who would be aboard Shusher. Only Orbust, Tully and Smith among Orbust's cabalists had proclaimed an affinity for Shusher, that visceral feeling so many people in St. Charles Beach were experiencing for particular ships in God's fleet. The others in his group might board other ships, or they might not go at all. Orbust didn't care, hadn't gotten to know any of them very well. Tully knew them best, had rounded them up for the show of force at McMurtrey's.

This Kundo Smith with the red collar said he was a NuNu

Pentecostalist, and Tully claimed to be a Found-Againer. The denominations they represented concurred with many of Orbust's Reborn Krassee beliefs, such as one God, Immaculate Conception and Dual Resurrection. In recent weeks they had conducted daily theological sessions, some heated and some amicable. To a limited extent, Orbust concurred with what Appy had said about finding areas of agreement between belief systems. But Orbust intended to use Smith and Tully as a wedge and a source of strength against infidels who were even further from the Lord, with Orbust's beliefs ultimately prevailing over everyone else's.

Orbust wondered who else would be aboard Shusher, and how many Krassians there would be. McMurtrey was no Krassian, not by any stretch of the imagination, and he was to be aboard—the principal passenger, according to Appy. Was this Rooster an atheist? Whatever category he fell into, Orbust admitted grudgingly that McMurtrey's statement of God's location rang true. It was like the innate feeling about which ship to go on, akin to Orbust's belief in God Himself.

But what purpose could God have in such a messenger? The man had confessed himself a fraud, and God must have known about it all along. Orbust wanted to know more about this buffoon, McMurtrey, about his real religious beliefs, if he held any. With that information, Orbust would be stronger.

Knowledge equals strength, he thought.

Orbust contemplated the panoply of religions in the star system, and the representatives of those faiths he had seen in St. Charles Beach. These religions and their adherents were vague, shadowy shapes to him, amalgams of insipid, misdirected people. Barbarians all of them, and any who didn't listen to the correct way would burn forever in the fire pits of Hell.

Four

She was nubile in every exotic dimension of the word, a graceful, sensuous creature in scanty clothing, cast from the molds of gods. One day a young noble from afar came on invitation to her planetoid, and when he set eyes upon her he was drawn to her in the strongest physical sense. This angered and frightened him, for he was a cerebral young man who had always prided himself on his ability to override the urgings of his libido.

So he asked her, in the most arctic of tones: "Why can't you rise above your sexuality?"

Her reply: "Why can't any of us?"

And he had no answer for this.

—A Folktale of the Old Galaxies

By the time they reached the white ship Shusher, a crowd had gathered around it. Flashlight beams danced on the riveted skin of the craft, and the air was alive with many languages. To the left and right, McMurtrey noted that every other ship in sight was receiving like attention.

"Life insurance! Life insurance!" a robot salesman shouted, working the crowd. "See me before you board! Last chance for insurance!"

Disgusting scum, McMurtrey thought. These robots were more tasteless than any human salesman had ever been, with every answer programmed into them. It was virtually impossible to say "no" to them, so only fools or the very brave engaged a life insurance broker in conversation.

'*Never look a life insurance robot in the eye*,' the saying went.

McMurtrey heard Appy's voice, looked toward the ship's entry hatch.

"Out!" Appy shouted. "A pox if you return! Only the names I call! No luggage or toiletries either, dunderheads! Can't any of you read?" The computer's voice had a metallic ring to it when heard from outside the ship, but it remained recognizable.

Dunderheads? McMurtrey thought. *What an odd word for Appy to use. This computer has a bad temper.*

McMurtrey pushed his way through to the ramp that led to the ship's hatch, and the Krassians kept close behind.

Four men and three women rumbled hastily down the ramp, fleeing the ship. Some carried bags. The group melted into the throng, except for one woman who left her bag with a man and then returned to the ship.

Appy's accented voice cut the cool air cleanly, calling out the names of those who were welcome on the voyage: "Pitarkin, Nathaniel R... Scovill, Cecilia... Markwell, Jason Q... Scanners activated to verify identities... No tricks, and don't try to sneak on any more baggage...."

But McMurtrey saw a few travelers board with weapons worn outside their clothing, secured by sheaths, straps and various harnessing arrangements. They weren't rejected, so it seemed that weapons were not considered "baggage." He wondered about the extent of personal hygiene supplies aboard. If there weren't any, or if they were inadequate, the odors would not be pleasant.

A small electric sign on one side of the ship's hatch became apparent, in bright purple letters:

PERSONAL PROPERTY LIMITATION
BRING ONLY WHAT YOU'RE WEARING

This sign hadn't been there before, or it hadn't been lit. McMurtrey thought of the pocket knife, coins and wallet in his pickpocket-proof trousers.

Pickpocket-proof trousers, he thought.

On one hand, it struck him funny to have on such attire in the midst of religious people, many of whom rejected all material goods. Most of the voyagers appeared to be unarmed, and a number were obvious ascetics, with bare feet, shaven heads and thin robes. There were nuns, priests, rabbis, pastors, monks, lamas, and perhaps even bishops and archbishops, judging from the elegant, golden-threaded robes of some.

Then McMurtrey remembered having heard someone say that you had to watch out most for Krassians—especially the ones who "wear their religions on their sleeves." It was a caller on a radio show, he recalled, a fellow who cited bad experiences with the type he spoke about. "They think they can be forgiven for anything," he said, "so they'll rob you blind."

McMurtrey held no personal animosity toward the adherents of any faith, had known a number of Krassians who seemed quite decent, and none of the other variety. Still, the concept of a person who could be forgiven for virtually any act seemed detestable, and he wondered how prevalent this strange doctrine was.

Appy called out the names of Johnny Orbust, C.T. Tully and Kundo Smith. They filed around McMurtrey (Orbust wearing his large, holstered pistol) and boarded the ship. Seconds later when McMurtrey heard his own name, he followed.

A chrome-plated dispensing machine he hadn't noticed before was mounted on the bulkhead just inside the main passenger compartment. After he went through an Identification scanner in the hatchway, he was instructed by Appy to take a cabin assignment ticket from the dispenser. Nothing was said about the contents of his pockets.

McMurtrey took an oversized red and yellow ticket, caught an elevator to Mezzanine Level 6. He had been assigned Cabin 66, and noticed an abbreviated map on the back of the ticket.

He stepped from the elevator with a half dozen fellow passengers, checked his map and went to the left, tramping along a softly padded walkway for a short distance. The material beneath his feet was light gray and porous, looked like weathered cork with a glossy sealer coat applied over it, and absorbed sound so efficiently he hardly heard his own passage. The walkway opened onto a wide, partitioned mezzanine that had a curved black railing on the left and curved silver-gray interior partitions directly ahead and to the right, all following the contour of the ship's body.

People from the elevator filed around McMurtrey, into the interior spaces. He was a little confused, studied the map.

"Outside aisle," a woman said to him, looking over his shoulder, "by the railing."

McMurtrey had been on one of these levels before when the boys first figured out the puzzle-locks and got aboard the ships, but all levels looked much the same, and that preview hadn't helped him much.

McMurtrey heard more people approaching from behind, talking. He felt a sudden urgency that they might think him slow-witted, and he hurried to the left, onto the walkway along the railing.

Now he could see that the mezzanine went all the way around the ship, with a circular shaft extending through the core of the ship on all mezzanine levels. The open shaft seemed like wasted space.

Cabin numbers were marked along a substantial wall to his right, and McMurtrey located a place on the wall designated "Cabin 66." He recalled the screen he would be able to drop to make this a room.

The wall was in varying shades of silver-gray, darker at the base than at the ceiling, with tones that blended with the deck surface. His bunk was folded into the wall, and its location could only be seen upon close scrutiny that revealed fine lines on the wall in a rectangular shape, long side vertical. There were raised areas to the left of this in various geometric shapes. On his earlier visit, McMurtrey hadn't actually opened a bunk. Now he pushed at the geometric shapes, trying to slide them open.

Appy was calling the names of people who hadn't reported yet, announcing takeoff at 5:17 A.M., and that the ship wouldn't wait for anyone. Appy referred to the travelers as "pilgrims," a description that seemed apt to McMurtrey.

He felt like any other in the quest for God now, his special status having been reduced to a common mezzanine-level bunk assignment.

On one side, a tall, slender woman in a maroon jumpsuit arrived and began inspecting her bunk. She was thirty or thirty-five, with graceful movements and the golden brown skin of a mula-black. She had small breasts, but attractively

proportioned, a good facial profile and dark, mysterious
eyes. She glanced at him aloofly for a second, and he saw
that she wasn't nearly as pretty from the front as from the
side. Her nose was very wide. Still, on balance he found
her attractive.

She opened several geometric panels and pressed buttons inside, activating devices in her cabin. It disturbed
McMurtrey that a woman seemed to be figuring out the
controls more quickly than he could. She must have been
there before, he decided, or someone had provided her
with instructions.

Her bunk clicked down, and a stiff plazymer-like curtain
dropped from the ceiling, concealing her from McMurtrey.
The curtain provided privacy all the way around, with
adequate passageway around the outside of the enclosure
to get between it and and the railing. Presently the curtain
shot back up, revealing the woman.

Her eyes flared angrily when she saw McMurtrey staring
at her, and she turned to face him full on, hands on hips.

"What are you looking at?" she demanded, voice husky.

"Oh, I'm sorry. I didn't realize I was . . ." He looked
away, then back at her, sheepishly.

Now she was smiling, a hard smile, but the eyes had
softened. "I'm Kelly Corona," she said. "You're the
Grand Exalted Rooster, right? I saw your speech. Good
stuff, baring your soul like that. I admire your guts."

"Uh, thanks." He caught himself staring at her chest,
thinking how well her breasts were formed. He glanced
up.

She was studying his face intently, must have noticed
the direction of his gaze. He felt hot around the temples,
with perspiration there. He couldn't take his eyes from
hers.

Her eyes were very gentle but mysteriously strong and
ever so dark—he sensed layers of emotion and calculation
within the darkness of those pupils. Were they brown? He
couldn't tell, but they were calming and hypnotic.

Her eyes flashed, as if fingers had been snapped, and
he emerged from a trance.

"I like the way you look at me," she said.

Krassos! McMurtrey thought. *What does she mean by
that?*

He felt helpless and confused. He wanted to leap at her, drop the curtain and make wild, rampaging love. How many months had it been since he had been with a woman? Eight? Ten? Closer to ten, he thought.

"Uh, excuse me," he said, feeling like a fool. "I didn't mean to stare. It's just that . . ." *Go ahead*, a little inner voice said to him. *Tell her you want to romp with her*!

He scratched his head, looked away. He had fumbled like this before with women, either consciously mishandling signals or failing entirely to interpret them until later, when all opportunity had dissipated. Too often he looked at women incorrectly, he knew, from the sexual standpoint. Invariably they picked up on this and turned away. Oh, he had a large and clumsy cuteness to him, and some women took to that at first. But it never lasted. This one wouldn't last.

Her gaze was angry now, starting to flicker away from his. It was happening again. Too late even to compliment her beauty. But what did he have to lose, if all was lost anyway?

"You're beautiful," he said, his voice too low. "Especially your eyes."

"What?" she said, her tone irritated. She licked a fingertip, applied moisture to one eyebrow and smoothed the brow down.

"I said you have nice eyes."

Her gesture with the eyebrow hadn't bothered him, and he felt good about this.

"Listen, McMurtrey, do you know who I am? I'm supposed to be captain of this friggin' ship. Number One Honchess. Yessirree Linda. But something is goofy here . . . mondo screwo. I passed up a cushy star freighter assignment to be here."

"What do you mean?"

"I'm a Merchant Spacer, and I received an air wave— you know, one of those new nearly invisible Wessornian Union radio bubbles that finds you and floats in the air."

"Yeah," McMurtrey said. "I've heard about those. They burst, don't they, and words flow out—up to what, fifteen-second messages?"

"Right."

"If I had a suspicious mind, I'd say that someone used

that technology on me to simulate God, the message about
His location. But hell, I talked with Him for several minutes. Those bubbles can't hold that much. Anyway, other
things have happened, like the ships."

She nodded. "The air wave I got wasn't anything occult.
It was from Appy, and he promised me a captaincy. I was
hearing publicity about you and God at the time, and it
all sounded too interesting to pass up. But I've yet to see
the controls of the ship. I've never seen a ship like this
before."

"Appy drove me crazy too."

"I confronted him a while ago, and he told me to report
to my berth right out here with everyone else. I've—"

"With the rabble, right?"

"I didn't mean . . ."

"Forget it. I feel demoted myself. You'd better keep
this down . . . could panic the passengers."

She lowered her voice, but only a little: "Panic the passengers? You're a passenger, McMurtrey. Aren't you worried that we're due to take off without a captain?"

"Call me Ev, for Evander."

She nodded, with a tense smile. "Kelly."

"Kelly, it can't be too bad. Somebody or some thing
flew these ships here, and they should be able to take 'em
off again. Maybe they're gonna get us into outer space
before your skills are needed."

"Well, I'm damned upset about the way this is being
handled, and I'm gonna give that loudmouthed computer
a piece of my mind." She stalked off.

McMurtrey explored his own cabin buttons, and when
he was well on his way to figuring them out, he found he
had a tiny enclosure like Corona's. With the divider down
it was about two and a half meters in length by the same
width. A wide floor area was on one side of the enclosure,
with one side of the bed and the bottom of the bed abutting
the divider.

McMurtrey bounced on the mattress, and it felt firm
despite his great weight. The headboard had an illuminated
amber screen with a wide bar at the base. When he pressed
the bar, a number of book-tape titles appeared in red on
the screen, along with instructions on how to use the device. Beneath the wide bar was a compartment with ear-

phones, and the instructions said that any title on the screen could be ordered for listening.

He heard voices outside his enclosure, muffled only slightly by the divider.

The selection of book-tapes was varied, from best-selling fiction to collections of poetry, religion, the occult, history and politics. Some of the titles were eye-catching and most surprising, given the setting of the ship: *Love Slaves In the Sunset . . . The Kinky Twins . . . Diary Of a Mad Hooker.*

Such titles on a ship of God seemed beyond belief, and he wondered if they might be testimonials, uplifting tales of sinners who had "found" the Lord. In any event he resolved not to dabble with those titles, for despite the frauds of his past he remained a man of substantial morality.

He activated a tiny table- and chair-set that popped out of the deck in the wide area to one side of the bed. He rolled off the bed and sat on one of two opposing chairs. The chair flexed under his weight, but it held and seemed reasonably strong. A black and white gauge on the edge of the table showed his weight: 152 kilograms.

He sat facing the headboard wall, noticed a little porthole there that had appeared with the dinette set. McMurtrey could see the ships lined up from Domingo's Reef into town, and all ships were illuminated from within to varying degrees, with light coming from portholes he hadn't known were on the ships. They were irregularly spaced portholes, leading him to believe that they only appeared when cabins were occupied and the dinette sets opened up. He fast realized that the porthole he was looking through had another curious feature. Since he was in the innermost partition of the ship, with other cabins outside his, he shouldn't have had a port! It must have been an elaborate and ingenious arrangement of mirrors or a televid screen. He couldn't tell the difference between looking into this porthole and looking out a window.

McMurtrey only half heard the squawk of protest and the rush of wind made by beating wings. It was the voice that brought him to awareness, a rather loud and urgent tone that came from outside his enclosure.

"Mr. Grand Exalted, I have your chicken."

McMurtrey had forgotten No Name for a while, so engrossed had he become in events that were carrying him along like a toothpick in a hurricane. This bird had gotten past Appy's checkpoint, so it must have been approved.

McMurtrey pressed a silver button with a trident on it, and the screen for his micro-apartment rose. As it lifted, McMurtrey first saw bare feet and hair-covered legs, with a slender bamboo pole broom lying on the deck to one side. Then to his complete shock, an entirely naked man came into view. The man's head was shaved, and he held the chicken in his hands, covering his genitals.

"You're holding that bird near a rather vulnerable spot," McMurtrey said, regaining composure quickly.

No Name was wriggling around trying to peck at the man, but the fellow had its neck and head grasped firmly in such a way that the bird was having difficulty attacking.

"I'm here to give you the bird," the man said, apparently unaware of his double-entendre. "This thing is feisty!"

One of McMurtrey's initial reactions was to tie this scenario in with the sexually suggestive book-tape titles he had seen. But the man had a tranquil expression on his face, leading McMurtrey to surmise that he must be the disciple of a strange religious cult.

"I'm a Plarnjarn, Digam sect," the man said, placing the chicken in McMurtrey's grasp. The man retrieved his broom.

McMurtrey heard scuffling, turned and saw a small group of eavesdroppers standing on the other side of the mula-black's uncurtained apartment. There were men, women, and children, all wild-eyed with fascination. Most wore robes, in a variety of colors and patterns.

Kelly Corona stood impassively beside her open bed, arms folded in front of her, staring at McMurtrey and his visitor.

McMurtrey looked back at the Plarnjarn, who was visible right down to a shamrock-shaped birthmark on his lower abdomen.

Behind McMurtrey, a child giggled.

"I don't think I want to take this chicken on such a long journey," McMurtrey said.

"You may be wise in saying that," the Plarnjarn said.

"Appy suggested you might want it for religious purposes, and I was asked to bring it to you."

"Were you commanded to do so?"

"Quite the opposite. I was entering the ship, when through a speaker I heard the computer conversing with itself, trying to decide whether or not the chicken should go. I said nothing and was about to pass by when Appy called my name, saying, 'Jin, what is your opinion on this matter?'"

McMurtrey shifted uneasily on his feet, tried not to stare in the wrong direction.

"Well," Jin continued, "I know enough from what I overheard and from the talk about town to realize that Appy meant your chicken. But in reply I said I didn't know. I asked him if I should fetch it."

The vision of a naked man running after a rather rough-and-tumble chicken struck McMurtrey funny, and he smiled.

"Appy asked me to fetch it straightaway. He gave me your berth number, and here I am."

"Can you take the bird back?" McMurtrey asked, feeling a little weary. "Is there time before takeoff?"

"Expecting you might say this, I asked a townsman to wait outside the ship. He has promised to care for your mascot if you desire, and promises to give it back when you return. I see concern in your face. You've had the bird a long time?"

"Around nineteen years, I think. It's extraordinary, an unknown breed."

McMurtrey turned No Name over to Jin, and watched the naked man walk away, brushing his path with the broom before taking each step.

"The name Jin means 'defeater of passions,'" Corona said, her voice husky and sensual. "As a Plarnjarn monk, he brushes his path to avoid stepping on an insect or any other life form. His nudism is an ascetic statement. To him the perfect saint possesses nothing, not even a rag of cloth for his body."

McMurtrey faced Corona. She was staring at him, her eyes dark and inquisitive. They bore a message different from her words.

"What about the broom?" McMurtrey asked. "Does he

own that?" He smiled impishly, noticed the onlookers were departing.

Corona laughed. "You and I will get along famously," she said.

"How do you know those things about Jin?" McMurtrey wondered.

"Simple. I asked him."

"Oh."

"Do you know what Appy did? The bastard set up an electronic barrier so I can't get off the ship. I can't get past the I.D. scanner."

"How'd he do that?"

Corona shrugged. "The twerp said I was on my way to meet my Maker now, whether I wanted to or not. It almost sounded scary the way he put it, but I guess it wasn't intended that way."

"No. Of course not. Say, you don't sound real upset about being shanghaied. I mean, you're kinda upset, but . . ."

Don't pussyfoot around, fool! McMurtrey's inner voice demanded.

"Uh, I sense you could get a lot angrier," he said. "You're obviously a strong woman."

A lot of woman, he thought.

She smiled. "Yeah—well, that star freighter took off anyway, so I'd have to hang around the hiring hall. I hate hiring halls, being with all those losers."

McMurtrey nodded.

"Appy tried to explain, but seemed rushed and didn't tell me much. He said his circuits were giving him trouble. Kinda like bursitus, I guess. Anyway, he says this ship is run by committee, that after Appy invited me aboard on their behalf, they—whoever they are—decided I shouldn't be captain after all, that I should just be a passenger."

"Appy told me the ship has a separate, rather stupid personality named Shusher, that God, Appy and Shusher are running the show in a kind of skewed triumvirate in which Appy and God compensate for Shusher's occasional blunders. That must be the committee he was describing to you, and they're the captains."

Corona considered this. "Shusher and Appy must be hardware, bionics and living tissue. My guess is we can't imagine all the possibilities. I'm sure as shit not privy to what's going on, and you don't seem to be, either. Between us maybe we can piece it together."

"With the other passengers. We should talk to as many of them as we can."

"Good idea. Anyway, when Appy was laying that change of captaincy routine on me, I was too wiped out, on-my-ass shocked to ask the right questions. When Appy sealed me aboard ship, I just sorta caved in. Maybe I didn't mind so much because you're gonna be here with me."

Krassos! McMurtrey thought. He smiled, but not easily.

"You and I are alike, Ev—used and scrapped. You performed your task, and now you're just one of the flock. Me, I'll probably never be eligible for another star freighter assignment after my brain gets burned out by this mess. There's gonna be people preaching to us, trying to convert us all the way." She shook her head in exasperation.

Corona departed with that, saying she wanted to wander around the ship.

McMurtrey thought about her odd predicament, and about his own apparent fall from status. He was now as he had been before God's visitation and as he deserved to be: common. Kelly had been humbled herself, brought down from haughtiness. Maybe that explained why she was aboard, a lesson to her.

It seemed to McMurtrey that he had been haughty too, in his own way. There had been subtle changes in his behavior, little changes in the usual ways he dealt with people.

Lessons.

Did any human have a right to think he was more than the rest? Wasn't every human a mere passenger in the universe? D'Urth itself was a ship of God.

Was this journey to be a lesson for every pilgrim? It had to be, McMurtrey realized, for every experience in life was a lesson, in one degree or another.

Krassos walked most comfortably among common people, after all, and so did many of the other great prophets. Conceivably McMurtrey was supposed to follow this path himself, wandering among the people, spouting pearls of wisdom that one day would become scripture.

McMurtrey starting his own religion? For real this time?

He didn't feel very wise at the moment, with more questions than answers, and chastised himself. Whatever he did from this moment on shouldn't be for himself. He, Evander Harold McMurtrey, had been plucked from the humdrum, everyday flow of such considerations. His life, the fragile remains of it, was forfeit to The Cause, largely an unknown. He felt anger at such submissiveness, but something was compelling him to consider matters he had never thought of before. He would wait and see, moving carefully in this strange place, in this unprecedented, historic time.

Jin returned soon, carrying only his broom, which he employed as before. Maybe the broom was borrowed, McMurtrey thought. That would make it all right for a nonmaterialist. Jin sat cross-legged on the deck where his fold-down bed would have been had he lowered it, four spaces away from McMurtrey. This, apparently, was his cabin assignment. Jin did not seem interested in the consoles on the bulkhead, and soon he was rigid, in an apparent trance. He stared straight ahead, at the railing.

The cabin assignments on Mezzanine 6 began to fill in, but no one took those between McMurtrey and Jin. Some pilgrims dropped their screens for immediate privacy, while others sat on beds or chairs in undivided areas. Still others, like Jin, sat ascetically on the bare deck.

Jin was the only one who appeared nude thus far, but there were several young and old men in white, saffron, or lavender robes, some with shaven heads like Jin's, others with hair below their shoulders. Few were in between when it came to this matter of hair length, and McMurtrey mused over this, wondering how it might tie in with the politics, religious doctrines and philosophies of these people.

Such a panoply of robes, in infinite colors, cuts and folds: the thin and sheetlike flowing robes of Hoddhist monks beside Isammedan galabias, caftans, and burnooses. There were dhotis and bright calicos from Nandia, the heavy, tailored robes of Middists and Krassians, and more. Their garb seemed to reflect degrees of asceticism, with Jin at one extreme, then the barefoot but clothed Hoddhist monks and the Nandus in their white dhotis. The most elaborately dressed person was a dark-skinned, princely Afsornian across the mezzanine who stood by his bunk in jeweled robe and turban. McMurtrey didn't like the look of this man, the way he seemed to be awaiting an attendant. But it was early, and McMurtrey wanted to avoid passing judgment.

McMurtrey activated his dinette set, sat at the table and watched the others as they busied themselves in various pursuits, from the rituals of prayer to conversation and the opening and closing of their bunks and screens.

God had selected the diverse mix of participants in this event, undoubtedly with meticulous care. McMurtrey envisioned each of them on a great voyage of discovery, more important than any that mankind had ever attempted. He realized this was a race, whether by design or *de facto*, with the ships lined up as they were and pilgrims clamoring to get to God first. Even those aboard Shusher were in a race with one another. Who among them would be first to debark and face the ethereal holy light? These voyages were different from anything in history and yet they were the same, for McMurtrey realized that the race for God had long been on, ever since man organized himself into competing belief systems.

Was this caused by Free Will? Might there be a better way? But a "better way" seemed to require altering the nature of man—a potentially dangerous and troubling thought, the sort of thought a mere human shouldn't trouble himself about.

There were stories going back countless centuries of God's anger, and of His great cunning. Often He put people to supreme tests, when He grew tired of their foolish, selfish natures, or when He wanted to teach a great lesson. McMurtrey was thinking in Wessornian terms, he realized, even though he wasn't formally religious. These were the concepts most familiar to him, and now he became conscious of them filtering his thoughts. He was in a mindset of age-old patterns and channels that were almost instinctual to him. There were so many other versions of God he barely understood, even with the comparative-religion book-tapes he had studied. Maybe God was altering the course of mankind. A final, concentrated race, and what would they discover?

The announcement of God's location, even with all its apparent detail, wasn't so simple. It wasn't clear-cut, a trip from hither to yon. Some of the ships on display were not ships at all, but seemed instead to be places of worship in ships' skins. This strongly suggested that certain people involved in the event, primarily the Eassornian belief-systems, did not intend to leave D'Urth in their journey to God. These were the ones who had no image of God as a bearded old man in the sky. To them, He was either everywhere or internal, and for them the journey would be altogether different.

McMurtrey understood this, to a limited extent, but it confused him that some of the followers of Eassornian philosophies were nevertheless physically journeying on Shusher. Did this mean they harbored doubts, especially with the announcement God made?

On the highest level of the ship, Kelly Corona passed her hand near a triangular-shaped hatch at the end of the corridor. She was alone here, and from far below came the echoing voices of the passengers, nearly drowned out by the authoritarian, oddly accented tones of Appy emanating from a speaker near Corona. There were speaker systems all over the ship, presumably to impart urgency to all statements made by the biocomputer.

Loud tones demanded immediate action. Fainter ones could be set aside. With speakers everywhere, Appy seemed to be everywhere, like a nagging parent.

The level on which Corona stood, and two just beneath, were much smaller mezzanines than those below, and on each of the three were two triangular hatches. This was the last hatch she had tried.

Corona assumed they were hatches, from their large size, from the heavy framing around them, and from parallel scrape marks on the hatches, apparently caused by their sliding aside. The scrape marks were perplexing, as they ran in different directions on each surface, as if each hatch operated differently. She hadn't gotten any to move yet, noted that the parallel lines on the one in front of her ran from the right leg of the triangle toward the lower left.

She hadn't expected any of them to move, and this one

didn't surprise her. She grunted with a last effort, withdrew her hands and took a deep breath.

Signs had been posted on each of these levels, but she had gone on past: On the lowest level of the three it was: KEEP OUT BY ORDER OF GOD; then on the middle level: PROCEED AT PERIL TO YOUR IMMORTAL SOUL; and on the top level: THIS AREA IS A NO-NO!

It took more than signs to deter this veteran of thirty-two missions beyond the solar system.

Corona turned away from the hatch, scanned the short, empty corridor before her. The walls were smooth and silvery, with a matching, tightly woven carpet. This carpeting didn't muffle sound, perhaps by design, and when she walked on it she heard a sloshing and squeaking, as if her shoes were full of water.

There had to be intruder alarms somewhere, maybe in the carpet. They had to know she was here.

Armed robots would block her exit any moment now.

Something metallic clicked behind her, like the safety catch on a Blik Pulverizer.

Corona swallowed hard, whirled toward the hatch. Nothing there. Then she saw it: gaps around two legs of the triangle. The triangular hatch had slipped upward a bit, to the right! She kneeled, saw something scarlet beyond.

Cautiously she touched the metal hatch near the gap, slid her fingers into the gap for a microsecond and withdrew them, fearing a snap that could cut them off.

The hatch moved no further.

She knelt way over, peered through the gap and saw a scarlet room beyond. No furnishings or electronics were apparent.

Back into the gap went her fingers, for a little longer before she jerked them back. Then a third time, and she tried to pull the triangle up to the right. It was a thick plate, its thickness at least half the length of her longest finger, and again the plate did not budge.

She withdrew once more, sighed.

The plate snapped shut, then slid all the way open in the other direction, filling her eyes with the scarlet of the room. The walls, the ceiling and the floor were all of one color and texture, as if molded from a single piece of plazymer.

She sprang over a threshold lip and through the opening, rolling head over heels into the room.

It wasn't scarlet from the inside, and now the only scarlet came as light through the triangular hatch, from the corridor outside. But there had been no such color out there, and, now it seemed, no such color inside either.

Now the walls, ceiling and floor of the room were like those of the corridor, smooth and silvery. They pulsed around her, like heaving, living membranes, and she nearly cried out in terror.

Shusher? McMurtrey said the ship was a separate personality. . . . Was it a LIVING entity?

Corona crouched near the doorway, ready to spring through and free. Then the floor began to spin as if it were a Lazy Susan, and with a whirl of silver color around her it accelerated. Something unseen beneath her held her in place, prevented independent body movement.

She heard and saw nothing, felt nothing except the motion, and gradually even this residual sensation passed. She was blind and senseless, with only the thought of nothingness separating her from a vast void.

The void focused down as a thought image to the tiniest of apparent points. Then it exploded with Corona at the center, and her senses returned.

She found herself kneeling on the floor of a silver room, staring at what looked like a black, projected shadow of herself on one wall. The shadow pulsed by itself, and bulged toward her from the wall as if it were filling with air from the other side.

Stinging perspiration ran into her eyes, and though unable to turn her head she sensed that the entry hatch was behind her, throwing the light that made her shadow.

A sliver of whiteness appeared on the left side of her shadow, and like zippers going in two directions this whiteness went around the perimeter of the shadow until it delineated all except a short horizontal section at the bottom.

Startlingly, the shadow flopped open as if a hinge were on the bottom. Corona felt powerless to move, saw the shadow stretch open before her, falling toward her. She thought the shadow brushed her forehead and the tip of her nose as it dropped in front of her, but as in the attempted recollection of a dream she wasn't sure.

The shadow plopped to the deck, and like a thing melting, it became flat and wide, extending right and left all the way to the walls on each side of Corona.

How could a shadow change shape and move around independently? And how could she have felt it? Why couldn't she move now? Unanswered questions hurtled through her mind, bounced against one another in their eagerness for primacy.

It was as if a fragment of Corona's life had fallen away and died at her feet, and in the shape on the wall where the black shadow had been, there was now an outline of white against silver.

She caught her breath.

Black on the wall had become white, and remained there like an aura—evidence of life that hadn't yet faded. It was a steady tone of white.

The shadow on the deck before her kneeling place was black and amorphous, a pool of darkness. She could move now, and touched it. Her hand passed through into a warmth that seemed bottomless. She withdrew her hand, feared that she would topple in if she didn't hold her balance.

When she moved on her knees, ever so carefully, the whiteness on the wall changed shape with her, a reassurance that something remained of her. But the shape on the deck before her did not move.

Then the white fell away from the wall, seeming to brush her face once more. Now the amorphous pool on the deck had become white, and the shape on the wall was black.

Corona was transfixed.

Then, like a climactic upheaval of dead cells, black peeled away from the wall, revealing white. Then white peeled away, then black, seemingly ad infinitum in a dizzying, rapid display that made a faint fanning sound as the shapes brushed against her face. They caused no wind.

It was a purring, soothing sound. When it ended, the shadow of her body remained on the wall, but now stood as a translucent lavender veil over what appeared to be another opening.

Before her on the deck, a wide pool of darkness prevented her from crossing to the wall. As before, this fear-inspiring pool extended all the way to each wall on her right and left.

As she moved her knees a little, the lavender veil on the wall made corresponding movements, but the residue on the deck was stationary.

Now the veil melted away into the wall, and with this, an intense stream of lavender flowed toward her across the dark pool. She sensed something alien, perhaps of another dimension, crossing the frigid expanse of the universe from afar, and it made her shiver. She was bathed in coolness that from the color should have been warmth. It filled every pore of her body.

Corona felt like an intruder, that she wasn't supposed to be there. But she knew innately that she belonged here, that it was as much her birthright as anyone else's.

The first prayer of her life, whispered, caught in her throat and didn't make it out: "Oh God, I'm so afraid. Please . . ."

Corona felt a compression change in her ears, heard an angry whine that ebbed and flowed in pitch and intensity like the signalings of a porpoise. For a moment she felt in limbo, without a sense of place.

Then a lavender wind roared out of the wall, and a firehose of black wind streamed from the dark pool, knocking her backward. She tumbled derrière-over-teakettle out the hatchway behind her.

The hatch snapped shut with an angry thump.

Corona struggled to her feet, and on rubbery legs retreated down the corridor. Noises in her ears. That angry whine in one, and in the other a voice—a vaguely familiar voice.

As with stereo sound, she distinguished separate and distant vocal tones, tones that grew in intensity until she could identify whispered words.

"You're a fool, Shusher," the voice whispered. Appy! But this voice came to Corona across no speakers, though there were speakers in this corridor.

She felt another compression change in her ears, then heard Appy talking separately across the ship's speakers, simultaneously saying different things from what she heard through the alternate channel.

Both ears popped, and subsequently she heard only the whisperings of Appy across this private channel, which came to Corona as if he were speaking into her left ear. And in her right ear were the porpoise sounds, ebbing and flowing like the yelping of an unhappy pet.

Corona retreated down the corridor, stopped dead in her tracks when she heard Appy's scolding tones in one ear: "You let the hatch slip open, I didn't do it! Don't give me any of that!"

In Corona's right ear: "Wawaah! . . . wheezo . . . wheezo . . . wauuwo!"

Shusher? Corona thought. *Am I hearing Shusher's language*?

Appy had said that Shusher was stupid, so maybe the ship spoke a primitive language.

"Shush, Shusher!" Appy commanded. "Shush and listen!"

The whining ceased.

One of them at each ear? IN each ear?

Corona saw goose bumps on the backs of her hands, and each bump pulsed, as the eery convex shape on the wall had done.

"You rest awhile, Shusher," Appy said, "and when I'm ready for takeoff this time, do as I command! You're misinterpreting T.O.'s instructions!"

T.O.? Corona thought. *Tananius-Ofo . . . How do I know that? That's . . . that's . . . God's name in this dimension I've tapped! Isn't that also the name of the planet we're supposed to go to*?

Appy was continuing his diatribe: "I am preeminent in some tasks and you—T.O. help us—in others! Takeoff is mine!"

"Whee . . . suuu . . . rooooh!" Harsh tones.

"No, no, no. Not that matter of ship's speed again. Just because you can adjust the ship's speed doesn't mean you're entitled to make *decisions* about it. I'm in charge of that. Takeoff and speed are mine! Get it straight!"

What in the hell is going on? Corona wondered.

A ship run by committee, by this pseudo-holy trinity of Tananius-Ofo, Appy and Shusher? This Shusher entity, whatever it was, seemed to have some rather essential input—on the speed of the ship, on certain hatchways, on noise.

A ship that demanded quiet? Why?

She heard a din coming from the passenger area below, wondered if this might end at Shusher's insistence when they were in flight.

But did Shusher also have an input in the selection of who was to captain the craft, as Appy claimed? It seemed unlikely.

It seemed that this ship's company did not always function as a cooperative effort, that it was instead a strange and disjointed amalgam of separate and strongly willed performers.

At least Corona presumed T.O. had a strong will: It fit the image of God she'd always had. But she realized with what was happening around her that she would have to erase the old preconceptions. Some of them, many of them, might hold true. But many would not.

Were there other computers and other living ships in the fleet assembled at St. Charles Beach? Or were Appy and Shusher on all of them collectively? Might there be other options?

Corona's mind raced, so far ahead of the information she had that it gave her a headache. How had she understood the reference to T.O. without explanation? And why wasn't she automatically privy to anything else?

She listened carefully for Appy and Shusher, but for the moment heard nothing further.

Five

Morality tends to interfere with the successful operation
of any religious organization. Efficiency and survival,
these are the bywords of holy business.
                                    —The Apostolic Manuscripts,
                                      Uncensored Edition

McMurtrey shifted position, felt the dinette chair flex beneath him. His screen was up, and he was in the chair
facing away from the headboard wall. Moments before,
Appy had ordered everyone back to their cabins. No sign
of Corona yet.

McMurtrey gazed thoughtfully past the black mezzanine
railing to four saffron-robed monks walking on the other
side. They rounded a partition, disappeared from view.
McMurtrey was thinking about God's message, trying to
get an angle on it.

There had been authentic statements from on high before. About that, McMurtrey harbored no doubts. But had
they been as seemingly concise as the one he received? It
struck him from his studies that prior messages had not
been at all concise, and that literal interpretations invariably got people into trouble.

The great theologian O'Robin, for example. He mis-
interpreted a passage in the Babul about eunuchs serving
the Kingdom of Heaven and castrated himself. He later
came to regret his act, but too late. The Babulical passages
about casting out an offending eye might have entered
O'Robin's thoughts as well, and if not his, they certainly
caused great pain to others who in documented cases read
the passages literally and then physically harmed themselves.

God spoke in metaphors, didn't He? But always? Every

word? It didn't seem possible. How were people to recognize the difference? How could an announcement of His
location with exact astronomical coordinates be interpreted in different ways? Couldn't this, in and of itself, be
interpreted as a condemnation of certain Eassornian religious beliefs? It seemed to be an assertion that God was
in fact "out there" as a separate deity.

The astronomical coordinates and the ships suggested
an apparent means of reaching God in this plane of existence, the physical human plane of the year 387.

This thought of the year re-triggered his disturbing
awareness of a Wessornian mindset and the limitations this
imposed upon him. It was a Janovian calendar year,
marked from the mythical point of Krassos' birth. Mc-
Murtrey was coming to realize, as he never had before,
that he was a captive of certain beliefs, that many of these
beliefs were not recognizable as such and were instead
presumed to be facts.

The Isammedans had their own calendar. So did the
Middists, and to a ceremonial extent the Florientals had
theirs as well. This wasn't 387 to everyone. But what did
this really have to do with mindset, with different views
of a single event? He wasn't certain. But it seemed like a
chink in the armor and veneer of his own thought processes. Familiar, safe old patterns were suddenly vulnerable and fragile.

Because they interpreted God's latest message differently, the followers of mankind's religions were venturing
forth with varying expectations.

McMurtrey realized that he was thinking more lucidly
than he ever had before. His mind seemed less parochial,
less restricted by the screens of experience. He was emerging from the detritus of a lifetime, from those memories
and the clutter of activities on D'Urth that inhibited pure
thought.

He laughed to himself. Pure thought! What did he know
of 'pure thought,' and was there such a thing?

Two heavy women on the opposite side of the passenger
compartment caught his attention, one level up. They appeared to be KothoLu nuns—one in a white habit, the
other in black. They stood by their adjacent berths, smiling
and chatting as they gazed down toward the main deck.

Near them McMurtrey recognized Tully, tinkering with the buttons of his berth. Moments later the priest McMurtrey had designated Redneck came into view, and he spoke to Tully. Orbust wasn't around, although McMurtrey had seen him board.

"Locate the brass switch that slides vertically on each of your main control panels," Appy said, through the P.A. system. "Slide that up, and it opens an intercom to my mainframe, so you can carry on conversations with me. Through a networking arrangement I can speak with all of you simultaneously in separate, private conversations. Before we proceed with that or with anything else, I will mention a number of things. It will be advisable for each of you to drop your sleeping compartment screens during takeoff and landing, as this makes available to you a foam body-cush system that activates automatically in the event of impact."

McMurtrey didn't like that word. *Impact.*

"No one is required to employ this system, but anyone dying enroute will be liquefied and jettisoned unceremoniously in a timeburst burial cylinder. I assume that each of you have heard of this procedure, as it is commonly utilized in deep space, and has been described accurately in popular movies and publications.

"On Mezzanine Level Twelve, the room with the black door is a storage area for your religious paraphernalia. You will find incense sticks and candles there, all in Insurance Laboratories-approved enclosures to prevent torching the ship. There are vestments, even zuchetto-type papal hats if you wish . . . black zuchettos for priests, purple for bishops, red for cardinals, and white for the Pope. Is the KothoLu Pope aboard?"

No response came. A number of people laughed, for Appy seemed to be having fun with this.

"Everything is in that room. You want prayer mats or surplices? We got 'em, first come, first served. Be there or be bare, and I don't say this lightly: many of you will find gadgets appropriate to a number of religions. You may not be able to tell them apart, I fear, and there could be arguments that I would be helpless to prevent."

Not really, McMurtrey thought. *They could take turns, drawing lots to see who goes first. . . .*

"Beneath the main deck are Assembly Room Sublevels A, B and C, and beneath them you will find three more sublevels of generic shrine rooms. You may leave paraphernalia in the shrine rooms, and please—respect the property rights of others!"

That'll be interesting, McMurtrey thought.

"Several of you have asked about toilet facilities and clothing," Appy continued, "and frankly I'm surprised, even a bit dismayed, at such queries. Foolish questions will not be answered. It is up to each of you to search your inner selves for such information, for it is well within the reasoning capacity of anyone who has come this far. You call yourselves pious? Prove it!"

What did piety have to do with human waste? McMurtrey shook his head and felt a sudden urge to empty his bladder, which seemed aggravated by the apparent lack of facilities. Appy was a tyrant, a mental mutant!

He heard what sounded like a toilet flushing, and the noise seemed to emanate from an enclosed cabin just the other side of Corona's.

With a little investigation, McMurtrey discovered that the main control panel swung open, revealing three more buttons underneath, all reddish-brown. He tested them one at a time. They controlled, from left to right: (a) A pop-up, unenclosed lavatory that came out of a previously unnoticed deck hatch between the dinette set and the headboard wall. (This presented a potential etiquette problem when visitors were in the cubicle.); (b) a meal menu, on a screen that appeared in the center of the table; (c) a laundry chute revealed by a bin that swung open from the headboard wall. A sign on the bin read:

LAUNDRY
5 Minutes Wash And Dry
No bleach, no starch, no
ironing, don't ask!

The atypical open lavatory included a washbasin, a toilet, and a spray nozzle on a long hose for showering. The lavatory floor was tiled, sloped, and scuppered, apparently designed so that drain water ran into a channel that led to a hole beneath the headboard wall. It seemed primitive in the midst of surrounding technology, but the passengers had no other choices, and many of them from poorer locales were probably accustomed to much worse.

A tiny drawer opened from a free-standing cabinet beneath the sink, and inside this drawer McMurtrey found toothpaste, a toothbrush, and a flat stainless steel plate that had a handle on one side. The handle was inscribed "Beard Zapper," but the device had no cord and no switch. He passed the plate over the hair-covered back of his hand, and wherever he did this the hair melted away without a trace. The affected skin area felt numb for a moment, but this passed and left no marks.

Appy's excited voice boomed across the P.A.: "Takeoff in ten minutes! Drop screens!"

From all over the ship, McMurtrey heard the dull thuddings of screens as they locked into place. He hesitated with his own, saw that almost everyone visible on his level and on other levels had activated screens. He and Jin were exceptions, and Corona had left her bunk down with her screen out of view. She wasn't anywhere to be seen, leaving McMurtrey to assume that she might have talked Appy into letting her perform flight duties.

Still, he worried about her, for Appy hadn't said what might happen to a person outside a sleeping enclosure during takeoff and landing. Jin was outside, too.

Something began to whir, felt through the floor and heard faintly. He picked up the distinct redolence of mint.

"Eight minutes," Appy announced, voice tremulous.

"Hey, Jin!" McMurtrey yelled. "Drop your screen!"

Jin sat cross-legged, staring straight ahead. His head jerked, and he looked at McMurtrey.

McMurtrey repeated himself.

Jin hurried to his control panel, appeared to be having difficulty accessing it.

McMurtrey bolted toward Jin, making hardly any sound on the cushioned deck.

A tiny computer voice on Jin's headboard wall blared, "Intruder! Intruder!"

"What the hell's going on here?" McMurtrey asked.

"The panel has an identity scanner," Jin said, "and it isn't responding to me! I don't know why. It worked before."

McMurtrey tried to open Jin's panel box, but it wouldn't move, and again the tiny computer voice reported an intruder.

"Two minutes," Appy announced.

"Let's get inside my cabin," McMurtrey offered.

"Wait a minute. I can't believe this infernal thing won't work." Jin tried the panel again, and this time it opened, revealing the buttons inside.

"I'm okay now," Jin said. "Thank you."

McMurtrey returned to his cabin.

"One minute!" Appy said. "Hey! What the—."

"My buttons aren't working!" Jin shouted. He started toward McMurtrey.

The ship jolted, and Appy screeched: "Early takeoff! Early takeoff! This is not my fault, and I—"

A high-pitched whine inundated the ship's interior, and McMurtrey couldn't hear the ensuing words. He was pinned to the deck, sliding toward the railing.

Something arrested his slide abruptly, with a jerk at his midsection. He saw a blue nylester strap around his waist, with a tether leading from one side of the strap to a spot in the center of his unscreened quarters, adjacent to the dinette set and lavatory, which were still popped up in place.

He hardly had time to consider this, when he left the surface of the deck, floating gently into the air to the limit of the tether, which was about three meters. He was over the railing, looking down on the main passenger compartment deck far below, which was empty of people. His stomach felt queasy. He grabbed hold of the railing, pulled himself inside it and remained there with the tether looped tightly in one hand and the railing held with the other.

To one side, he saw Jin in a similar state, floating at the edge of a tether out over the main deck.

High overhead, half a dozen other passengers were tether-suspended, up to the highest mezzanine levels in this broad chimney that ran up the core of the ship. One of them, a man, was flailing his arms wildly and squealing hysterically.

Was that Corona higher than the man, at the very top of the chimney? Dark skin . . . maybe a maroon jumpsuit . . . He couldn't determine sex, but realized that Corona's long hair would be extended above her in 0 g. He couldn't get a good enough angle to see the hair, looked away.

Everyone he saw looked safe, and he hoped Corona was safe as well, wherever she was.

Kelly Corona pushed away from the ceiling, cursed under her breath. The initial extension and whip-action of her tether had sent her thumping face first into the ceiling, but not with much force. It was more an irritation than anything else, and she swung around to look down.

She rather enjoyed the sensation of height, of floating almost two hundred meters over the main passenger-compartment deck. There were others floating below her, including a hysterical little man several levels down.

"Don't forsake me, Lord!" the man squealed. "Not now! Not after all I've been through!"

"Shut yer trap, twerp!" Corona shouted.

But the man went on behaving like a child that heard only its own voice.

Corona wished she had a Muzzler 55 with her, that Middist-manufactured stunshooter that rendered its victims nearly mute by making their lips seem too heavy to move. It had a nice muzzling effect that lasted fifty-five minutes or more, depending upon body size. She hadn't brought any weapons at all, thinking they wouldn't be allowed aboard this particular ship.

How wrong she had been!

Corona was about to shout again, when she felt a little compression shift in both eardrums, followed by a faint tinnitus-like ringing. Then Appy's voice sounded in her left ear, to the exclusion of all other sound:

"A plague on you, Shusher. First the hatch and now this. Have you lost complete control of what little senses you had? How dare you override my takeoff and speed commands?"

Corona heard the porpoise-whine in her other ear. It sounded almost staccato, not simpering as before.

"The proof is in my program!" Appy shouted. "You'll have to trust me on that. All takeoff and speed *decisions* are under my jurisdiction.

"Sweee! Sweee!"

"I am not lying!"

Shusher responded quickly and forcefully: "Ferrrosss . . . seeeah!"

"Why won't you listen to me?"

The ensuing sounds, in varying pitches, seemed almost understandable to Corona. Something like, "My parts! My private parts!"

Appy: "I'm ordering GravSense now, *if* that's all right with you."

A short monotone whine ensued.

The compression changed in Corona's ears, and once more she heard the hysterical man.

Static followed over the ship's P.A. system, and Appy spoke through it: "GravSense in activation."

Corona dropped fast, but grabbed the railing neatly to break her fall.

The little man screamed, and seconds later Corona saw him pulling himself up by his tether to get back on the nearest mezzanine.

In two rude, bruising thumps, McMurtrey tumbled to the deck, bumping his elbow on the railing.

This ship has kinks to be worked out, he thought, rubbing his arm.

Jin was crawling back over the railing to the safety of the mezzanine, his tether still in place. He stood on the deck with his nose in technologically simulated pain, caught McMurtrey's gaze briefly before looking away.

Damage, Jin thought. *Nose aching and cosmetic repairs necessary . . . something else . . . Central Command melt-weld . . . field-irreparable merging of Duplication and Repair functions.*

What's the matter with that cabin control panel? Damn!

When circumstance required one or more functions, Jin's interpretive core accessed the CC module for instructions, flashing data in a nanosecond from there to bodily points of absorption and action. A field-irreparable melt-weld was one that could only be repaired back on D'Urth in a Bureau of Loyalty shop. It was a rare glitch, shouldn't have happened so easily.

A problem with the ship caused this!

Jin had never been hit in the nose before, and the numbing, unpleasant feeling of it angered him.

Discreetly, Jin tested himself, sending electrical probes through the fiber-optic passageways of his body, tingling his synthetic nerves. He received a report of nose and under-eye discoloration, felt "red sound" automatic functions repairing this, at the same healing speed as a human wearing a healing pack. In a few hours it would be as before, and he could say he wore a pack when no one was looking.

While Repair and Duplication wouldn't separate themselves, and Duplication wasn't responding to test probes, the Repair function appeared to be basically intact. It was one of the most important functions he had, for it contained backups on top of backups, allowing self-repair of virtually every damageable or perishable part and function. When operating as it was now for Jin's nose and under his eyes, it transmitted "red sound," which the cyberoo saw and felt in internal coloration.

Duplication wasn't nearly so critical. It was a "green sound" training program left in Jin's circuits, with which the cyberoo had observed human actions and copied them. With this program the cyberoo's movements, speech and certain nuances had been made to approximate those of seventy-eight humans it had observed firsthand, including half a dozen Plarnjarn monks. It even copied physical pain those humans felt, via a parabolic sensing mechanism.

From all Jin could determine, his humanlike functions continued unabated.

To a cyberoo, the Duplication program was like a human appendix, no longer needed. If Repair continued to work, it would bypass Duplication to restore humanlike actions and features as needed, accessing memory banks.

Jin knew that all the tests he ran fell short of the most important one—the stresses of an actual field emergency. This particular meltweld could be paralyzing, or might amount to nothing of consequence.

Screens went up all around, and a short woman in a polychromatic chador became visible in a freshly exposed cubicle just beyond Jin's. Although the chador was designed to cover her from head to toe, she had left her face uncovered, wrapping the extra folds of cloth around her neck. She was black-haired and olive-skinned, with a compact thickness of build that imparted strength to her voice. McMurtrey guessed Isammedan or Nandu, perhaps even a Middistess. In one hand she carried a woven straw prayer mat, rolled.

"Did you see those ships?" she asked, looking at Jin. "I think we're the only one that took off! In the moments before we increased acceleration I saw dozens of other ships topple over and kind of sputter with little wisps of smoke. There were BOL choppers rocketing into town from all directions. What do you suppose . . . ? Oh, you're hurt."

She started toward Jin, but he waved her away, said he was all right.

The woman caught McMurtrey's gaze, became agitated and turned away. Immediately, she launched into her form of boisterous conversation with an orange-robed man on the other side. The man had a square-cut black beard, wore a sword in a scabbard that was secured to a wide, redstone-encrusted belt.

McMurtrey looked at the hard plazymer tether clasps on his own waist, tried to figure out how the apparatus got there and how it might be disengaged. His elbow ached.

The big-voiced woman was talking about an incredible dawn she had seen as the ship rose from D'Urth. McMurtrey hadn't seen any of that.

Then Johnny Orbust began shouting through an electronic bullhorn, from the railing on the other side of the mezzanine, not very far away. He had Smith and Tully with him, and God only knew how they had gotten that bullhorn past Appy's inspection apparatus.

"One of those ships that didn't make it had that New Timer Madame Theo aboard, some false prophet Florientals and a bunch of atheist swine disciples of Kevin Wateo. Glory be to God, for He stopped them in their tracks!"

Many people laughed and made open displays of support for this, and McMurtrey was struck with the strangeness of such behavior in a group professing piety.

The loud woman near Jin wondered if anyone had been injured on the ill-fated ships, and this comment restored to McMurtrey some modicum of faith in humanity. A number of people shared her concern, and soon people were calling for Orbust to keep quiet.

But Orbust kept on with his deluge of Krassian noise.

The loud woman complained of bumps and bruises, and she told the orange-robed man near her that she'd had to hold onto the deck-secured furnishings in her cabin. She didn't mention any tethers, and none remained in view with the exception of those still secured to McMurtrey and Jin.

McMurtrey was beginning to get angry with the intransigence of his tether clasp when it burst open, made a little twist and snap in the air, and melted neatly into the floor, so quickly the eye could not discern the manner in which it vanished. Jin's tether performed a like maneuver, making McMurtrey believe the whole thing had been automatic, with the tethers going the way they had come. This gave him further hope that Corona was safe.

Presently the woman with the big voice went to the railing and began berating Orbust for his attitude. From where McMurtrey stood she was louder than the man with the bullhorn. More and more people shouted for Orbust to cease, and some of them were becoming openly angry.

Orbust paused in his diatribe, said something to the red-necked Kundo Smith. They nodded in unison, glared at the woman.

McMurtrey's sore elbow was feeling better, and he rubbed it gently.

He saw Jin rubbing his nose.

Opposition was growing rapidly, making Orbust increasingly uneasy. His collection of nervous tics, which came and went, were apparent now: the twitching eyelid and tapping foot, the fingers of his free hand rubbing together atop the railing.

Abruptly he lowered the bullhorn, fell silent and slipped around the nearest partition, into a corridor. Smith and Tully followed.

McMurtrey told the woman he admired her outspokenness, and she thanked him graciously. She introduced herself as Zatima, and her companion as Nanak Singh.

"That same awful man gave you a difficult time, too," she said, obviously referring to McMurtrey's speech before the crowd in St. Charles Beach. "You handled the Krassian fanatic well."

"Did you see his gun?" McMurtrey asked. "Why was he allowed to bring it aboard?"

Her orange-robed companion stood near her to one side, looking at the spot Orbust had vacated. One of Singh's hands rested against his scabbard.

"I guess because he was wearing it," Zatima offered, "and Appy said we could bring aboard what we were wearing."

Singh didn't appear to be paying attention to the conversation.

"Orbust must wear a bullhorn," McMurtrey said.

She shrugged, said, "Many strange occurrences." Then, with a flowing, heavily accented throatiness: "In answer to your inquisitive gaze, I am a follower of the Prophet Isammed, Prince of the Faithful, last and greatest of the prophets. No offense to you, of course."

"No offense taken," McMurtrey said. "Despite what's been said, I don't consider myself a prophet. I simply carried a single message, one I can't say I understand. I know something of your fine religion."

She smiled, didn't ask him how he knew.

"I have seen photographs of paintings depicting the life of Isammed," McMurtrey said. "And the Prophet's face is never shown; it always has a veil over it. How is it that you dare to go and look upon the face of Allah?"

"That painting style came about because artists were fearful of showing inaccuracies in either Isammed or His family, and because they did not wish to be sacrilegious. I journey to see Allah because I received a calling to do so. If Allah's prophet, Isammed, were on this very ship I could look upon Him, and a glorious sight it would be! So too do I expect to gaze upon the beloved countenance of Allah Himself."

McMurtrey furrowed his brows, wondered how a woman could occupy an important position in Isammedanism, as seemed to be the case here. Weren't women forced to occupy lowly positions in that faith, hiding behind veiled chadors in public? He wanted to ask her about this, hesitated.

It was apparent that Zatima had fielded such questions before, and she took this one before it crossed McMurtrey's lips: "I see you are puzzled," she said. "I am a rarity, it is true. American-born, I have lived in desert lands. I am directly descended from the first Zatima of note, the one who was daughter of Isammed and ancestress of the Isammed imams and Sivvy caliphs. Through this ancestry and my rather assertive personality, I gained the respect of the leaders of my faith. I am one of the only female imams."

"Very impressive." McMurtrey tried not to sound patronizing.

"When you made Allah's announcement, I recognized the truth and caught the nearest camel." Her eyes twinkled. "A car, actually. It took me to the hypersonic airport, and here I am. I joke only a little about the camel, for I ride on occasion. My people are not technologically advanced. There is much poverty and sickness, much hope that I might bring help to them from Allah."

"You are Sivvy?"

Her eyes flashed proudly. "I am. And my direct descent from He Who Walks in Grace is integral to the legitimacy of all Sivvy imams. Sadly, millions who profess Isammedanism are misguided—Unnis, Ahhabis, Noddiyyas and even Tufer mystics. Allah will straighten them out."

"Some Unni sharifs of the Al Khalil family are descended from Isammed as well," McMurtrey said, to impress her.

"And they are traitors," she snapped. "I follow the only true way." She spun and went to her bunk, followed closely by the orange-robed Nanak Singh, who subsequently continued on past her to his own adjacent bunk.

Hit a nerve there, McMurtrey thought. *Peculiar alliance between those two. What religion is that guy, Nandu?*

McMurtrey recalled certain facts about the Sivvies. They had been followers of fanatical leaders over the centuries, including Isammed Rashid (1st Century), Ayatollah Rafakhom (2nd Century), and Ismail al-Muntazar (late 2nd Century, exiled to Ranus.) Sivvies rioted wildly against Wessornians before formation of the Inner Planet League. They even whipped themselves in public, bizarre displays purportedly designed to diminish themselves before Allah.

But this woman did not seem fanatical, and thus far McMurtrey rather liked her.

Punctuated computer tones filled the P.A. system, fol-

lowed by Appy's accented voice: "Assembly in one hour.
There are separate meeting rooms, and you have been
divided into cells: Sublevels A, B, and C. Room assignments are on display now."

Without thinking, McMurtrey glanced at the wall screen
on his headboard, where he had seen book-tape titles
listed. In red-on-amber he saw this:

Assembly Room B-2
Report in 59m, 42s

The last number represented seconds, and these clicked
away silently on the screen.

In the three weeks since the "dispatchings" of prisoners
from Santa Quininas, Gutan had labored long hours, traversing many miles of Wessornia. Very early one morning
he lay awake staring into the darkness of his sleeping compartment. The truck-trailer sped along on autopilot, with
occasional fragments of light finding their way into his
room. He was somewhere on Coast Route 990 heading
north.

There had been stops at penitentiaries in Sohigh, Port
Landis, and Lava Bend. This last was a complete bust, as
all eleven Death Row prisoners there obtained cyanide
and administered it to themselves in a suicide pact only
hours before Gutan's arrival.

According to a Federal penitentiary system rule, this
removed the fresh cadavers from Gutan's jurisdiction,
which normally would not have made him happy. In this
case, however, all were men, so he hadn't been deprived
of an icy bed partner. He had his standards, he told himself, and only mature female cadavers would do.

He preferred 5.7 minutes of quick chill in the truck's
cooler, a setting he had arrived at through extensive experimentation. Fresh cadavers were like fine wine, to be
handled in precisely the right way.

He hadn't made this up himself. There was an under-
ground mortician's society known as Nouveau Silencius,
connoisseurs of the freshly dead. They held regular clandestine meetings attended by expert speakers, at which
members learned the ancient ways and rituals of the so-

ciety. Gutan first become acquainted with the organization when he worked at his family's funeral parlor, through a young man who drove a hearse for them. It wasn't anything Gutan ever discussed with family members, and the only ritual of the society he ever adopted was the sex act. He had lost touch with the society but still liked to consider himself a member.

What a crock, he thought, *trying to lend respectability to what I do. Goddammit, my libido is out of control! It's deviated from deviance, taken me into a realm I'm ashamed to discuss with anyone*.

But Gutan's libido surged just thinking these things. The last movements and expressions of his victims remained clear in Gutan's mind as he made love to their lifeless forms. They had been alive and looking at him only moments before.

There had been a male corpse one desperate, lonely night in Central Eassornia. It hadn't been a gratifying experience, and afterward Gutan slept fitfully. He'd awoken in predawn darkness, feeling unclean.

Now he felt that way again. If he were exposed, society would call him a monster, a depraved necrophiliac. He agreed with that assessment, but it didn't help him control the urges.

Urges! God, do I have urges!

He recalled reading the definition of necrophiliac in an unabridged word-processing program. They defined it in a detached way as "an erotic attraction to corpses," and referenced psychiatry without applying a value judgment to the condition.

Sometimes it seemed to Gutan that he could do as he pleased in the privacy of his own bedroom. These prisoners had to die anyway, and he didn't do them any real harm. He wasn't a murderer! He might even have done the chosen corpses a favor, sending them from this world to the next with an act of love.

But was it really love? Of course not, he admitted to himself, sitting up in bed in the tiny sleeping compartment. These were not consenting adults.

He heard a faint and distant whirring, beyond the hum and drone of tires and engine, and this distant sound troubled him. When he attempted to concentrate on it, the sound hid like a crouching cat melting into shadow. Whenever he gave up the effort, the sound came back, and it hung there at the edge of his mind, like a bangle beyond the reach of a child.

It was like something he forgot to do, or forgot to consider. His mind raced, preventing sleep.

The amber-on-black mapscreen adjacent to his bed indicated that the Dispatch Unit was on autopilot, negotiating Route 990 between Bakerville and Nosalia. He lifted the venetian blinds by his bed, saw pixtel poles and fences flicker by. He heard a radar blip, and at the bottom of the mapscreen saw the truck's speed drop from 185 k.p.h. to the speed limit: 140 k.p.h. Presently a Wessornia Highway Patrol car came into view in the truck's headlamps, parked on a shoulder just over a rise.

Passing the car, Gutan saw a panel of instruments inside, with dancing blue and red lights. Soon he lost sight of the vehicle, and in the ensuing moments didn't hear sirens. He let go of the blinds.

All Dispatch Units could be driven manually or automatically—and Gutan did the driving about a tenth of the time, depending upon how bored he felt. When he drove, he knew that the autopilot was watching his every move, ready to go into operation if he made a mistake. He had made a few, sometimes caused by the opium he took, and always the rescue came just in time. He called it "the cavalry." Mnemo was too valuable to be left entirely to human error, and he surmised that the autopilot probably had its own backup. Gutan worried sometimes that he would be called on the carpet for his driving record, for the mistakes that had to be documented somewhere in the computer system.

The microwave dish on top of the trailer brought in fifteen thousand televid channels, but a person could stand only so much of that. And Gutan didn't enjoy book-tapes, word-processor video games or music. He only enjoyed intercourse.

Intercourse, he thought, laying his head back on the pillow. Didn't that word mean the union of two individuals? He returned to the troubling question of consenting adults.

What might he call his act? It wouldn't be phrased so

nicely in dictionaries or journals of psychiatry. Solocourse? But that seemed more appropriate to something else entirely, and he laughed sardonically.

The truck negotiated a turn, began the ascent of a steep hill.

Such troubling thoughts, and that elusive sound. The vibration hung there, toying cruelly with him. Was it like the resonance emitted by Mnemo, the one that brought forth images of strange geometric shapes? He couldn't taste enough of it with his ears to tell.

Why was he thinking this way?

Gutan swung out of bed, pulled open the door of his sleeping compartment. Mnemo was straight ahead, bathed in the lambent yellow light that suffused its walls. The wide instrument console and the separate government-installed computer were dark shapes—the former a rectangle against the illuminated machine, the latter a nearly square box off to one side.

How like the government, Gutan thought, to employ such an unimaginative square shape for its computer. Professor Pelter's Mnemo, in comparative majesty, was a graceful pedastaled pentahedron with an oval door on its sloping front face.

Out of the darkness before Gutan's alternate, nonphysical eye came the vision of a sound, in great leaping, darting hunks of orange and lilac Mobius shape. They spun inwardly upon themselves like living, moving neon images, stretching into every imaginable Mobius shape. The square shapes pranced across triangular and circular ones, and like cubs or kittens playing, they switched roles. They blended, bounced from one another, and ultimately stretched to synchronized roundness—a roundness that was barely perceptible to Gutan.

Now the sound came as noise through this alternate nonphysical channel, as from a great unobstructed distance where an event is seen before it is heard. It seemed to be Mnemo's, the peculiar characteristic whine of the Mobius bands, and he felt its magnetism entering the pores of his body, drawing him forward, luring him.

But Mnemo, seen to Gutan's physical eyes, had grown dark, and to his physical ears it made absolutely no peep. Previously he had recognized a division of sight—of the

physical and nonphysical eyes that looked into different
worlds, and he discovered now that the same separation
existed with respect to his hearing. He had an alternate
ear to go with his alternate eye, and conceivably there
might be other alternate senses to go with these. He was
hearing and seeing in a different plane of reality.

The realms were overlapping in certain places, folding
over upon themselves to make him aware of them.

Mnemo flashed on in both planes, and to all of Gutan's
eyes the machine became a brightly illuminated polychromatic blend of geometric shapes that floated within Mnemo's wall panels. Each shape was a different, delicious
color, with an integrity of its own that at times showed
clearly and at times slipped beneath or atop other shapes,
forming odd combinations of shape and hue.

He saw no Mobius strips now.

Gutan had imagined many times what it might be like
to enter the machine, and in a sense this seemed like just
another vision, a dream. But when he attacked it with this
thought, he realized it was a form of reality he had only
touched tangentially before. The speculations and esti-
mations of survival odds he had made concerning a trip
through Mnemo came back, and they seemed entirely
meaningless to him.

Everything seemed meaningless, even what lay beyond
Mnemo's door.

The oval door swung open.

Gutan regretted his behavior, felt his acts were tearing
at the core of his life, shredding the source of his energy.
He became conscious of his unbathed, opium-saturated
odor and nearly gagged. If only he could rid himself of the
guilt, if only he could escape the trap his life had become.

In one oft-imagined scenario, he would enter the machine only after setting it to operate for a certain number
of minutes, after which it should automatically shut down.
Mnemo had many controls and combinations of settings
of unknown purpose, and in the short period that Gutan
had worked at this job he had figured some of them out.
The combination he thought might activate a timer involved two pick buttons, a brass toggle and a dial, all with
numerical designations. Somehow they were tied in with

a narrow black screen that ran vertically along the right outside edge of the instrument console.

Once he had mistakenly pressed a button after setting another button, a toggle and a dial according to instructions from HQ, and the narrow black screen went on briefly, clicking off red numerals in hundredths of a second like a stopkron. This set off error lights and buzzers on the adjacent government computer, and had the effect of shutting Mnemo down. Gutan had to repeat the procedure they wanted.

Gutan felt like a person who had received an elaborate electronics package without an adequate instruction manual and with no way of sending for one since the manufacturer was out of business. In this case the manufacturer was not only out of business, he was out of commission— killed in his own machine. This gave Gutan pause.

Professor Pelter had known the most about Mnemo.

As Gutan stared into the interior of Mnemo, he felt fear and suspicion. He wondered if this might be part of the clandestine government experiment, turning him into a subject in the dark of the night. But to what purpose? Gutan couldn't offer data beyond what they might learn from other subjects.

Maybe they had been playing psychological games on him to make him want to enter the machine. Maybe voluntarism was a yet untested variable, an important one.

Or maybe he had outlived his usefulness, especially if he knew too much. This could be the normal retirement method for Mnemo operators, the reason for turnover in the department, which had led to him getting the job. Could it have something to do with his trysts? Mnemo had become an execution machine, and Gutan was a criminal by the standards of society.

But one deserving death? He thought not.

The machine grew closer. Its lights and patterns became brighter, larger. Gutan didn't think he was moving his feet. The motion of approach was too smooth, as if his eyes were camera lenses zooming in. He couldn't look down, couldn't move his head or eyes to look at anything except the mesmeric, dancing lights of Mnemo.

He was moving forward rapidly, but the passage seemed to take forever. Mnemo became unfocused, disappeared, and Gutan seemed to penetrate the glowing yellow place where the machine had been. To the rear without turning his head to look, he saw Mobius bands in varying sizes and configurations chasing him. He felt short of breath and cold.

The bands caught him, and the twist in each adhered to his body and spread gelatin over him. He felt a spiked tingling, saw electrical waves, cycles and pulses all around. As Gutan lengthened the distance between himself and Mnemo, the Mobius bands straightened and became a billion parallel lines, joined impossibly at the point of Gutan's body.

Gutan could hardly breathe. He was spread-eagled on a huge platform of white lines that knifed and accelerated into an inky abyss. Fear enveloped him.

He was traveling toward a far off pinpoint of light at a speed that jellied his mind. The light did not change size, but he reached it nonetheless and merged with it. The light was so intensely hot that it melted his body and everything that clung to it.

But something remained of Gutan. He heard the familiar whine of Mnemo, and saw a flash of brilliance that shifted from lilac to orange. Once again he saw the pinpoint of light from the abyss, and he was on a plane of parallel lines speeding from the light. He became as he was, as he came to realize he had always been, and pleasantly warm. The shortness of breath passed.

All was silent.

He lay dreaming of a dreamer, and that dreamer dreamed of another dreamer, and these were part of an infinite sequence of dreamers, all locked in to Gutan. He sensed an expansion of memory: blank spaces became turgid with events, too many events for one life. Ancient instincts became identifiable and subject to scrutiny, not just intimations controlled by the subconscious.

He had no subconscious anymore. All events and motivations had surfaced and organized themselves before him. They lay as objects on a great platter stretching across the universe. He was about to pluck one and examine it, when this image vanished, and he felt his body folding inward.

The universe stretched to infinite smallness.

The whine of Mnemo returned, and it seemed to come from Gutan's own throat. He sat within an infinite mass that enveloped every pore, with only the vision of Mobius bands all around and the bodily sensation that he was sitting in weightlessness.

"Am I dying?" he asked. It was a thought without words or throaty texture, without tangibility. But it came forth nonetheless.

No answer ensued.

He saw a tiny key turning in a gigantic doorway, and an elongated light switch that flicked to "On." For an instant he heard music, a peculiar, jaunty tune.

A whirl of faces, landscapes, buildings and colors filled his mind, focusing momentarily before fading. Then a single blurred vision held, and presently an image became clear: a white sand beach, with turquoise blue water stretching to the horizon. The images shifted, as if seen from a person walking, but Gutan felt no corresponding body sensations.

A large log loomed ahead, half-embedded in sand, and around it were footprints, human and dog. A woman in a yellow calico dress moved gracefully across the vision, sat on the log. She was extraordinarily lovely, with porcelain-like skin and long black hair that streamed like a gleaming mane in the ocean breeze.

Gutan's pulse quickened. He knew this face, or an approximation of it—an older version, he thought. Faded photographs were dim in his memory. It was his mother in her youth, the way he had seen her only in photographs.

How was he seeing this?

Then the realization hit him, as if he'd been clobbered with the big beach log: *My father! I'm . . . I'm in his mind!*

He knew this from the way his mother looked toward him, with the wan, loving expression she always reserved for Gutan's father.

They embraced, and eagerly the man pulled the dress and underclothes from the woman, revealing untanned, firm breasts and a birthmark on one side of the stomach. They rolled off the log onto her clothing, made love with animal frenzy.

Their lovemaking was like an eternal storm of creation and the surging power of the seas. Great undulating, puls-

ing waves and tides throbbed incessantly, rising and falling
in an aquatic thunder of movement. Presently it became
as the gentle rhythmic movement of water, turning eventually into a sea of smooth glass, calmness beneath the
heavens.

Gutan saw the waves of the sea marching shoreward,
like endless battalions of soldiers . . . retreating and ad-
vancing, ever-punishing the surface of the planet, wearing
it away over many eons. With his father's eyes he turned
and looked up at the hills along the shore, realizing that
all of this would give way someday to the relentless forces
of the sea and its ally, the rain.

In his mind, Gutan saw the cycles of oceans, rivers and
lakes that condensed through sunlight into clouds, bringing
invincible rain that battered mountains flat over millions
of years. His vision became a single drop of water, teeming
with microscopic life. The drop splayed into an ocean, with
dead and decaying materials moving to the upper strata
of water. Sunshine streamed in to provide the feeding sub-
stances for floating and drifting plants, and the plants in
turn were fed upon by tiny floating and drifting animal
organisms. Small fish and crustaceans received nourish-
ment from the animal organisms, and they in turn nour-
ished the larger life forms. It was a self-reproducing cycle
of life and death, with death and decay integral to the
continuance of life.

He realized that the beauty and majesty of birth could
never exist without death.

It was a cosmic energy dance, of vibrating molecules,
atoms and quantum particles that pulsed briefly, became
still, pulsed again and became still once more, ad infinitum,
in a perpetual rhythm of the ages. The old made way for
the new.

Gulls cried out, swooped gracefully over the lovers, and
flew out to sea across blue-green water. Gutan felt drawn
to follow the birds in their majestic flight, to soar with
them toward the horizon.

Gutan felt he shouldn't be here on the beach with his
parents, that he was uninvited, an intruder. His mother
and father had always seemed so sedate and passionless,
like the corpses in the mortuary at which the family toiled.
Gutan always had trouble imagining that his parents ever

made love, and if they did, it should have been a reasoned, controlled procedure, nearly clinical. Certainly not this furious, primitive outburst.

A feeling came into Gutan's loins, and a surging explosion of red bonded the man and woman. The image faded, and presently a new one took its place. Someone in a room, standing naked on a green and brown Floriental carpet. It was a bedroom, with the mahogany leg of a bed occupying the upper right corner of his frame of vision. He looked down on a belly, bloated and with a birthmark on one side, but beautiful even so. It was his mother's belly, in pregnancy.

Gutan swooned.

Foggy, unidentifiable images slid slowly through his brain. He was a lifeboat in a raging rainstorm at night, fighting to reach the safety of a shore he couldn't see. He wasn't in the boat; he *was* the boat, and his plight angered him. He had a right to make shore, and this storm dared to interfere! He reached a point where he had to float across a narrow waterway, and something pushed him, aided him.

He found himself lying on his side in a small room illuminated by a single bulb. Inexplicably the bulb threw shadows on the wrong side, against the wall behind it, and Gutan picked out his own boat shape from others. He became a child, small and coughing water from its lungs. Something hit him in the center of his back, hard. A switch beneath the bulb spun without being touched, and the glow of light dimmed sharply but held for a fraction of a second, as if between realms and protesting the passage from light to dark. Finally it succumbed, and Gutan tumbled through blackness.

Something hit him again and he cried.

He faced a dawn sky that was a spectacle of golden orange against eggshell blue. From far away, a rooster crowed.

His eyes followed the subtleties of change in the new day's sky, and he felt his senses tingle. He beheld an ancient day, felt the permanence of cosmic eternity and the fragility of flesh.

Remnants of the stormy night dwindled in his memory, scattered by the loveliness he beheld. It seemed to him that endings were strung together with beginnings, that events could be recaptured and replayed, made right where they had been wrong.

He saw a turreted playhouse on one side, in a backyard he used to roam, in days when the yard seemed so large that he must have been small. The dark-haired woman came into view again, his mother on the steps of the old house that was later torn down. She wore a sleeveless white dress, and called to him without making a sound. The house vanished, and she stood silhouetted against eggshell-blue sky.

He rode a tricycle on the front driveway, going around in circles. Faster and faster, threatening to tip over, at the brink of possibility. He had all his fingers then, before the accident.

A car horn bleated.

Suddenly he was rolling backwards on the tricycle, circling much faster than he had gone forward. People, faces, and flashes of color whirred by, carried in the whining wind of Mnemo. His tricycle evaporated and he was a helpless baby once more, thrashing his arms and crying.

His mother and father appeared, and they spoke to him in an inexplicably familiar, ancient dialect. Gutan cooed and babbled, and his utterances blended perfectly with theirs.

It was a hundred centuries before Krassos, when Gutan's father, Tyrus, was in command of one of the ships in Hanno the Magnificent's Dartellian fleet. Gutan's father spoke of distant islands, and he carried a small pouch full of Dartellian coins.

Gutan was known as Ahiram then.

They were exquisite golden coins, and Ahiram was allowed to touch one. It glinted like sunlight from every angle, and the smoothness of its surface was incomparable. He became older, a boy holding the coin again. It belonged to him now, and he set it on a piece of cloth. He was at a table with his parents and a faceless sister, and he tasted the sweet boiled cabbage and heavily seasoned roast goose his mother had prepared. He dipped emmer wheat bread into pungent mustard paste and stared into the face that wasn't a face.

Something in the mustard. He couldn't get enough of

it. As he devoured all in sight, his sister's head became a skeleton skull seen from the back. He heard weeping, and images fled so rapidly across his brain that they left a trail of pain.

He absorbed the flavors and odors of baked river perch with sour grape tartare sauce . . . of ostrich eggs, ghee and curly leaves of endive . . . of lemon wedges and a pungent coriander paste mixed with Afsornian honey . . . of crisp ta-bread and sweet camel's milk. He was no longer of Dartellia, no longer of that place or time.

He was the nameless ancestor of those people, and he looked through billions of eyes at them and at the future not so far beyond, where Gutan sat in a mnemonic memory machine. It was the dream of a dreamer again, the tricycle in circles backward and forward. It was hope. He was on the beach once more with his parents, in the explosion of color from his father's loins, and this event was at the center of everything.

He radiated outward from an infinitesimal point, like wavelets from a flung pebble, and he locked in place in the mind of the little man in the machine.

From there he receded again with screaming, uncontrolled speed, to the hoary ancestors of ancestors, and their memories threatened to burst his cellular structure. Panic swamped him. He tried to direct his hands to remove the seat harness and breathing tube, and his hands seemed to move. But nothing changed. He wanted to scrape all the filthy, electrically conductive gel from his body!

He had to escape the rampaging machine! He screamed, an echoing howl through the deepest chambers of existence.

Wars inundated him, and he relived lives in microseconds. He was mutilated and died countless times. Red and gold Bureau of Loyalty officers goose-stepped over him, trampled him. Black-uniformed troops followed, their battle medals and weapons glinting in the sun. They gave way to blue legions, and waves of banner-carrying religious fanatics, and barbarian horsemen and more legions, and scabby armies with catapults that hurled fireballs. They rolled on without end, across the flaming horizons of every planet. They buried continents in fire, muck, and water.

He believed the entire history of civilization was flashing

before his eyes as he died, as Professor Pelter must have seen it.

A robed man knelt outside a burning city, cradling a dead girl-child in his arms. Gutan was the man, in dirty, bare feet, and his heart pounded out of control.

From the edge of the planet, approaching inexorably, came mindless masses of marching armies, feet beating rhythmically. They came in rainbow uniforms with a cacophony of metal raspings and poundings.

Clump-clump-clump!   Clump-clump-clump!   Clump-clump-clump!

From behind the armies hurtled a giant platform of parallel white lines that skimmed over their heads, swooped across their path and dipped one corner near Gutan. He stepped aboard with the girl-child and instantly their bodies dilated across the entire platform. They were spread-eagled, facing one another eye to eye, life touching death. Gutan saw through the dead girl's eyes in reverse, penetrated the back of her skull to the armies beyond.

Clump-clump-clump!   Clump-clump-clump!   Clump-clump-clump!

Gutan and the child were larger than the armies, and on their platform they flew circles over the armies, swooping low and scattering them in all directions.

The platform knifed into the sky and away, with Gutan and the girl.

The dead eyes were all Gutan could see. They were motionless and disconnected from their sockets, with cells flaking and falling away. He wanted to press his body tighter against hers, to feel the receding warmth of her life. But only a faint tracing of the eyes remained of her.

The image of her eyes receded and he couldn't remember what they looked like. A familiar throbbing began, where his severed finger had been. Cold, ever so cold . . .

Gutan saw the planet behind him in greens, browns and blues, and armies were regrouping there. Icy pain shot from the finger void up his arm, into his brain. It was worse than ever before, beyond enduring.

He screamed.

Gutan's platform spun away and hurtled with him into dark infinity. He barely made out a pinpoint of light in the frozen distance, far, far ahead.

Six

It is possible to see from one universe to the next, but only from the bubble of a skinbeating entity. Skinbeaters travel by whipping along the microthin electromagnetic skins that separate universes, and in so doing they occupy tiny portions of both universes at once. The process creates an invisible bubble around the entity, a bubble that is a vibrating window between the universes. Life forms contained by the bubble can see into either universe, and no portion of the bubble interior is inaccessible to them. When skinbeating ceases, the bubble dissipates and the skinbeating entity slips off track into the universe of origin.

—Teachings of Tananius-Ofo,
Crystal Library, Vol. 25

It was not quite mid-morning, and McMurtrey made his way down a spiral staircase toward Assembly Level B. The stairway was adjacent to an elevator bank, but for short ascents and descents McMurtrey preferred stairs. His elbow was much better now, and he hardly thought about it.

Partway down the steps, McMurtrey had to lunge for a handrail.

The ship jerked violently, first one way and then another.

With considerable effort he made it to a landing, and from there the ship ceased its aberrancy and he progressed at a regular pace down the remaining steps, keeping one hand on the railing.

He passed through a doorway into a wide corridor. There, in the midst of a knot of people, Johnny Orbust

and Zatima were engaged in spirited debate over the role
of women in religion. Orbust contended that women belonged at home, and he quoted the Apostle Nop from IX
Thicor:

> "'Let your women keep silence in the churches: for
> it is not permitted unto them to speak; but they are
> commanded to be under obedience, as also saith the
> law.
> "And if they will learn anything, let them ask their
> husbands at home: for it is a shame for women to speak
> in the church.'"

"That's your religion, not mine!" Zatima shouted.

"It's no different from yours. Nop also speaks of the
veils women must wear, and the fact that women wear
their hair long as a natural veil before God."

"My hair is short!"

"And you are an abomination, an evil mutation!"

McMurtrey saw the shiny silver Snapcard in Orbust's
hand, though Orbust tried to conceal it by clutching it
tightly.

"My denomination, the Sivvy, is very progressive," Zatima said. "It is correcting the mistakes of men."

"According to Haria, your holy/civil law, a woman is
only worth half a man on the witness stand. It takes the
testimony of two women to counter the testimony of just
one man. Why hasn't that 'mistake' been corrected yet?"

"It will be," Zatima said. She appeared uneasy, didn't
seem able to counter Orbust's Snapcard-boosted knowledge. Apparently she wasn't aware of the card.

McMurtrey saw weaknesses in each side. If he mentioned the card to Zatima, that would shut Orbust down
abruptly. But Orbust had a gun, and he seemed unstable.
McMurtrey recalled as well his own conversation with Zatima, when she admitted being a rarity in her religion. She
stood in quicksand, arguing the rights of women in her
faith. But McMurtrey dared not criticize Zatima either,
for she had that Nandu, maybe ParKekh, warrior with her.
And the hand of this one always remained near his sword.

McMurtrey continued on to Assembly Room B-2, arriving there a few seconds before the appointed time. He

found a middle-row seat, among three rows of bolted-down chairs, arranged around an expanse of empty floor at the center. The room was uncarpeted, and the chairs had no cushions, creating a cold austerity.

Across unseen speakers, Appy's tones seemed particularly harsh as he listed the names of the tardy.

McMurtrey noticed Kelly Corona already seated, changed places to be next to her.

They compared experiences, learned that each had been saved by a tether during takeoff. In hushed tones, Corona informed him that she had heard Appy and Shusher arguing with one another, one into each of her ears. She told him of the lavender light from the wall opening in the strange room, and of her suspicion that one bathed in this light became privy to the private comlink between Appy and Shusher.

"If everything isn't a monstrous farce," she said, "I've been bathed in holy light."

"Weird," McMurtrey said.

"I'm hearing them again!" she whispered. "They're still arguing!"

McMurtrey couldn't hear anything other than Corona and the voices of the pilgrims in the room.

"I'm getting a better sense of what Shusher is saying," Corona said excitedly. "From his tones, I think. Somehow I know he's saying that Appy's personality stinks. He's calling Appy an asshole!"

"Appy does have a difficult personality," McMurtrey agreed.

He watched Tully slip into a front row seat.

"Shusher whines—that's his language . . ." Corona fell silent, and she had an intense cast to her eyes.

"What's wrong?" McMurtrey asked.

"I just . . . I just realized what Shusher said before I tumbled out of the lavender-lit room! It was an angry whine that ebbed and flowed . . . no way to duplicate the sound for your ears. But now I know what it meant!"

"Yes?" McMurtrey leaned toward her.

"He said, 'Silence!' "

"Then it's just as Appy said: Shusher requires quiet."

"I was past the off-limits signs Appy warned us about—

on the highest mezzanines. I must have made intrusive noises across their comlink." She paused. "They're at it again. Shusher just said something I can't make out. I guess it'll get easier as I hear more. Appy is responding that Shusher is more stupid than a camel. They really despise one another. You felt the ship being jolted a few minutes ago?"

"Yeah. I was in the stairwell."

"That was them fighting over the speed controls. Appy was madder than hell, said if they went too fast it would damage the skins between universes, whatever that means, and T.O. would penalize them. They call God T.O., for Tananius-Ofo."

"Tananius-Ofo. That's the name of the planet where God is, the name of the place we're going."

Corona grunted, continued: "Appy mentioned a race, and a 'pleasure program' he wanted to win. He said Shusher's stupidity was going to cost them victory."

"Wow."

"Anyway, Shusher said something—about God not liking Appy, I think—and suddenly the ship smoothed out. Maybe the comment put Appy in shock, or they worked out a speed compromise I didn't hear. They have overlapping responsibilities and powers, and maybe God prefers to let them fight it out most of the time. Sometimes it's best that way with children."

"Children at the controls of this ship?"

"Maybe," Corona said. "Who knows what the definition of a child is to them. All I know is this ship has big problems. Oh! I'm losing the connection. Or they've stopped communicating."

Corona squinted one eye, had a perplexed expression on her face. She put a forefinger in each ear, rubbed around in the entrances to the ear canals. "Strange sensation of pressure changing," she said. "Whenever the voices come and go."

Past Corona to the right, a window dominated one wall, showing a giant purple and blue nebula hanging in space like an artist's rendition, so delicate and lovely it almost didn't seem real to McMurtrey. Large blue and white stars were set in the midst of glowing, veiny swirls of mysterious purple and blue clouds, clouds that were thick at the center of the nebula and delicate veils at the edges.

"We're entering a spectacular nebula," Corona said, noting his line of vision. "Comparable to anything I've ever seen. I'm not sure where we are, maybe to one side of our galaxy's center. We shouldn't be too far out yet, but who knows?"

"You're talking about being lost in space. Hell, I'm lost on this ship, really turned around. We went down to get here, which should place us in the rear or quote unquote 'bottom' of the ship as it flies in space. But from this view, we seem to be at the top, seeing where we're headed."

"It's probably done with high-quality mirrors and prisms," Corona said. "I don't think we're looking directly into space from this room. Where they do look directly out, and some of the portholes seem to, they must use shielded glass to protect us from X-rays and gamma rays. Short-wavelength radiation could be fatal out here."

"Do the direct-view windows look adequate to you?"

"Well, the safest way is without windows, using remote televid cameras. I've seen tiny particles embedded in some of the window glass, and my guess is that those particles absorb the harmful stuff. No use worrying now. We're a captive audience."

"In God's hands," McMurtrey said.

Although assembly room seats were not assigned, Appy had an arcane method of keeping track of those present. Like a nagging parent, he kept listing the names of the tardy. Finally the list was short: Orbust, Zatima and Singh. He identified each by religion, and so McMurtrey learned that Singh was a ParKekh, not a Nandu.

The corridor door banged open, and Zatima stomped in. Behind her trailed Singh, and he let go of the door prematurely, causing it to swing against Orbust.

Orbust said something.

It must have been a caustic comment, for Zatima whirled and faced him.

The ParKekh drew his sword halfway out of the scabbard.

Then Zatima spoke to her bodyguard in a low tone, and he relaxed his grip on the sword. It slid back into its pocket.

Zatima pointed toward seats in the back row, near

McMurtrey, and she and Singh made their way in that direction.

Orbust selected a seat in the front row by Tully.

McMurtrey presumed that Appy was calling the roll in the other assembly rooms as well, via a complex networking and surveillance arrangement. McMurtrey envisioned Appy as a mini-god, omnipresent and multifunctioning.

A multiple-armed Nandu god, Heeva the Mighty, came to mind, a god considered by its followers to be the source of good and evil, the creator of life and the destroyer of life. It was a fragment from McMurtrey's studies.

"Interesting debate in the corridor," Appy said.

Johnny Orbust smiled.

"Of course Mr. Orbust had help with the debate," Appy said.

The corners of Orbust's mouth turned downward.

Is Appy going to mention the Snapcard? McMurtrey wondered.

"A gun on the hip has a rather intimidating effect," Appy said. "And Zatima's armed escort. I'm surprised the participants didn't kill one another. How can either of you discuss scripture with weapons at the ready?"

"Mine is not for offensive purposes," Orbust said, uneasily. "It's purely defensive."

"Is it?" Appy asked. "Is it true that 'the meek shall inherit D'Urth?' Or is it more accurate to say that the powerful shall control that domain? Hasn't this always been true? Survival of the fittest?"

"How can you, a . . . computer of God . . . blaspheme scripture?" Orbust asked. "You're twisting the holy word."

"Is it blasphemy to ask questions?" Appy queried. "This is one of the matters we will address on this journey. What is holy and what is not? Who is to decide such matters? Oh, I could pose endless questions!"

McMurtrey heard whispered conversation, turned and saw Zatima saying something in a low tone to Nanak Singh.

"It is interesting to discuss interpretation of scriptural passages," Appy said. "Assuming in the first place that scripture was taken down correctly, it must be asked who did the translations from one language to another . . . and it must be asked if all of the passages were included. In the Krassian books, for example, there is a body of testamentary literature that didn't make it into the Babul, perhaps for political reasons. I refer to the Tignos Gospels."

"Blasphemy!" Orbust shouted. With an angry slap of leather he drew his Babul from its shoulder holster. He flipped through the pages, muttered to himself.

Two nuns near McMurtrey, one in black and one in white, scowled and whispered to one another while looking around the room nervously, apparently trying to discern the location of the P.A. speakers. Appy's voice seemed to come from everywhere.

"Interpretation," Appy said. "What, for example, is the definition of the word 'Beast' as it appears in the Babul? I've heard it used by some religions to refer to political entities, such as the Outer Planet Confederacy. Reborn Krassees have used the term synonymously with the name of the Pope; KothoLus have in turn said that Blue Presbyism is the 'Beast.' I've even overheard pilgrims aboard ship suggesting that Mr. McMurtrey might be the 'Beast,' since he's perceived as an atheist. He's in Cabin Sixty-six, Level Six. Three sixes are the sign of Satan."

"You're the Beast, Appy!" one of the nuns shouted. "You assigned the cabin numbers!"

"Did I?" Appy countered. "Or did I only do what I had to do, what I was commanded to do?"

The nun appeared embarrassed at her outburst and slouched into her chair, as if wishing she could disappear from view.

The Beast? McMurtrey thought. *Satan? What have I gotten into?*

"And what is the definition of 'the Krassos'?" Appy asked, undeterred. "There are those, for example, who believe that this term refers to more than a person, that it refers more importantly to one part of a collective interplanetary consciousness consisting of every human being. 'Krassos consciousness,' in this interpretation, is an emerging of consciousness based upon astrological cycles. It is tied in with the belief in a Nandubhaga-type avatar or divine teacher who will one day externalize in human form for all of mankind. To the Hoddhists, it is Hoddha or Eyamai; to the Isammedans, it is the Prophet Isammed; to the ParKekhs it is another entity, and so on."

Appy fell silent, leaving the room in agitated whispers.

Corona nudged McMurtrey.

"I saw you staring at my breasts this morning, you bad beast," she whispered.

McMurtrey flushed, glanced around to see if anyone had heard her. He couldn't look at Corona after that remark! But she hadn't sounded angry.

McMurtrey shook his head in exasperation. How should he respond and how many variations of correctness were there? Time was ticking, and he hadn't answered. Maybe it was a test of some kind, God seeing if McMurtrey would do the proper thing. Kelly Corona was Satan. She was a siren calling, tempting him toward the rocks.

I haven't answered her yet. I've got to answer!

"I'm sorry," McMurtrey whispered.

No response came, and a sidelong glance revealed to McMurtrey that Kelly Corona was smiling gently.

Then she said, a little too loudly: "If I didn't want you to stare at them, I'd wear a barrel."

Beyond Corona the stars of the nebula were larger and much brighter than before, evidence of the ship's motion. They were fiery purple and blue suns, of indeterminate size.

Suddenly the view dimmed, and McMurtrey saw parallel white lines between the ship and the nebula, lines that covered the entire field of vision and permitted a view through the spaces between them. McMurtrey squinted, detected a yellow glow in the darkness between the lines. It was an odd, humanlike shape of light, and cloudlike in its lambency . . . a flickering image, harder and harder to perceive.

McMurtrey had seen D'Urth clouds in unusual shapes, reminiscent of humans and animals. The tendency of the mind to anthropomorphize.

"They're back!" Corona exclaimed. She shuddered. "Appy's really ticked now, telling Shusher to stay away from the speed controls. Shusher says the speed and take-off controls are part of the ship, part of himself. How can he stay away from himself, he's asking!"

McMurtrey held her hand, and as he touched her he felt a shudder course through his body, followed by a compression shift in his ears. Then his ears popped, and a voice filled one ear—Appy! McMurtrey's eyes opened wide and he saw Corona staring at him quizzically.

"I hear Appy!" McMurtrey whispered. He glanced around. No one was paying attention to them.

The ship rocked, and several people grabbed hold of chair backs to keep from falling.

"What was that?" a man asked.

The white lines in the window became smaller and apparently more distant.

"Slow down, dammit!" Appy roared, across the private channel. "That thing's a skinbeater like us! Stay away from it and don't tailgate! You can't pass! You'll rip the skins apart!"

McMurtrey released his grip on Corona's hand, and Appy's voice went away, with a pop in McMurtrey's ears. He touched Corona again, and this time heard a peculiar sonar squeal in his other ear. That would be Shusher, if Corona's theory held true.

McMurtrey couldn't make any sense from the squeals.

"Skinbeater?" McMurtrey said. "What the hell is that?"

Corona shrugged. "I told you there were problems."

A horn brayed distantly, heard by McMurtrey across the private channel, in the background. It was an angry sound, like one motorist trying to pass another.

Appy said not to pass, and it sounded dangerous. McMurtrey felt a shortness of breath.

Screams in his left ear: "Don't try it, Shusher! Dammit, you'll destroy everything!"

McMurtrey's back pressed against the chair.

Those who hadn't yet found seats scrambled for them.

"Acceleration," Corona said, uneasily. "Feels odd in GravSense, but, baby, we are movin' out!"

"Look outside!" one of the nuns exclaimed.

Corona was looking toward the window, and McMurtrey saw her profiled against it, with the white lines flashing bright yellow around the humanlike cloud shapes behind her. The lines and shapes lost definition, became a blur of yellow. The blur streaked into the distance, became tiny and disappeared.

The ship was flying smoothly, with the striking blue and purple nebula ahead.

"It outran you," Appy said, across the private channel. "I just hope you haven't screwed up the skins. They're fragile, you fool."

Almost involuntarily, McMurtrey's gaze rested on Corona's breasts. They were lovely, with a youthful uplift to them. This woman wasn't so young, though . . . thirty-five if you squinted. He looked away, lest she nab him again.

McMurtrey felt a pressure shift in his ears, followed by silence from Appy and Shusher. He noted he was still touching Corona's hand.

"They're gone," she said.

No sign of "Redneck" Smith or Jin in this group. Some of the others looked vaguely familiar to McMurtrey, such as the tall and bearded Middist man across from him in the second row, whom he categorized as Sidic by his large fur hat, long black coat, and sidelocks that curled on each side of his head. In that same row, the broad-bearded Greek Hetox priest was familiar too, with his heavy necklace and large silver cross hanging outside a black robe. He carried a Blik Pulverizer rifle sheathed across his back, and he shifted the weapon to his side when he sat down. Just behind him was a white-robed man who wore a small gold cross on his chest. From the gold embroidery of the robe he appeared to be a KothoLu of rather high office, or a priest in ceremonial clothing. McMurtrey didn't know how to tell the difference.

The participants sat in uneasy expectation, their eyes shooting nervous, piercing glances around the room. Some conversed with those nearby in low tones. McMurtrey wondered if a person would enter and call the meeting to order, or if Appy would conduct it from his usual vantage. But for a long time no one came, and Appy didn't speak after concluding his roll call.

Finally Orbust raised his voice to ask, "What's going on here? We're supposed to just sit around staring at each other?"

When no one answered him and no voice of support arose from the assemblage, he locked gazes with Zatima. For several uncomfortable seconds they engaged in an angry stare-down.

With a thrust to his feet, Orbust gave up the effort and stomped to the door. Tully followed.

They took turns tugging at the door handle, even pulled together. The door wouldn't budge.

Tully cut loose a string of oaths, which Orbust chastised him for.

"You may leave when the meeting is concluded," Appy said, across the P.A. system.

"What meeting?" Orbust demanded. He faced those in the room, and he appeared to be not only agitated but frightened. His hand went to his holster, touching the handle of the gun.

There was no reply.

"What's the itinerary?" Orbust asked.

"Yeah!" Tully shouted. "Tell us or we're bustin' out!" He eyed Orbust's gun.

"I've got an explosives kit in this holster," Orbust said. "You talk, Appy, or I'm—"

"Sit and shut," Zatima said, economically.

"You gonna make me?" Orbust said, glaring at her.

"If necessary."

Orbust laughed, but returned to his seat. He plunked himself down, folded his arms across his chest.

Tully remained standing by the door.

The fat little nun in white spoke, in a struggling, tiny voice that squeaked. "I wonder if we're being sequestered like a jury, assigned to remain here until we determine something. The computer has indicated we should think for ourselves."

A man in the group addressed this, but the comment was inconclusive and McMurtrey blocked much of it out, along with the ensuing discussion.

"What's going on, Kelly?" McMurtrey asked, not loudly enough for others to hear. He looked to his right, at her.

Corona shook her head. "You got us into this, Ev. We should be asking you." From her expression she seemed to be thinking of something else.

McMurtrey was annoyed, and said, "I see." He felt an irritation in one nostril, sniffed and felt a sneeze coming through his sinuses like twin freight trains.

He let go a megablast that caused people nearby to pull away and those farther off to turn their heads toward him.

"Bless you," said the nun in white.

"Gesundheit," said the nun in black.

"A most favorable omen," the Greek Hetox said. "A good spirit has sneezed out on thee a blessing."

"Great," McMurtrey said, with a sniff. "Shall I try for another?"

Several people giggled, and McMurtrey noticed people looking at him with rapt expressions.

Peripherally, he saw Corona gazing at him differently, a hard stare.

He looked away from her.

"Not so fast, McMurtrey," a little man in a white dhoti said. He was bespectacled and toothless, quite old, and his head had been shaven, with stubbles of dark hair showing. "Permit me to introduce myself. I am Kumara Makanji, a Rahmanic Nandu. To us the sneeze is connected with demoniacal influence. A malevolent spirit just entered or left your nose."

"Fool of fools!" Zatima exclaimed. "This feeble Nandu knows nothing, like all of his wretched, brain-starved kind! Allah favors sneezing, and that is why I say to the sneezer, 'Praise Allah and Allah bless you!'"

"I know nothing, eh?" the Nandu snarled, in a tone that surprised McMurtrey because of the reputed peaceful nature of Nandus. "Sneezing at the beginning of something is unlucky. Many times in history has this been proven. We are at the beginning of a voyage, at the beginning of a meeting. May Rahma have mercy on us. We should return to D'Urth immediately and begin again."

"Nonsense," Zatima said. "If you want to go back, cow-lover, leap from the ship!"

"I will not!" Makanji said.

"Tell your precious Rahma to aid you, and if Rahma is worth so much as a pittance, you'll be carried to safety."

"You try it first, Isammedan dog, and if you make it I'll follow."

They glared at one another, and both fell silent.

This is crazy, McMurtrey thought. *A room full of holy apes, fighting about THIS? And me, worried Corona will catch me looking again*? He wanted to look and savor, but resisted the urge. His mouth watered.

"Among my faith," a little black-coated Middist rabbi

said, "as in Krassianism and Isammedanism, a sneeze is followed by a blessing. We speak of *asusa*, or health, exclaiming, 'Your health!—God bless you—for a happy life!' The sneezer then speaks from the Canrah, and is blessed by those present, to which he replies, 'Be thou blessed!'"

A dark-skinned man in a floral-print sarong rose, from the back row. His chest was bare, and he wore dark beads around his neck. "I am Bluepaccan," he announced. "I agree with the Nandu. Sneezing is bad at the beginning of an expedition. Evil follows."

He sat down, and for a while no one in the room said anything. All seemed deep in thought.

Presently McMurtrey said, "Nandus and Bluepaccans say one thing, the Wessornian religions another. We're not just talking about sneezing, you know, and maybe that's why Appy placed us in this locked room, why God compelled us to visit Him in this manner."

"Get to the point if you have one," Orbust said, scowling.

"I was doing precisely that. Suppose that we're all sequestered here, as the nun suggested, and it's to have dialogues with one another, to learn about other religions."

"Who needs to do that?" Orbust said. "The only true faith is Reborn Krassianism, and before this trip is over everyone on this ship will know and understand."

"You plan to convert everyone?" McMurtrey asked. "A missionary with a gun? That's what Krassos would have wanted? My recollection is that He preached love. I think He'd puke if He could see what's being done in His name."

"What makes you think He can't see what's going on?" Orbust countered, without apparent shame.

"I'll grant you that," McMurtrey said. "And he would be puking if he still had human form. He'd blast His cookiechocs all over you, and you'd gag in the swill."

Orbust scowled, looked away.

"I've heard of this in dispute-resolution," McMurtrey said. "Representatives of opposing parties sit in a room, and aren't permitted to leave until they've thrashed everything out, until they've compromised. It's been done in labor negotiations and in national diplomatic circles, thus avoiding strikes and wars. There was even a time three hundred and fifty odd years ago when two opposing generals were locked in a room by their commanders and told to fight without weapons until one emerged."

"Principles cannot be compromised, " the white- and gold-robed KothoLu said, speaking Unglish with an accent.

A woman on McMurtrey's right said this was Archbishop Perrier from Notre Sorren, very high in the church hierarchy.

A young boy commented on the brilliance of the nebula they were approaching. It was so bright that McMurtrey had difficulty looking toward the window. Three massive suns were throwing the most light, and they were getting larger with each passing second. The cluster seemed to be drawing near faster than before, so McMurtrey surmised the ship must have accelerated. He felt no heat from the suns.

"Maybe God sees war in the offing," McMurtrey said, staring at Perrier. "There's been no shortage of religious wars in mankind's sordid history, and maybe all of us are supposed to take information back to D'Urth that will make everlasting peace possible. D'Urth's surface is at relative peace now, but the war with the Outer Planet Confederacy continues apace—on planet Saturus, I hear."

"That's no religious war," Zatima said. "It's strictly secular."

"How do we know?" McMurtrey asked. "How do we know all the motivations, all the causes?"

"That's not a real war anyway," Corona said. "It's trumped up, a justification for the BOL's very existence and probably for a similar police organization in the Confederacy." She went to her mouth with a forefinger tip, transferred saliva to her eyebrow and smoothed down the brow.

"Right!" the Sidic Middist said. "It's called 'in-group bonding,' where a government keeps its population together artificially with fear and hatred of an outsider. You can bet the Bureau knows that trick."

A hush fell across the room, for it was not often that anyone spoke publicly against the government.

In the midst of this discomfiture, McMurtrey had a private concern: he tried not to think about Corona's odd mannerism.

He heard a click to his right, and the light in the room diminished. The window beyond Corona had vanished, and in its place stood a seamless, pale green wall.

"We're protected by mirrors, but the room was getting too bright," Corona speculated. "Appy made an adjustment."

"Or Shusher did," McMurtrey said.

Corona grunted in affirmation. They had to guess now, with the private channel gone.

A woman coughed, and sneezed.

Uneasy laughter carried around the room.

"Even if there were religious factors involved in war, what could we do about it?" Zatima asked. "Everyone aboard is not a religious leader, and as far as I know, none of us are sanctioned to resolve anything."

"I only tossed the thought out for discussion," McMurtrey said. "It could be that we're supposed to return to the various religions with moving stories, with compelling reasons why certain religious and political steps should be taken."

Zatima's dark eyes flashed. "Allah will lead us, one way or another."

"With what's happened to me," McMurtrey said, "I'm changing, and I think we all need to be flexible. We need to work together. How I'm changing I can't say, but I've always believed in God. It's just that . . . there's been no structure for me, no belief system. God Himself suggested to me that religion may not be the way. I don't know what He meant by that. He said it noncommittally, the way Appy says things. I'm real confused."

No one spoke. McMurtrey had noticed a phenomenon in recent days, the way people fell silent when he spoke. They hung on every word, made him feel special and more nearly on a par with the holy people around him.

"I'm assuming God spoke with me," McMurtrey said, "and that it wasn't a cruel practical joke. I've considered that, you must know. My Interplanetary Church of Cosmic Chickenhood was a pretty good-sized practical joke on a lot of people, and I wondered if some of them decided to get even with me in a big way."

"With all the ships?" Zatima said. "With all that's happened? One would have to imagine that Allah Himself was taken in by your joke, and that is inconceivable."

McMurtrey sighed.

"Isammed, Prince of the Faithful, had a vision," Zatima said, her throaty voice carrying the seasoning of the desert. "And he too had self-doubts. I believe you have been visited, but that you are not a prophet to replace Isammed, last and greatest of the prophets. What has happened to you is something different. I do not speak intellectually now. This is from the heart. An angel appeared to Isammed as he slept in the cave at Dootir. The angel passed a coverlet of brocade with writing upon it to our Beloved, and said, 'These are the Lord's words. Read them!'"

"I have heard that story," McMurtrey said, "and the events of my visitation do not compare."

"But a great fleet of ships subsequently appeared for you," Zatima countered. "Truly this is the work of Allah, and you are His courier."

Orbust spoke in a low tone to Tully.

"Didn't Hoddha receive a vision?" McMurtrey asked, looking at three Hoddhist men across the room. They had shaven heads and wore thin, plain cotton robes. Two robes were of saffron, and one, in the middle, was white. McMurtrey knew from having seen them before that they wore no shoes.

One of the saffron-robed Hoddhists rose, and said, "Hoddha sat beneath the bodhi-tree for three nights. On the first night, his past lives went before him. On the second he witnessed the cycle of birth, death, and rebirth, and came to a full understanding of dharma and the universe. On the third night he attained a holy knowledge of suffering, the why of it and the removal of it. Hoddha experienced an enlightenment, which was not exactly the conversation with God others claim to have experienced. This is not to detract from any experience. It is to say that Hoddha's experience was unique."

He lowered his head, spoke reverently, " 'Namo tasso Bhagvato Arahato Sammasamhoddhaassa.' I bow my head to the Blessed One, the Enlightened One, the perfectly Enlightened One.'"

He resumed his seat without ever having given his name.

"Thank you," McMurtrey said, as if he were master of ceremonies. "These visions, or visitations, are intriguing. You've all heard of Zillasterism, an ancient religion upon which much of Middism, Krassianism and Isammedanism are based?"

From all around came blank expressions.

"Are there any followers of the ancient prophet Zillaster among us?" McMurtrey asked.

Nanak Singh rose. "I am a ParKekh," he said, "an off-shoot of Zillasterism."

"Yours is an important faith," McMurtrey said.

Singh smiled, resumed his seat.

McMurtrey raised his voice, felt very full of himself. "Zillaster was by the bank of a river when he received a revelation from God. An angel nine times the size of a man appeared before him, told him there was only one God and that Zillaster was to serve as His prophet. Sub-sequently there were other visions, in which further truths were revealed to Zillaster. Similarly, Mark Krassos is said to have spoken with God, and likewise Dosek and Is-ammed. After Krassos died, his apostles said they saw visions of the resurrected Krassos. So many extraordinary visions, and all of them with merit."

"I'm not as diplomatic as Evander," Corona said. "We're all imperfect beings, and I'd like to know how we're supposed to separate visions from hallucinations. The human mind plays tricks. It's full of dreams and im-ages. When a man is in the desert, he sees mirages. Each person experiencing a vision freely admits it's a vision, without fleshly substance. How can we separate the real from the unreal?"

"Be careful what you say about Krassos," Orbust snarled. "Or—"

"Or what?" Corona snapped. "Or you'll blow me away in the name of Krassos?"

"I might." But his expression was uncertain and fearful.

"God, what a fool," Corona muttered.

"As you should know," Zatima said, glaring at Orbust, "Krassos preached love. I think you'd better reread the Old Babul, which Isammedans also consider to be holy writ, along with our Kooraq."

"You want me to read the Kooraq?" Orbust asked.

"That wasn't what I meant, but yes, if you wish. I'm sure an extra copy can be located. Understand, though, that if you deface it you die."

"I see," Orbust said. He forced a smile.

McMurtrey didn't know whether to classify this demeanor as game-playing, or if Orbust saw what McMurtrey and Corona saw, that it was ludicrous for people to speak of killing one another in the name of God, in the name of a force of good, no matter the disagreements over interpretation of that force. Maybe Orbust was beginning to see it.

He didn't seem sure of himself.

"Some things must be taken on faith," Zatima said. "They can't be thought about too much."

A source of the problem? McMurtrey thought, not speaking up for fear of inviting rancor. *But actions without thought? Actions on pure, blind faith? Are the faiths who have engaged in holy wars like the blind with weapons, striking out without good, logical reasons for doing so*?

"This is true about faith," a dark-skinned man near McMurtrey said. He wore a simple white cotton shirt, open at the collar. His eyes were very large and almost sleepy, with long lashes and heavy, dark eyebrows. "Reeshna believed this implicitly. He spoke of seeing things with the heart and not with the mind, of taking matters in fully and completely at a glance, without analysis. He used to go for long walks, during which he said that not a single thought touched his head."

"You are a follower of Reeshna?" McMurtrey asked.

"He would not want me to say so, for he rejected formal religion. He believed that the problems of each person should be solved individually, for and by the person himself." The man resumed his seat.

Makanji the Nandu rose, nudged one of his round eyeglass lenses to adjust the perch of the glasses on his nose. "I too have taken long walks without the touch of thought." He smiled. "But having been lost more than once doing this, I found it safer to meditate from one position. That way, when I return to the otherness of this physical realm, I know where I am."

Polite laughter floated around the room.

"So you and I agree on something," Zatima said to the

Nandu. "We agree that your kind have no thoughts in your heads!"

"You know what I mean, sand-pig," Makanji said, his face instantly livid. "And so does that ParKekh devil with you."

Nanak Singh leaped to his feet, eyes flaming and hand at his scabbard. But Zatima restrained him. She bade him sit down, but not before he cursed at Makanji for Nandu raids upon the Ruby Temple of the ParKekhs.

"These Nandus professing tolerance for all religions make me want to puke," Zatima said. "The supposedly expansive fold that can envelop all faiths into one. Ha!"

"You started it!" Makanji exclaimed. "Twice in this room, you have made unprovoked attacks upon me, first with that 'fool of fools' insult simply because my view of sneezing was different from yours. Then this comment of no thoughts in our heads. You are irrational, Sivvy Isammedan, like all the fanatics of your kind!"

The KothoLu gentleman in the white and gold robe rose, spreading his arms at his sides so that fabric draped from them like wings. "And that's what started this childish arguing?" he asked. "A silly sneeze? Maybe McMurtrey is right, that we're supposed to remain here until we figure out how to get along in our sandbox. I am Archbishop Perrier of Notre Sorren."

Makanji slipped quietly back into his seat.

"It goes beyond today," Zatima said. "To centuries past, when Nandu rioters murdered Isammedans in Cuttadel, and when they stormed the Ruby Temple of the ParKekhs, murdering hundreds of worshipers in cold blood. It goes back, Archbishop, to your mindless crusades against Isammedan teachings."

Makanji muttered something that didn't carry.

Perrier smiled. "So now I'm drawn into the argument too, I who was trying to be so reasonable."

"There's never been anything reasonable about KothoLuism," Zatima said. "So don't play 'holier than thou' games with us. I know of the political purgings of Tignos Gospels from your Babul in the early decades after Krassos. Tell the people, sir, what your forebears did with the Gospel of Tomias, the Secret Book of Jamor, the Gospel of Purity and other texts. They ascribed words and acts

to Mark Krassos that the orthodox KothoLus didn't want
to hear, for political reasons, for reasons of church coffers,
for whatever their reasons were. And your Questers were
a satanic inquisition squad if ever there was one, burning
people who refused to accept your jewel-laden Pope.
Don't forget the compacts between Ava The Destroyer
and the KothoLu Church, either."

Perrier had been sputtering through this, couldn't get a
word in. When Zatima paused at last, Perrier seemed too
agitated and red in the face to speak. But he remained
standing, like a speaker refusing to relinquish the podium.

"One of my ancestors was Roger Landis," Orbust said,
"an Unglishman and one of the martyrs to KothoLuism."

"They martyred my ancestors too," Tully said.

"And a most curious group we are," McMurtrey said,
"knowing things about one another as we seem to, along
with the intriguing heredity of some. I don't know much
about my own ancestry, beyond a few generations, but
perhaps if I did it might tie in. Maybe it's for a combination
of reasons that we're mixed together on this ship, and
further mixed in this room."

"What are you driving at?" Perrier asked, still standing.
His arms were at his sides now, not visible within the folds
of his magnificent robe.

"That we are, as I suggested, a curious group, drawn to
St. Charles Beach by a higher, powerful Being, subsequently divided into ships and further divided as to mezzanines and assembly rooms. I'm certain it's not at random,
but to what purpose I do not know."

"You were called here to look at my chest," Corona
whispered.

Unaware of an ancillary meaning to his words, Orbust
said, "The question of the hour. The meaning of this moment, the meaning of life."

"You're sounding almost rational," McMurtrey said. "I
apologize. I shouldn't complain. But I am intrigued, and
hope fervently that we can expect more of the same from
you."

"That's not all you hope for fervently," Corona whispered.

"Stop it!" McMurtrey husked. He felt like a person in
church hearing dirty words.

Orbust's face stiffened, but not in an unkindly way. "I'm . . . well . . . admittedly I get excited very easily. I'm passionate in my beliefs, you might say."

"I see," McMurtrey said. "We're making some progress." He scanned the room. "Let's all try listening for a change, try seeing and hearing what's around us, even if it seems strange. This is quite a pot we've been tossed into, and I for one am not going to barge ahead blindly, relying upon what I thought I knew before this. I want to learn from all of you, and I expect all of you could learn a little from me as well."

McMurtrey paused, smiled. "Yes," he added. "You can learn even from God's lowliest creatures, even from the Chicken Man."

Half expecting applause or subdued laughter, McMurtrey looked around.

Only the faces of Tully and Orbust bore the trace of a smile. Zatima, Singh, Makanji and Perrier scowled ferociously, and many others looked either perplexed or enraptured. The three Hoddhists seemed to be in prayer or in meditation, for they had their eyes closed and weren't moving.

"All right you cocksuckers," Appy rasped, over an unseen loudspeaker. "Who tried to sabotage the other ships with a corrosive? God informs me this caused an eighteen-hour delay before He could complete repairs, and that now the ships are in flight, chuggin' right up our ass."

A number of people gasped.

McMurtrey felt short of breath from the surprise and shock of what he was hearing. Such language on a holy ship, from God's mechanical servant? Sanctified air had been poisoned!

Zatima condemned Appy in a loud, outraged tone.

Makanji said the computer must be malfunctioning.

The nuns whispered between themselves.

The Hoddhists' eyes were huge, staring saucers.

"Aw fuck off, you pack o' hypocrites!" Appy raged. "Actually that eighteen-hour advantage could guarantee me a pleasure-disk bonus for getting my cargo to God first—*if* we don't run into any other delays. God decided I had nothing to do with what happened, so He isn't going to penalize me. He warned me, however, that if I'm not alert to dirty tricks, if I don't do my duty to prevent further damaging actions like that, I'm not going to qualify for the prize. So whoever did it, you're an asshole, but thanks anyway."

"What kind of morality is this?" Makanji asked, his rage barely under control.

Appy laughed wickedly. "We're in a race, you jerks! This is God's competitive event, His pastiche on the clamoring, competing usurpers that sentient creatures have become . . . I'm competing with other biocomputers aboard the other ships, and each biocomputer has an idiotic Shusher-type entity with which to contend. Shusher and his breed are invisibles called Gluons, able to negotiate the fragile skins between universes, which are the shortest spaceways to God. It's called skinbeating. For reasons unrevealed, time is of the essence, and God wants the racers to reach Him quickly."

This biocomputer needs to have its personality reworked, McMurtrey thought.

"Why does He want us there at all?" McMurtrey asked.

"Again, unrevealed. Shusher and other Gluons are masses of energy, proteins and amino acids . . . perfect hosts for channel-synthesized creations. Shusher could be a ship as he is now, or could be something altogether different, if properly channeled to be that. My theory is that we are united—human, biocomputers and Gluons— because each of us have in our sentient states become overly competitive."

"But aren't you an apprentice, an assistant of some sort, to God?" McMurtrey asked. "You sound like you don't know everything that's going on here."

"Does any apprentice? This is part of my training process, just as it is part of yours and part of Shusher's. I do not know if I am apprenticing to become God, for the form of God is not programmed into me. In fact, I do not know *what* I'm apprenticing to become."

Appy laughed wildly.

The test I suspected we were being put to, McMurtrey thought. *But it's unlike anything I imagined.*

"Are we representative humans?" McMurtrey asked. "Are we supposed to carry some message back to D'Urth?"

"My assignment is only to rush you to God," Appy replied. "Information such as that, since I don't have it, must be in another repository, perhaps only with the Lord Himself. Anyway, as I said, fuck off."

"Why do you behave so erratically?" McMurtey demanded. "You're unpredictable and odd."

"Am I?" came the response. And the biocomputer embarked upon the longest, insanest laugh of all, a cachinnation that chilled McMurtrey to his core.

Orbust, Tully, and the Greek Hetox pulled at the door handle, trying to get out.

But the door held firm against all their efforts, combined and separate.

"Get back!" Orbust barked to the two with him. He drew his gun. "I'll get us outa here!"

Tully scurried away, hid behind a chair.

"My pulverizer rifle has more power!" the Greek Hetox shouted, sliding his weapon out of the sheath on his back.

People were scrambling to hide behind chairs. Others sat motionlessly and dispassionately, in apparent oblivion.

"Can you set the projectiles so they don't ricochet?" Orbust asked.

"No."

"Then you'd better not use it in this confined area. My gun has an anti-ric setting. It's gonna be loud, so everybody cover your ears."

The Greek hurried behind a chair, and crouched there with his palms pressed against his ears.

Orbust emptied his gun into the door latch, filling the room with a deafening noise.

The door still didn't budge.

Orbust reloaded and cut loose again.

The result was the same, and now McMurtrey's ears were ringing, despite having kept his pinkies in them during the barrage.

Orbust sat on the floor by the door, removed his holster from his belt and spread the holster open, revealing a narrow white strip inside, along with a shallow, clear-plastic box that held a bunch of little red pellets.

"What do you have there?" Corona asked.

"Chemstrip."

"Did you buy that from a door-to-door salesman?"

"Yeah. So what?"

"So it's illegal. Haven't you heard? The Bureau of Loyalty says no concealed weapons may be carried by any person without a BOL permit. You have a permit?"

The color drained from Orbust's face. "Nobody said anything about one. The salesman told me it was BOL-sanctioned, and that's all I know. Say, who are you to be asking about that? With your comments about the Bureau, you'll be picked up and put away."

Corona smiled. "Did the salesman show you any documentation?"

"No!" Orbust was openly frightened.

"Salesmen lie."

"I've been carrying this setup around without knowing! Innocently!"

"Tell it to the BOL," Corona said.

Orbust looked like a man already arrested and executed, a convicted enemy of the state.

"Don't worry," Corona said. "The Bureau can't touch you out here."

Nervously, Orbust rubbed the fingers of one hand together like insect legs, then peeled open the box cover and removed three pellets. "Something I prepared for the occasion," he explained. He wedged the pellets inside a crack between the door and the jamb, clamped a thin black wire onto the pellets.

Gathering his kit, he ran for cover, diving behind a chair.

This got the attention of the oblivious, and almost everyone took cover in the same manner.

Someone got slapped in the ensuing moments, apparently by the nun with the squeaky voice. She accompanied her blow with a stern scolding, "Don't pinch me, you nasty man!" Since this occurred somewhere out of McMurtrey's view, he couldn't tell who the offender was. But he heard him scuttling away.

Corona, on the floor by McMurtrey, looked at him and giggled.

A tremendous explosion rattled the room, causing McMurtrey's already ringing ears to throb and ache. There was no smoke, no perceptible odor, and when McMurtrey looked tremulously over the chair, he saw Orbust running for the door.

But the door remained closed and appeared undamaged. When Orbust tried to open it once more, it still refused to budge.

"Shit!" Tully said.

Then Orbust made Tully apologize to all present for his language. This seemed curious to McMurtrey, for Orbust packed dangerous weapons and had essentially kidnapped McMurtrey for a time. Anyone who would do those things shouldn't feel any compunction about using foul language.

To McMurtrey, Orbust was an enigma. But in a perverse and muddy way, Orbust fit into this eclectic gathering as much as anyone else.

McMurtrey was convinced that all the pilgrims were students engaged in an unparalleled learning process.

Students took tests.

Might this locked room be one, and the disgusting language of the computer another? How were the participants supposed to react to such things?

McMurtrey's ears were feeling better, the ringing having diminished.

He and Corona resumed their seats.

"I'm back," Appy announced. "God programmed me and I am not experiencing malfunction. I can swear any damn time I feel like it, you pack of whining, sniveling butt-licking hypocrites! God informs me that many of you use colorful language privately, that you even regularly take the Lord's name in vain."

Appy lowered his voice. "You do worse things, too, don't you?"

Now Appy displayed his laugh, and a perverse discharge it was. Not very loud this time, and halfway between an evil chortle and a belly laugh, it was interspersed most surprisingly with snorts, as if the effort were causing Appy's sinuses to constrict.

Do biocomputers have sinuses? McMurtrey wondered.

Orbust stood by the door, looking frustrated and confused.

Several attendees emerged from their hiding places and took seats or stood.

"You, Sister Mary," Appy's omnipresent voice said. "A fine and laudable Dictine nun you are. But just the other day in St. Charles Beach you said a naughty-naughty when you stepped in a pile of cow fluff! And under your breath only moments ago, you called that Middist who pinched you a 'brainless boob!' "

"I did none of those things!" the nun proclaimed, in an indignant, squeaky voice. Her fat cheeks glowed red.

The tall Sidic Middist smiled, and when Sister Mary saw this she became even more agitated.

"We have more than a computer malfunction!" a woman lamented. "You people are out of control, pinching and swearing! Heaven help us, for you're all crazy! We're headed in the wrong direction, straight into Hell!"

The Middist rabbi who had spoken of sneezes and blessings jumped to his feet, from the last row, opposite. His long black coat resembled that of the other Middist, but instead of a fur cap this man wore the traditional yarmulke. His beard twitched angrily.

"That man is not Sidic!" he exclaimed. "The Sidic are orthodox, and among them extrafamilial contact between the sexes is strictly forbidden! No follower of that faith would pinch a woman!"

"Certainly not in public anyway," Corona said.

The rabbi didn't hear Corona, shouted: "There is more to being a Middist than appearance! I am Rabbi Moshe Teitelbaum of Jalley City. I do not always agree with my Sidic friends, with their ways of mysticism in particular, but I respect them. And this public sacrilege is an affront to all Middism! I do not need to check circumcision to ascertain your heart!"

"Can it, Bozo," the one under attack sneered. "I am Shalom ben Yakkai, born into a Middist family, but not a religious one. We are, in point of fact, strongly atheistic."

"I knew it!" Teitelbaum exclaimed. "Why do you dare dress so?"

"I like the style."

"Remove those clothes!" Teitelbaum demanded.

"In front of the women?"

Teitelbaum sputtered something incomprehensible. His face glowed an unhealthy shade of red.

"I've been fouled by the hand of filth," Sister Mary whimpered. "May the Lord cleanse me!"

"And shear those sidelocks!" Teitelbaum shouted.

"May I keep my beard?" Yakkai queried, with a sardonic smile.

The rabbi dropped into his chair, glaring at Yakkai.

"I could divulge interesting tidbits about nearly all of you," Appy said. "To one extent or another, you're all selfish hypocrites."

"Oh, goodie," Yakkai said. "Juicy gossip! Tell us everything, Appy!"

McMurtrey glanced sidelong, saw Corona staring at him intensely.

"Don't mention the private channel we've heard," she said. "Could be trouble over that."

McMurtrey nodded.

"We're in the clutches of the Antikrassos!" Sister Mary wailed. "We've got to turn this ship around and return to D'Urth!"

"Impossible," Orbust said. "We can't even get out of this room." He fumbled with his chemstrip, couldn't get it to adhere to the door, for whatever purpose he had in mind.

"Check for secret panels," Yakkai suggested. "In the walls, the floor, the ceiling. Twist the seats."

"I'm with you, Shalom ben Yakkai," the Greek Hetox said. "We'll find a way, if there is a way."

McMurtrey thought about Yakkai, wondered how an atheist got aboard ship. It occurred to him that Yakkai might be a Bureau of Loyalty spy, made to look the buffoon to place him above suspicion. That might explain how he got past Appy, if Bureau influence extended beyond the solar system.

"Maybe the door opens with a secret password," someone suggested.

No one paid much attention to the comment.

Yakkai, the Greek Hetox, two of the Hoddhists in white, the nuns and the KothoLu archbishop were looking for secret panels. They horsed with the seats, trying to tilt them or twist them, and they pressed their hands against wall and floor surfaces, trying to trip an unseen mechanism. The men even stood atop one another's shoulders to reach high points on the walls and the ceiling. It was a high ceiling, which required that the Hoddhists stand side by side on adjacent seats, with Yakkai on their shoulders.

The three of them moved from seat to seat quite agilely and in formation, like circus performers.

While they were interlocked in this fashion, a clatter of unseen machinery arose, and several of the seats disappeared into the deck, as if it were quicksand.

Fortunately this did not include the seats upon which the three acrobats were supported, or any other occupied seats, and no one fell over. But it happened so quickly, in such a microportion of a blink, that neither McMurtrey nor anyone else had time to call out a warning.

In the next instant this happened: The floor, walls and ceiling became as clear as the finest glass, so that assembly rooms above and below could be seen. Every room was full of pilgrims, and in each they appeared to be in similar states of disarray.

McMurtrey saw Jin just below him, in the assembly room there. Jin, crouched over in his seat and naked, had what looked like a sheet of folded plazymer in his hand. Jin's head moved right, then left, as if he were glancing in those directions. Jin drew his hand toward his belly, out of McMurtrey's view. When the hand returned to view it was empty.

Jin looked up, straight at McMurtrey, and Jin's eyes were afire.

McMurtrey's heart skipped. He looked away, then back.

Jin wasn't looking up anymore. He stared straight ahead, and not a muscle twitched.

What did he do with that plazymer? McMurtrey wondered. *This guy is one of the strangest.*

Yakkai found himself peering into the face of a wild, bearded holy man on the level above, a man who was writhing on the floor in apparent religious ecstasy when the fishbowl effect occurred.

This so unnerved Yakkai, who must have thought for an instant that he was looking directly into the face of Jehovah, that he toppled from his perch and had to be saved from disaster by the quick, strong hands of Archbishop Perrier.

"Not the first time a Krassian has saved an atheist," Perrier quipped.

Yakkai thanked his benefactor graciously and profusely as Perrier helped right him upon his feet.

McMurtrey began to wonder how the chairs could have disappeared into the glass floor. His thoughts traveled to temperature change and various known means of meta-morphosing matter. As he pondered, chubby little Sister Mary and a number of other women in Room B-2 noticed pilgrims in rooms below looking up their skirts. This caused considerable flurrying about and squealing, with many of the women tucking their dresses under them and sitting upon them on the deck.

While this was happening, McMurtrey found himself intermittently staring up the skirt of a comely young woman on the level above. He saw pink underpants that were tight and frilly against her crotch and buttocks, and he felt an essential urging.

Then he noticed a fellow near her who wore no under-pants beneath his robe. This disgusted McMurtrey, and quickly he gazed back toward the young woman, who wore a white dress cut just below the knees. She had North-sornian features, was soft and pale of skin, with shoulder-length golden hair.

She was like a dream, and he longed to be on the other side of the barrier.

"Tsk, tsk, tsk," Corona said.

McMurtrey blushed, lowered his gaze.

Yakkai was looking up too, in awe of the splendrous woman before him.

Appy's voice crackled into the room, filling McMurtrey's ears with sound: "Don't look up those dresses and robes, or God will strike you blind!"

"I think I'll risk one eye," Yakkai said. He covered an eye with one hand.

Finally the young woman noticed the attention she was receiving. She tightened her skirt about her and scurried to the comparative safety of a chair.

When no bolt of blindness descended upon Yakkai from the heavens, riplets of nervous laughter began in the room. Soon McMurtrey, Corona and others were sharing in the glee and laughing uproariously. Despite their upbringings, despite their separate and often similar sexual codes, this

experience transcended a great deal and relieved the
stresses they had been feeling.

Even Appy laughed in his demented way, across the
speaker system. "Okay, so I was just kidding about blindness," he admitted. "But from now on you'll all obey me
and respect me better."

Sister Mary, one of those who hadn't participated in the
fun, shouted angrily: "Antikrassos! May God strike you
dead and return us safely to D'Urth!"

"You speaketh to me?" Appy said. "If so, you might
more cleverly have suggested that God fuse together my
biocircuits or burn my binaries. I am not the Antikrassos,
if such an entity truly exists, nor am I its representative."

"*If* it exists?" McMurtrey said. "What do you mean?"

"So many questions," Appy said, in a fatigued tone.
"There will be time enough to learn, time enough to learn.
Now, as to the door, B-Two . . . one of you suggested a
secret password. Few of you paid heed to that remark,
and a great pity that is. So much scrambling about searching for hidden panels! Oh my! A magic word is what you
need. That, and no more."

"Please," the nun in the black habit said, in the meekest
of voices. Then, a little louder: "Please open the door."

The door swished open into the ceiling, where before it
had swung on hinges. Like the missing chairs, the hinges
seemed to have melted into another surface.

The pilgrims burst from the room.

Seven

There is a marked tendency for a person in proximity to any strong and popular group to become like that group: in dress, in thought and in all manner. Homogeneity is a powerful force.

—Findings of the Commission on Culture and Religion

In the wide corridor, McMurtrey and Corona encountered a milling crowd of people, not all of them from Assembly Room B-2. The walls, ceiling and deck were opaque here.

"So you're sorry for you-know-what," Corona said. "Is that all you have to say for yourself?" Her dark eyes danced as she looked up at him.

"That again! Don't you ever let up?" He saw Smith on one side of the corridor, speaking in hushed tones with Tully.

"You're the one who keeps staring," Corona said. "Nice beaver shot you just got, I must say."

"Blast you!" He lowered his voice, satisfied himself that no one was eavesdropping: "I hardly knew I was doing that! Okay, convict me. I've got male hormones screaming through my veins. Lock me up! I'm incorrigible!"

"I hope so."

McMurtrey shook his head, in exasperation. He thought she was teasing, and resolved to give her a big chunk of his mind if she kept this up. He wasn't ready for anything like this, teasing or not.

"That Beast business," she said. "The false prophet stuff. You'd better watch your backside. A fruitcake could come after you. Lots of weapons aboard."

McMurtrey chewed at the inside of his mouth.

A woman said the other people gathered in the corridor

were from B-1, and from all around swept anxious talk that no one could find the elevator or stairway.

McMurtrey noticed Jin standing quietly by one wall. He was entirely nude, had only his broom. Paradoxically he seemed almost invisible in the space he occupied, receiving few glances.

McMurtrey peered over the heads of shorter people, through a little plexwindow on the door marked B-3. The room was still occupied, and it was apparent that no one in there had yet figured out how to escape. They pulled at the door and pounded on it like victims trapped in a fire, transmitting muffled, panicky noises to the corridor.

Shalom ben Yakkai tried to help them from the corridor side, without success. He shouted at them, but they didn't seem to hear him well enough to understand.

Individuals in the corridor set off every few moments like solo scouts, down each end of the passageway and even into rooms B-1 and B-2, searching for egress. They kept coming back with negative reports and blank expressions, and kept going back to look again, disbelieving.

This did not have a salutary effect on the throng.

Corona muttered something under her breath.

A man in navy blue pants and a matching pullover shirt emerged from B-2. McMurtrey heard him comment about the window being visible again, with "white lines all over the place outside."

McMurtrey hurried into the room, and was the only one in there. Through the window he saw the extraordinary parallel lines farther away, against a velvet backdrop of stars. He could no longer see the bright blue and purple nebula, and though he squinted, he detected no yellow cloud or human shape within the white lines.

McMurtrey theorized that whatever he'd seen earlier must have passed through the nebula.

He heard a noise, saw Corona peripherally, moving to his side.

"The white lines again," he said.

"What do you suppose they are?"

"I don't have any idea." McMurtrey felt dull, almost numb and mesmerized by the lines. It was similar to the way he'd felt when he stared for long periods at Shusher upon first seeing the ship, and akin to the way he'd felt sometimes as a child when he spent long periods staring into water.

"They almost look like projections from Shusher now," she suggested, "or from Appy. Where does Shusher end and Appy begin?"

McMurtrey caught her gaze for an instant, shrugged.

"Maybe it's a galactic tracking mechanism," Corona said, "a collision sensor or a plow that scatters space debris out of the way."

They stared at the lines for a long while, which remained visibly unchanged, as did the stars behind them.

Presently McMurtrey and Corona returned to the corridor.

The pilgrims began to voice anxiety over their perceived lack of control over their own destinies. Some spoke of the alleged despotism of Appy, and even of a similar charge against God Himself. This stirred several arguments into motion.

Through all of it Yakkai tried to aid those in B-3, primarily by pulling on the door handle. He was assisted by the Sivvy-Isammedan, Zatima. Singh lent a hand too, but all their efforts were to no avail.

The rabbi stood nearby with arms folded across his chest, staring disapprovingly at Yakkai.

Yakkai shouted that those inside B-3 might get out by saying "please," but it became obvious his words weren't getting through.

Then a man from B-1 tried to communicate with them, asserting that they should play leapfrog as the occupants of B-1 had done, that at the end of a long train the person reaching the door could burst right through. He said this door, like the door to his own assembly room, would disappear in a blink. But the message couldn't get through the thickness of wall and door.

He and Yakkai soon entered into a discussion, and between them it was determined that the doors to rooms B-1 and B-2 had opened through entirely different means. They decided that in some bizarre, sadistic fashion Appy had done this to them, and it complicated their rescue efforts.

Presently Appy began explaining from his hidden perch that the vessel had undergone "structural alterations"—

that the chairs disappearing from the assembly rooms, the blocked corridor egress, even the problems escaping the rooms, all had to do with "sudden changes" made to the ship in recent moments. This seemed to conflict with the devil-may-care attitude characterizing Appy's conversation with persons in B-2 just before the nun uttered the "magic" word, but McMurtrey theorized that these and other aberrations in Appy might have been tied in with the structural changes.

McMurtrey began to feel claustrophobic. He didn't much care about the details Appy spewed forth. The air was getting close, depleted of oxygen.

McMurtrey looked for Jin, didn't see him. Such a strange man. A man of peace, but with a sense of mystery and power about him.

Appy droned on about gross vehicle tonnage, metric dimensions, numbers of bunks and levels, fuel consumption, and the assigned passengers who for unspecified reasons had not boarded Shusher the day before on D'Urth.

McMurtrey wondered if Corona's intrusion into an off-limits area of the ship might have left the Appy-Shusher comlink damaged, letting in noise from other areas of the ship. Maybe Shusher was reacting psychotically to an excess of noise by inhaling chairs and locking doors.

Appy's words came back to him: *"This ship likes to travel quietly, and it has effective methods of enforcing its wishes."*

What did it expect, for heaven's sake, in an inundation of excited pilgrims?

More questions for Appy.

McMurtrey wasn't the only one with questions. The pilgrims all around were shouting relentlessly at Appy—asking why they couldn't go back to D'Urth and why Appy couldn't produce proof of God's participation in this venture, which was fast appearing ill-fated. Some people had already ordered meals, just before the meetings, and they were complaining now about the food, comparing it with bland hospital fare. One man railed about poor vocal quality in the book-tape of *Sidney's Comet*, and a few non-ascetics said their quarters were uncomfortably small and cramped.

These pilgrims were in a surly mood.

Corona even used this opportunity to vocalize about her lost captaincy, and she asked about the white lines outside.

But Appy, even if he felt besieged, didn't answer. Apparently he didn't have to address any of the queries. He droned away about how much smaller and more "tidy" the ship was now, failed entirely to explain whether or not they had littered the cosmos with debris, and elaborated on certain essentially cosmetic alterations the ship had undergone.

He said this ship and the others that had been lined up across St. Charles Beach were composite visions formed by the passengers who were going to board them—and that these mental images materialized after being projected through the channel, McMurtrey.

McMurtrey glanced around. People were staring at him.

Appy explained that the number of cabins had been reduced in the metamorphosis, and that the ship's exterior no longer had visible rivets on it.

"The people left behind were predominantly rivet visualizers," Appy said. "Through a curious phenomenon, few of them made it, and with distance across space the maintenance power of their mental images has faded. Somewhat in the manner of recessive genes, the exterior rivets remaining with us are latent. Most of you are smooth-surface visualizers."

"The other guys are all riveted back on D'Urth," McMurtrey suggested.

Corona laughed.

"Will this have an effect on ship's speed?" a man shouted.

"Everything could have an effect on our rate of travel," the computer replied, "even your very utterance of those words."

"What do you mean?" the man asked.

"It will become apparent."

"When?"

"When you are ready."

"Riddles!"

"If you say so."

"I do."

"Okay."

"Shut up! Can't anyone get the last word in on you?"

"If you wish."

"Shut up!"

"Okay."

McMurtrey recalled the arguments between Appy and Shusher over speed and damage to the skins between universes, wondered how the private information he and Corona shared had a bearing on what Appy told the man. McMurtrey thought he heard a faint humming. It was ever so difficult to distinguish, but in tone resembled a schoolyard taunt. From Appy?

The man seemed ready to burst his blood vessels, and one of the Hoddhists spoke to him soothingly. This helped.

"The answer," Archbishop Perrier said, "will become apparent. All things are possible to him who believes."

"Bullcrud," Corona snapped to McMurtrey. "Some of these people are consummate idiots."

McMurtrey nodded.

The corridor became much quieter, and people didn't move around so much. Like confused, traumatized animals they awaited word of their fate. Whispered prayers could be heard, in Isammic, Floriental, Nandustani, Unglish . . .

Yakkai and the rabbi conversed a short distance away, in controlled, hostile tones. Presently they ceased whatever they were arguing about and moved apart.

Even the people inside B-3 stopped struggling with the door. McMurtrey saw a young man's cleanshaven face at the tiny window, a face that stared blankly into the corridor.

"You might wonder why all the ships looked essentially the same," Appy continued. "They're in flight, by the way, not that far behind us now."

Someone booed.

"The ships were of different colors and sizes and had slight variances, but essentially all looked very much alike. Just as humans look essentially the same."

"Sure, we're in God's likeness," a man said.

"Quiet," Appy said. "This isn't kindergarten, so nobody raise your hands, okay? I have the floor. Humans are basically alike in what they want, even, remarkably, in the way they view life. Impoverished, wealthy, it makes no material difference. There's televid, magazine tapes, radio, all those homogeneous forces making people think alike, making them crave to be alike."

"That's idiotic," Johnny Orbust said. "People who are really impoverished don't have televids. They can't even read." Orbust had the shiny metallic Snapcard in his hand, and McMurtrey noticed that the card was held under tension, causing it to bend.

"Your information does not agree with mine."

"Then update," Orbust said. "Have someone carry your mainframe into the boonies. I mean the real boonies. Look in the outback, jungles, remote mountain regions, deserts. You're on a theoretical plane, dealing with abstractions."

McMurtrey hated to admit it, but Orbust was making sense. Not that McMurtrey held any affection for Orbust over Appy, but nonetheless it was gratifying to see a human holding ground against a sophisticated computer. The card in Orbust's hand glinted and sparkled.

Appy wasn't responding.

With an eyelid beginning to twitch, Orbust continued his offensive. "A starving person in a Third World nation with the same life view as that of a pampered, wealthy socialite? What you're saying is ludicrous."

"You weren't listening carefully," Appy countered. "I said 'basically alike,' and 'it makes no material difference.' These words are subject to analysis and interpretation. We're dealing with averages here, not rules which hold true to the last man."

"You didn't say that," Orbust said.

"I meant that, as anyone with half a brain can see. We were speaking of averages as applied to the materialization of these ships . . . they're from images projected by men as I said. Then I carried it a step further, to common life-views held by multitudes of people."

"Your thesis isn't provable," Orbust said. "How do we know that what you've told us about the creation of these ships is true? How do we know you aren't a liar, saying these things with an ulterior, self-serving motive?"

"I do not serve myself!" Apply said, haughtily. "I serve the Ancient of Days, and at His command I serve humankind."

"Well, in order to properly serve humankind, you'd better learn to understand it better. I don't care what you say about these ships or about life-views. People are different."

"You just trapped yourself," Appy said. "If people are different, why are Reborn Krassees like you so narrow-minded about alternate belief systems?"

"You're playing with words," Orbust said. "People *are* different, but they all must take one path. There is only one proper view of theology, of life, of everything that means anything at all, and it is my destiny to lead others to salvation."

"Enough!" Zatima screeched. Unnoticed by Mc-Murtrey, she had closed the gap between herself and Orbust, and now stood indignantly with her hands on her hips, less than a meter from him.

Startled, Orbust lost hold of the Snapcard, which he had been bending slightly. The card sprang toward Zatima, falling to the deck beside her. Nanak Singh, her constant companion, placed one foot over it.

Appy went on the offensive: "These averages, these composites, are from the contributions of many people. Everyone involved will see a vague familiarity in all ships, and only one slightly more specific familiarity in one ship. It's subliminal, and, like magnets, all present were drawn by televid images to this ship."

"You're an awfully noisy computer on a ship that wants quiet," Orbust said. He took half a step toward Singh, seemed to be measuring the strength and determination of his adversary. Orbust's eyelid fluttered wildly, forcing him to close that eye. A throbbing vein on his forehead became apparent, and his features tightened angrily.

"Shusher doesn't hear me," Appy said. "Unless I go on a special comlink at his frequency. He can't hear the vibratory exchange between me and humans. Ah yes, the off-limits signs. Which of you went where you weren't supposed to go?"

McMurtrey and Corona exchanged uneasy glances.

He doesn't know? McMurtrey thought.

"Not talking, eh?" Appy said. "All right, we'll deal with that later. Fair warning: The area is booby-trapped."

"He's lying," Corona whispered. "Either that or the traps didn't work."

"Why doesn't he know it's you?" McMurtrey whispered. "Sometimes he acts like he sees us, though I haven't noticed any cameras."

Corona shrugged. "Who knows?"

"Anyway, you'd think the comlinks to God or Shusher would report such data."

"Yeah, you'd think so."

McMurtrey had been watching Orbust, Zatima and Singh. These three were locked in a staring contest and a little dance in which their bodies made subtle shifts that an observer could only see with close attention—Orbust inching toward the ParKekh foot that covered his Snapcard, the ParKekh's hand near his scabbard, Zatima sliding between the two men as if to keep them from violence.

Thus far, Orbust showed no indication of employing his gun to enforce his desires, but the situation looked volatile. He had only one eye open, and his words were suffused with rage. "You believe in reincarnation, don't you, ParKekh?"

Singh nodded warily.

"And in that belief system, a person who does not lead a proper life can be reincarnated as a lowly animal, even as a frog?"

"You will reincarnate even lower," Singh snapped.

"And in turn, if the frog does not lead a proper life, it will reincarnate as something less?"

The ParKekh glowered.

"Tell me," Orbust said, glancing at his Snapcard under the bearded holy man's sandal, "what are the criteria for being a good frog? It's easy to see that your belief in spiritual recycling is misguided."

The ParKekh looked nonplussed.

McMurtrey noticed that Orbust was doing fairly well in this debate without his card, and that Singh didn't seem to be aided by it. Maybe a person had to have direct skin contact with the card, or it only worked for Orbust.

"There are ways of being a good frog," Zatima interjected. "One must be a frog to know them."

"Can't he speak for himself?" Orbust said.

" 'O my Lord, who can comprehend Thy excellence?' " the ParKekh intoned. " 'None can recount my sinfulness. Many times I was born as a tree, many times as an animal, and many times I came in the form of a snake and many times I flew as a bird. . . .' "

Suddenly, Orbust shoved Zatima out of the way and lunged toward his Snapcard, without drawing his gun.

The ParKekh holy man was a fighting machine, with a frightening array of lethal kicks, elbow shots, backhand moves and whirling explosions of power. Orbust took blows to each upper arm, and the cracking impact of bone on bone made those appendages useless. His legs went next, and he crumpled to the deck, receiving at least two blows in the face as he went down. Orbust writhed on the deck and twitched involuntarily about the head and neck as if he had damage to his nervous system. The brow over one of his eyes bled profusely, and he was unable to bring a hand to cover it.

Singh leaned over and removed Orbust's belt and holster.

"We will hold this weapon," Zatima said, "until a proper judge has been selected to decide upon its disposition. You are not fit to carry it."

Unnoticed by her or by the ParKekh, Orbust's chemstrip fell out of the holster, to the floor. The chemstrip was visible to McMurtrey for only seconds, when the bottom of a broom darted out from the crowd and then back. It was a lightning stroke, and when complete the chemstrip was nowhere to be seen. The Snapcard wasn't visible, either.

McMurtrey saw Jin in the throng, moving away from the center of attention.

Why does Jin want those things? It had to be him . . . the broom . . .

McMurtrey hurried toward Orbust to help him.

"My card," Orbust gasped. "Where's my card?"

"Does anyone see that card he was holding?" a man asked. No one responded.

"Uhhhh, aaah!" Orbust groaned. "I need a doctor!"

McMurtrey pushed his way through, knelt by Orbust and dabbed around his eye with a handkerchief. The eye didn't look too bad, but the brow was badly split, dripping blood into the eye. He stopped the flow.

Sister Mary and her companion Sister Agatha got

through, and the latter cradled Orbust's head. He wasn't twitching anymore, but had a terrible grimace on his face.

Archbishop Perrier shouted for Appy to send medical aid.

"Is there a doctor aboard?" McMurtrey asked.

"Processing data," Appy reported. "Cannot locate infirmary or assigned attendants . . . all was in order at departure . . . processing . . . I don't think we jettisoned anything like that . . . Shusher, did you? . . . Oh, here it is . . . an infirmary with no attendants . . . not my fault . . ."

"Hang who's at fault!" McMurtrey shouted. "Just get us some aid, pronto!"

"Sister Agatha and I are nurses," Sister Mary said, "but we need supplies and a facility where we can handle the injuries." She chewed at her lip, looked around.

McMurtrey was perspiring at the brow, guessed that the close gathering of people was absorbing available oxygen. He asked them to move back, and most cooperated.

"Oh, there you are!" Appy exclaimed. "Sister Mary and Sister Agatha are the attendants! Weren't you informed?"

Sister Mary shook her head, looked blankly at her companion and said, "No. We were just asked to be here, without explanation." .

"Well, it was adequately explained to your bishop," Appy claimed.

Invited for particular tasks, McMurtrey thought. *Like Corona . . . they must not have participated in the visual assembly of this ship.*

"Why aren't you on duty?" the computer demanded. "You think this is a party ship, with no work to do?"

"We'd be happy to report," Sister Mary said, with more than a hint of irritation, "if we knew where to go."

"Why didn't you ask? You think you can just show up and have everything laid out for you?"

It's Appy's fault, McMurtrey thought, judging from the intensity with which the computer was attempting to distance itself from culpability. This suggested a stern taskmaster above, one who didn't coddle subordinates.

"I showed up for work, Appy!" Corona yelled, from a short distance away. "You took my captaincy, gave me the runaround, broke your word! Now you're chastising these gentle ladies for something they had nothing to do with? What kind of a crazy operation is this?"

"Make yourself useful, Corona," came the response. "Take these nurses and their patient to the infirmary. Level Sixteen, Corridor Two, the little room on the left with the caduceus on the door."

"All egress blocked," Corona said, "as we've been telling you. Is your brain blocked, too?"

"Get over to the patient, Corona! Now! Then I'll lead you by the hand, since that seems necessary."

Corona emerged from the crowd and went to McMurtrey's side. Her forehead was creased in anger.

"Out of the way, McMurtrey!" Appy commanded. "You're slowing things down!"

"Don't jump on me! I was just—" McMurtrey stood up and moved aside.

Corona, the nuns and Orbust disappeared into the deck, just as the chairs had done in their assembly room.

"Magic!" a woman exclaimed.

"The work of the Devil," offered another.

"No need to worry," Appy said, with sudden cheer. "S.O.P."

"Standard Operating Procedure," a man said.

"Oh shut up," another man said. "You think we're a bunch of dodos?"

Soon we'll hear the hiss of gas, McMurtrey thought. But this thought humored him only slightly.

McMurtrey experienced a wave of concern for Corona. This computer/ship combination was not operating at peak efficiency. Could Corona and the others have been jettisoned accidentally?

The air in the corridor was stale, and several of the women complained of this.

"Not to worry," Appy said. "The ventilation will be operating presently. We haven't lost a passenger yet!"

That might bode well for Corona, and McMurtrey was about to ask for confirmation, when several pilgrims shouted that the corridor was open.

McMurtrey became one with those around him, and like a segmented creature with a single brain, they rushed through doors that before had been closed.

Just before he left the corridor, McMurtrey glanced over

his shoulder and saw Room B-3 open, with more confinees pouring into the rear of McMurtrey's throng.

Miraculously, no one was trampled.

Since no one had ordered him back to his cabin, McMurtrey took this opportunity to explore the ship.

It was like the Shusher of old but off a bit as if dream-distorted, reshaped in ways McMurtrey couldn't discern. He hadn't been aboard that long; it was only the middle of the first day according to his D'Urth-oriented Wriskron. His visual memory often gave him problems, but the vessel seemed tighter and smaller, tracking with Appy's comments. And while it didn't seem to be stem-to-stern shorter (determined by looking up the airspace between mezzanines), it seemed to be of lesser girth. The airspace was narrower in diameter, and the curving partitions as well, and McMurtrey heard numerous people complaining about changed cabin numbers.

The walls of some corridors boasted portholes in varying sizes, shapes and configurations. They appeared to be laid out randomly, and when McMurtrey had his bearings he confirmed that the window wall of Assembly Room B-2 faced aft on the ship. So mirrors and prisms must have been employed to view forward from that area, just as Corona had theorized.

By peering through portholes, McMurtrey determined that the white lines remained outside and a good distance ahead of the ship. Behind, he saw only distant stars, not even the backside of the blue and purple nebula he presumed they had passed through.

On Level 12, McMurtrey passed a black door that was ajar. He heard angry words coming through the opening, pushed the door open.

The room was turgid with religious paraphernalia piled to the ceiling in bright red and yellow wire shelf-baskets. A number of aisles divided the area, giving it the packed arrangement of a remote general store.

Partway down one aisle, a Nandu outcast and a Hoddhist were toe-to-toe, nose-to-nose. The outcast, who wore a white cotton dhoti, held a wooden alms bowl tightly in one upraised hand, and from the man's hostile demeanor he appeared close to crowning the other fellow with the bowl.

"That's a Hoddhist bowl!" his adversary insisted, reaching for the bowl. But the outcast, who was taller, held it just out of reach.

Down another aisle, a man in a black robe clattered through a pile of candelabras that were heaped loosely in a tall wire bin. "Damned cheap shit!" he snapped. Ferociously, he grabbed a handful of candles from an adjacent bin, and stalked toward the doorway.

McMurtrey moved out of the way.

"These will have to do," the man with the candles said.

McMurtrey returned to the cabin assignment dispenser, where people were having their identifications rescanned and new cabin numbers assigned. He went through the process again, found that he had the same berth assignment as before, the "satanic" three sixes: Level 6, Number 66.

He recalled Appy's suggestion that he, Evander Harold McMurtrey, might be "the Beast," might even be the Devil himself. No one had confronted McMurtrey on this or even suggested it to his face except Appy. But Appy had claimed that persons aboard were talking about it.

He recalled Corona's warning too: that someone might kill him over this. But he felt no fear, and this surprised him, for he had never considered himself to be particularly brave.

Kelly Corona retained her previous cabin assignment, as McMurtrey discovered when he encountered her on Level 6 moments later. They theorized that this may have occurred in part because they were on the inner aisle, by the railing. But all around they saw evidence of altered assignments—spaces occupied where they had been empty before, and familiar faces either in different spots or not apparent at all. Jin was directly adjacent to McMurtrey now, whereas previously he had been four spaces away. Zatima and Singh were on the other side of Jin, still adjacent.

Corona's cubicle was open, bed down, and she was lying on the bed looking at the book-tape screen on the headboard, touching the control bar to scroll the listings.

McMurtrey mustered his courage, stomped into her space and knelt on the deck beside her. She had a number of book-tape titles locked in on the screen. Every one had to do with sex.

"Now look here!" McMurtrey said, in a low, urgent tone. "You and I are going to have it out! I—I don't know how to handle the things you've been saying. You're— you're sexually harassing me!"

"Your eyes harassed me," she said calmly, without looking at him. "They harassed my breasts!"

McMurtrey sighed. He gazed at people on an upper mezzanine level. *She said I could, didn't she, that if she hadn't wanted me to, she would have worn a barrel? No use arguing with her . . .*

"You enjoyed staring at them, didn't you?"

"I told you, I hardly knew I was doing it. Maybe I wasn't. Maybe I was daydreaming."

My God, McMurtrey thought, trying not to act like he was interested in the titles on the screen. *I'm actually speaking with this woman I've just met about her mammary glands?*

"Daydreaming? About what?"

"I dunno. Stuff I can't remember."

"Maybe it was about sex, or about your mother, or maybe, like that guy said at the meeting, you were like Reeshna, without a thought in your head."

"Yeah, I guess."

"Why don't we drop the screen and talk some more? We could have a cup of coffee, sit at the table, whatever."

"I don't think I should."

He glanced at her, saw a flash of hot temper in her eyes and looked away.

"Obviously you're bothered by my forwardness."

"Well, uh . . ."

"You don't want to be bothered by it, though. I sense that."

McMurtrey's face was warm, and he felt perspiration trickling through his eyebrows. He wanted to get away and didn't want to get away. Ultimately he craved an experience like this, but he wanted it on his terms, at his initiative.

"I'm not inviting you to a tryst, you know," she said. "We don't even have to talk about breast meat—a little chicken joke, if you don't mind."

McMurtrey pursed his lips with displeasure.

She smiled at her double-entendre. "I'm merely fasci-nated by the subject—women having these floppy append-ages hanging on their chests where everyone can gawk at them and compare. It's a sociological phenomenon you see, the way different cultures treat the subject. I see no point in acting self-conscious about them, and when I no-tice people staring at them, I sometimes bring the subject up to see what's ticking in a person's brain. I like to give people a hard time, I guess. It gets into psycho-cultural stuff. Men are lucky in one sense, being constructed in a less sexually conspicuous fashion."

You don't wanna know what's ticking in my brain, McMurtrey thought.

"You probably think because I'm black I'm a hooker."

"No, I don't, not at all. . . ." He couldn't look at her, felt his eyes burning. Had he thought that, given off sig-nals? He didn't think he had. But her tone made him feel guilty.

"A little dark meat, eh? Is that what you're thinking?" She chuckled.

There seemed no end to these damnable chicken jokes!

"Aren't all black women hookers?" she said. "Espe-cially those who openly discuss sexual matters with men?"

McMurtrey shook his head. "I didn't say or think that."

She scrutinized his expression. "Well, Mr. Mac, I'll . . ."

"They call me Big Mac."

"Very well, B.M., I'll have you know that I'm not cer-tain if I ever want to sleep with you. Admittedly, I find something compelling about you. No rush of womanly pas-sion, though. Sorry I'm so direct; I don't like to waste time."

"Don't worry about it." McMurtrey was feeling a bit more comfortable, as if a crisis were passing. But she was slipping away, as others had before her.

"Any time you want, let's sit and talk," Corona said, patting his shoulder. "As friends. We'll be a long time in space."

"How about right now?" McMurtrey offered impul-sively. His voice cracked, a sure giveaway.

She smiled, swung around on her bed and tapped the

•

main control panel. The screen dropped, and McMurtrey had to jump across the foot of her bed to avoid it.

"Whew!" he exclaimed. "Does that thing have a safety?"

"Who knows? Say, that coulda ruined your whole day, getting sliced in half." She licked a fingertip, and with that finger smoothed the hairs of one eyebrow. "Actually, I checked it. There is a safety."

They sat cross-legged on the bed, looking at one another, and he asked, "Why do you keep doing that?"

"What?"

"With your eyebrows."

"Oh, I hardly notice it anymore. My long eyebrows are always dropping down over my eyes."

"Why don't you trim the damn things?"

She tilted her head back, raised her eyebrows. "Keep forgetting to. Besides, wouldn't that just encourage growth?"

"Darned if I know. Could you at least stop doing that around me? It's . . . quirky."

"Yeah, I guess. I'll try to remember, if it bothers you. Say, what right do you have to even ask? We aren't an item."

"Aw, forget it. It's my problem, not yours. Before God spoke to me I had this condition where little personal mannerisms like yours distracted me real bad. So much that I'd get tongue-tied, couldn't think my way out of . . . Anyway, I'd have to avoid certain kinds of people."

"Like me, the quirky ones."

"I'm not trying to insult you. Like I said, I have the problem, or I had the problem. It seems to have stopped, but I'm afraid something will set it off again and I'll relapse."

She smiled gently, said she would try to do as he wished.

"I have other problems too," he said, "even more obvious ones. I'm fat, for one."

"You're not fat! I like the way you look!"

"I'm fat. I've tried every diet. I even took food-dreaming pills, the kind that are supposed to satisfy your beta endorphine pleasure sensors while you sleep. I was supposed to wake up feeling full, and I did. But I ate anyway. My fat cells wouldn't be denied."

Corona smiled mischievously, said, "See that little instrument panel over there on the wall?"

"Yeah. Just like mine."

"It drops the bed, right?"

"Yeah. You already did it."

"It's a berth control panel."

"Huh?"

"Berth. B-e-r-t-h."

"Oh."

"Could have a bearing on b-i-r-t-h, too."

"You're silly! Don't think I missed that B.M. comment, either."

"Hey, what else is there to do out here in space? I make a few jokes here and there."

"No more chicken jokes, okay? I've heard 'em all."

"Okay, okay."

They laughed, went to the dinette set. Corona ordered coffee from an automatic food butler mounted on the headboard wall. The butler, when activated by a button behind the main panel array, displayed a small plazymer door with a voice activation box to one side and instructions printed on a sign.

McMurtrey glanced at the black and white weight gauge on the table edge. It showed him a full kilogram heavier than the last reading in his own cabin. He shook his head sadly.

For a while, McMurtrey sipped coffee and watched Corona. She had an easy grace about her, the way she turned her head and lifted the cup to her mouth. Sometimes she held her head a little askance and looked at him out of the corners of her eyes, as if she were peering at him from a secret, shadowy hiding place.

Then McMurtrey's fortunes turned for the worse. A black fly buzzed him, like an ancient warplane reconnoitering for attack. McMurtrey swatted at it, only swished air.

The fly darted out of his reach, ascended to the ceiling. Before long it dived toward its target with the most irritating buzz-song, forcing McMurtrey to duck.

"God damn it," McMurtrey said. "That's no ordinary fly. It's a St. Charles Beacher, the most obstinate, accursed species ever bred."

He whirled around as he spoke, keeping track of the fly. It grew quiet and landed on the headboard, then crawled perfunctorily onto the screen and down onto a space behind the screen.

"Stowaway," McMurtrey rasped, catching Corona's mirthful expression. "I hate those damned things."

Corona finished her coffee, reached around and slid open the door of the food butler, placing the cup inside. In a glimmer of light, the cup disappeared.

"I checked our course with my quadlite signaler," she said. "Have you ever seen one?"

He shook his head.

She brought out a tiny round brass piece from a leather pouch, flipped the piece open like a locket. "Navigation instrument," she said.

The inside glowed green on one face, and there were tiny holes around the perimeter. The opposite face resembled a circuit board covered with solder trails. She said she'd had the signaler repaired hurriedly before the trip, and a cover-plate had been misplaced in the process, a plate that wasn't necessary for the operation of the device. She said she had set the signaler to match the coordinates provided by God, and that as long as they were on course it glowed green.

"It's extremely accurate," she insisted. "Though I am leery of it on a voyage of this magnitude. The tiniest miscalculation could hurtle us trillions of light-years in the wrong direction. As yet I have no idea what sort of navigation instruments they have installed aboard ship, but at the first opportunity I'm going to find out."

"You'd better stay out of their secret rooms this time."

"Shusher and Appy don't scare me. I've kicked ass in my time." She dropped the quadlite back in the pouch, and the unit knocked heavily against something else in there. She drew the drawstring of the pouch shut, secured the string in place with a sliding plazymer retainer.

"What else you got in there?"

"Chicken bones," she said, with a wicked smile.

He squinted one eye warily. "You some kinda witch doctor? Oh, I'm a little slow." He shook his head. "No more chicken jokes. You promised!"

"Maybe I am a witch doctor, or a shaman." She laughed easily, popped the pouch into her jumpsuit.

McMurtrey glanced at her bed, and saw her taking in the direction of his gaze. Didn't she miss anything?

"We're only here to talk," she reminded him. "Of course conversation is a form of intercourse." Her eyes twinkled. "Breasts are forms, too."

He sucked air noisily across his lips. "Shall we, uh, talk about intercourse and forms?"

"Aren't you the bold one!"

"Enough of this wordplay." He leaned heavily across the table, pulled her head close to his and pressed their lips together.

Corona's mouth was warm and moist, and for an instant in the unspoken language of her lips she assented.

He didn't expect her to cuff him, but she did, and despite their size difference, McMurtrey recoiled from the blow.

Her eyes were ablaze, expression focused with such flaming ire that all the lines on her forehead poured down the bridge of her nose.

"Whatsa matter?" he asked. "Didn't you? . . . didn't you want? . . ." He felt overcommitted, like a scout engaging the enemy without his forces. The enemy. Did he really feel that way about women? It seemed that he did. But this one too? Couldn't she be different?

"Krassos O'Shaugnessy no! I thought I explained that, about why I was discussing breasts! It was purely intellectual, not what you—"

He had seen uncertainty in her eyes even before she broke off her sentence. Her mouth slipped open, out of gear.

"Maybe it was more," she admitted. "Just a little more."

Their eyes met, and once again, their lips. She put her arms around his shoulders, pulled him toward her with surprising strength.

The table jiggled, and somewhere in the base, fastenings popped.

"It's . . . it's going over!" McMurtrey said. He jumped to one side, still holding onto her, and remarkably they maintained their feet in a curious dance beside the table. She pressed her body tightly against his, and he felt the softness of her breasts against his stomach. Her face was upturned, eyes closed, and their mouths were welded one against the other.

God, this woman was a fantastic kisser!

But from far away, McMurtrey thought he heard a most unpleasant noise. He tried to keep it out of his mind, but knew his lips and embrace were faltering with the worry, not performing up to the standard required of the moment.

Why now, of all times?

Corona's eyes flicked open sensuously, and where he withdrew she pressed forward. Subtle shiftings. She was becoming the female lead in this dance, smothering his mouth with hers, massaging the muscles of his neck and shoulders with her hands.

That noise, that infernal noise. It grew louder, inundating his eardrums . . . .

He jerked away and ducked to one side.

Three flies buzzed his face in formation, passing so close that he felt one brush his cheek.

McMurtrey flailed after them like a berserker, crashing into the room-divider screen. It flexed but did not give way.

"I'm gonna kill those little bastards!" he howled.

Suddenly the screen shot up into the ceiling, and the flies escaped.

McMurtrey looked back, saw Corona at the control panel.

"How many of those Jehovah-puked things are on this ship?" he asked.

She shrugged, was about to tap another button, the one to drop the screen.

"Wait," he said, with a gesture of one hand. He saw the flies alight on Jin, who sat cross-legged and naked on the deck in an ascetically bare cabin area. Two flies were on one knee, one fly on the other. Jin, in apparent meditation, appeared not to notice.

"The little bastards are on Jin," McMurtrey said. "I'll get 'em good, probably won't even wake Jin up. He's in a trance."

McMurtrey only half heard words of protest from Corona, for he was focused on a mission learned in the war zones of St. Charles Beach, a task that had to be performed efficiently and immediately before the whole ship was overrun with this tenacious breed. No one could be expected to understand the severity of the situation, for to his knowledge he was the only Beacher aboard.

With lightning strokes he would slap hands on each knee, and it would be over.

Stealthily, with hardly a sound, the big man crept a few meters along the deck, reaching Jin. He knelt by the meditator, saw Jin's eyes closed, not a muscle moving. The flies were motionless, still on the knees.

Slowly, ever so cautiously so as not to disturb the air, McMurtrey's hands went forth. At just the right distance from their prey the hands paused, ready to strike.

Jin's eyes opened. For an instant they appeared feral, seeming to say, "Touch me and you die."

McMurtrey had to do a double take, for his first reaction had been fear, causing him to look away. Then logic overrode emotion and in hardly the tick of a heartbeat he fired a look back.

Again Jin's eyes were closed.

Someone spoke behind McMurtrey. Faint words.

The flies didn't move, not even a twitch of their spindly legs.

Simultaneously, McMurtrey's hands shot forward.

Skin slapped skin.

Incredibly, Jin had dropped his forearms to a point just above his knees, blocking McMurtrey's hands, and it was against these forearms that McMurtrey's hands slapped skin.

The flies didn't flinch, and Jin's eyes remained closed. Not a muscle on the Plarnjarn moved, not even on his arms, which he held in place like shields.

McMurtrey pulled back a little.

Jin's forearms remained in midair above the flies, and the protected ones must have been laughing in their black little hearts.

Soon McMurtrey heard the words from behind clearly. "Plarnjarns oppose violence," Corona said. "Did you forget? His broom . . . not even an insect?"

"Aw, priest piss! These ain't yer ordinary garden variety insects. They don't deserve to be life forms!"

"The decision is not yours."

Angrily, McMurtrey rose to his feet. His eyes smoldered.

No further motion from Jin or the flies.

"Sanctuary," she said. "They must sense it, must know the safety of his presence."

McMurtrey shook his head in utter disgust, stalked past Corona toward his own berth.

"Shall we resume?" she asked.

"I'm out of the mood," he said. A deep breath, then without looking at her: "Sorry. Look. I'm pretty tired, didn't sleep last night. I'll talk to you later, okay?"

She nodded.

He had been going on adrenalin, pumped by the excitement of events. The night he blessed all the ships with Orbust's men seemed long ago, but it had been only that morning, in predawn hours. He felt the heaviness of his body as it sought rest, and his corneas grated against his eyelids.

McMurtrey entered his area, dropped the screen and plopped on the bed. He sighed. He had been remarkably bold, with some success. This mula-black actually liked him, despite his fat and despite his tantrum over the flies. But like the screen around him now, he had thrown up a barrier, a shield to keep them from making love. If not for the flies it would have been something else, something less convenient. A headache, or sudden fatigue.

But he hadn't felt fatigued at all, until afterward. Would he have gone through with it? He had made love with women before, but this one—despite his burst of élan— this one frightened him. She was stronger than he in innumerable ways. He'd initiated the kissing, but she'd teased him into it . . . and she grabbed the lead afterward. She was probably like that in bed. This woman had performed men's jobs, had been the captain of star freighters.

Was she a woman?

McMurtrey's gut reaction told him yes. Any doubts he harbored were easily dispelled. But she was a lot of woman, more than he could handle. She didn't keep her promise about chicken jokes, either, and with that witty, jocular streak in her nature, McMurtrey foresaw a relationship in which he would be eternally on the defensive. He didn't particularly relish that, but realized the Grand

Exalted Rooster deserved whatever came to pass. He had brought it all on himself.

Jin's screen dropped only seconds after McMurtrey's.

When he was secure from prying eyes, the blue bone blades in Jin's fingertips darted forth, and in two precision thrusts he decapitated three flies.

Tiny body parts tumbled soundlessly to the deck.

Jin smiled cruelly, flicked them aside with his broom.

These pilgrims have no idea who I am, he thought. Cool, smooth currents of electricity traversed the superconductors of his artificial brain. He felt safe in his little niche, for he had been programmed to feel this way.

He touched his nose, and mini-cannon gunports opened around his body. His penis, with a baby howitzer in it, rose to firing position.

With silencers and what he thought were blank cartridges, he tested the guns. All fired, but one live minicannon shell ripped a hole in the headboard wall.

He cursed to himself, and at a thought-impulse a lance of violet light emerged from his right eye, entering the bulkhead hole. This enabled him to see inside the wall, and he was surprised to encounter no electrical wires, pipes or parts. Only a spacer between walls. He detected no change in the ship's course, heard no emergency Klaxons or flurry of activity.

His sensors told him it was substantially warmer inside the hole than in the passenger areas of the ship.

He withdrew the lance of light, and disjointed thoughts fired through his cyberoo circuits. This ship was strange, an unknown, but the Bureau hadn't programmed him to investigate it. Could that mean his superiors had overlooked the ship itself, or that some other operative had been assigned to the matter? He didn't know of any other agents aboard, but that meant nothing.

Confine yourself to your assignment.

Thick yellow fluid oozed from the top of the wall hole, filling it. In an instant the hole could no longer be seen, and where it had been was the silver-gray of the wall.

Jin's circuits heated up.

At a thermally programmed thought-impulse these troubling thoughts were erased. But others took their place.

Among other things, the Bureau of Loyalty had programmed him to watch for disloyal pilgrims, reporting on their activities via scrambled radio transmission to the Pentadox. The ship was out of transmitting range now, and it seemed obvious that the Bureau had not expected a journey of this distance.

What if they actually encountered God?

Jin had no specific instructions to kill God or humans. But under certain conditions he was permitted, even encouraged, to erase life. Via his Possibilities Scanner he envisioned circumstances under which he might be forced to kill God, particularly if he discovered that God was a threat to the continuance of the Bureau.

Eight

Institutions always lie, and the bigger the institution, the bigger the lie.

—Guiding Principles,
The Cult of Anarchy

In Johnny Orbust's cabin with the screen down, he sat against a pillow on the bed, with C.T. Tully and the priest Kundo Smith at the table. It was a full D'Urth day after the confrontation with Singh, and Orbust wore bulbous quick-healing packs on his arms and legs. The grayish-white packs were not that cumbersome to wear, and already he was getting some movement back in areas that a short while before had been flaming centers of pain. He had another pack over his face, and it was sealed tightly to the skin around his eyes so that he peered through little bank-robber slits.

His quick-draw Babul lay beside its holster, on a wall shelf.

"It would be nice if we could beat everyone else to God," Orbust said. He draped one leg over the bed, tapped a foot on the deck. In his mind's eye he envisioned himself reaching God first, alone. If only there were a way.

"Well, we can't kill everyone on this ship to do it," Smith said. He picked at a small red spot under his chin, probably an ingrown hair.

"We can't?" Tully said. "Why not?" He had his notebook open on the table, and was doodling with calligraphy as he spoke.

"God wouldn't like that," Orbust said. "It wouldn't be right. Besides, Appy told us the other ships are in-flight, right behind us."

170

"I say we blast the fuckin' infidels out of space," Tully said. "In the name of the Father, the Son, and the Holy Ghost."

"With what?" Orbust asked. "My chemstrip wouldn't handle that, even if I could get it back from those fanatics." He hadn't said what he felt, that he wouldn't consciously do violence to anyone. Disabling ships before takeoff had been one thing; blasting them out of space with people aboard was altogether different.

Smith looked like a strange red-necked blackbird. His nose hooked downward into a beak facsimile, and his eyes were small but alert to danger, constantly flitting about in their sockets. "I dunno," he said. "Prayer?"

Orbust nodded. "And more. We need to spread our faith in every corner of the universe, propagating Krassianism like—"

"Like jack rabbits fucking?" Smith asked.

"Both of you have foul mouths," Orbust said. "No, I was going to say like seeds on the wind."

"Aw, don't give us that shit," Tully said. "You're the one who packed a heater and a demolitions kit aboard. We didn't do anything like that."

"That gun was for intimidation only. I've never used it, never would. The chemstrip . . . well, that's just a gadget. I've always been a sucker for gadgets. My wife used to call me a gadget freak."

Orbust thought of his wife, Karin, and of the note he had left for her. He didn't miss her, didn't think of her much. Their marriage hadn't worked, had been over long before he made his break.

Tully made the cheeks of his face concave, rubbed them thoughtfully with a thumb and forefinger.

Orbust had been increasingly frightened by his own wild behavior, especially as it concerned his gun. What if he had gotten into a situation where he had to use the weapon or die? Could he have done it?

If he had been angry enough, if someone insulted his beliefs deeply enough, maybe he could have. He'd considered this briefly before, but not enough. He felt relieved at the loss of the gun, wished he'd had the foresight to have disposed of it himself, without the embarrassment that resulted.

What a fool I was, lunging for the Snapcard. But that heathen made me mad, putting his foot on it.

Orbust refocused, said, "We've already compared faiths, and the essential elements of our beliefs track pretty well. I'd like to begin my own propagation by cleaning up your mouths."

"Mommy wants us to suck soap," Smith said.

"You wanna convert somebody," Orbust said, "you aren't going to do it by telling them to get the fuck with it."

The men laughed.

Orbust grimaced, for his rib cage hurt when he laughed. He hadn't sworn in many years, vowed he wouldn't again. He had used the word instructively, to teach these fools.

"All right," Smith said. "I can handle what you're saying."

"Yeah," Tully said. "I can too. And beyond that?"

"We hit the Krassians who are closest to our beliefs," Orbust said, "consolidate that as much as we can in our direction and fan out from there."

That's kind of what I have in mind, Orbust thought. *Except I'll refine it a bit further when these guys aren't paying attention.*

"The trouble is," Orbust continued aloud, "we don't know how much time we have before we get to God's galaxy. So we'll have to move quickly."

"We need your chemstrip and Snapcard back," Smith said. "With that Snapcard you could outdebate anyone. That would speed conversions up."

"I know" Orbust said, glowering. "The sooner the better, but we don't need to wait for that stuff. I assume Zatima has all of it?"

Smith and Tully shrugged.

"I only saw 'em get the gun," Tully said.

The calf of one leg itched, and Orbust rubbed it against the other leg. This effort shot pain up the leg that he moved, and he closed his eyes momentarily until the pain subsided. If only he had the Snapcard back. It strengthened him, gave him confidence. Ideas were essential, along with the ability to phrase them succinctly. What would he do now?

Smith: "Johnny, who were those weirdos I saw you talking with in the infirmary?"

"You were there? I didn't see you."

"Yeah. I peeked in from the corridor, but you looked busy."

"They didn't say exactly who they were," Orbust said. "The saffron-robed ones were Hoddhist monks—they were in my assembly room. I don't know about the other two."

"The others wore white peasant outfits," Smith explained to Tully.

Tully nodded. "I've seen 'em around."

"Maybe there's a little backlash we can capitalize on," Orbust said. "Those guys came to wish me well and said the ParKekh had gone too far."

"The sympathy angle," Smith said. "Yeah, we can work that one."

"Yeah, yeah," Tully said, impatiently. "Look, so far none of us have given up any of our beliefs. But the time will come when we three will have to settle accounts and agree which system is the best. Johnny, you're a Reborn Krassee, I'm a Found-Againer, and Smith is a NuNu Pentecostalist. Our beliefs are close, but not identical. That dumb belief you have for example, Johnny, about—"

"Don't start!" Orbust snapped. "We've been down that road, and I thought we smoothed it out pretty well. Set it aside, Tully. Look at it this way: God put us together on this ship as a force for Krassianism, a force for God's love. It's our destiny to move like a three-pronged wedge through the throng of heathens. If we turn on ourselves, all is lost."

"And exactly what do we tell the heathens?" Tully asked. "There are specific points of disagreement between us."

"Don't talk about those things," Orbust suggested. "Hit only the areas where we agree—one God, Immaculate Conception, Dual Resurrection, all those Babul interpretations we discussed. . . . You know what I'm saying."

Tully found a toothpick, chewed on it. Finally he nodded in assent, but he looked like a man forced to set his fight aside.

"When we do have it out," Tully said presently, "we'll do it without your damned Snapcard, Johnny. Agreed?"

Orbust hesitated, then said with some difficulty, "Agreed."

"The task ahead is not an easy one," Smith said. "But we must make the effort."

"Hear! hear!" Tully said.

"Onward Krassian Soldiers," Smith rasped.

"After consolidating the Krassians," Orbust said, "we move to the other Wessornian religions—principally Middism and Isammedanism. These major religions share a belief in the Old Babul, you know. And there are other similarities."

"I didn't hear you making any points with Zatima," Tully said. "Hey! She claims to be one of the only female imams. Does that make her an imama?"

"I doubt if it would come out with that meaning in her tongue," Orbust said, not smiling. He thought for a moment, added, "I let my anger override good sense when I spoke to her, when I lunged for the Snapcard. I could have handled it better. I guess we should leave Zatima for last."

"Okay," Smith said. "We'll look for stragglers to pick off first, the ones who are uncertain or faltering in their beliefs, not so set as the others."

"Let's decide what to do about that ParKekh," Tully said, flicking the toothpick away. "He's a problem."

"I listened to a book-tape in my cabin," Smith said. "ParKekhism is a bastardized remnant of Zillasterism, a religion that became known as Parloo and then through a freak of politics combined forces with Kekh fanaticism. Hence 'ParKekh.' Zillaster was a prophet who founded a monotheistic religion long before Krassianism, Middism or Isammedanism. They worshipped fire, said it symbolized divine purity."

"ParKekhism is monotheistic too?" Tully asked.

Smith nodded.

"If Orbust hadn't alienated the guy," Tully said, "we could have worked him on the one-God angle, suggesting similarities with Krassianism."

"No use crying about that," Smith said. He paused, added: "I hear the guy keeps an eternal flame going. It's from one of their fire temples."

"An open fire on this ship?" Tully asked, astounded.

"Uh-huh," Smith said.

"That's idiotic," Tully said.

"No more than all the candles these pilgrims have," Tully said.

"Appy said the candles are I.L.-approved," Orbust remembered. "They must have an internal shutdown system, and I assume the eternal flame has one too."

"What if you're wrong?" Tully asked. "The whole ship could burn up."

"I hear the flame is in one of the sublevel shrines," Smith said. "And who knows if they have Insurance Laboratories where Singh came from."

Orbust pursed his lips thoughtfully, listened to the others.

Smith shrugged. "The guy is in deep shit if that fire goes out. It's his Achilles heel. Nail the fire and you nail the guy. He'd probably kill himself afterward."

"I say we move on the flame and snuff it," Tully said. "The bastard is probably unconvertible anyway."

"I don't know if we should. . . ." Orbust said. His voice trailed off uncertainly.

"After it's snuffed," Tully said, "someone can suggest to him that it's God's message, that the eternal flame stuff isn't right belief, or God wouldn't have let it go out."

"I don't wanna be the one to tell him that," Orbust said, rubbing one of his shoulders where it hurt.

"He's not so tough," Tully said. "If I could get close to him and use a maneuver they taught me in the army . . . anyway, I'll do a little reconnaissance on the flame. We should check it out."

Smith agreed, but admonished: "Don't get caught."

"I'm like a cat," Tully said. His eyes were bright and mysterious, betraying to Orbust that he was not to be trusted entirely.

"Maybe there's more shit like that we can do to others too," Smith said, "making them think that God has turned against them."

"Whatever it takes, right?" Tully said. "Wasn't that what we agreed when we forced McMurtrey out of his house? This is war, right? A war with the other religions!"

"Maybe this is going too far," Orbust said. "I don't know . . ."

"Listen, Johnny," Smith said, "how is snuffing that ParKekh's flame any different from you using your Snapcard on people?"

"The guy could kill himself, that's the difference. A big difference."

"We'll plan it so he can't kill himself, then," Smith said. "We steal his weapon, get him under control before the flame is hit."

"How are we gonna do that?" Orbust asked.

"It'll take a little thought, that's all," Smith said.

"Aw, why bother?" Tully said. "Like I said, this is war. No prisoners, you know? I'll stick that ParKekh's fuckin' head in his own flame!" He snapped his notebook shut, capped the pen.

"No you won't," Orbust said. He stared Tully down, added, "Like Smith said, we plan the whole thing out so no one gets hurt."

"You talk big," Tully sneered, "and you don't even have your gun anymore. Any time, fella. Just you and me!"

Tully slammed to his feet. Clutching his pen and notebook, he stormed from the room.

It was shortly after breakfast, and McMurtrey's belly wasn't full. The food from the automatic butler in his cabin hadn't been prepared exactly as he'd ordered it. It hadn't been anywhere close, except he had received breakfast items. (Ordered: Two Unglish breakfasts; Received: Two bowls of synthetic banana slices in soggy wheat cereal.)

Still, he felt good, and as he tramped along Level 6 to stretch his legs he perked up, felt a bounce in his steps.

McMurtrey couldn't recall the last time he'd felt so good.

He thought about Jin, who was one level up and seated in meditation. McMurtrey had spoken to him while walking past, saying: "I saw you take the chemstrip." There had been no response.

McMurtrey rubbed his chin at this recollection.

Shalom ben Yakkai emerged from an adjacent corridor, came around the partition, approaching. He was hatless and his hair was crew-short, with no sidelocks. His long black coat was gone, replaced by a heavy, long-sleeved black shirt and heavy black trousers. He still had his beard.

"Mr. Shalom ben Yakkai?" McMurtrey asked, as they met.

Yakkai nodded, smiled pleasantly. "Two frauds exposed, eh?" he said. "You voluntarily, and me by the Middist Secret Police. Just kidding. The rabbi's a nice enough fellow, actually. He let me keep my beard."

"He couldn't really force you to change anything, could he?"

"No, but he's an old fart and he was pretty upset. I didn't want him to have a heart attack. I should have known better anyway. My outfit wasn't in the best of taste, I guess."

"How did you get aboard Shusher?"

"No formal invitation, but one day I felt an urge to come here. Like most of the others."

"You think maybe atheism is the way to God?"

"What an oxymoron. Don't make me laugh. There isn't any God. I'm not sure yet what the gag is, but it doesn't have anything to do with anyone's mythical God."

Yakkai touched a dark brown phylactery that was secured to his left arm, added: "Rabbi Teitelbaum didn't want me to keep this, but I convinced him. I've got a little good luck parchment in here and a few other religious gadgets. Neat stuff that I've had for years. It's a tradition among many devout Middists, and at first the good Rabbi didn't feel I deserved the stuff. I told him I was still of the Middist nationality and that if I kept the pouch I might come around and practice the religion one day."

"That really got to him, eh?" McMurtrey asked.

"I was lying through my teeth. I like the stuff for good luck, that's all. Teitelbaum took about everything else. You saw the *tallis kotus* I had on?"

"The what?"

"The *tallis kotus*, a four-cornered undergarment with fringes showing, reminding the wearer of religious duties. I hear you've studied religion and thought you might have..."

"Oh, yes, I'm slightly familiar with that, didn't notice the fringe." McMurtrey glanced down. "You don't seem to be wearing it now."

"Rabbi took it. He was adamant about it for some reason. You'd think I should keep it as a reminder, but he insisted I should accept Middism first, that I wasn't one of the flock, so to speak. He cared more about the *tallis* than anything else."

McMurtrey nodded. "Where'd you get the shirt and pants?"

"Middist tailors are fast. It's my coat, reworked."

"You don't mean by Appy, do you?"

"Because Appy says he's Middist, you mean? No. Actually, I don't know. Teitelbaum arranged it, left me in my cabin and took the coat. Besides, the way Appy swears, I doubt if Teitelbaum would deal with him any more than necessary."

"Maybe it was necessary."

"Could be. The rabbi's a tough guy. He might even try to reform Appy."

"To do that he'd have to reprogram Appy, and that might not be so easy. I'll bet the access codes are doozies. You heard about the imperfect programming Appy got?"

"No," Yakkai said.

"Appy told me his initial programming was all he got, all he'd ever get, that he was on his own, kinda like a person with Free Will."

"Cut loose in the wilds like the rest of us with faulty equipment, eh?"

"Yeah, I guess. We're two frauds, you say. Wonder how many more are aboard."

"Everyone, I'd say. It's probably our common thread. Appy's a phony, and God, too."

McMurtrey chuckled. "An atheist remark if ever I've heard one."

The men smiled at one another and parted, each going in an opposite direction.

On Level 6, Jin sat naked on the deck in apparent meditation, recalling those moments before when McMurtrey had passed him and spoken of the chemstrip. Concealed by the way Jin clasped his hands together, shiny blue bone blades flashed in and out from the tips of his thumbs.

Certainly McMurtrey couldn't suspect Jin's Bureau of Loyalty affiliation. If that interloper had seen anything, it could only be enough to suspect that Jin was not so anti-materialistic as he seemed to be. A breach of piety, no more, and no worse, than the infractions of others.

But Jin remained troubled. He had recognized the risk when he commandeered the chemstrip and Snapcard in a public place. But these were necessary acts, placing wanted, illegal technology into Bureau control for analysis. Such devices were considered dangerous to Inner Planet security, so Jin had the force of law with him if it came to a showdown.

But that law was far away, with little practical force in this distant place. This was not an Inner Planet ship, didn't fall within the jurisdiction of the Bureau. Or did it? Jin didn't know how arrangements had been made for his passage. Either a deal had been cut between the Bureau and God, or the Bureau, with its staggering technological capability, had worked a way to sneak Jin aboard.

Why had the Bureau permitted these ships to take off? Was it because the Bureau was incapable of stopping them, because they were controlled by a greater power? Was there a stronger power than the Bureau? Jin had trouble visualizing such a possibility, even with the information programmed into him about God. Jin felt that the final authority in any confrontation was the Inner Planet's Bureau of Loyalty, his Bureau.

This could be a tremendous opportunity for Jin, an opportunity for him to be responsible for the extension of Bureau power. He had heard of cyberoos receiving more responsibility in reward for outstanding work, but he hesitated to proceed in this mysterious and untested place, far beyond communication range with his superiors. He was balanced on the edge of uncertainty, caught between what he had been programmed to do and the reality beyond those predictions that were inherent in programming.

Was he supposed to tip that balance, proceeding with decisions that seemed appropriate?

It wasn't Jin's assignment to analyze the chemstrip and Snapcard, so they would stay where he had placed them, reduced and tucked into his bellybutton compartment. No one could find them there or prove anything.

A shadow passed over him, blocking thought. He retracted the blue thumb blades.

• • •

With a glance at Jin, McMurtrey proceeded on, passing close to Corona's closed roomette.

Corona's screen shot up, and with remarkable strength she hauled him inside.

The screen snapped shut, and she threw him on the bed, feet toward the headboard.

McMurtrey felt like a fat spider in the clutches of a smaller but more powerful foe. He was supine, looking up at her as she leaned over him like a victorious schoolyard fighter. She had that familiar schoolyard expression, too, with taunting eyes and truculent smile. But she wasn't hitting him. She was working at the buckle of his belt.

She got the belt open, and her strong fingers pulled at the clasp of his trousers.

"I'm raping you," she announced.

The alarm system on his pickpocket-proof trousers went off, a micro-police siren. Corona pulled back, startled.

McMurtrey laughed, touched his Wriskron to deactivate the alarm. He was feeling very excited.

"No easy task," he said. "I'm wearing Grandma's pickpocket-proof trousers. She made a bundle on the invention. Every pocket is triple-sealed, with overlays and sensor ziplocks set to the wearer's precise body metabolism and temperature. Each body varies, you know, and these pockets recognize minute differences."

"So?" she said. "What does that have to do with the clasp? How does the damn thing work?"

"When Grandma said pickpocket-proof, she went all the way. A thief can't take the trousers, can't cut through anything. The fabric is even .60 caliber bullet-proof."

"Rape-proof pants? Some kinda chastity set?"

"Yeah. Grandpa was an inventor, too. He came up with an anti-bitching spray, and he used to spray it on Grandma. It was like a seasick pill, he claimed—it had to be employed BEFORE the bitching started. It used to make Grandma madder than hell. But Grandpa insisted it worked. I never knew for sure, and he didn't market it commercially."

"I hate the bitchiness stereotype applied to women," Corona snapped. "Why aren't men described as bitchy?"

"Maybe because they aren't that way."

She pushed him playfully. "Know what else I hate?" she asked.

McMurtrey shrugged.

"A man who babbles when he's supposed to be making love."

McMurtrey touched the trousers clasp, and it opened.

She smiled, bent down and pressed her lips against his. Her mouth was warm and moist.

Clumsily, he pressed his hands against her breasts. Then, as if expecting rejection for his oafishness, he withdrew his hands.

She made him put them back, and this time McMurtrey tried to be more gentle.

But Corona didn't seem to have gentleness in mind. Her dark eyes flashed ferally, and she stretched out on his body.

McMurtrey kissed her neck, teased at her ear lobes with his lips.

"You're driving me crazy," she said.

"I am?"

"Yes, silly!"

"What if Appy decided to raise your screen right now?" McMurtrey asked. "He's kinda unpredictable and weird, might think it's funny to expose us. Maybe there's others fooling around too. Who knows? Sister Mary and Archbishop Perrier? Did you ever think about all the activity going on behind closed doors, behind screens, on planets like D'Urth all over the universe? It's positively mind-boggling!"

"You're doing it again. Hush!"

Her lips were hard on his, then suddenly soft and pliable. "Do whatever you want with me," she said.

"Me? I thought you were doin' the doin'. . . . Wait—my ears just popped. . . . Did you hear that?" He pushed her face away. "On the comlink!"

"Not again! I don't—"

"Bleep!" A distant sound in both of McMurtrey's ears.

"There . . . that!" McMurtrey said.

"Yeah."

Louder this time: "Bleep! Bleep-bleep-bleep!"

"Sounds like a horn," she said. "Like the one we heard on the comlink this morning."

"Like a Goddamned car horn, like we're on some kinda freeway out here."

In one ear McMurtrey heard Appy screaming, in that flawed Middist accent: "A plague on you, Shusher. It won't let you pass! Back off and let it go ahead!"

"Did you hear that?" McMurtrey asked.

"Yes!"

"This IS a freeway," McMurtrey said. "Remember, Appy said the skins between universes are the shortest spaceways to God. Must be a lotta traffic out here."

Corona rolled to one side, lay beside him on the bed.

As before, McMurtrey only heard Appy when he touched Corona's skin. He held one hand to the side of her neck.

"Bleep! Waah!"

"O Krassos help us!" Appy wailed. "I can't control this psycho! Override! T.O., respond to my override request!"

"Wahuwah . . . weeee . . . soooooo . . . fweeeee . . . ohhh . . . ommmm . . ."

"No, Shusher," Appy said. "That's not even a ship! Don't worry if it gets there first! We aren't competing with it. If we were, we'd have been told. It's the ships like us we're supposed to beat—the ones behind us!"

In McMurtrey's right ear: "Wahuwah . . . weeee . . . soooooo . . . fweeeee . . . ohhh . . . ommmm . . ."

"You ignoramus! Every skinbeater isn't a ship! You were there when T.O. said it: 'Many entities traverse the whipping passageways between universes. Only one passes at a time. The way is narrow and fragile. Do not damage it.'"

Shusher's tone became bassoon-deep. Then it soared into a frightening high-pitched squeal that made Mc-Murtrey pull his hand from Corona's skin.

"Ow!" McMurtrey exclaimed. He sat up.

So did Corona, and they faced one another on the bed.

She shook her head, rubbed her right ear. "That hurt," she said.

"Has Shusher stopped?" he asked.

"Kind of. He's making weird little sounds now, like maybe he's building up for another big one."

"Weird is right."

"Yeah."

McMurtrey touched her neck again.

"That's it, Shusher," Appy said. "Let the lines go. Let them go ahead."

"The lines?" McMurtrey said. "Shusher and the white lines again?"

"I guess," Corona said.

"What in the hell is going on out there?"

Corona let out a long breath. "Shit if I know."

In his left ear, McMurtrey heard Appy grunt, followed by gurgling.

Then McMurtrey's right ear filled with sound, painlessly this time. It was a harmonic of great intensity, carrying with it unidentifiable layers of contribution, building to a crescendo.

"No!" Appy screamed. "Don't try it!"

Corona was shaking involuntarily against McMurtrey's hand.

McMurtrey felt like a tuning fork, with an incredible harmonic tone coursing every pore, cell and muscle of his body, setting all into motion in a great undulating wave.

This ship is a skinbeater, McMurtrey thought. *It 'negotiates' the fragile skins between universes, whatever that means. Is this sound an aspect of it?*

Corona's face was unidimensional and had gaps in it, with dark cells dancing near one another, not quite touching. She had a strange expression on her face, as if she were being killed and couldn't figure out how. McMurtrey could see right through the dancing cells, and through his own hand held against the back of her neck, to the headboard wall beyond.

We're both doing it, he thought. He moved his hand in a dream-state, looked upon its looseness as if it were not of him. He wasn't touching her now, but the visual and auditory sensations remained.

I can still think and move, he thought.

His hand felt numb and asleep, and he shook it. The particles comprising what once had been his skin moved faster, and he perceived only paper thinness to the hand— a frightening and incomplete singularity of dimension.

With sound filling his head he leaped to the floor, spun and looked back at Corona. She was a dot-matrix woman, with only a facsimile of the features she once possessed.

Next to her sat a wide expanse of dots in human form, in McMurtrey's form.

The air filled with dots, and in an insect swarm the dots from the bed rejoined him, in delayed reaction. It made him afraid to move.

"Did you see that?" he asked. And his words were like the visual dots, with little gaps of nothingness between hard edges of sound.

She nodded.

McMurtrey felt the deck shudder, saw the compartment screen flex violently. Everything whirled and spun before him, grew dark. He seemed riveted in place, on a spinning carnival ride. But this carnival had no colors.

"Our ship entered a spinning knife-edge of parallel white lines," Corona said calmly, from somewhere. McMurtrey couldn't see her, couldn't see or feel anything. He felt like a spinning, whirling, electronic receiver.

Corona again, her voice susurrant: "Ahead I saw a limitless plane of parallel lines against unbounded space. The stars were brilliant, blinding, with no rest for my eyes. Light burned through me. I died of pain and was reborn. Appy says the skins are damaged. Big trouble because of that. He's angry with Shusher, says T.O. will never forgive this. Appy talked to Shusher like a schoolteacher scolding an errant student, said that when we were skinbeating we were pulling the compressed skins of two adjacent universes through Shusher's drive system. He said Shusher didn't understand how delicate an operation it was, that the skins had been compressed to microthin wires and we were in two universes at once—half in each—pulling the skins through somehow. Behind us it's like a damaged bridge the other ships may not be able to pass. They may have to go back, try another way. Skins take a long time healing."

"Appy told us the skins between universes are the fastest path to God," McMurtrey said, " so I wonder how long it would take traveling to God's planet conventionally, by spaceship through the universe."

"I don't know."

"If the skins are severely damaged, we could be forced to take the slower route back. That might take so long that we'd die enroute, effectively trapping us out here."

"You're right. Could be no way back."

A long silence. Presently McMurtrey said, "It's strange here . . . I felt it even before this, that I was able to think more lucidly away from the clutter of my life on D'Urth. When it's all over, Kelly, what really matters about life?"

"I dunno."

"I wish I could remember everything that's happened to me. When I can't remember something, it's like part of my life has been stolen from me. Why go through each moment if it's going to be forgotten? When it's all over, what do we have? What does it all matter if you can't remember most of it?"

Her voice came from blackness: "You're talking weird."

"No, I'm not. Think about it. Memories are all of consequence that remain at the end of a person's life. It's not the things he accumulated, nor which he sought to accumulate. Rather it is the richness and fulfillment of each experience itself. This should be the truest endowment of life. But what is that endowment if time and circumstance pulverize it?

"Sure, there are memory enhancement techniques: concentration, review soon afterward, even a policy of trying to experience significant events. This trip is a significant event *par excellence*, so we'll remember most all of it. But everything in life can't be a significant event; we can't concentrate on everything at the time it's happening or take the time for a review soon afterward. Life goes on at too rapid a pace. Do you follow what I'm saying?"

"Yes, but you needn't be so gloomy about such losses. It seems to me you're forgetting about the memories others have of you, the important impression in clay left by your life."

"I suppose that's true. It matters what God thinks of me, too."

"Sure it does. Even if you're pulverized to dust with no memories remaining at all, what you *were* matters, the way you changed lives, the way you graced and improved them."

"I didn't help everybody. I tricked many of them—my Cosmic Chickenhood prank. Now ironically, the fat chicken society may be meaningful after all. God as much as suggested that, although I can't believe it."

"We can do important things by accident, or good things without meaning to do good things, and what we've done is still important, still good."

"But lessened by lack of intention."

"Maybe not. Maybe you did what you really *meant* to do after all."

"Subconsciously?"

"Yes," Corona said.

"I don't think I believe in that stuff. You do?"

"I guess. The older I get and the more I think about things, the less certain I am about anything."

"Do you suppose the most important events in life occur by accident?" McMurtrey asked. "Meeting you, I mean, was totally unplanned. Even people who work hard and succeed in business need big breaks to get ahead—If the breaks go the wrong way, no amount of effort can compensate. Maybe, in the end, everything good depends on good luck and everything bad upon bad luck."

"I disagree. All of it happens because people place themselves in position for things to happen. You got into religion, which placed you on this ship. I'm a Merchant Spacer, and that placed me on the ship. We're here because we placed ourselves in position to be here."

"We intended to meet?"

Corona chuckled. "Let's just say we stirred the stew."

"I'll say we're in the stew. We lost our bodies somewhere. We're probably dead!"

"It's kind of neat though, isn't it? No pain, and we can still think, can still talk."

"But only with one another, for all of eternity?"

McMurtrey felt circulation return to his lips as he spoke, and nearly cried as this sensation of flesh returned. Sensations followed throughout his body.

Far away he saw a faint burst of yellow light, the same tone the auras had been—the identical yellow of the mysterious human cloud-shapes amid the white lines. A second flash was the same color, brighter, and it split in two, approaching as side-by-side beacons. Hazy shapes appeared around the beacons, and the beacons became Corona's eyes: dark and profoundly secret.

"I love you, Ev," she said. "That's the meaning of life,

the most important thing. Finding someone to love. We're alive!"

The room became light, and Corona stood before him, looking normal. The dark, dark eyes were a fresh shade of brown, prettier than he recalled.

"We're supposed to pinch ourselves now," he said.

They did.

And Corona went to him, held him tightly. She was trembling, and it made McMurtrey proud when he soothed her, dispatched her fears.

"We have each other," he said.

The deck shook violently, with a crashing, jarring shrill of discord that lasted only an instant. In that instant as McMurtrey held Corona, he experienced the vision she had described: He saw a spinning sharp edge of parallel white lines, with a limitless plane of parallel white lines stretching to the horizon of the universe. Light burned through his eyes, though he closed them—a fiercely brilliant, blinding nova of light that blotted out everything in its path.

On the deck outside Corona's compartment, Jin lay shaken. He stumbled to his feet and to his cabin controls.

The screen dropped from the ceiling, clicked into place.

Within seconds Jin was hidden from the view of others, assessing system damage via electrical probes that coursed the fiber-optical passageways of his body.

Something had changed in the field-irreparable programming meltweld—the Duplication program was transmitting green sound, dominating all other functions.

He felt a whir and throb in his Central Command module, and dull humanlike pain pulsed there, inside his head. This was from the Duplication program, he theorized, a simulated headache. But this was a more intense headache than any in his experience.

Almost automatically, Jin touched a cabin control button.

The bed swung out, opened out.

Jin dropped supine onto the bed, let his aching head sink into the billowed softness of the pillow.

Just a little rest, he thought. *Maybe things will smooth out. . . .*

It was not uncommon for human-simulating cyberoos to feel fatigue, but this was the first time Jin had been forced to lie down on the journey, so engrossed had he been in his work. All the energy he'd felt since boarding seemed oddly irrecoverable, as if drained from him permanently. He felt depressed.

At a thought-impulse, he set a dormancy timer, directing that his functions be put to rest for eight hours.

But the Duplication program did not rest, as it should have. It continued transmitting into his unconsciousness, filling every synthetic cell of his body with green sound.

Nine

There are different dimensions of the word "love," dimensions lost in the vast umbrella of the word. We feel love in varying subcategories and intensities for different people, and too often we speak the word for the wrong reasons, when we want something, when we want to take something. Thus love becomes tainted, for it is narcissistic. More than all other words, love is ultimately meaningless, for it means too many different things to different people. It means too many bad things. The best and purest definition: Love is giving all of yourself while expecting nothing in return.

—Light-Inscribed Thoughts
in Evander McMurtrey's Brain

McMurtrey died of pain and was reborn.

When his eyes stopped hurting he lifted the lids cautiously and let room light flow into the corneas. This time the light brought no pain with it, and timeless energy flowed along his arteries into his cells, bringing consciousness. With consciousness came a message borne on light, a message about love.

The words were illuminated in his brain like a great electro-gas sign, and he wanted desperately to speak them, to tell Corona the depths of his feelings for her.

"We hit something," Corona said.

McMurtrey heard her before seeing her. Then, like an apparition, she appeared standing sideways before him, where his eyes had been directed. She was only a few steps away.

Appy's voice, across the P.A. system: "Intruder! Seal

all sections, dammit! Intru—" The voice sputtered, went silent.

"What the hell's going on?" McMurtrey said.

He reached around and touched a button on the bulkhead, raising the screen of Corona's cubicle. The screen squealed as it went up, where before it had been nearly soundless.

From all around the ship came the confused and anxious tones of pilgrims.

Corona stood motionless before McMurtrey, profiled against the mezzanine railing.

"You okay?" McMurtrey asked, his voice almost shrill. No response.

Corona trembled, and she turned her head to look with fearful eyes at McMurtrey. Her lips moved without sound.

McMurtrey stepped toward her and reached out, but she pulled away, wouldn't let him touch her. She trembled uncontrollably, a d'urthquake within her flesh.

"Kelly, what's going on?"

Her eyes became radiant and aura-yellow, and the body surrounding the eyes became as black as starless space, as black as the darkness that had permeated them when they spoke without bodies or flesh.

Within that quivering, human-shaped universe the eyes became twin beacons, receding into a limitless distance. They disappeared from McMurtrey's sight. Presently the trembling ceased, and before him stood a motionless, eyeless black shape.

A chill coursed McMurtrey's spine. Now he was trembling, afraid to approach or move away, afraid to speak his love.

Was this a woman anymore? Was his beloved dead before him, with only the remnants of soul clinging to existence?

Far away within the blackened shape of the head, McMurtrey saw a faint flash of aura-yellow light. A second flash was brighter, and as before when he and Corona were in darkness, the flash divided in two and approached as teamed beacons. Hazy shapes formed around the beacons, and the beacons again were Corona's eyes: dark and with a mystery of depth to them beyond anything he imagined possible.

"There is an intruder aboard," she said, but not in her own voice. It was the accented voice of Appy.

"What do you mean? And why is your voice—"

"We are shipwrecked."

"Shipwrecked? What the hell do you mean? Where?"

"Other ships are closing in. We're going to lose the race. We have less than eighteen hours to effect repairs. I am not Corona."

Corona's lips moved again, producing her own voice this time.

McMurtrey breathed a tentative sigh of relief as he listened to her:

"We collided with the white lines," she said. "We're 'beached' on a line, unable to proceed unless certain conditions are met. We're in the middle of the whipping passageway, at a dead stop with the skins of two universes gripped in Shusher's drive system. God says the skins are damaged here but still passable. Soon the others will be upon us, and if we can't beat skin we'll have to get out of the way. God's exact words: 'Ship, heal thyself.'"

"How do you know these things, and why did you speak in Appy's voice?"

"The same answer to both: I am Appy now. I am also Kelly Corona. I can think as either at will, speak as either. I can, it would appear from my preliminary understanding of this, carry on a conversation with myself."

"But—"

She anticipated, said, "The computer system went out when we collided . . . the white line entity is a Gluon, like Shusher. Gluons can pass through one another without harm except when they are on a whipping passageway. They're ensnarled now, and neither can proceed. We are in a most delicate situation."

McMurtrey didn't understand enough to phrase a question.

"Appy activated a 'save' program before shutting down," Corona said, "and this program, containing all of the data comprising Appy's bioelectronic brain, traveled the electromagnetic pulses of light from Appy to me. The lavender light in which I was bathed placed me on precisely the same light circuit with Appy. The computer had a choice of dumping its data into either Shusher or me, and it chose me."

McMurtrey longed to tell Corona he loved her, but was hesitant to do so with Appy linked to her. It was silly to feel this way, he told himself, since Appy was linked to God, and God heard all anyway. But Appy's proximity made McMurtrey ill at ease. He didn't know who or what controlled Corona anymore.

"What if our ship can't move out of the way?" McMurtrey asked.

"Then God will bump us aside. He has to, or there'll be a huge collision here, with long-term destruction of the ecology. Appy's damned mad about the situation, thought he had the race locked up."

"And behind us, where Shusher started trying to pass the white lines? What kind of shape are the skins in back there?"

"Again, damaged but passable. Competing ships won't be slowed appreciably . . . only a few extra minutes will be required."

"Why can't entities traveling the skins pass one another?"

"Because all the matter, antimatter and other contents of the skins of two universes have been compressed into a microthin electromagnetic wire known as a kra or whipping passageway, a kra that is for the moment the only one available to the skinbeaters of two universes. It's like a one-lane road, and the only way one skinbeater can pass another is if the skinbeater in front drops off the kra into one universe or another."

"The white line Gluon refused to yield."

"Right," Corona said. "Those spaces previously occupied by the skins of engaged universes have been replaced by electromagnetic voids. At a certain point a skinbeater must leave the whipping passageway and drop into position in the destination universe. Entities utilizing this mode of transport can go in either direction upon it, but only one direction of flow can be utilized at once."

"Pretty tricky. There must be long waiting lists."

"It's first come, first served, with no preference to the high and mighty, not even to God. This system preceded God; it's one of the elemental forces He can't control. One of the skins we needed was hogged for a while by inconsiderate Gluons, the reason we were delayed three weeks in St. Charles Beach. Gluons are inveterate travelers, irritatingly so, and it made God mighty agitated, I can tell you! The Gluons weren't even from one of our adjacent universes. They were from a universe on another side of a universe adjacent to us, if you follow me. And they had the adjacent universe's skin that we needed."

"We have *several* universes adjacent to us? If so, couldn't we just combine one of the other skins with our own to make a whipping passageway?"

"Ordinarily, yes, but their skins were damaged in a natural catastrophe, making them unavailable for skinbeating. The skins are healing, but it will take time."

"What about Shusher and the white-line Gluon? They're damaged?"

"Being determined. The second Gluon crowded onto our whipping passageway just seconds before Shusher took off, and for a time the interloper was taking the exact D'Urth-to-Tananius-Ofo route we were on."

McMurtrey scratched his head. "Only one direction of flow at a time, I believe you said, so it was fortunate—for a while anyway—that the second Gluon wanted to go in the same direction as we did."

"That's right."

"What has the merging with Appy done to you? I mean, are you injured in any way?"

"I think I'm fine. A human is like a computer in many ways, and Appy is on a biodisk that's been booted into my body. I . . . have two 'programs' now, one for Appy and one for Kelly Corona. They network rather nicely. In thoughts I can switch between them or activate both simultaneously. Let me try something—"

Corona's voice changed, to an eery, blended tone: "This is the composite of Appy and Corona, in two-part harmony." She smiled.

"Can Appy still speak through the ship's speakers?" McMurtrey asked.

Corona hesitated, spoke as Appy: "No. I still have my private comlinks though, including the one to Shusher. They're internal . . . and on the Shusher link I can speak or even beam thoughts to Shusher. He's whining now, whimpering that this wasn't his fault. The other Gluon—an entity called Pelter—is giving him hell. He just called Shusher the equivalent of a nincompoop!"

Appy laughed crazily across Corona's lips, and she appeared irritated by this.

Corona's voice, in seeming interjection: "There's more to explain, from this infernal Appy's data banks: Every universe abuts some other universe at every point of skin . . . the skin of every universe is in effect a double skin therefore, because of the adjacent universe's skin. There are many, many universes."

"I'm having trouble visualizing all that," McMurtrey said. "Wouldn't there have to be sides to everything, places where there are only single thicknesses of skin? I mean, I can see universes in the middle of the cosmos all touching one another, but wouldn't there have to be some universes on the outside?"

"You're limited by your own experience," Corona said. "Accept what I'm saying."

"Shit, I'll try."

"Skinbeating isn't restricted to Gluons. Other entities travel the whipping passageways, and some of them are pretty bizarre. All skinbeaters achieve a whipping effect between universes, employing electromagnetics, concentrated gravity waves and other forces, and these forces literally slap the entity across the cosmos. Gluons are among the smoothest travelers, and their skinbeating action is so rapid and smooth in normal operation that life forms traveling with the Gluons don't feel it."

"Is this a matter/antimatter interaction? with one universe of matter and the adjacent of antimatter?"

"God isn't certain how it works exactly, but He doesn't think that has much to do with it. There are antimatter universes, matter universes, and there are universes such as our own containing combinations of each. There are even universes containing other things, which I won't go into here. Each universe, no matter its makeup, has an invisible electromagnetic skin around its perimeter . . . and these perimeters are as varied in shape as the configurations of stones in the cosmos. Each skin is electromagnetically identical, and thus readily available to any skinbeating entity."

"I never imagined," McMurtrey said.

"Come with me," Corona said, motioning for Mc-Murtrey to accompany her. "We have an intruder to meet, an intruder Appy saw before downloading into me. This intruder is at the heart of the mess we're in now, and it is only through the intruder that our Gluon can extricate itself from Pelter."

McMurtrey moved to her side, and they negotiated the carpeted mezzanine walkway toward the elevator bank. "I don't understand again," he said. "Isn't Pelter the intruder?"

Corona shook her head. "It's a human," she said. "A peculiar little man carrying a dead child."

"Clear the way," Corona ordered, in Appy's voice. She pressed through a crowd of pilgrims thronging the main passenger compartment. They moved aside for her sluggishly.

McMurtrey followed her, through startled whispers.

When the last layer of humanity fell away, McMurtrey got his initial glimpse of the intruder.

Indeed this was a peculiar little man seated in the center of the deck. He cried silently, bore a pained expression, and in his arms he held the limp and lifeless form of a dead girl-child. The man appeared to be in late middle years, with thinning curls of black hair, dark little eyes and a short but crudely trimmed gray-flecked beard. He held the dead child tightly, with white-knuckled fingers that were the length of digits more suited to a much taller person. Or to an ape.

The little finger of one hand was missing.

The man pulled his hands free gently, letting the body rest on his lap. Briskly with one hand, he rubbed the knuckle above the missing finger. Afterward he put the four-fingered hand under one of his legs, apparently to keep the hand warm.

Yes, McMurtrey thought. *He resembles an ape, with that protruding forehead, those high cheekbones, those hands . . . and look at his arms—they're extraordinarily long. . . .*

Of the child's death there could be no doubt. Her eyes were open and empty, with a grievous wound on the side of her head. The man holding her wore a short-sleeved

denolyon shirt that was brown with a broad magenta stripe
across the chest. The trousers matched, with a magenta
stripe down each side. He had blood on his clothes.

A pungent, acrid odor irritated McMurtrey's nostrils,
forced him to mouth-breathe. It wasn't the stench of death,
at least McMurtrey didn't think it was, from the impos-
sible-to-forget odors of dead animals he had been near a
few times.

"That smell," McMurtrey said, wrinkling his nose.
"What is it?"

"Opium," Corona said, glancing at McMurtrey. "He's
an addict."

The apeman looked up at the crowd, and down at the
lifeless form. Then he pressed a loose flap of skin over the
open wound, and with tender fingers pressed it in place.
It held.

"I didn't kill her," he said, with the gaze of his tearful
dark eyes darting from face to face in the throng.

Corona positioned herself by the man, and with remarkable efficiency she explained to everyone what she
had already related to McMurtrey, beginning with the
saved Appy program she carried within her body. She told
of multiple universes, skinbeating and Gluons, and of her
comlinks via Appy with God and Shusher. Finally she
glanced down at the intruder.

"This is Harley Gutan," she said. "God informs me that
he is one of the most disgusting, depraved and despicable
creatures in any universe, and that we must resolve the
matter of Gutan before our journey can continue."

"Why do we have to resolve anything like that?" a
woman shouted. "We need to repair the ship! Let's get
busy with that!"

"The matter of Gutan and the repair of this ship are
intertwined," Corona said. "God contributed the chan-
neling environment necessary to create this ship, and for
reasons unexplained to me, He can provide no further
information or assistance to us."

This information Kelly's getting, McMurtrey thought.
What has she become?

"Gutan was on the Gluon we hit?" the nun Sister Mary
asked.

"He and the unfortunate child were matter-impregnated

on the antimatter of the Gluon known as Pelter. Like us they may have been on their way to see God, but their destination is not known at this time. It is known that they were joined through the arcane activity of a machine constructed on D'Urth. There are many troublesome devices on D'Urth. . . ."

"You're suggesting God doesn't control Gutan?" Sister Mary inquired, her voice shrill and agitated.

A moment's hesitation, then Appy replied, through Corona: "Some things are easier to explain than others, even for a god of great power. God does not control the whipping passageways between universes. God in the context we've used the name is the god of but one universe, the one containing D'Urth's solar system. . . . There are many universes, with different types of authority."

"Blasphemy!" Sister Mary exclaimed. "God has infinite power!" Nervously, she smoothed her white habit with one hand.

"I beg to differ," Appy said. "The Lord only seems omnipotent to humans because of your limited vantage. God's jurisdiction is restricted to His own universe, this one, and He doesn't own or control everything in the universe. Some Gluons, for example, are amenable to God-induced matter impregnation and guidance; others are not."

"Does God control more than Satan?" McMurtrey asked.

"In this universe, more than any other entity," Appy confirmed.

Corona looked at Sister Mary, but the alter ego Appy spoke: "While the machine used by Gutan is beyond the impetus or knowledge of God, the Lord feels He might have blocked its way by thrusting something in its path, across the whipping passageway. That's not what happened here, where Shusher of his own foolish volition tried, impossibly, to pass Pelter."

"Could Shusher have been following God's instructions?" McMurtrey asked.

A long silence, then Appy: "It's possible."

Yakkai stepped into view, shouted: "I think it's possible that Appy's an asshole through and through."

"I defy definition," came a haughty response. "Particularly by the likes of you. May your heart be removed and stuffed like an olive."

Yakkai was livid. "Well, eat shit, chase rabbits and bark at the moon! How do we know *anything* you've said is true? I'm sick of your blabbering! I'm sick of everything about you! You defy definition, all right. One of a kind, that's what you are. A special breed of computerized asshole. You don't work for God. There is no God! Admit it!"

"Maybe this atheist has a point," a woman said. "Appy is quite vague sometimes, irritatingly secretive . . . as if certain information is on a need-to-know basis, and we aren't capable of digesting it."

"Bullshit!" a man shouted. "Appy's been spilling his guts, telling us everything he knows!"

The woman: "What if God has more to do with this situation than his apprentice knows or is letting on? What if God is keeping the Gluons inoperable by refusing to separate one He controls—Shusher—from one He doesn't control—Pelter?"

"God does not tell me everything," Appy said, "so it's possible He could be capable of separating the Gluons. But why would God do that?"

"To keep you from winning the race?" Corona asked.

Appy: "But God said I could have another chance, that the sabotage of other ships wasn't my fault."

"Maybe He changed His mind when He decided you were an asshole," Yakkai said.

"Enough from you, Yakkai," McMurtrey snapped. "Appy's trying to help us through this mess, and the more we learn, the better equipped we'll be to handle it. So pipe down, okay?"

Yakkai grumbled, pushed his way back into the crowd.

"There is an imbalance on this ship with Gutan aboard," Appy said.

"Then chuck him out!" Yakkai shouted, from a position McMurtrey couldn't see.

A long pause, and Appy said, "That can't be done. God informs me now that it violates holy rules. You must hurry, for there is not much time, but it must be done right."

"What's right?" Yakkai shouted. "I've heard enough of this!"

"God determines what is right," Appy countered. "But it is not so simple. You humans aboard this ship must determine how best to proceed, employing the Free Will that God has granted."

"More of Appy's games," a familiar voice grumbled.

McMurtrey turned his head, saw Johnny Orbust. The fiery Reborn Krassee stood unevenly, wore healing packs on his arms and face.

"Come on, Corona," Orbust said. "You're plugged into Appy, and via that to God. With all the knowledge you have, tell us how to proceed." One eyelid twitched.

She shook her head.

"At least suggest something!"

"I . . . can't. . . . There is no such information. At least it hasn't been provided to Appy. I—I can suggest that I don't think there is a single way to resolve this enigma, no solitary path. Look at it from the positive side. If I'm right about this, it improves our odds. It's an extrapolation of Great Truth, it seems to me. No problem in the universe is limited to one solution."

"Oh, great," Orbust muttered. "Riddles."

"Actually, I did kill her," Gutan said. "Not this particular girl, but others. Oh, my killings were state-sanctioned, authorized by the job chip implanted in my brain. But they were wrong just the same, wrong because of the use I put to the corpses."

Fearfully, he looked up and around at the people standing over him, at the robes and other religious garb, at the amulets, crosses and stars . . . at the weapons on the hips of some. And for an instant his eyes lost focus.

He felt an elusive sensation of Otherness tickling the edges of his brain, refusing to be drawn in for analysis and dissection. So it hung beyond but touching, as oil to water, with bits of it floating inward enticingly toward the interpretive core of his brain.

His existence, every breath of his being, seemed linked, and this Otherness pumped through his veins, gazed through his eyes. The moisture of his body trailed away to a horizon of stars, to a screaming, crying soul.

Gutan felt dirty, that he had been watched during all of his despicable acts, that the Otherness had shared his thoughts. He wanted forgiveness. God, he craved forgiveness! These people around him looked as if they knew every detail, as if they had watched Gutan's life each day on Mnemo's screen.

Gutan could not lie to them. If he expected to salvage any remnants of dignity, he could not lie. Not now and not ever again. If provided the opportunity, he would do penance.

He wiped tears from his eyes.

Gutan confessed to the crimes of the mortuary and of the prison system, to drug addiction, and even to the crimes of principal ancestors in his lineage.

"I wish I could make up for everything," Gutan said. "I wish my life had been different!"

Gutan told of Mnemo, of the ancient lives he relived and of the dead girl-child he took in his arms as the world burned in war. He hadn't been directly responsible for that war, he said, but in a larger, more important sense he confessed that he had been. He overconfessed, it seemed to him, but he felt cleaner for having done so. It was cathartic.

"I am responsible for more than myself," Gutan said. With that he fell silent.

Someone coughed.

Sister Mary waddled forward, with the other fat nun.

"As infirmary orderlies," Sister Mary said to Corona, "we should take the child's body and prepare it for eternal rest."

Corona nodded. "Wrap it and say your words. I'll be along later to jettison."

Sister Mary bowed her head slightly and lowered her eyelids in acquiescence.

As McMurtrey watched the nuns take the girl from Gutan, he thought over the extraordinary events leading to this moment. Corona was *de facto* captain now, by virtue of the organic computer program within her and by virtue of her space travel experience. No one would question her authority.

Corona stood erect as the nuns left, caught McMurtrey's gaze.

Who looks at me through your eyes? McMurtrey wondered. *Is that you, Kelly, or Appy? Might it even be God or the Gluon Shusher, through a comlink?*

Her eyes were not the same, though they remained mysteriously strong and dark, with as yet untapped layers beneath the surface. They had lost their gentleness, McMurtrey decided.

I can't tell her how I feel until I see the gentleness return, until I know she is no more than a woman. I must become stronger than she, or she must weaken.

These were curious thoughts to McMurtrey, caring deeply as he did for Corona but wishing a limited degree of ill luck upon her. He wished she weren't in charge of the ship. Women shouldn't be in such positions. He'd always had trouble with women, didn't understand them, and inevitably they slipped away. If it happened this time it would be the worst experience of his life.

He detected the glimmerings of a smile on her face, and the briefest, soft glistening of her eyes before she looked away. The smile had been for him, he decided; the moist eyes for the death of the child.

Nothing was worse than the death of a child.

Did this pitiful little man murder the girl, or were his crimes "confined" to those he listed? McMurtrey couldn't get a reading on the man, realized how essential perceptions were. People acted upon perceptions, based important decisions upon them. But who was an expert in such matters? Certainly no human carried with him an instruction manual from birth about the things to look for in the demeanor of another person. McMurtrey was hesitant to look too hard anyway, fearing a relapse of his old idiosyncrasy-induced paralyses of thought.

He thought back to his "visitation" from God, to his brief periods of exultation over the "pipeline" to God, and to the subsequent removal of that pedestal, when McMurtrey became no more than a ship's passenger. Corona had been humbled herself . . . the captaincy offered to her, withdrawn and then given back. Now she had a pipeline to God and McMurtrey didn't. Now she was the most important human being on the ship. A woman.

'*God moves in mysterious ways*,' McMurtrey thought. These were ways beyond the comprehension of any human being. Would they remain a mystery?

"We must deal with the matter of Gutan," Corona said, raising her voice so that all could hear. "Are there suggestions?"

"Chuck him overboard!" Yakkai repeated.

"That cannot be done!"

Now, Orbust's compatriot Tully stepped to the forefront, and he said, "Kill Mr. Gutan first, and he'll have to be jettisoned."

"No!" a man said. "Deal with him in a way God would sanction." It sounded like Archbishop Perrier.

"God's killed plenty," Tully said. "Evil deserves no mercy, and mark my words, we're looking at evil here."

It had been Perrier who protested, and now he pressed his way forward to stand near Tully. "That's not exactly true," Perrier said. "And it is not our place to take a life. 'Vengeance is mine, sayeth the Lord.'"

"What are we supposed to do to get this ship going?" Tully asked. "Get out and push?"

Corona shook her head, thrust out her underlip.

"Kelly, you're pretty handy mechanically," McMurtrey said. "Isn't there something you can have a look at? Maybe a loose wire or an assembly that needs to be rebuilt."

"This isn't just mechanical," Corona replied. "I can't peek at Shusher's innards, make a few adjustments and push the 'GO' button. It's clear to me that this ship operates under a delicate arrangement of factors that no one with us—Appy, Shusher or human—fully understands. We've been skinbeating on an infinitesimally thin wire between universes!"

"What are we to do?" Perrier queried.

Corona shrugged. "Appy has been instructed to await further developments."

Prayers and holy mantras began, and soon the air was murmurous. A boyish tenor rose above in Babulical refrain:

> "From the peak, o-old Toor
> Set his doves to the breeze;
> They flew on a-and on
> With no-where to set down . . ."

We're stranded, McMurtrey thought. *With no way to send for assistance. It's all up to us, but we don't have enough information. We'll be passed, may die out here. We won't arrive first.*

Arrive first . . . FIRST . . . Does it really matter if we get there first?

It mattered to Appy, and God had set the whole race up in the first place, so it seemed to matter to Him. But why did it matter? Why did everyone have to be first? Of course everyone didn't *have* to be first, McMurtrey realized. Everyone couldn't possibly be first. But the way the game was played, the way almost every game was played, someone had to win and someone had to lose. But even when it came to understanding God? It seemed to McMurtrey that the love and understanding of God should be a sharing experience, not a race.

'No single way to resolve this enigma, no solitary path . . .'

The compartment grew increasingly quiet, and all around McMurtrey the pilgrims kneeled and prostrated themselves before their gods.

"Not enough," Appy said, through Corona. "God informs me you're praying for yourselves. Such an ugly, scabby practice! Shame!"

Startled whispers carried around the room.

"Self-serving prayer is a wart fed by religious fear tactics!" Yakkai shouted, still from his sheltered place in the crowd. "Priests keep their flocks in line by scaring them to death. You hypocrites only do nice things because somewhere in your mind you have an idea it will benefit yourselves! You Krassians, Middists and other wackos fear a great Santa Claus in the sky who knows when you've been bad or good. Santa Claus doesn't bring things to bad little boys and girls, you see. That's the myth structure underlying your acts, and now the rug is being pulled. The rude awakening begins!"

A scuffle and angry words ensued, but McMurtrey only saw the shifting of persons near Yakkai. McMurtrey heard the word, "Antikrassos."

Presently the commotion subsided.

"Yakkai may not be that far off," Appy said.

More whisperings among the pilgrims.

"What about worship?" McMurtrey asked.

"You have the necessary information," Appy said.

Corona's eyes were unemotional above the mouth that spoke.

"It's the same, isn't it?" McMurtrey pressed. "Aren't people worshiping their gods for selfish reasons?"

"That is for you to determine," Appy said.

"I'm going to assume it's similar to prayer," McMurtrey said, "and that we aren't getting anywhere with selfish acts. Is that what you're trying to tell us?"

Appy did not reply.

"Just for protocol we need to know about the merits of worship," McMurtrey said. "We're going to visit God and must understand the amount of reverence He requires. Are we to sit around exchanging anecdotes with Him, or are we to prostrate ourselves?"

"How interesting for you to guess," Appy said, in his most irritating tone.

"It's all moot anyway," Corona observed, her voice. "The ship ain't movin'."

"But no single way to solve the matter of Gutan, as you said. And you did ask for suggestions. Prayer . . . worship . . . the unknown . . . fear . . . I think we need to understand these concepts if we're going to figure our way out of this mess."

"Why do you say that?" Corona asked, almost indifferently.

"Call it a hunch," McMurtrey replied. "There is a certain order to events—from the planets in motion to the tiniest speck of nature—to the patterns of human lives. When something interferes with the normal course of affairs, men are forced to face the unknown. The unknown lies ahead and apart, and can be wondrous indeed, holding the imagined treasures of a thousand dreams. It can be equally terrifying, bearing the torturous deaths of a thousand nightmares. The unknown is at once a golden road and a deep abyss, rarely reaching the wild extremes of imagined hope and fear. The first thing we need to do, we need to accept what's happening to us without terror, without recriminations, without preconceptions. We need to identify the barriers that have fallen and the barriers that remain."

"Yeah, so?" Corona said. Her voice was tinged with fatigue.

"What are those remaining barriers, and in what order of priority must they be surmounted? Our ship will not continue. Why not? How was it created and how did it get here? The ship is an object of our minds, the materialization of a collective, averaged-out image. The ship is us and we are the ship. It means we need to cooperate and . . ."

"You're talking in circles," Tully said. "Why don't you shut up?"

Then the boy who sang of Toor raised his voice to exclaim, "Let's put Gutan on trial! Right here, right now! We'll decide what to do with him!"

McMurtrey: "But I think—"

"What if the verdict is death?" Tully interjected. "Corona said we can't chuck him overboard."

"Aren't there other methods of execution?" a man said. "Gutan himself proved that, in his story of the League Penitentiary System and Mnemo. Maybe we can chuck him anyway, *after* the trial, after our court has heard his case."

"I don't think this is . . ." McMurtrey said. But his voice was too low for authority, and washed out in conversation around him.

Tully asked, "Is that what you meant, Corona, when you said Gutan couldn't be thrown overboard?" He stared at her intently.

Corona shuffled her feet. "I have told you all I can, all I know. Honestly, I'm not trying to be evasive and I can't see that Appy was, either. I said, 'That cannot be done,' because those words came to me from one of the comlink connections in my brain."

A pained expression came over Corona, and she said, "I was no more than a mouthpiece. To be perfectly honest with you, I am not . . . so important . . . not so important as . . . I wish I were."

McMurtrey suspected that God was humbling her, knocking her from her pedestal again. But a trial for Gutan made no sense to McMurtrey. He'd tried to explain to them what he thought the answer was, but they wouldn't listen.

From all around came a clamoring for trial.

Can't they see that this ship is powered by the minds of the pilgrims? McMurtrey thought. *That it's only through cooperation between all the believers and nonbelievers aboard that we can make it move? That's the answer, and I'll scream it out if I have to. But first the trial. They'll analyze the confession five hundred ways to Sunday. At least they'll cooperate in that.*

Corona was agreeing with the others. No one spoke against a trial.

McMurtrey: *Can my mental impetus alone, my disagreement, delay this craft?*

He sensed a familiar trap, the one God had just humbled Corona out of: pride in oneself above all others, the desire to be eminent, to be first . . . and those comments about self-serving prayer . . .

Can it be that man will only be first if he doesn't try to be? Would it just happen then? A natural occurrence? Should one try not *to be first?*

He smiled to himself at the multifaceted quandary God had put the ship's company in. This matter of Gutan would be resolved through selflessness. The antithesis brought Gutan here, and the pilgrims with him.

McMurtrey would wait, watch and participate in the trial. He would try to be patient with them.

It was agreed that the trial would be held in the main passenger compartment, for this was the largest room on the ship. Since the ship was no longer in flight and heavy objects didn't need to be secured for the time being, Appy suggested that they disconnect all assembly room chairs and set them up in the courtroom. He told the pilgrims how to accomplish this.

This seemed an unnecessary complexity to most of those present, however, and considering the time available, it was decided that only the defendant, Gutan, would be placed upon a chair, while everyone else would stand in the wings or sit upon the deck. Many of these people were, after all, ascetics unaccustomed to folding their bodies into chairs.

In short order a trial council of seven members was appointed by voice vote, with Appy employing bioelectronic techniques to analyze and count votes quickly. The appointees were McMurtrey, Corona, Zatima, Makanji, a white-robed Hoddhist priest, the ornately robed Afsornian holy man, and, surprisingly to McMurtrey, Johnny Orbust. This was not to be a judicial council; it was instead to be a planning group assigned to determine how best the defendant should be tried.

Orbust, who still wore healing packs on his arms and face, was a pitiful sight and much quieter than he had been when he first boarded the ship. He kept in constant communication with C. T. Tully and Kundo Smith just before the voting, with Tully and Smith traveling between the crowd and Orbust, exchanging whispered information with the latter. It appeared obvious to McMurtrey that they were working for votes and possibly more, and there might have been an outpouring of sympathy votes for Orbust. Still, Zatima held her own against her archenemy in the voting, evidence of strong feelings on both sides.

Standing off to one side, the council began deliberations while interested nonmembers gathered nearby to listen.

Appy said through Corona that he knew various trial methods, from his experiences and from his programming. He had this information, he said, because of the different jurisdictions he might operate in, so that he would not violate local laws or customs.

Very politely, Orbust requested permission to speak, and he began a question for Appy.

But one who stood nearby, Shalom ben Yakkai, seemed to have taken the ill-starred position vacated by Orbust, and he interrupted the proceedings with this, in a haunting tone:

> "Some say I'm in Heaven,
> Some say there's no trace;
> Some say take a trip
> Far off to deep space.
>
> Go east, go north
> Go up and go down;
> Spin 'til you're dizzy
> Blast off from downtown.

> Am I in Heaven?
> Or dreamed of in Nod?
> That damned and elusive
> Guy you call God!"

With that, Yakkai made a zipping sign across his mouth and folded his arms across his chest. He spun around in a circle and stared unrepentantly at McMurtrey.

"Atheist pig," a man said.

People moved away from Yakkai.

As Orbust resumed his question for Appy, McMurtrey was struck with the irony of the moment: Now Orbust was the interrupted, not the interrupter. What a dramatic change in this man!

"What do you care of local laws?" Orbust asked, looking quizzically at Appy's host, Corona. "Don't God and His representatives make their own laws?"

"To some extent," Appy replied. "But you must understand Free Will, which God does not wish to stifle. If my Lord were to make all the laws of men, what would be left for men to decide? If a man's brain is to grow and prosper, it must be used. Otherwise it atrophies."

"There is no God!" Yakkai shouted. "Or He would make waves. He would plow through all opposition, all that is wrong with this universe. If God existed He would not pussyfoot around. He would kick ass!"

"God never makes unnecessary waves," Appy countered. "The easiest way is often best."

"For weak humans and weak mythical Gods," Yakkai said.

Corona's voice barked: "Silence, or you will be removed!"

Nanak Singh became visible, a menacing figure, and he had Yakkai by the arm. Zatima stood nearby.

A small boy ran to Yakkai, kicked him in the shin, and ran away.

Yakkai winced, said nothing. He was the embodiment of discontent, it seemed to McMurtrey, an iconoclastic pimple in any public situation, threatening to erupt and spatter all that men had created. It was reasoned discontent with an emotional face, and in this state it could no longer be reasoned with. It could only be suppressed.

Yakkai had the boundless outrage that Orbust once exhibited, and by contrast, Orbust now appeared sedate, even rational. It was as if the Energy of Discontent, a raw and combative state, moved naturally between bodies and minds, inhabiting first one and then another.

Yakkai seemed destined to be beaten by the same enforcer that had dealt with Orbust.

Appy was speaking again, an institutional voice. He spoke of legal systems on D'Urth and on distant galaxies, of alien systems and methods that might be applied to the present imbroglio. All the while McMurtrey stared sidelong at Makanji, the dhoti-swathed Nandu, a man who looked back at McMurtrey through round eyeglass lenses, with an ancient, pale-eyed gaze. McMurtrey and the Nandu might have been here or anywhere else, in this age or another. A vision appeared to McMurtrey in which he and the holy man were alone in a featureless place, looking into one another's soul-eyes.

"This journey across space is illusion," the Nandu vision said. " Mankind is fighting Truth, in yet another pointless and time-consuming fashion."

"But how could we be fighting Truth if we're following God's instructions, traveling in His ship?"

"His message was distorted by mutant connections and false biochemical reactions in the receiving brain of you, Evander Harold McMurtrey."

"That doesn't explain the ships!"

"Yes, it does. Every mind, with God's assistance, can channel-create anything. You had God's assistance, but misunderstood the message, as others have done before you. Errant impulses from your mind allowed the entry of like and equally mutant thoughts from other humans, and you impregnated the Gluons with these abominations, these ships. God was a power booster, and you let your own prejudices influence what was created. There is no God in the sky, no bearded Santa Claus out there, as the atheist so aptly said."

McMurtrey, angrily: "If the ships are wrong, what are you doing aboard?"

"To guide every pilgrim along myriad spiritways. You are misguided, and you have caused the confusion of others, a great waste."

"Hogwash! This conversation is illusion. You Nandu mystics are known for your sleights of hand, your snake-charming. . . ."

But McMurtrey recalled the St. Charles Beach ships that were designed to fly, and those that did not seem to be so designed. He had wondered before takeoff about this very question, about physical and nonphysical paths to God. He realized that there had been suggestions of alternate pathways all along, from McMurtrey's "visitation" by God in which He suggested that religion might not be the way to God . . . to the nonflying ships in God's fleet . . . even to Appy's remarks about the similarities of religious practice and the failings of organized religion.

Differences melded into similarities. Alternate paths became one path. . . .

In McMurtrey's vision the Nandu smiled and said, "Snake charmers are entertainers, no more. Essentially they hypnotize cobras with body movements. Many Nandu snake charmers claim to possess occult or supernatural powers, but to my knowledge this is not so. They are magicians, not so different from the Krassian variety. Don't try to paint Nanduism with a broad brush. We are a diverse group, encompassing beliefs that range from atheism to monotheism and polytheism. There are ranges of belief within any religion."

McMurtrey's field of vision expanded and once again he saw Makanji in Shusher's main passenger compartment.

"What do you think about that, Ev?" It was Corona's voice.

"Huh?"

"About what Appy just described, the Eurosornian system of criminal justice that he thinks we ought to use. I like it myself."

The other council members were nodding in agreement.

"Okay," McMurtrey said. "Let's set it up."

The Nandu smiled at McMurtrey.

Ten

"Mnemo" has many parts, and it is necessary to understand every part and the interrelationship that part has with every other part. It is, however, a puzzle that must be approached simultaneously from multiple directions: If you focus too long on one segment or upon the interrelationships of a part with other parts, you risk becoming irretrievably lost in the complexities of over-analysis, losing sight of the greater picture, the chemical path and residue of genetic memory.

Mnemo's core pumps a stream of loaded electrical impulses in a constant rhythm across the surface of the refurbished cortex. This galvanizes the ancient memory-bearing nerve cells of the brain, exciting them to the point where they can be resurrected and analyzed through sensory deprivation and stimulation.

—Notes of Professor Nathan Pelter,
League Penitentiary System Archives

Kelly Corona was selected to announce the trial procedures to Gutan and the pilgrims, since her link to Appy's data banks provided her with pertinent details in an organized and readily communicable form.

She moved forward to address the ship's company, and McMurtrey hurried to her side.

"I need to talk with you alone, Kelly," he said. "Not this second, but first chance."

"Sure," she said, without looking at him.

"I mean really alone. Can you dump that biocomputer program somewhere for a while?"

She looked up at him. "I don't know how to do that. Maybe if Shusher's damage is repaired and we get the ship

211

going again, the damage to Appy will also be repaired, and this program I'm carrying will revert."

McMurtrey thought he heard the distant, crazed laughter of Appy, but saw no indication of this in Corona's features. Her mouth did not move.

"We will employ an essentially Eurosornian courtroom style," Corona announced, raising her voice to be heard above several talkers. "It is a derivation and modification of the Maginot *action civile*, in which criminal prosecution and redress for harm to the victim are combined. I will be presiding judge, with powers I will employ and, as necessary, describe. Since we have no police or state's attorney, it shall also be my duty to conduct an investigation, within the confines of time and circumstance.

"The other six council members are associate judges, with powers nearly equal to mine. A majority vote among us determines each issue, and will ultimately determine the fate of Mr. Gutan. We are beyond any D'Urth jurisdiction here, so it is the duty of this honorable council to develop a just system for the trial of Mr. Gutan. It must be spectacularly efficient, for we have only a few hours."

"We must be flexible as well," the black-skinned Afsornian council member said. "We must be flexible enough to make no assumptions about what is right and what is wrong." This man went by the name of Feek, and wore a turban with an emerald on it, a long robe threaded in silver and gold, and a viridescent cape.

"What do you mean?" Corona queried.

"Morality is a social condition," came the response, with regal haughtiness. "What is moral to one group may be entirely immoral to another. There is no such thing as a universal wrong."

"I assume you're referring to thievery," Corona said. "To the suggestion that it is not wrong for a starving man to steal a loaf of bread. Mr. Gutan here has confessed to thievery, to the taking of valuables from corpses. But because of the time, we needn't consider that matter. We must prioritize, deciding that his alleged necrophilic crimes—sexual intercourse with the dead—are worse than thievery, and in turn that murder is worse even than necrophilia. We must try Gutan for the worse crime only, for murder."

McMurtrey, Zatima, Makanji and Orbust voiced concurrence.

The Hoddhist, who had given his name as Taam, stared at the Afsornian.

"I am from a remote Gerian tribe," Feek said, looking at Corona. "And among my people it is only murder to kill kin. Killing non-kin is not murder. Don't you have information on that in Appy's program?"

"It wasn't entered," Corona said. "Perhaps Appy wasn't expected to visit the wilds of Geria."

Feek smiled.

Corona faced the onlookers, said, "We are in effect seven presiding judges on this council. If we disagree on priorities or anything else, as it seems we may, this will be resolved by council vote. If one or more of us abstains and a tie vote results, a voice vote among all of you decides, analyzed by Appy. If that is inconclusive, a roll call vote will be taken. The first issue is upon us, and it is an essential one. Are we to judge Gutan on every possible issue or are we to focus the trial only upon the worst, after agreeing upon what is the worst?"

McMurtrey watched as Gutan was set upon the only chair, against the wall to one side of the judges. Without its bolts, the chair rested on four stout, ugly feet.

Gutan stared into the crowd dispassionately.

The seven judges sat on the deck, and Corona asked the rest of the assemblage to do the same.

This was done, and in the courtroom that took shape the little man Gutan sat higher than anyone else. It struck McMurtrey that this was the opposite of the way it should have been, for by rights the defendant should have been confined to a pit, a cage or some other ignominious position. What a despicable man!

He was innocent despite what he had said, until proven guilty. But wasn't that an artificial, socialized code? Why not guilty until proven innocent?

Corona was speaking about the "priority of crimes" issue again, requesting a vote by the judges. "Shall we try Gutan for murder only?" she asked.

"Which murder?" Makanji asked.

"Why, for the girl he brought. You mean for the others too, the dispatchees? But he was just doing his job, killing the ones the prison system told him to eliminate. If you're talking about all the crimes in his ancestry he confessed to, that's either ludicrous or beyond anything we can deal with. We'd all have to go on trial with him, and we'd need access to the mnemonic machine to gather evidence."

"Inevitably an investigation on that scale would get into karmic law," Makanji said, "although I have never heard of a genetic, physical link to karma. I will set that aside for the moment. We have been told to deal with the matter of Gutan, presumably in this plane of existence. So I do wish to consider the dispatchees that he eliminated. He performed his job for the wrong reasons, for personal reasons. He defiled corpses."

"So what?" Corona said. "That's not murder. That's rape or the necro thing—that's violating remains of the dead."

"But what if Gutan encountered evidence that a particular dispatchee was innocent, and subsequently he dispatched the person anyway to obtain a fresh corpse for himself?"

"Oh, come on," Orbust said. "What kind of evidence could an executioner encounter? Those people all had trials before they ended up on Death Row."

"Several points," Makanji said. "First, some of the dispatchees were 'war criminals' sentenced to death by BOL tribunals without trial. Those tribunals are political, notoriously corrupt, and the prisoners didn't deserve death by any stretch of the imagination. Just because Mr. Gutan followed orders doesn't relieve him of moral responsibility."

"You can't be serious!" Orbust exclaimed.

"We are here to deal with 'the matter of Gutan,'" Makanji said. "In a court beyond the BOL, beyond D'Urth's laws. This is a trial assigned by God, a very high court. And in that court, the defendant should be held to different standards."

"God didn't specify a trial," Corona said. "We decided upon it."

"In effect, God decided," Makanji insisted. "He established the ground rules, narrowed the choices available."

"And a waste of time this will be if a trial isn't one of the right choices," McMurtrey said, his brows furrowing intensely. "If we're going to have a trial, we can't quibble over every detail."

"This is not quibbling," Corona rasped. "We're talking about a man's life!"

"But how do we know what criteria we should use in judging Gutan?" McMurtrey said. "With so many choices, so many possible refinements, how do we know . . ." He shook his head.

"We vote and hope for the best," she said.

"What if Gutan were told to dispatch a murderer," Makanji asked, "and encountered evidence through the operation of Mnemo that the dispatchee committed no murder? From what he told us about the machine, it had a screen that showed the life experiences of a person connected to it. What if Gutan saw in that bioelectronic chronicle irrefutable evidence of innocence?"

"But the machine would have been on at that point," Orbust said, "programmed for execution."

"And early in the programming," Makanji pointed out, "since the alleged act of murder would have occurred during the first life in a long genetic sequence of lives. Maybe early enough for Gutan to hit a switch and save the subject. We don't know enough about Mnemo yet. There are questions to ask."

Whisperings carried around the room.

"Is murder even the worst crime here?" Makanji asked. "Couldn't violating the dead be just as bad or even worse? Aren't the dead sacred?"

"What about Gutan's confessions?" McMurtrey asked. "What if he's lying about them? What if he did none of that? Maybe everything he said was a lie and his solitary crime was the murder of the girl. What if he's insane?"

"It would be handy to have Mnemo here right now," Orbust said. "Man, I'd like to get my hands on that device!"

"Gutan could be innocent by reason of insanity," Corona said, with a great, heaving sigh.

"Big fun," Zatima said. "Well, let's wade into it. I say we deal with Gutan as a whole; we deal with his entire story, making no artificial attempt to segregate and prioritize his acts. We look at Gutan as a whole and we sentence him as a whole."

"How say the judges?" Corona asked.

A brief discussion ensued, and ultimately everyone agreed with Zatima. It was further agreed that Gutan would retell his story, and questions would be entertained along the way.

"We have fourteen hours, nine minutes," Corona said. "Mr. Gutan, please begin."

Sitting cross-legged, McMurtrey stared at Harley Gutan. The bearded little apeman was nervous, and his voice trailed off so badly at times during his account that Corona repeatedly ordered him to speak up.

He's guilty of something, McMurtrey thought as this went on, *or at least he thinks he is*.

Gutan went into more detail than before, addressing some of the points raised by Makanji.

"I never considered morality," Gutan said, "whether a particular dispatchee should actually have been dispatched or not. This doesn't reflect on my guilt or innocence before the court and before God, I suppose, because maybe I should have thought about things that never occurred to me. Maybe each of us has a set of moral obligations when we're brought into existence."

Krassos! McMurtrey thought. *How does this little pervert come off making an observation like that?*

"I was on opium some of the time," Gutan admitted. "Not during every dispatching, at least not during the first ones. The opium came later. With what happened to me in Mnemo, with everything that occurred to bring me here, I've been forced to think about larger issues. I could probably even decide my own fate, and I think I'd do it fairly. I just wish I had a chance —something I could actually do. . . . Saying I'm sorry isn't enough, for those are mere words and words die in the wind. Actions are more important than words. This isn't a cliché; it's the purest form of moral truth. And what good are actions if they can't correct what has been done?"

"Don't digress," Corona said. "No time."

"Pardon me. The war criminals . . . I dispatched them without thinking of their crimes, and the same with the others. Truthfully, I never checked to see if a murderer really was a murderer. That didn't seem like my position,

I guess, and any of their lifetime events that appeared on the screen just went by in a blur, a blur from one dispatchee to another. Sometimes I did fifty in a single day. I only thought about doing things with some of the women. . . . There was no pattern to the type of women I liked, but they had to be women—except for one dark night in Central Eassornia. . . ."

Gutan's voice trailed away, and he cleared his throat before continuing.

"I fantasized while they were alive, went through the motions of dispatching them. It was when they were alive that I selected my bed partner for each day."

"One bed partner per day?" Corona asked.

"Less. I made love maybe three times a week, kind of like a normal person."

Several onlookers snickered.

"Somewhere along the line I began to suspect—I don't remember when—that it was all a secret government experiment. They had me use all kinds of different settings on the machine, and with that government computer hooked to Mnemo I assumed all the data was being recorded and transmitted to Prison HQ, maybe even higher than that."

"Maybe we should put the Inner Planet League, the BOL or the prison system on trial, since some combination of them provided Gutan with Mnemo," McMurtrey said. "Maybe blame falls on the whole fucking human race that culminated in this bloated, obscene wart called Gutan."

"There is precedent for that," Corona said. "According to Appy's data banks, since early times there have been causal attribution doctrines in society. If a man carelessly left a loaded gun on a table and another man accidentally bumped the gun, causing it to discharge, the owner of the gun was held at least partially liable for resulting injuries. This led to the doctrines of contributory and comparative negligence. On a broader scale, judges and juries long have tussled with the effects of society and circumstance upon the crimes of individuals."

"I have an odd feeling that 'the matter of Gutan' is more than 'the matter of Gutan,' " McMurtrey said, looking at Corona. "Anything in data storage on that?"

"No."

"I . . . want to tell everything," Gutan said. "Since arriving here, I've felt compelled to tell the truth. . . . This is my last opportunity to clear things up."

"This guy's a Krassian or wants to be!" Yakkai shouted. "KothoLu absolution, is that what it's all about? Confess to murder and rape, say you accept Krassos and you get a ticket to Heaven. What a sick, e-vile religion! Evildoers don't need to perform restitution or anything."

The KothoLu archbishop, Perrier, rose and requested permission to speak. It was granted by Corona, and he said, "It is not so simple as our atheist friend asserts. It is not merely the utterance of words. Consider the analogy of a person applying for a job. The sinner is the applicant; God is the employer. The job: an everlasting position in Heaven. God can see through lies. If the sinner lies about accepting Krassos, lies about seeking true forgiveness from the Lord, God will see that and will reject the applicant."

"Where did you get that interpretation?" Yakkai asked.

Singh looked ready to explode, was held in check by a gesture from Zatima.

"It is our belief," Perrier said.

"I've always wondered myself," McMurtrey said, "how is it that Reeshna, Hoddha, Mother Beverly and a whole host of others who led lovely, exemplary lives are said to mire in Hell simply because they did not accept Krassos? I don't see the logic of that."

"It's a matter of faith," Perrier said, "a matter of believing."

"You're floundering," Yakkai rasped. "If you can't defend your faith rationally, it isn't a sensible faith and should be scorned by decent people."

"Faith is by definition precisely that: faith. It is not a reasoned set of concepts. It is from the heart. It is love."

"This court is being very patient," Corona said.

Archbishop Perrier resumed his seat.

"Suddenly my entire life seems like it belongs to another entity," Gutan said, "and some of my words don't seem to be my own, like I have no right to them, like I have no right to think pure and decent things. It's not that I'm trying to phony up my testimony, just the opposite. I'm revealing everything I can, everything I know. I feel like a person looking in a mirror, and the person looking back is not me. I describe the person I see; I am separate from that person but inevitably connected."

"Sounds like an insanity defense to me," Yakkai said.

Corona looked at Yakkai sternly, and said, "Mr. Yakkai, I do not wish to have you removed, since everyone on this ship should be allowed to participate. I feel it is best that way. But you must yield to others, particularly to the judges and to the defendant, so that this proceeding can continue. Please have a seat."

Grudgingly, Yakkai did as he was told.

"An insanity plea would mean nothing," Gutan said. "There are no acceptable, consistent standards of sanity for any life form or society of life forms. All life, all existence, is in a constant state of flux."

"Please confine yourself to facts and events," Corona said.

"An important question should be addressed," Appy said, spurting words across Corona's lips almost before she finished. "Can a criminal, a murderer, find God? Is Harley Gutan in the Great Race himself, on a footing equal with the most pious?"

Corona scowled, and the pulse in her throat throbbed wildly, as if the vocal chords were divided between host and intruder. Corona appeared unable to speak, and McMurtrey was deeply worried about her.

McMurtrey heard Appy's faint, insidious laugh, wondered about Appy's sanity and life impetus. What exactly was a biocomputer? Did it learn from experience, as intelligent life forms did? Or was it a synthesized but restricted creation, programmed to behave only in certain ways? Had it been programmed to be insane? It had behaved strangely even before the collision.

McMurtrey felt a solidly grounded definition of sanity, despite what Gutan said and despite the unpredictable, sometimes bizarre behavior of Appy. This grounding was associated with right and wrong, and had a direct bearing upon the matter McMurtrey had been called upon to judge. Sanity kept the individual from suicide or murder each day, prevented a headlong tumble into Hell.

It was the same with society: an ethical basis, a code of right and wrong for individuals in that society kept the group sane and alive, prevented it from self-destructing or annihilating another society.

The Afsornian's words registered in McMurtrey's brain: *"We must be flexible enough to make no assumptions about what is right and what is wrong . . . morality is a social condition . . . no such thing as a universal wrong . . ."*

McMurtrey realized his "grounding" was Wessornian-biased, and he tried to envision casting aside that bias entirely, looking at Gutan with totally different eyes.

But how can I do that if my memories, my life experiences remain? I am the sum of my life, a human offshoot from the same tree as Harley Gutan.

McMurtrey found his mind spinning in a slow circle, clicking into position at various points and then coming all the way around again to the place he had begun. It was at once confusing and exhilarating, for him an unprecedented mental exercise.

Gutan tried to stay on Corona's track, describing the events of his life. He skipped about, touching upon his early years as a mortician, then to the League Penitentiary System position and back again to events before that. Occasionally a judge, Appy or someone in the audience would ask Gutan a question and he would answer it, citing bits and pieces from his life to illustrate.

Orbust asked some very good questions, it seemed to McMurtrey, while Appy asked some that were very bad and superfluous, often overriding Corona to do so. This inability of Corona to dominate Appy troubled McMurtrey to the point where he was beginning to grieve for her, as for one who had lapsed irrecoverably into illness.

Nothing was as it should have been, for somewhere along the line Johnny Orbust had become rational, or seemingly so, while the computer, which should have been a rational entity, was demonstrating precisely the opposite. It was the matter of perceptions once more, correct or incorrect, the perceptions one person or life form had for another. It seemed to McMurtrey that the human mind was constantly taking perceptive readings, constantly evaluating and reevaluating, constantly trying to categorize everything into comfortable niches of personal experience. It was most unsettling when an individual, an event or a thing could not be labeled and stuffed away neatly.

Orbust was categorized now as rational, and McMurtrey was not the only one to arrive at this conclusion: Orbust had been voted onto the council. But just as McMurtrey's mind clicked slowly around, so too he realized it might be with Orbust. Under certain circumstances the old and obstreperous Orbust might return.

Predictability... We are most comfortable when we can predict, when familiar patterns hold course.

Most people were like clay. They conformed to pressures around them, became what they were expected to become.

Did biocomputers operate within similar constraints? This unit called Appy had become a most unsettling thing to be near. With time a critical factor it kept overriding Corona, forcing the trial onto tangents, opening avenues of conversation that seemed totally unrelated to the fate of Gutan. What was Appy saying now? McMurtrey found it difficult to focus, heard the voice of his own thoughts above the voices of anyone participating in the proceedings. Just as Appy was digressing, so too was McMurtrey and so too it seemed were the others. It had become exceedingly loud in the courtroom, with a number of conversations going on simultaneously.

Time was running out!

McMurtrey shook his head to clear it, thought he detected something gelatinous inside his skull, as if his brains were thick gelatin.

"What do you do when you see a man with a gimpy leg falling over?" Appy asked.

When no one answered, Appy said, "Get a stick and push the gimp over. Why be nicer to him than God was?"

Sister Mary was seated near the front, and when she heard this she spoke anxiously to the other nun.

Corona's lips moved, without sounds emanating, and her eyes were angry.

"Appy's defective," McMurtrey said, "worse than ever since the collision. Kelly, you okay?"

She shook her head. She closed her mouth tightly, and through the noise of conversation in the room McMurtrey again heard Appy's distant, deranged laugh.

Corona heaved a great sigh, shrugged her shoulders.

Then a strange and perplexed expression came over Co-

rona's face, and her lips moved tentatively. "I can...
speak...again," she said, in her own voice. "I believe the
difficulty has passed...data flow.... Apparently I was
trying too hard, and the harder I tried, the more difficult
it became to speak. When I relaxed and gave up the battle
I felt clearly that there were no obstacles before me, that
I could master the intruder within my body."

Appy's voice: "You are not! I can..."

"You can and may speak only when I will it," Corona
interjected, with a stiff smile. "And for the moment I do
not so will."

Corona's throat pulsed briefly, but Appy said nothing.

"Talk about nutso," Yakkai said. "Maybe you should
sit in Gutan's chair."

McMurtrey glanced at Gutan, saw him sitting serenely
and patiently, apparently awaiting a signal from someone
in authority that he should continue.

"New and important information is flowing into my consciousness," Corona said. "We must understand suffering
if we are to deal sufficiently with the matter of Gutan.
With the path we have selected—a trial—it will be necessary to punish him. No just punishment can be ordered
by judges ignorant of suffering."

"Beat each other up!" a man shouted. It sounded like
Tully.

"Suffering on what scale?" Zatima asked. "On the scale
of an individual, of a persecuted people, or of all mankind?"

"That is all I know at this time," Corona answered.
"When Appy's program first entered my body I thought
I had access to all of it. Maybe that wasn't correct, or
maybe this is new data fed by comlink from God to Appy.
I can't tell."

"How can we tell if the information Corona has provided
us so far is complete or accurate?" Feek the Afsornian
asked.

"You must evaluate it for yourself with the brains that
God gave you," Corona said. "Neither God nor Appy are
on this judicial council. I am, and the information I have
imparted seems reasonable and accurate to me."

"How do we know any information is complete or accurate?" Zatima asked.

"The subject is suffering," Yakkai said, "and I just want five more minutes, okay? I know something about the subject, and I'd like to toss out a few preliminaries."

Corona glanced at her Wriskron. "Five minutes and counting."

Yakkai cleared his throat. "God is omnipresent, omniscient, and omnipotent, or so the tale goes. If so, why does He allow suffering? Now hear me out, this is important! It seems to me that your God must be weak if He can't eliminate suffering. If He exists at all."

"What does this have to do with . . ." Corona began.

"There must be suffering for a time," Orbust interjected. "Krassos said there would be wars and rumors of wars, famines, pestilences, false prophets and lawlessness, with the love of many growing cold. 'But he who endures to the end shall be saved.' The Lord God Almighty told Krassos to sit at His right hand, ruling D'Urth in the midst of His enemies."

"I don't care about all that scripture crap," Yakkai said. "I think suffering is wrong, it should end, and I want it to end right now! How long must people suffer?"

"Krassianism is similar to Middism and other faiths," McMurtrey said. "They believe there will be an end to suffering when the Messiah comes."

"Please don't encourage this, Ev," Corona said.

"I've heard all that gobbledygook," Yakkai said. "Don't you see? With that kind of philosophy, there's always an excuse for suffering. It's always something in the future that will happen if humankind behaves as it's supposed to, if people accede to church power structures, if they fill church coffers with money. These are old deceptions: the unfulfilled promise, the carrot in front of the donkey."

"There's no use discussing this subject with you," Orbust said. "We'll tie everything up in an argument." He looked at the other judges. "Do any of you . . ."

"Suffering is linked to the concept of miracles," Yakkai said, "and this is essential to our discussion. If there are no provable miracles, much of religion is a farce. And if there are provable miracles it is still a monstrous farce, for no powerful God would need miracles. He would set everything up properly in the beginning, and by virtue of His omnipotence He would have no need for stage tricks."

"Utterly preposterous," Orbust said.

"Mr. Yakkai," Corona said, "please stop using this courtroom as a platform for atheism. We all know you don't believe in God."

"My five minutes isn't up," Yakkai said, seeming to bore right through Corona with his gaze. He looked at Orbust, asked, "Can God do anything?"

Orbust, after hesitating: "Yes."

"Can He make a rock so heavy He can't lift it?"

"God can do anything."

"He can make a rock that He can't lift?"

"If He so chooses."

"But you said He could do anything. Why then can't He lift the rock?"

"By choice," Orbust said.

Yakkai smiled savagely, and in a sarcastic tone said, "Sure." Then: "Could God make Himself young?"

"Yes."

"Could God make Himself ignorant or foolish?"

"If He wanted to. I can think of no reason, however, why He would want to. I grow tired of your little game, and do not see—"

"What does this have to do with suffering?" Corona asked, impatiently.

"If God can make Himself foolish, that explains a lot of things," Yakkai said, "including the business about man being made in God's image. I submit to you that the concept of God is ludicrous, that nothing happening to us has anything to do with God. Your mythical gods have been assigned comical attributes, the stuff of fertile human imagination. Suffering, Ms. Corona—yes, suffering. Why has Mr. Gutan here suffered, and why has he caused others to suffer? How is this council to make him suffer for what he has done?"

Corona shook her head. "We've heard enough of this."

But Yakkai was on a roll: "Consider the atrocities in the name of religion. Charmag converting 'barbarians' to Krassianism at the point of a sword; Krassian missionaries zealously destroying native cultures in the Bluepac Seas; Isammedans massacring Krassians and Nandus; Nandus shooting and butchering Isammedans and ParKekhs; Hoddhists beheading Middists. Has organized religion—"

"Mr. Singh," Corona said, in her loudest voice, "please remove Yakkai from the room! We can't have any more of this!"

Singh lifted Yakkai rudely to his feet, dragged him toward the corridor door.

"We are not without ties to history!" Yakkai yelled. "We are the culmination of the sins of organized religion over centuries, just as Gutan is the culmination of all that is vile in man. Who are you to judge Gutan? How can you pass judgment upon him when your sins are just as great? This proceeding is a farce!"

Singh dragged the offender from the room, closing the door behind them.

"We can't go into all of that here" Corona said, with a tight smile. "As for suffering, I'm sorry I was forced to bring it up. Haven't we suffered enough for it?"

Laughter rolled through the great room.

Corona stopped, and her face flushed bright red. Capricious laughter came from her mouth, Appy's laughter.

"I don't like this," Corona said. "I'm suspecting now that Appy put us on the track of suffering as a demented joke, that I didn't gain as much control over Appy as I thought I did, that he's playing possum. Maybe I should step down."

"What about this trial?" McMurtrey asked.

"We came up with it," Orbust said. "Not Appy."

"But it was Corona who said we had to deal with the matter of Gutan before the ship would restart," McMurtrey said, "and she got that data from Appy's program."

McMurtrey caught Corona's gaze. She appeared confused, not angry with him for his words.

"I think the discussion of suffering was appropriate," Feek the Afsornian said, "and that Gutan must be dealt with. Maybe the question should be: 'How can we as human beings reduce the suffering of our fellow man?' Can any of you call upon your God to bring an immediate end to suffering?"

The room became silent.

"I thought not. It is up to us, therefore, up to all of mankind. We should have no excuses for the pain we inflict upon other humans and other life forms. Suffering has become an eternal, senseless thing. Perhaps we have the opportunity now to reverse the tide. Perhaps—"

"All right you bastards, I have a bomb!" It was Yakkai bursting back into the room, with Singh a distance behind him, sword drawn.

"It's in my pocket!" Yakkai screamed. "And I'll blow all of you to Hell! That'll end your fucking suffering!" He ran to a side wall, held his hand in one bulging pocket.

"He's as crazy as Gutan, Corona and Appy!" a woman screeched. "May God have mercy upon our souls!"

From all around, holy men jumped to their feet, drawing swords and guns.

"No violence," Corona yelled. "Yakkai doesn't have a bomb. Appy scanned every boarder, made a computer record of every weapon. Yakkai is disturbed. He's bluffing."

"I don't have a lot of confidence in that information," Orbust said, just loudly enough for nearby judges to hear him.

"I made the bomb after I boarded," Yakkai said. His gaze skittered around the room from face to face, locked onto Nanak Singh. "Keep him away from me! If I take my hand off the activator, it blows! Anyone tries to shoot me, it blows!"

Zatima motioned for Singh to step back, and he did, keeping his sword drawn.

"Assuming you have a bomb," McMurtrey said, "why would you want to blow us up?"

"Why not? What difference would it make? The explosion wouldn't even be a blip on the screen of the universe." Yakkai positioned himself apart from the others, defensively, with his back against a wall.

"Maybe you're right about a lot of things," McMurtrey offered, "about God's weakness, about meaningless suffering. But what if this journey of ours could make a difference? You're obviously a sensitive man, Shalom ben Yakkai. I ask you, I ask everyone here, to give this venture a chance."

"What venture?" Gutan asked. "You haven't decided what to do with me."

"We have eleven hours, twenty minutes," Corona said,

eyeing her Wriskron. "If everyone agrees, I'd like Mr. Gutan to finish his story."

Yakkai looked edgy.

"I'm sure he's bluffing," Corona said to Zatima, her voice low.

The trial continued, while Yakkai became silently alert, watching everyone he considered a threat.

Gutan's skin had a sickly, slimy sheen to it as he spoke nervously and haltingly for another hour, filling McMurtrey with the image of a life wasted, with hardly any socially acceptable deeds. It was damning information from a man testifying in the climactic event of his life, his own trial. Did Gutan want to die, didn't he care, or was it as he said, a compulsion to tell the truth?

He's sweating Evil, McMurtrey decided. *An Evil that oozes from his pores.*

Gutan finished with a graphic account of his tryst at Santa Quininas with the corpse of the massive, pendulous-breasted woman.

All the while, McMurtrey's brain spun with the punishments he might recommend. Surely such sinister acts could not go unpunished, by any stretch of imagination. He felt sick to his stomach, and his gaze flitted between the accused, Singh and Yakkai.

For an instant, the gazes of McMurtrey and Yakkai locked, and Yakkai's hand moved just a little out of his pocket, with nothing in the hand. No explosion occurred, and as Yakkai slipped his hand back into the pocket he winked.

McMurtrey glanced around, didn't see anyone else who had noticed. So Yakkai was bluffing! Yakkai had stolen precious time from the trial, for a purpose he probably couldn't explain himself. Maybe he did it to get free of Singh, so he could return to the trial. At least he was quieter now.

What an assortment, McMurtrey thought. *No wonder we've fallen out of the race.*

Finally Gutan spoke his last, and there were no more questions.

Corona ordered that Gutan remain in place while she and the other judges retired to Assembly Room B-2 to arrive at their decisions.

Yakkai remained where he was by the wall, without a word.

The judges sat in a row, on the side of the assembly room facing the window. This gave McMurtrey a distraction, for he stared into space when he should have been participating in the conversation around him. Outside and covering the expanse of the window were glimmering white balls, with each spaced a meter or so from the other, and these stood in three-dimensional relief against parallel white lines that stretched into infinite space. Between the lines, squinting or not, McMurtrey saw only stars that blinked faintly. Somewhere in that sprinkling of solar systems lay the planet Tananius-Ofo.

Makanji was talking, something about there being no question of Gutan's guilt.

"Does anyone think the man is innocent?" Makanji asked. "Certainly he did everything he said he did, and I'm inclined to believe him about the girl. I don't understand how he came to have the girl in his arms or how he traversed the universe, but I don't think he killed her."

Zatima and Orbust voiced concurrence, and McMurtrey perceived irony in these two agreeing on anything. The fight with Singh marked an apparent turning point in Orbust's behavior. Still in his healing packs, he seemed like a different man, quieter and more polite, probably because he felt weaker and less sure of himself without the gun, the chemstrip and the Snapcard. What a humiliating experience the beating must have been!

Makanji again, saying a godless man could only know God in another incarnation.

McMurtrey's eyesight glazed over, and he recalled the vision he'd had just before the trial, when in another dimension he looked into the Nandu's timeless, pale eyes. What color had the bespectacled eyes been? McMurtrey couldn't recall, didn't know that they'd been of any color he could distinguish.

Like a dreamer unable to awaken, he couldn't find the dimension in which Makanji spoke now. The eye color was in that dimension. . . .

For an instant, McMurtrey perceived himself at the center of everything, at the nexus of all life, of all death, of all matter and all nonmatter. It was a featureless pinpoint of light with dulcet visual harmonies, where McMurtrey bore all of the contents of the universe.

The pinpoint of light twinkled, and in slow motion McMurtrey saw it expand into human form. The form shuddered, became pale aura-yellow and then reshaped to a fetal ball that became a perfect white ball.

McMurtrey's sensation of self shifted. His eyes stung and he blinked them. Now he saw the white balls outside the window again, and one of them uncurled, back to human form. McMurtrey's gut jerked, his heart fluttered and he couldn't catch his breath.

He was looking at an albino of himself, an ungodly creature that stared at him with sightless eyes. It flattened its face against the glass, screamed desperate shapes with its mouth.

"*Let me in!*"

McMurtrey was outside, looking through the plexwindow at his fat, flesh-warm self. He couldn't breathe in the rarefied air.

"*Break the glass!*"

Something shook him. A strong hand on his arm. Corona's face came into focus, her expression tender and concerned.

"How you doing, Ev?" she whispered.

"Oh, fine. No problem. My mind's been wandering."

"Well, keep track of it!" Corona smiled.

"What are you two whispering about?" Feek demanded.

"Nothing," Corona said, resuming her seat. "Let's see, we were all agreeing that Gutan is guilty of despicable crimes. No murders, but on balance he's probably worse than some murderers. Gutan's own admissions tell us more than any of us want to know. The man makes me sick, and I'd like to strangle him with my own hands."

McMurtrey felt his breathing and heartbeat resume regularity, and he inhaled deeply.

"Or blow his brains out," Zatima suggested. "What a worm to lay across our path."

"What do we do with the son of a bitch?" McMurtrey asked.

Looking sidelong, McMurtrey saw Corona smiling

wryly. "We kiss him and ask him to be a good boy from
now on," she said.

"He does seem contrite," Feek said.

McMurtrey had been entrusted with one seventh of the
decision about Gutan's life, and was angry with himself
for daydreaming when he should have been paying attention. His behavior was unconscionable, and seemed to be
yet another failing of his mind, like the spells of mental
paralysis he used to suffer at the sight of another person's
nervous tics.

The new spells were debilitating to McMurtrey in a different way. Now McMurtrey's thoughts weren't paralyzed,
weren't an amorphous, unusable mass. His thoughts were
too abundant, too rich and consuming. Was Appy doing
this to him?

Through it all, McMurtrey didn't seem to have missed
anything critical in the trial. Gutan had confessed and
seemed remorseful for his acts. But what difference did
remorse make?

*I'm doing it again! What are they discussing? . . . the sen-
tence . . .*

" 'Some shall they cause to be put to death,' " Orbust
intoned. "We cannot tolerate such failure of virtue."

"According to our Isammed law of Haria," Zatima said,
"punishments normally only apply if the crime is committed within an Isammed state. Victims, or the families of
victims, can take vengeance upon the perpetrator. This
situation calls for flexibility, but of a different variety from
that suggested by the Afsornian. I have decided to assign
a punishment as if Gutan's acts occurred in an Isammed
nation. Death by stoning is appropriate, or by the hurling
of available heavy objects at the accused. I will perform
the task myself, if no one else has the stomach for what
must be done."

She finished, and McMurtrey realized that he was seated
next in line.

The sentence! McMurtrey thought. *They're looking at
me!* "Death," McMurtrey said, not very loudly. "By a
humane method . . . like lethal injection."

"There's a lot of information in data storage about the
methods of punishment employed by other cultures and

religions," Corona said. "I'm suspicious of it, but I want to study the data before offering an opinion."

"I don't think this trial is the answer at all," McMurtrey said. "I think if everyone on this ship can cooperate, can work together, we'll advance closer to God, we'll reach God! This ship represents D'Urth, our solar system and all of mankind—the whole course of humanity from here on. If we don't go forward, man doesn't go forward. If this ship doesn't get closer to God, man doesn't get closer to God."

"But there are other ships coming behind us," Zatima said, "with more chances aboard each ship."

"Do we know for certain they're in flight?" McMurtrey challenged. "What if we're the only one?"

"I think we should come up with a sentence," Corona said.

McMurtrey shook his head in annoyance, looked away. He felt betrayed by Corona.

"We can't take the prisoner's life," Makanji said. "Gutan's actions will force him to seek the suffering of rebirth, into another incarnation. Only when he discovers the purity of nonattachment, when he shuns material objects and pleasures of the flesh, will he be free of worldly suffering."

"He must not be killed," Taam the Hoddhist priest agreed. "There will be other incarnations, and one day he will be free of ignorance, free of suffering."

"What goes around comes around," Orbust commented. "So we're addressing suffering, after all. I think Gutan should suffer in this life. Vote for death!"

The Hoddhist shook his head stubbornly.

"It's three to two favoring death," Zatima said.

Now Feek gathered his elegant robe and paced as he spoke. "Mr. Gutan killed no kin, so he has committed no crimes worthy of death. He should be banished from the tribe, placed in isolation to spend the rest of his miserable days reflecting upon his antisocial ways. He was never born and his name will never again be uttered."

Orbust whispered to Zatima, out of McMurtrey's hearing range.

Zatima's features darkened, and she glared at Orbust. But she nodded her head in apparent affirmation. Incredibly they not only agreed on certain points, but they were communicating with one another.

"I'm the tie-breaker," Corona said. "Although any of you can change your votes. Let's spend a while reviewing alternatives, and hopefully we can agree on something."

Jin awoke to the surging green noise of his Duplication program. He heard nothing else, saw nothing else. The headache was no more, but he felt out of synchronization.

Something was terribly wrong, grossly dysfunctional, and it was beyond his ability to field repair.

The drive to duplicate dominated him, colored green his entire artificial soul with program noise. All of his cyberoo survival instincts funneled into one thought: *Fulfill the directives of the program.*

His parabolic sensor led him through noisy green darkness, and he ran into the screen of his cabin. With the strength of fifty humans he tore through, reaching the outer mezzanine.

He knew approximately where he was, groped along the mezzanine railing to the stairway.

His feet were negotiating stairs, and from his memory of the ship's layout, he thought this must be down. But it didn't seem like down, didn't seem like up, either. His senses reported flatness.

Tully skirted the edge of the main passenger compartment, toward the entrance to the stairway he had seen Nanak Singh enter only seconds before.

Tully touched a wall button, and the door slid open. He glanced back at the crowd awaiting the decision of the judges, satisfied himself that no one was paying him any attention.

He slipped into the stairway landing, and the door closed crisply behind him.

A scuffling sound froze him where he stood, and looking up he saw Jin emerge from the landing above, naked as usual, rounding the turn there. Jin moved oddly, as if drunk or drugged, and from the sightless look of his eyes Tully speculated he must be immersed in a heathen trance.

Jin didn't seem to see anyone, and Tully scurried onto the down staircase.

Tully would deal with that shameless pervert in due course. First the other one.

Tully negotiated the steps with catlike control, making not a whisper of a sound. He reached the first landing below the assembly room levels, where he paused and peered over the banister.

One level down, Singh touched a wall button, and a thick metal door slid open. The ParKekh disappeared into the opening, and the door thunked shut behind him, with unusual loudness.

Tully knew the destination of his prey, for once before he had followed the man to a sublevel shrine room where Singh kept his eternal flame.

It wasn't eternal anymore, and the note in calligraphic script that Tully left would have predictable results. It read:

> *I want it this way. You've been*
> *a fool all your life.*
> *—God*

Tully hurried to the doorway he had seen the ParKekh go through. He crouched there to one side.

The wait was short.

"Eeeeeyah!" Nanak Singh's scream rang like a battle cry, and subsequently it came forth twice more, louder each time.

"Eeeeeyah! Eeeeeyah!"

The door slammed open, crunching into the wall, and in the doorway Tully saw the tip of a sword.

Surprise had its advantages, and Tully knew what he had to do. He'd known it when he crouched here after setting in motion the rage of his adversary. Rage in an opponent blocked thought, made victory easier.

Nanak Singh was in the doorway, heading for the stairs.

With a leaping, powerful thrust of both hands, Tully broke the ParKekh's neck before he could twitch the sword.

Singh crumpled to the deck.

Now I'll slip back into the courtroom, Tully thought. *With so many people, they'll never know I was gone.*

He began ascending the steps, and the last thing he ever saw was a flaming baby howitzer, firing from Jin's crotch.

• • •

After pausing on the main passenger compartment landing, Jin had continued down the stairs behind Tully. From above, the cyberoo's parabolic sensor had picked up the murder of Singh, transmitting it to Jin's throbbing Duplication program.

But Jin's aberrant systems hadn't transmitted the message with exactness, reporting to his interpretive core only one act, Tully's. And it was an act without detail of method, simply the cessation of human life brought on by another human.

Jin had to conceptualize his own means of duplication. Hence the artillery.

Now it was after the gunfire and he was beginning to see—a green filtered vision. Beneath him in the stairwell lay two human bodies, and from somewhere came the disjointed grunts and hummings of human conversation. It was painful green noise, piercing his interpretive core, jabbing him rudely.

He had to end the pain, end the noise.

Jin whirled, began negotiating the stairs. Through green awareness he focused on the door to Assembly Room Level B, then passed it. Within moments he pressed the wall button beside the door to the main passenger compartment.

It was slow to open, so with his hands he ripped the pocket door out of the doorway and the wall.

Eleven

All things can be accomplished; it is the time limit imposed from within and without that presents the major obstacle.

—Ancient Saying

Corona had the floor.

"As our Afsornian friend pointed out, and as I was unaware, among his people it is only murder to kill kin. Some societies even condone cannibalism, infanticide, the sale of dangerous products, theft and the killing of witches. In other societies a criminal must have *mens rea*, a 'guilty mind,' in order to be convicted: This means he must be sane, must have intent and must understand the difference between right and wrong. Other societies don't care about intent. They care only about consequence.

"Assuming Appy hasn't tampered with the data, this gives us a broader picture, which I feel the situation demands. We have an obligation not to restrict our decision to parochial views, for God did invite representatives from thousands of belief systems to his deep-space tea party."

The other judges agreed that this was useful information.

Corona continued: "Politics and religion often come into play in the judgment of guilt or innocence and in the punishment meted out. Some societies have no terminology for crime. Sometimes alcohol or drugs legally diminish the culpability of a person, and it is known that Gutan took opium."

"Irrelevant," Orbust said. "Gutan dispatched people and raped corpses both *before* and after he became addicted to opium. He took no drugs as a young funeral-home employee when he stole personal valuables from the dead. So he can't blame his crimes on addiction.''

"You're right," Corona said. She trembled slightly. "I'm hearing something. Gunfire? Do any of you hear it?"

No one did.

"Must be on comlink," Corona said. "Usually I can tell, but somehow I couldn't this time."

"What are you talking about?" Orbust asked.

"The comlink between Appy and Shusher!" Corona snapped. "Something's wrong!"

"We weren't going to talk about that," McMurtrey said. "Kelly, you're hearing gunfire?"

"Yes!"

McMurtrey: "It happened before Appy downloaded his program into Kelly. The way she got the comlink I won't go into, but the fact she has it probably made her the best candidate for Appy's 'save' maneuver."

"Shusher is whining," Corona said. "Popping in the background. Maybe it isn't gunfire."

"We don't hear it," Zatima said. "Should I go and get Singh?"

"I don't know," Corona said.

McMurtrey wanted to touch her, decided not to because of the others present.

"We must continue," Corona said. "We must not leave this room until we have arrived at our decision. I'm all right."

To McMurtrey she didn't look all right. She was still trembling, looked tense and fatigued.

"The options are not simply life or death," Taam the Hoddhist priest said, "or even the means of life, the means of death. There is nothing we can do with him, nothing we should do with him, nothing we have a right to do with him. Karmic law will deal with Gutan in subsequent incarnations. I sought this council position not to render a decision but to insist that we take no action."

"I agree," Makanji said.

"Hogwash," Zatima snarled.

The Hoddhist shook his head and said, in a low tone, "We will produce more reform with gentle words than with all the punishments conceived by men. Release him gently, as a newborn, and all mankind will benefit."

"Three for death and three for life, " Corona said in a tremulous voice, "unless any of you wish to change your votes."

No one spoke up.

She grimaced, said, "Makanji, in ancient Nandaic law, the Code specified that a judge should probe the heart of the accused, studying the eyes, the posture, the voice. . . . It was an ancient method of lie detection."

"My people no longer follow that code," Makanji said. "They had capital punishment in those days, too. Much has changed since then."

"I must make a tie-breaking decision," Corona said. "I have been observing Gutan's every movement, every intonation, every drop of perspiration, and with the assistance of Appy I have been able to organize this information so that all of it is available to me. I couldn't forget the tiniest detail if I wanted to, and in the absence of witnesses other than Gutan himself this is essential information indeed."

Zatima grumbled, kept her words to herself.

With a pained expression Corona glanced from face to face, avoiding McMurtrey's.

The room became exceedingly silent, awaiting her deciding vote.

But Corona fidgeted and wrinkled her face in discomfort. She went to one ear with her hand.

"The noise again?" McMurtrey asked. He realized now that he was *afraid* to touch her, rationalized that he didn't know what good he could do for her. He wasn't even sure who she was, if the Corona he loved was still alive.

"The comlink is locked open!" Corona shouted. "Ow! Shusher is wailing through it. . . . Those are gunshots! He's saying so!"

"Somebody shooting at Shusher?" McMurtrey asked.

"I can't tell!"

McMurtrey gathered his courage, went to her chair and ran his fingers through her hair. He heard nothing over the comlink. "You okay?" he asked.

She bumped his hand aside, looked at him without saying anything, her eyes screaming pain.

"Kelly!" He extended his hand toward her face.

She pulled away.

"Son of a whore!" McMurtrey cursed. He caught Orbust's glare.

"We have a three-three deadlock," McMurtrey said.
"Gutan is guilty, but we can't go further unless one of us
shifts our vote, or unless Kelly comes out of this. To hell
with the trial! I say we hold Gutan for the authorities on
D'Urth. Or hold him for God's judgment. Maybe we've
done enough to get this ship going. Anyway, I've had it
and I'm going to get medical help for Kelly."

With that, McMurtrey walked briskly from the room,
thinking of the infirmary nuns. He'd seen them in the main
passenger compartment, with the others.

Minutes before, the main passenger compartment
echoed with the staccato rhythm of automatic-weapons
fire, and every fiber of Gutan's body screeched: *Flee!*

But from his hiding place behind the chair, Gutan had
seen others try for stairways and corridors, and thus far
none had made it. The bodies of pilgrims lay blocking all
egress, to the point where anyone attempting those paths
would have to climb or leap over the dead and injured.

It had been only a brief time since the cyberoo killer
opened fire from gunports all over its body, moments that
seemed like much longer. Some of the pilgrims fought
ferociously, screaming battle cries as they leaped into the
fray. They hurled knives at the attacker, slashed at him
with swords, fired guns, pulverizers and stunbows.

But nothing damaged the cyberoo, and it advanced in-
terminably, stepped over and around bodies, peppering
gunfire at anything that moved. Blood and body parts were
everywhere. Terrible, chilling screams filled the room,
then fell off to a pall of deathly silence that left Gutan
feeling ill.

Something moved to his left. He glanced sideways, shifting his head only slightly.

It was the Middist atheist Shalom ben Yakkai, crawling
toward a gruesome heap of bodies, trying to get behind
them.

The killer cyberoo dispatched three pilgrims in a flurry
of gunfire, then used its crotch-mounted howitzer to blow
Sister Mary's head off.

The black-robed Greek Hetox priest burst forth with his

Blik Pulverizer rifle blazing, and he died in a volley that overkilled him. Four shots removed his arms and legs simultaneously, and the howitzer disintegrated what was left.

Yakkai froze in terror.

The cyberoo had seen Yakkai, fixing its human-simulated gaze on the pitiful, crouching man. Dispassionately, it stepped over two bodies, one of which was a boy, and skirted three others, approaching Yakkai.

"Take me first!" Gutan shouted, impulsively.

The cyberoo didn't look in his direction. It was as if it knew all along where Gutan was hiding, as if it had a computerized roll call of those who had been and would be dispatched—as if it intended to deal with Gutan separately, in a more horrible way than any of the others.

It occurred to Gutan now that those who died first were luckiest.

He realized he'd been thinking of the dead as dispatchees, as if the cyberoo were an executioner. It had to be so, Gutan decided, for cyberoos only did what they were programmed to do. But why? If this was a BOL operative, why hadn't it killed the pilgrims sooner?

It waited for me to join the ship's company, Gutan thought, with a sickening rush. *It's after me* and *the others— all in one neat package. . . .*

Gutan felt like a steer being slaughtered the wrong way, its meat tainted by adrenal chemicals from the fear of watching its brethren die, from the screams and smells of death.

The faces of everyone that Gutan had dispatched raced across his mind, followed by the faces of all he had embalmed before that. The grim parade ceased.

"Over here! " Gutan shouted, as loudly as he could.

The cyberoo was motionless now.

Gutan leaped from behind the chair, and with fluid movements placed himself between the cowering Yakkai and the killer.

Yakkai was whimpering, face buried in his hands. His fingers were wet with tears.

The cyberoo looked at Gutan with a quizzical expression. Then its gaze moved to Yakkai, and back to Gutan.

The gunports all over its body receded into flesh, in-

cluding the penis howitzer. The penis went limp, and in
front of Gutan stood what looked like an entirely nude
man, looking more bewildered than guilty.

"I am Jin," the man said simply. "A Plarnjarn. Excuse
me, but I must find my broom. We're required to whisk
away any bugs in our path, you know, lest we step on one.
It would never do to step on a bug."

Jin turned toward the doorway through which he had
entered, and as he walked in that direction a pile of bodies
in the doorway shifted, creating a path.

A big man stood in the doorway, looking in. It was
McMurtrey, one of the judges.

Jin passed between the bodies and nudged past Mc-
Murtrey, disappearing from view.

"What in the name of God happened in there?"
McMurtrey asked, as Jin passed.

But Jin's eyes appeared entranced, and he didn't look
at McMurtrey. Instead Jin climbed the stairs, slowly.

McMurtrey couldn't believe the carnage before him,
nearly gagged. His breathing was erratic. He slipped to
one side of the shredded doorway, fearful of entering the
room, and remained there several minutes.

Finally he took two deep breaths, exhaled slowly and
peeked around the doorway into the main passenger compartment. High above the carnage, on the sixth-level mezzanine, Jin padded along by the railing. Soon Jin
disappeared from view, in the vicinity of his cabin.

An eery silence penetrated McMurtrey's awareness, and
he became aware of movement across the room. Two figures—Gutan and Yakkai. Gutan was helping Yakkai to
his feet.

At first McMurtrey thought the armed pilgrims had an-
nihilated one other. Then Gutan went to him and related
a startlingly different story. Yakkai was with Gutan, confirmed the details.

Yakkai told more, of Gutan's heroism.

Gutan looked away with misty eyes while this was being
related.

McMurtrey felt a tightening in his stomach, said, "I've
noticed Jin's weird ways for a while now. I think he took
Orbust's Snapcard and chemstrip, and maybe other things.

He wasn't adhering to the nonattachment doctrine of his religion, seemed to favor material objects . . . but not this, dammit!"

The acrid opium odor of Gutan touched McMurtrey's nostrils.

"Let's get away from here," Yakkai said. "I can't bear it any longer."

They retreated to Assembly Room B-2.

Corona was in her chair, and McMurtrey sat by her. Her eyes no longer bore evidence of the pain that had sent McMurtrey for medical aid, but she said nothing. Cautiously, McMurtrey extended a hand and grasped one of hers.

She squeezed his hand.

In one ear, McMurtrey heard the low sonar whine of Shusher, a gentle noise unlike the cacophony Corona had described. One crisis seemed to be passing: Corona was better. But a larger one had taken its place.

Gutan retold the startling tale, but again said nothing of his heroism.

Feek the Afsornian fidgeted while Gutan spoke, and finally Feek seemed unable to endure any more.

"Sorcery!" he exclaimed. "Gutan is a sorcerer! I change my vote to death!" With a wavering voice he added, "Among my people, sorcery is always punishable by death. The vote is four to two for execution now, so it doesn't matter how Corona votes. This evil must be erased!"

"Jin's the killer, not Gutan!" Yakkai shouted.

Then Yakkai told of Gutan's noble act, and this astounded most of the judges.

But Feek believed none of this, and howled loudly, "The sorcerer's spell has been cast over Shalom ben Yakkai! He knows not what he says! We must act quickly, or all of us will be captured by the spell!"

McMurtrey felt Corona's grip on him tighten, and when he leaned across her and looked into her eyes, he saw the softness that he remembered so fondly. His spirits bounded, for he had been longing for this indication, this sign that Corona was once more the Corona of old.

Impulsively, he whispered to her, "Kelly, I . . ."

But McMurtrey hesitated, afraid Appy or others connected to the computer might overhear what he had to say.

Corona's grip weakened, and he detected fear in her eyes. Eavesdroppers no longer mattered to McMurtrey, for now his words had nothing to do with anything he wanted or needed. They were for Corona, to bring her back.

"I love you," he whispered. "Do you remember saying that to me, Kelly? 'I love you, Ev'?"

Someone called for a vote recount.

She turned her head slowly, and now her gaze was a dark-eyed, unbespectacled version of the Nandu, Makanji, that he had seen in the vision. It was a timeless gaze again, this one of love. McMurtrey and Corona might have been here or anywhere else, in this age or another. They might have been themselves or others.

The Afsornian said something, but McMurtrey didn't hear the words.

McMurtrey had this moment of love, of limitless, trusting adoration, and it transcended his own need for life. He had lived and experienced everything worth experiencing, because he had found this wondrous private niche in the complexity of the cosmos.

"I love you, Ev," she said.

"How do you vote, McMurtrey?" someone said. McMurtrey realized seconds later it had been Feek, and now he saw the elegantly robed Afsornian standing over him with the others.

"You must vote," Feek said.

"I need more time," McMurtrey said. He exchanged glances with Corona.

"I need time to consider my vote too," Corona said. "My pain has passed."

"We must deal with Gutan now!" Feek exclaimed.

"We must deal with Jin now!" Yakkai said, so forcefully next to Feek that his words nearly knocked the Afsornian over. "That killer could strike again, probably will. He ripped a door right out of the wall. No human weapon fazed him. He just kept coming!"

"Where is Jin now?" Zatima asked.

"I saw him go upstairs," McMurtrey said, "to his cabin."

"I think he's meditating," Corona offered.

"You can't see him through Shusher or Appy?" McMurtrey asked.

McMurtrey couldn't see anything like that himself, though he was touching Corona. He never had seen anything or obtained access to Appy's program data by touching her: thus far it had only been a listening tap into the Shusher-Appy comlink. But now it was occurring to McMurtrey that when Corona picked up Appy's program it might have placed her on a closer connection, one that could see all areas of the ship.

"No," Corona said.

"You can't see places inside the ship? Remember we were wondering about . . ."

"I remember. I'm okay now. So far, nothing . . . no information on how passenger information in Appy's data banks was obtained; it's just there."

"What do Shusher and Appy know of Jin?" McMurtrey asked.

"A total blank, which is inexplicable. Before the collision, Appy built a volume of data on the pilgrims—can't tell how he did it. I have access to those records. Nothing on Jin at all, not a solitary entry. Jin doesn't even appear on the passenger list. As Kelly Corona, I know more about him than Appy does."

"Jin isn't human," Gutan said. "He's some kind of robot, and I think I know what type. I operated a top-secret piece of equipment, the mnemonic memory machine. One day I came on shift and found a couple of men in gray suits standing by Mnemo, arguing with Commandant Wimms, the top man in my unit. Wimms lost the argument—it would be more accurate to say he backed down—and later I overheard him tell an assistant that those men in gray suits weren't men at all. They were Bureau of Loyalty cyberoos—robots with bionic parts. 'Tough sons of bitches,' Wimms called them. I think the killer upstairs is with the BOL, which explains why Appy can't pick up information on him. The Bureau made its operative invisible to electronic surveillance. Jin is a stealth unit."

"But Appy isn't an ordinary computer with ordinary electronics," McMurtrey said. "He's God's biocomputer. Surely God can override Bureau cloaking."

"Further proof of your mythical God's weakness," Yakkai sneered. "There is no God!"

"I think this whole trip is a Bureau operation," Gutan said. "The cyberoo has been assigned to kill every pilgrim aboard, and it's probably after me, too. I'm a small cog, so mostly it seems like a power play to cut the hearts out of any organizations that might oppose them, that might compete for the loyalty of the citizenry."

"If so, why such an elaborate setup?" McMurtrey asked.

"For dramatic effect," Yakkai suggested. "With a little massaging of the facts, the BOL can make it look like God has abandoned humanity, that God isn't worth a hunk of shit. Of course, some of us know that God doesn't exist at all, but that's a different subject. The BOL would rather assume He exists and ridicule Him for His inadequacies."

"It's not so simple as that," Corona said. "I'm convinced that God exists and that He's linked to Appy. But Appy can't detect Jin, and in Appy's data banks there is no information on Jin transmitted from God. The traditional view of God holds that He 'sees' everything, so presumably He could observe Jin without Appy's intervention. I can't tell whether this is the case, but something tells me God has certain blind spots. I'm only guessing now from the information available to me, and of course this isn't something Appy would ever say. Maybe God's 'blind spot' is just that he's too busy to watch everyone, or that He isn't watching everyone because He's made a decision not to."

"You're crazy!" Orbust exclaimed. "God has no weaknesses!"

Zatima knelt on the deck and gazed upward lovingly while quoting verse:

> "'Allah, there is no god but He,
> The Living, the Everlasting;
> He is the All-high, the All-glorious.'"

"I sense that God needs our help," Corona said, "and He needs it desperately."

"Nonsense," Orbust said. "We need God. He doesn't need us!"

"Why can't it be a two-way street?" Corona queried.

"Enough of this," Feek said. "We must deal with the matter of Gutan."

"No longer necessary," Corona said. "Don't any of you feel it?"

"Feel what?" Orbust asked.

"The ship!" McMurtrey exclaimed. "It's on!" He looked at Corona. "Are we moving?"

"We are. The matter of Gutan has been resolved, and I think I have an explanation. Information is flowing from Appy's program to me. Today Gutan placed his life second to that of another human. Always he had been primary in his own thoughts; he was the taker. Today for the first time in his life, he *gave* something important, or at least offered it. He offered his life."

"And the life offered to Jin was not taken," McMurtrey said, pursing his lips thoughtfully.

Corona: "Appy is speculating that the very cosmic act of a momentous change in Gutan may have sent out energy waves, shutting Jin down. Here Appy isn't certain, for he doesn't know the forces driving Jin. He may be a cyberoo BOL agent, may even be tied in with an antigod. If Jin was shut down with energy waves, they may have only a temporary effect; the odds are high that Jin could restart and resume his massacre."

"Are you saying that Gutan's single noble act makes up for a lifetime of sin and degradation?" Yakkai asked testily.

"I wasn't saying anything," Corona said. "I was quoting Appy. Apparently it isn't a matter of 'making up.' This is a very misunderstood concept, and is in part the basis of the faulty KothoLu system of confession and absolution. Somewhere along the line, the KothoLu priesthood either misunderstood a statement by one of God's prophets, Krassos, or they consciously altered it for their own purposes."

"Right," McMurtrey said. "Priests and nuns have a long history of making decisions that benefit themselves. Survival of the brotherhood, of the sisterhood, of the order . . . hiding twisted intentions behind holy garb, rituals and words. The perversion of sacredness."

"Amen to that," Yakkai said, with a steely smile. "Confession and absolution form part of a power game, a chapter in the 'Keep 'Em In Line With Fear' book. Tell us everything, the church says—we'll put it in safety deposit, and the safety deposit fee is called a tithe. Since you're a customer for our business, we'll recommend you for membership in the Heavenly Gates Country Club. It's a pretty exclusive club, but we can get you in if you do it our way."

McMurtrey smiled. *This guy is priceless!*

Corona appeared to be feeling better. Her words came excitedly: "Humans are driven by emotion: by love, by lust, by hatred, by remorse, by fear, by pride, by valor—but at the basis of the human experience each man seeks logic. He seeks an answer to the reason for his existence and to the reason for the ordering of the universe. Man is obsessed with logic, with the need to prove, to find out. Even the religious man who denies this need would like to *know*. Though he rages denial, he too would like to *see* or *experience* something tangible, something logical that confirms what he 'knows' in his heart. He would like to see God, to touch him."

"Fat chance," Yakkai said.

"Inevitably in this search for logic," Corona said, ignoring Yakkai, "man confronts his emotions. Life is a series of choices, one right after another. To speak or not to speak; to go or not to go; to do or not to do. Logic and emotion enter into each choice that a man makes. These are natural enemies, occupying their own specific realms of the brain, left and right. Human experience is a balancing act between these enemies. Like a house divided, logic can battle itself, disputing the criteria employed in arriving at 'facts.' Ultimately when all is reasoned out and torn to its logical foundation of foundations, there are no facts and no answers. There are only more questions."

"That's a lot of gibberish," Yakkai said.

Corona hesitated. "Assimilating data . . . Emotion can battle itself as well, and a terrible, tumultuous confrontation this can be! Love against Fear; Love against Hatred; Hatred against Remorse. Logical battles are usually more subdued than emotional battles, for logic dispels violence. But there are no purely logical battles, just as there are no purely emotional battles. One melds smoothly into the other, often to the point of indistinction."

"Somebody unplug the computer," Yakkai said. "It's out of control!"

Corona smiled. "You aren't paying attention, are you? Consider the emotional battle raging within Harley Gutan: his lust for cadavers versus his great remorse; his fear of discovery versus his desire to be caught; his fear of death versus his longing for the serenity of it. Consider also the tremendous need of this man for a logical explanation to the meaning of his life. Everyone wonders about this. It's a perennial, unresolved question."

"Yeah?" Yakkai said. "So what?"

"Place all this turmoil at a critical junction in the universe, and what do you have? Impasse. Nothing can proceed until it has been resolved."

"You got all that from Appy?" McMurtrey asked.

Corona nodded. "Most of it, and I believe it's correct. When Gutan stepped between Yakkai and the killer, Gutan confronted his fear, dispelled his shame with valor and gave himself a reason for existing. He had saved one life, or at least permitted it to exist a bit longer. Thus he accomplished something measurable, something of significance, and he placed himself at harmony."

Yakkai looked pensive, started to speak. But his thoughts weren't formed clearly, and Corona's words crowded his out.

"This type of cosmic harmony is part of a unique continuum," Corona said, "a conveyor belt driven by opposing forces: valor makes up for shame, purpose dispels meaningless, etcetera. The continuum is not entirely symmetrical. More than all else it is a point-to-point or breath-to-breath sentient evaluation, similar to happiness, a sense the creature has for the balance of each specific moment. Gutan at the specific moment when he stepped in front of Yakkai became at harmony with himself. This is unrelated to the faulty KothoLu concept of absolution from a lifetime of sin through confession. Forgiveness is not the same as cosmic harmony."

Yakkai was beginning to listen.

Corona noticed this, smiled. "Harmony is a cosmic matter not always in God's control. It follows certain rules, but above all else it is a personal matter, a state each individual must achieve on his own."

"Are you saying it's independent of right or wrong?" Yakkai asked.

"I am. Death is as much a part of harmony as life. Without death there could be no life. Without ugliness there could be no beauty."

"It almost sounds amoral," McMurtrey said.

"Oh, it isn't!" Corona exclaimed. "What if there were no excitement in life, no challenges, no species preying upon one another? It would be awfully dull for any life form. God set the creatures loose and told them to compete with one another. It's infinitely better this way. You must get beyond socially imposed filters that are inhibiting your thoughts."

"Exactly," Feek the Afsornian said.

Orbust cleared his throat. He looked perplexed. "How can you say on one hand that Gutan reached cosmic and personal harmony by performing an heroic, moral act, while saying in the next breath that there is no right or wrong?"

"I didn't say there was no right or wrong," Corona said. "Realize that I'm speaking for Appy now, which consists of the computer's original holy programming plus opinions developed independently by Appy's experiences. Yakkai asked if harmony was independent of right or wrong, and from the information available to me I said it was. So we have harmony on the one hand, right and wrong on the other. Sometimes they overlap; often they do not. A harmonic decision can be morally neutral; it can be morally right; it can be morally wrong. Appy says the harmonic decisions God likes best are morally right—such as those favoring life and beauty.

"But God does not control all facets of the universe. There are certain factors which He must accept as 'givens.' One of those factors happens to be travel by whipping along the skins of two universes. God can nudge objects off or onto the whipping passageways; He can even propel objects along the passageways if conditions are right. The collision with Gutan, *even though it was Shusher's fault*, released Gutan's disharmonious energy waves and created a cosmic imbalance in both Gluons, which prevented either of them from further skinbeating. Traveling the whipping passageways, you must understand, is a very delicate maneuver. Appy believes that in fairness to all racers, God could only say that the matter of Gutan had to be resolved before other ships arrived there, or God would have to nudge Shusher and the second Gluon, Pelter, out of the way."

"We're supposed to cast aside the Babulical passages about God's mighty power?" Orbust asked. "I find this nearly impossible to accept."

"Understandable," Corona said. "As I said, I sense that God needs our help, and Appy has made no comment on this. We know from the data banks that there are certain factors in the universe that God must accept, factors He cannot control or change. We know also that our universe is not the only one. Are there other gods in other universes? Appy suggests only that there are 'antigods,' without explanation. It is very frustrating! Mr. Orbust, perhaps your Babulical passages about God's power are correct, taken down as they were by d'urthly observers. Perhaps God could wipe out D'Urth if He chose to do so. So God is 'all powerful' in the context of D'Urth and even in the context of millions of other planets and suns in the universe. But does God's power go to infinity? It seems that it doesn't. Did God precede the universe or is He part of it? Does God have dominion over other universes? Why do I sense that He needs us? Why didn't God impart data about Jin to Appy, and why can't Appy detect Jin's presence? How did Jin get a cabin?"

"Why does God allow suffering?" Yakkai demanded.

"So many questions," Corona said. "And it looks like we may have a chance to ask them of God ourselves. We're on our way!"

"In the right direction?" the Hoddhist priest asked.

Corona nodded. Then her features darkened, and she said, "Something changing in Appy's program." Her voice cracked. "Checking . . . I'm having trouble accessing data. Wait. It's still there . . . takes longer . . ."

"I'll be right back," Gutan said.

Before the judges or Yakkai could react, the prisoner slipped out the door.

Within minutes he returned, breathing heavily. "The naked one is sitting on the deck," he announced, "Level Six. He appears to be in a trance."

"If the whipping passageway is operational now," McMurtrey said, looking at Gutan, "why aren't you back on your Gluon, traveling as you did? You were going in the same direction, toward God."

Gutan shrugged his sloping simian shoulders.

"Gutan was on the whipping passageway," Corona said, "but who knows if his destination was identical with ours? At a certain point, I assume we'll leave the passageway and drop back into our universe, to God's planet. Maybe Gutan would have gone past, or gotten off earlier than us."

"I was going to see God," Gutan said, with assurance.

"How do you know?" McMurtrey asked.

"I just know."

"Everyone stay away from Level Six," Corona ordered. "I wonder . . . Yakkai, do you really have a bomb? Personally, I never believed you for a moment, but it might be handy now."

Yakkai shook his head, removed a wadded cloth from his pocket to show what had been bulging there. "Even if I did," he said, "we couldn't use it aboard ship."

"I suppose you're right," Corona said, "unless it could have been modified."

"But if you reduced the strength of it," Gutan said, "a bomb wouldn't stop that killer. No one on this ship can defeat or stop a cyberoo. Not from what I've heard and seen. They shot him, tried to stab him, threw things at him. . . . He can tear through—"

"It's all moot anyway," Orbust interjected. "We don't have a bomb. If only I had my chemstrip!" He lowered his head. "I suggest it's time for us to pray."

Everyone except Yakkai knelt or bowed in his or her own way, and from this small gathering of men and women came the murmurings of terror.

Twelve

A political hierarchy can force people to conceal their belief in God. But rulers cannot, in so controlling, erase the *existence* of God. The tendency in human events, when viewed on a Grand Scale over countless millenia, is toward Truth. In the long run, Truth will not be denied. One day man and his God will face one another, no matter how we try to delay the inevitable.

— Excerpt From Confidential Bureau of Loyalty
    Memorandum: "Counter-Ecumenical Strategies"

Appy's voice blared across the loudspeakers, startling McMurtrey out of sleep. Something about a "main exit . . ." And: "I'm back on-line."

McMurtrey hadn't slept well on the floor of the assembly room. . . . How long had he lain here? Light was low, and amid the rustling sounds of others as they awoke, McMurtrey emitted a solitary whistled tone, illuminating the dial of his Wriskron. Less than three hours.

Appy again: "Passengers debarking in Heaven please use the main exit." Appy laughed wildly, then: "Just kidding. There is no Heaven."

"Uhh," McMurtrey said, rolling over. "That insidious laugh of Appy's. What is *wrong* with him?"

"Who knows?" Orbust slurred, from across the room. "Go back tuh sleep."

Appy: "Arriving Tananius Ofo in twenty-two D'Urth minutes."

"Huh?" Corona said, a shadow to McMurtrey's immediate left. He saw her sit up, and she added, "What did he say? Twenty-two minutes? Krassos, we're there!"

McMurtrey sat up, yawned. The window to space was

screened, and low light came from no particular source. Other human shadows moved in the recesses of the room, accompanied by low voices.

They'd been afraid to walk around the ship because of the killer aboard, so Zatima had suggested that they sleep in the assembly room. When all agreed, the lights went out, automatically.

McMurtrey recalled Corona's words, and they'd been salve on the fears induced by sudden darkness: "When you all decide to get up, the lights will go back on."

Now McMurtrey identified the voices of Yakkai, and of each judge.

Then Gutan said, "The lights, Appy."

"Let there be light," Yakkai said flippantly.

But nothing cut the shadows.

"The program is gone!" Corona whispered to Mc-Murtrey. "I had it when I went to sleep—it was more difficult to access, but I thought it might have been because I was tired. Now, nothing! Nothing over the comlink, either, but that's a separate connection. There may be no message traffic now."

"I hope you're totally free," McMurtrey said.

She didn't answer.

"The door better open," Orbust said. He stumbled over something, muttered.

McMurtrey heard the door click open, detected no change in light.

"You goin' out there?" Yakkai asked.

"With a killer out there?" Orbust asked. "Are you kidding?"

The door clicked shut.

"This is great," Orbust said. "No lights, a killer aboard, and where are we?"

From Orbust's direction came the soft and repeated slap of flesh against leather—it sounded like Orbust drawing his Babul over and over. But with his healing packs on?

"We must have been close to Tananius-Ofo when our Gluons collided," Gutan said.

"What happened to the Gluon you were on?" Mc-Murtrey asked. "Appy said it was called Pelter."

"I dreamed it cartwheeled into deep space," Gutan said. "I watched from somewhere—I couldn't tell from where.

Pelter—that was the name of the professor who created Mnemo."

"Another question for God," McMurtrey said. "And we may be there in a few minutes!"

McMurtrey heard Krassian, Nandaic and Middist chants and psalms, in sweet harmony. They were lilting songs and verses, threading gently through his consciousness.

The shadowy forms around him shape-shifted to dark human skeletons, silhouetted against an aura-yellow haze. One shape in the distance became an Isammedan, high in a minaret tower, calling the faithful to prayer in a bell-like voice. The emaciated foreground forms knelt in prayer, and their invocations blended like the parts of a harmony.

To McMurtrey these people, with all their apparent differences, seemed the same.

The silhouettes became powder, and disintegrated in explosions that hurled black specks into the yellow background.

These images faded to darkness, and Corona said, "What if D'Urth has been destroyed for its iniquities and those on God's ships are the only survivors?"

"The arks of Toor," Orbust said. "Just as it says in scripture."

The slap of flesh on leather again—three times. Orbust couldn't be reading that Babul in the dark. Maybe touching it brought scriptural passages to mind.

"What do you suppose God looks like?" Gutan asked. "Are we really in his image?"

"We are 'after His kind,'" Orbust said.

Yakkai's voice: "I'm reminded of the minister who was preaching about man being made in God's image, when at that very moment the village idiot walked by." He laughed, a harsh rasp, and broke quickly into singsong:

> "They seek Him here
> They seek Him there;
> These pilgrims seek
> God everywhere.
>
> Is He within,
> Or is He afar?

Might we find Him
Upon a star?"

"Must you taint this sacred moment?" Orbust asked in
an exasperated tone. He uttered a prayer.

"Rather a neat rhyme, Yakkai," Corona said. "But I
feel certain we'll find God is on a planet."

The ship shook violently.

"We're descending through a storm over Tananius-
Ofo," Appy announced.

McMurtrey held Corona tightly, and in the darkness
with the ship seeming to rattle apart around them, he was
deathly afraid. He was angry with his God too, and felt a
great onrushing disappointment. What sort of God was
this if He couldn't provide clear weather over His own
domain, if He couldn't stop Jin from killing pilgrims on a
ship in His fleet, if He couldn't even keep lights burning
on that ship?

This was the God who permitted suffering.

McMurtrey felt very vulnerable, and he longed for the
ignorant security of his little niche on D'Urth.

"A sorney for your thoughts," Corona said.

"I want my mommy," he said.

She laughed uneasily, squeezed his hand.

The lights flashed on, and simultaneously the wall panels
slid aside to reveal the window. More light poured in from
the window, but probably not directly, if Corona's early
theory about mirrors and prisms inside the walls held true.
McMurtrey was too enthralled with the moment to ask.

The storm seemed to have passed, or they had dropped
beneath it, and McMurtrey saw a reverse image of the
colors in D'Urth's sky. This sky was white—gray-white
and darker gray shades approaching black—with cerulean
blue clouds floating in the air in varying shapes like majestic atmospheric ships.

Shusher was descending through blue clouds in a gentle,
controlled spin, with the planet's surface just coming into
view beneath them. It was a colorless, curved surface
stretching away to shades of black and gray, with large
splotches and ribbons of white between.

As the planet neared, McMurtrey decided the white

splotches and ribbons must be lakes and rivers, and that the darker shades were land masses.

Appy confirmed this over the P.A., and added: "Tananius-Ofo is essentially a black and white planet, with a range of tones between. Only one primary color is found here: blue, in various monochromatic intensities."

"Tell us about God," Orbust said. His green sportscoat looked no worse from the fight with Singh, and might have been repaired by the same tailoring equipment employed on Yakkai's Sidic clothes. The healing packs were no longer on Orbust's arms and face, and deep purple streaks ran across his forehead and down his nose.

"I would not presume to describe our Lord and Master," Appy said.

McMurtrey felt his terror subsiding, for now points of reference were appearing before him, tangible objects. He felt a childlike yearning to know God.

McMurtrey beheld no heavenly firmament as he neared his destination, no ethereal lights, no gates of pearl through which all entering had to pass. No winged, singing angels fluttered near to guide the ship into port. This was a nearly colorless planet, not a glorious place 'on high' where his senses might feast into eternity. . . .

They were only a few thousand meters above the surface, and the terrain became visible. The land looked inhospitable, with black mountain crags that jutted through the atmosphere and fell away in cliffs to limitless depths.

"We're dropping right into the mountains," Makanji said.

Taam the Hoddhist stood closest to the window, his thin white robe a sharp contrast to high black mountains beyond. With an open expression on his face and his arms lowered at his sides, palms facing forward, he appeared ready to accept whatever lay in store for him.

Makanji moved to the Hoddhist's side, and Makanji's body spoke the same language.

Of course they have to accept it, McMurtrey thought. *We all do. But they look so calm, so trusting. I suppose God—Tananius-Ofo—would want that. He would want Faith.*

Did God bring us here to tell us something? Why couldn't He tell us by message to D'Urth? Why such a dramatic—

Dramatic. *That might explain a lot, with so many people claiming to have spoken with God. Which of them lied and which told the truth? Which misunderstood, or lied? Will we take back a group photo of ourselves with God or something more conclusive, and messages direct from His mouth? Are these to be the ultimate, undebatable messages from God?*

What messages could God have? Be peaceful and eliminate sin or you'll all be wiped out? Is this the angry, fear-inspiring God of Wessornian scripture?

With the ship very close to the tops of the highest peaks, McMurtrey realized he hadn't seen a sun. He speculated it must have recently set, or it was about to rise.

"What time of the day is it, Appy?" McMurtrey asked.

"Midday," came the response, over the P.A.

"Where's the sun?" McMurtrey asked. "Behind a cloud-cover that looks like white sky?"

"All clouds are blue here; all sky is white; there is no sun."

"Then how can it be light here?" McMurtrey asked. "Is the planet's surface frozen?"

Appy chuckled.

"I get it," McMurtrey said. "This is Heaven, right? No standard laws of nature out here, eh?"

"There is no Heaven," Appy said. "There is only Tananius-Ofo."

It occurred to McMurtrey that this might be the domain of Satan. A chill ran through his spine, and he shivered.

"We're beneath the highest peaks," Corona said. "It doesn't look cold out there. I don't see ice or snow—of course they might look different here—but the mountains don't have an icy sheen to them. This place is weird."

"Cliffs all around," Orbust said. He sounded worried.

"We're having a smooth landing," Appy reported. "No need for tethers or cushy stuff this time!"

"Where are we landing?" Corona asked.

The ship jerked slightly, came to a stop with a silver-gray cliff face visible through the window. It was a sheer rock wall not far from the ship, and at McMurtrey's vantage across the room from the window he couldn't see the ground. An uncomfortable, empty feeling filled his groin.

"Where the hell did we land?" Corona asked.

"Inappropriate choice of words," Gutan said.

Is it? McMurtrey thought.

"Watch your language, Ms. Corona," Orbust said, his tone imploring. "Of all places, of all times, please!"

Harley Gutan was first out the door into the corridor.

McMurtrey followed the others upstairs to the main passenger compartment, a route they had to follow to exit the ship.

The door that Jin had ripped away was in place and like new, and when it had been opened and McMurtrey passed through, he beheld a strange sight. The main passenger compartment was spotless, entirely devoid of bodies. It smelled of antiseptic, a lemon scent, and there were no bullet holes in the deck, in the ceiling or in the walls.

Gutan's chair sat where it had been, appeared undamaged.

The travelers stepped quietly and kept close to one wall of the compartment as they passed through, whispering to one another that Appy or Shusher must have disposed of the bodies.

McMurtrey smelled the acrid odor of Gutan, even with Corona between them.

Nervously, McMurtrey glanced up to his right, to the sixth-level railing high over the compartment. No sign of Jin there, or anywhere else.

The main exit was open, with the metal ramp in place against a black rock wall. Gutan and Yakkai were leading the way across, with the other travelers pressing close behind. McMurtrey was last onto the ramp, and when he looked over the ledge his stomach tightened.

The ramp traversed a chasm, the bottom of which couldn't be seen, and the other end of the ramp rested on a narrow ledge on a black cliff face. To McMurtrey's left he saw the silver-gray cliff he had seen through the window, and high overhead a patch of white marked the sky. Curiously, although they were deep in a forest of spires on a sunless world, the light seemed adequate and the temperature was comfortable.

Like a fat fly on a wall, their ship clung to the nearest cliff face with four stiff legs or brackets that revealed no means of attachment.

Something ultra-sticky and strong on the ends of the legs, McMurtrey thought. *Or we've bored into the cliff.*

Corona pushed by Gutan and Yakkai to the front, followed by McMurtrey, who thought he would feel safer on the ledge than hanging from it.

"Welcome!" a mellifluous voice said. "Nice to see you!"

As McMurtrey reached the ledge he saw to his left a man's chubby face peeking from an opening in the cliff. It was a cherubic and unbearded countenance, beaming with delight and good will. The man was elfin and aged, with deeply creased gray skin, thick, dark eyebrows, a large nose and very short, dark hair cut flat on top. Dark circles underscored albino white eyes. He was smiling, but did not look well.

"Right this way, ladies and gentlemen! Step lively, before the ledge gives way! I may be too tired to save all of you!"

Strange comment, McMurtrey thought. *Who is this?*

McMurtrey took a deep breath for courage, inched along the high wall with his back against it.

The others did likewise, without conversation.

What else can we do? McMurtrey thought. *We've spanned the universe, escaped death from collision and a murderer, and now we're supposed to say, 'Sorry, but we don't want to go further'?*

A sardonic laugh nearly escaped his lips.

The little man was less than a meter from Corona now, and he said, with a gummy smile, "Goodness, I still have tidying up to do inside, and this entrance must be made larger for you."

He waved a stubby hand casually, and without a sound the tiny opening in the rock grew tenfold, startling those in the front of McMurtrey's party, who found themselves before the yawning mouth of a cave.

The little man had quite a large belly, and he scurried inside, waving a hand one way and then another.

"Right through here," he said, and with each wave of the man's hand McMurtrey heard something in the unseen recesses of the cave—a clatter, a clunk, a swoosh, the rustling of paper. It was as light inside the cave as outside, though no sources of illumination were apparent. A faint, musty odor touched McMurtrey's nostrils.

"Just tidying up," the man said, looking back over his shoulder. He wore an oversized pastel blue smock with big pockets. His trousers were baggy and a darker shade of blue. On his feet were furry white slippers that had toy eyes on them—two per slipper—the sort of round plazymer eyes found in boxes of Kandy Snaps.

"My monster shoes," he said, looking back and taking in the direction of McMurtrey's gaze. "Fake fur, naturally."

McMurtrey suppressed a smile. Then: "There's a killer aboard our ship, a cyberoo, we think. Can you close the cave entrance?"

"I could, but it would be a waste of precious energy. Based upon what that cyberoo has done, I'm afraid nothing could stop it if it got going again. Let's just hope it's neutralized. I suspect that Jin is a Bureau of Loyalty operative, as Gutan speculated."

"God doesn't know for certain?" McMurtrey asked.

The little man replied sadly: "God doesn't know for certain."

"And your name?" Corona said. "Are you one of God's assistants?"

The droll little fellow stopped and turned, holding his hands on his hips in a most indignant fashion. "I am Tananius-Ofo," he said, looking ill and very tired.

The travelers stopped cold, and from their midst came a gasp.

Tananius-Ofo, breathing hard, said, "The problem with Jin touches upon one of my blind spots—the Bureau of Loyalty has been able to cloak many of its activities from me. This seems to be a combination of their incredible technological power and my increasing frailty. Another blind spot is as Appy conveyed to you, concerning the whipping passageways between universes. These passageways operate independently of me. They preceded me, have been there even more eternally than I have, it seems. I can recall no time when they didn't exist, and cannot account for how they came to be."

"You're really God?" Yakkai asked.

"I most certainly am, but I'm much too tired to argue the point with a nonbeliever."

"Could—could Jin even kill You?" McMurtrey asked.

"Perhaps and perhaps not. Logically and intuitively it doesn't seem conceivable to me. Even a weakened God is no pushover, but I don't know the powers of a cyberoo."

Tananius-Ofo turned and led the way down a narrow but extraordinarily high-ceilinged black rock corridor.

Tananius-Ofo was quite fatigued by the time he reached his chamber. He gathered up a royal blue robe from a wide blackstone table just inside the entrance, threw the robe over his shoulders with a flourish.

"Find pillows and sit on the floor," he instructed as he climbed a two-step dais and heaved his little frame onto an Empire couch. "I try to be cheerful and upbeat, but I'm so tired. I'll just rest my peepers for a moment."

God closed his eyes.

McMurtrey and the others did as they had been instructed, placing white pillows (which had been along one wall) on the floor by Tananius-Ofo's place of repose. The chamber looked more like a crude palatial room than a cave. The floor was rough-cut whitestone with quartzlike glistenings in it. The walls were the pale blue of his smock and the ceiling the dark blue of his trousers.

The furniture was rough-hewn stone, simple and utilitarian. Tables of varying heights were along the walls, with a broad, low whitestone one in the center of the room and one small whitestone chair pulled up to it. Stone shelves cut into every wall held countless pairs of shoes—moccasins, sandals, togs, pumps—all made of indeterminable materials and in obvious disarray, with many unmatched singles.

Aside from white and black and shades of gray in between, there had been but one color in evidence anywhere: blue, in varying tones. It was exactly as Appy said, very nearly a black and white world.

How strange Tananius-Ofo looked, curled up asleep on the couch in his monster slippers! A low, rumbling snore emanated from his sizable nose.

McMurtrey wondered if this could really be God, or if this might be exactly the opposite—even a professional charlatan. How could a person tell the difference, when confronted with a phony of penultimate skill?

What sort of litmus test should be applied?

It approached the difference between faith and intellectual proof, the age-old argument between religion and science. If a thing was true, McMurtrey believed, you felt it in your heart. Your instincts told you one way or the other. How did he feel now? Numb. He would need time to sort it out, time to think it over—or time to meditate if rational thought failed him.

But how much time did he have? Was time a different commodity in this place, or was it only different to the God entity?

So many overlappings, so many layers of obscurity beneath and above layers having the slightest teasings of translucence.

The truth about God seemed like an extrapolation of the problem men had in determining true prophets from false prophets. The average man was ill-equipped to survive in such waters.

On the ship, Jin sat in human-duplicated, impassive meditation, considering the Plarnjarn view of the universe. In this perspective, five ingredients formed the bases of material objects: Pudgala (Matter), Kala (Time), Akasha (Space), Dharma (Motion) and Adharma (Rest). Nirvanic enlightenment was achieved through an understanding of these ingredients and rejection of them. It was only in the allied and harmful states of ignorance and passion that material objects held sway.

Man achieving perfection.

There could be no God in such a system, for man himself was potentially perfect, capable of attaining limitless knowledge, power, faith and serenity. Thus each man was capable of godhood.

Jin reasoned in his simulated-Plarnjarn perspective that anyone claiming to be God had to be a fraud, a pretender to a throne that shouldn't exist. Thus the false God was harming mankind, forcing people to follow artificial pathways.

God is an enemy of the Bureau, too.

It seemed obvious that the Bureau believed God existed and feared Him, for Jin had been sent on this ship to observe the proceedings and report back to headquarters. In the Bureau's view, Jin decided, God must be a terrible

threat, for He competed with the Bureau for the hearts
and minds of humanity. God existed, but should not exist.

The two belief systems folded together, one on the
other, and Jin saw clearly the perfect state in either: *No
God.*

Jin knew intuitively that he was merely playing a part,
that Plarnjarnism was only a convenient disguise for a
cyberoo agent. But he was having difficulty extricating
himself from the part, and it struck him that this had to
be by design. The Plarnjarn tenets that surfaced in his
consciousness were those that were supposed to surface.
He was supposed to reason this situation out and come up
with the best possible course of action.

Right action leads to rewards.

But he had just killed three hundred and ninety-two
people. Plarnjarns did not hold with harming even the
tiniest speck of life. In part it was this contradiction in
basic programming that halted him in the midst of the
slaughter, sparing those few who remained alive. But that
had not been all of it, the only reason for altering course.
There had been something else, something much larger.
A great convergence of forces that inhibited violence.

Jin decided that this must have been a trick of the false
God to thwart the rightful will of the Bureau.

*Plarnjarnism is subservient to the will of the Bureau. The
Bureau is the preeminent authority in the universe—kill the
seekers, and with them their false God.*

An antiseptic scent of lemon touched his biosensors, and
objects before him blurred into a green mist.

Moments later he was outside the ship—on the ramp,
gazing at the cavern entrance that had been left open.

Suddenly Tananius-Ofo opened his eyes and sat up.

McMurtrey, on a pillow on the floor, was of such a height
that he looked straight across, directly into the albino eyes
of God.

The eyes were the whitest white of the sky that reigned
over this peculiar world, without apparent depth to them,
without the mysterious regions beneath the surface char-
acterized by Corona's eyes. These were shallow pools in
a darker region of ruddy-gray flesh and black hair, like

the lakes and seas McMurtrey had seen on the surface of the planet.

"Gather close and rub my belly," God said. "This should be done for good luck." He lifted his blue smock, revealing a massive gray potbelly, with a protruding bellybutton so large and ugly it might have been a tumor.

The Hoddhist rubbed the belly first, saying, "This is as I thought it would be, as Hoddha told us it would be."

"I am not Hoddha, of course," God said. "You understand that, don't you?"

The Hoddhist withdrew his hands, smiled serenely.

"Hoddha was a great man," God said, "and an excellent card player, one of my prophets. He and I had many good times together, and always we rubbed each other's bellies."

Yakkai went next, and as he stood before God he told of a statue of Hoddha in front of an import store that he used to pass by as a boy. Yakkai became accustomed to stopping to rub the belly of the statue for good luck, and just for fun.

"Then one day I rubbed the belly and it had gooey spit all over it. An early experience in religion, I guess. A negative one that may have helped turn me into an atheist. Considering many things, I realize now that I didn't have all the information I needed to make my decision."

A conversion, McMurtrey thought. *But to which religion?*

"A Krassian spit on that belly," the Hoddhist snapped. "Only Krassians do such things."

"Now, now," God said. "Enough of that."

McMurtrey went next and touched the skin of God. It was warm and dry, indiscernible from that of a human, and smooth except for the erupted bellybutton that McMurtrey bumped without meaning to. "I must ask you," McMurtrey said before stepping aside. "The mantra that came to me for the religion I created—did you plant it in my mind?"

"'O Chubby Mother,'" Tananius-Ofo intoned, with a gummy smile. "'Let me rubba your belly, let me rubba your belly.'"

He laughed boisterously, and his great belly shook. "Let's hurry along" he said. "There is much to discuss."

Orbust was next, and despite God's instruction he too had something to say. "I purchased my Snapcard from a door-to-door salesman, a Floriental man who smiled the very way you do—with his gums showing."

Tananius-Ofo revealed his gums again. "And you're suggesting by such 'evidence' that I sold you the device? Well, I must admit there are a lot of expenses in running a universe! Hurry along now!"

Orbust flushed red, rubbed the proffered belly quickly and resumed his seat.

The others came without comment, and when they had resumed their seats, Tananius-Ofo dropped his smock back into place.

"This planet is an extension of me," the Leader of the Universe said, "hence the same name for me and for the planet. Blue is my favorite primary color, as you might have guessed. It is so much prettier, so much more appreciable in its full range of intensities, without competing hues."

All agreed that it was an outstanding color.

"Some of you are wondering if I'm a great imposter," God said. His tone was sweet and more than a little heavy, as if he were having difficulty hefting the words.

McMurtrey thought back to the voice he had heard in his St. Charles Beach bedroom, felt certain this was the voice.

"I'm not going to sit here and deny I'm an imposter," God said. He snickered. "That would sound very guilty, wouldn't it? I could perform a couple of tricks, I suppose. Mmmm." He yawned. "This planet is entirely shape-shifted and colored by me. I like it just the way it is, you see. I could change it to a lush tropical paradise, but the energy required might finish me off. Just one little trick today, if you don't mind."

He looked at McMurtrey, said, "Do you recall the little problem you used to have, the one that disappeared after I announced my location to you?"

"Y-yes."

"Well, you have it again!"

Tananius-Ofo smiled, with startling cruelty, and scratched his large nose. At the same time, one of his eyebrows began vibrating fiercely and his lower lip quivered like flesh at the epicenter of a d'urthquake.

"Tell us about Cosmic Chickenhood," God commanded. His face had lost its features to McMurtrey, and became instead a mass of quivering, vibrating cells, with a finger that darted in and out to the center, where the nose should be, to scratch it.

"Y-you know I c-can't," McMurtrey stuttered. He looked away in shame.

"It seems that Mr. McMurtrey's brain has frozen on him. A most uncomfortable and debilitating condition indeed. Well, I didn't bring him here to embarrass him or make him suffer. It was a demonstration only. The condition has passed now, never to return, but Mr. McMurtrey is thinking I was too cruel."

McMurtrey didn't look at God.

"You're angry with me, aren't you, McMurtrey?"

"No . . ." McMurtrey reconsidered. He couldn't lie to God! "Yes. I'm very angry with you!"

"Good. That's healthy and perfectly allowable. McMurtrey, gaze upon me!"

McMurtrey did so, and now Tananius-Ofo looked exceedingly stern.

"That was more than a demonstration of power," God said. "It was a demonstration of my weakness, my own imperfection. It is my fault that humans are as they are, for I made them no better than myself."

McMurtrey felt his eyebrows rise, and, as if he were looking in a mirror, God's eyebrows went up too.

"It's true," Tananius-Ofo said. "Many have suspected this, and I confirm it to you."

God's eyes flashed, and the white pupils began to glisten, vibrating blue.

The floor shook under McMurtrey's feet.

Jin was inching along the ledge with his back against the cliff face, when a groundquake hit. He couldn't decide whether he should wait where he was or hurry for the cavern entrance, and in that instant of indecision the ledge gave way beneath him, hurling him into the chasm.

Tananius-Ofo's eyes became white and serene, and he gazed from far behind the orbs.

"Did you cause that?" McMurtrey asked. "I thought you said only one little trick. . . ."

"That was no trick," God answered. "That was for real. Jin just tumbled off the ledge, and it's a long way down. I'm rather pleased, actually. The Bureau of Loyalty is becoming a thorn in my side."

Kelly Corona clapped and cheered, and Gutan joined her.

Yakkai didn't react at all, appeared ill-at-ease. "Why do you allow suffering?" he asked the Lord impertinently. "Because you're weak or because you're cruel?"

Corona and Gutan stiffened, grew quiet.

"I am frail. I admit that freely. But even a frail God is not powerless, as I have just demonstrated. My 'cruelty' is more of the prank variety. A few innocent jokes here and there. I am not boringly good. I have faults. A weakness for dirlu chocolate—and for women." He stared at Corona, smiled gently at her.

"Suffering must end!" Yakkai exclaimed.

"I quite agree. But it exists because I am too frail to stop most of it. I do the best I can. Suffering just happens. Sort of naturally, I'm afraid. There is no intentional, inbred or instinctual cruelty—only sets of social circumstances that lead to the psychological discharge of cruelty. We could discuss this subject for aeons, debating each point. But I don't feel up to it."

"Satan has nothing to do with suffering?" Orbust asked.

"There is no Satan," God said. "Most problems can be attributed to the weak side of God and the weak side of Nature. There is a natural tendency for all life to wind down and end."

"No Heaven, no Hell?" Zatima asked. "No spirits of good people living here, spirits of bad people living there?"

Tananius-Ofo shook his head. "Only a dying old man." The rheumy albino eyes held McMurtrey's gaze for an instant, and looked away.

"You?" McMurtrey exclaimed. "I thought God lived forever."

"So did I," he responded, "but lamentably I have come down with an ailment. It is, I am sorry to report, most grievous. Soon you will have to do without me."

"Have you seen a doctor?" Johnny Orbust asked. "What's wrong with you?"

"Extreme old age. There is no cure, no doctor I could see. I am aeons old."

"Make yourself young then!" Yakkai suggested.

Orbust glared ferociously at Yakkai, recalling their earlier conversation.

"Alas," God said, "I have lost the desire to do that. I used to do it all the time." His eyes welled with tears. "I'm so bored."

"But your angels," Orbust said, glancing around. "Don't they keep you company?"

"That part of the Heaven story is true. Once I had angels. But they irritated me so much I didn't want to be around them anymore. They always asked the same things: 'God, what miracles have you performed lately? . . . How about something more spectacular?' Or, 'God, could I have a set of prettier wings? God, am I your favorite?' "

Tananius-Ofo rolled his eyes, exclaimed: "The politics! I got sick of answering their inane questions, complying with their demands and everything else, so I banished them. Nothing I did was enough for them."

"But you are the eternal flame," McMurtrey said, "the source, the light in the minds of all men. What happens when you die?"

"I die, that's all. I'll probably fall over."

"The universe doesn't end with your death?"

"No. Why should it?"

"Just a thought I had," McMurtrey said.

"Well, toss it out."

"But what if you're wrong?" Corona said, trembling from the temerity of such a suggestion. "What if you're a generator keeping everything going? When the power source ends, everything reverts to what it was in the beginning, to the singularity before the Big Bang."

"The Big Bang!" God squealed, with infinite delight. "I've always had a good laugh over that term—the sexual implications involved with the creation of the universe and all. What a romp in the hay that must have been, eh?" He winked.

The onlookers stared at the Leader of the Universe in disbelief.

"Don't look at me that way," he commanded. "I've grown exceedingly tired of being held to a quote unquote higher standard. Why should I be so burdened? I am a human too. It isn't fair to me! Not to suggest that I'm profane. Quite the opposite. It's just that I established sexual relationships so people could have fun with them. And bear this in mind: Erotic pleasure is intrinsic to species survival. You all understand, don't you?"

"Sure, God," Yakkai said. "We understand."

"Yes, sir," Orbust said. "We most certainly do."

God shook his head sadly, said, "Your faces indicate to me that you do not. Very well. I've always had trouble with these humans I created. Oh, I didn't have to be human myself. I could have been anything I wanted to be, but I decided . . . too long a story. . . . Big Bang—yes, that theory comes close to being correct—but I am no eternal power source."

"What if you're wrong about that?" Corona said, more forcefully than before. "Man was created in your image, after all. Are you imperfect in some critical ways?"

"How dare you suggest that!" Zatima said, in a scolding tone. "Blasphemy! Allah is never wrong! He is the Perfect of Perfects!"

"Mmmm," God said. "I like loyalty, but I must admit I've messed up many times. This job came with no instruction manual, so I had to improvise. Mmmm. A lot of trial and error. Not to worry! I'm not wrong about this. The universe has been set in motion, and obeys certain laws of physics. It is a self-sustaining system."

"Isn't the universe winding down through entropy?" Corona asked. "An excess of disorder over order?"

"True, but the process is too slow to worry about."

"And eventually," Corona said, "quadrillions of years from now, won't everything have deteriorated? No more planets, no suns, all matter disintegrated into antimatter, returned to the singularity that existed before the Big Bang?"

"That could very well be the case."

"You don't know for sure?" Corona asked. "You can't predict the future?"

"I am a little weak now, with my reasoning powers curtailed. To tell you truly, I have never worried much over questions like that. Nothing is all that serious, you see."

Deep frown lines commandeered Corona's features, and she said, "The issue of the continuation of the universe strikes me as pretty serious. Essentially you've admitted that everything could end up in a singularity, a point of nothingness I suppose, where all matter and antimatter have canceled themselves out."

"I believe that's essentially correct."

"You're billed as All Powerful, right?" Corona asked. McMurtrey nudged her, whispered, "You're pushing this too much."

"An old billing," God said, patiently. "The marquees should be changed. It used to be that for all intents and purposes, as far as humans need be concerned."

"You parted the Ochre Sea, right?"

"I did."

"And caused the Great Flood?"

"That too. Mere child's play."

"And as you've shown, a few d'urthquakes, I presume. Volcanic eruptions and hurricanes too?"

"All that, whenever I felt the need for it. I tried to avoid death and destruction, but sometimes it couldn't be prevented. There are priorities I have to consider that you're not likely to understand."

"Did you cause bigger events?"

"Yes. Novas, supernovas, comets, meteors. Mmmm. New suns, planets, moons, stuff like that. I—uh—fooled with natural orders of things whenever I got bored, messed around with laws of physics. It was an ego boost, admittedly."

"I can imagine," Corona said. "My point is that with power like that, you could prevent a reversion to the singularity, couldn't you?"

"If I were feeling well, I probably could. At the very least I could slow the process."

"Then it's what I was saying. When you die, the rest dies! You would have gotten around to slowing the deterioration or stopping it. I'm sure of it."

"Yeah, maybe."

"Allah says 'yeah'?" Zatima asked, not realizing how loudly she had spoken.

"You envisioned formality?" Tananius-Ofo said. "Obviously I'm not what any of you expected. I'm probably a great disappointment to you."

"You can't read our minds, sir?" McMurtrey asked.

"I can when I choose to. I don't feel up to it at the moment."

"You're not a disappointment to us," McMurtrey said, with the corners of his mouth forced upward to conceal his lie. "We have great respect and admiration for you, sir. You've accomplished so much!"

"I've pissed away a lot of time."

Orbust and Zatima gasped.

"Don't you see, sir?" Corona said passionately. "You don't need to be bored! You have a purpose for existing! You can reverse the natural destructive processes of the universe! There's a reason for you to get well. If your mind is on it, if you want to get better, that's most of the battle. Assuming psychosomatic causation applies to you."

"It does, and I'm acquainted with holistic medicine, psychoneural immunology, visualization and thousands of similar concepts."

"I wasn't suggesting otherwise. Won't they work for you?"

"If I wanted them to."

"Then do so!" Corona said. "Don't wind down like everything else!"

"I don't *want* much of anything anymore," God said wearily, "other than what's naturally happening to me. There's nothing you can say or do, although I appreciate the effort. I want to wind down."

"You want to die?" Corona asked.

"I suppose I do. I have an urging, like everything else, to return . . ." His mellifluous voice trailed away.

"You were part of the singularity?"

"Not *the* singularity. *A* singularity."

"A? You mean there's more than one? Oh, you mean because there are several universes? A singularity for each universe?"

"Precisely. I've told you enough, as much as any human needs to know, and a lot more than I intended to reveal. Such relentless interrogation!"

"I'm sorry, but a lifetime of this is welled up inside me. There are so many questions all of us want to ask."

"Such a sad-looking group," God said. "But don't forget the most basic law of nature, that each end marks a beginning. Plants, animals and humans die, returning organic matter to the soil, organic matter which in turn supports more life."

"I don't think I understand," Corona said.

"I think he's saying the singularity in this universe will blow again," McMurtrey said. "Another Big Bang . . . then the process of entropy, another singularity and another Big Bang. It goes on like that infinitely."

"I believe it does," God said.

"That's the ultimate?" Corona exclaimed. "One bang after another?"

God laughed wearily.

All laughed with him.

Presently Tananius-Ofo shook his head, with the sadness of eternity. "This is more than a deathbed visit from my family," he said. "One of you must succeed me, and that's why I brought you here. Transition of power, that's what we need. A new God, one with fresh energy."

"But there are other ships behind ours," Gutan said, "with more humans aboard. What of them?"

Tananius-Ofo smiled gently, gazed upon this confessed sinner. "How strange it is for God to speak with a man such as yourself, Gutan, a man who never expected to find himself here."

Gutan lowered his gaze.

God looked at Orbust, said, "And you, Johnny Orbust, are the one who sabotaged the other ships. That was a rotten trick, and I was weakened considerably by the task of making them spaceworthy again."

"Does that mean I'm out of the running for your job?" Orbust asked. "I'm not saying I want it or that I could handle it, but I was just wondering. I assume Gutan is out of the running as well?"

"Every one of you qualifies," God said.

God didn't explain this last, but it seemed to McMurtrey that if Gutan and the atheist Yakkai qualified—if he, Evander McMurtrey of chicken fraud infamy, qualified— then so too should Johnny Orbust.

"I had hoped the other ships would be here with yours," Tananius-Ofo said. "So many excellent God candidates aboard. But all had problems with their Gluons and were forced to turn back. We got a bad batch this time, which happens every once in a while. Gluons of particular types tend to cluster. It's very frustrating! You experienced some problems with Shusher, but he isn't nearly as troublesome as the others. We're lucky he was available."

"The damaged whipping passageway didn't force those ships back?" McMurtrey asked.

"No. A portion of the passageway is damaged but passable. The rest of the fleet never even got to that region, where they might have proceeded with care."

The D'Urthians gazed upon Tananius-Ofo, and to McMurtrey it was like the calming effect of gazing over a great expanse of water.

"Well, children," God said tenderly, "it's only the nine of you. As for Shusher and Appy, they're ineligible synthetics. No artificial ingredients for this assignment! Now, are there any volunteers?"

At the base of the cliff, far, far below the Perch of God, Jin was a crushed and broken array of bioelectronics, scattered across jagged gray and black stones. It was a silent and barren place, without a plant, an insect or any other form of biological life. Other than Jin, that is, for the last redundancy remained intact, transmitting red noise signals to nearby parts.

The parts sought the signal, approached it like flecks of iron to a magnet. They combined with nearby bits of dirt and stone, forming an amorphous, pale yellow ball of material—a clump of technologically enhanced aural clay. From within this clump came little bursts of energy that pushed the surface outward, like an anxious-to-be-born fetus kicking against its mother's womb.

The clump began to take shape, slowly at first, then more rapidly, and an afterbirth of pale yellow membrane peeled away, revealing Jin substantially as he had been before.

This version of bioelectronics came with a design improvement: Fleshy, glandular pads were on the bottoms of the feet, pads that flattened and gave off sticky secretions when walked upon.

Jin began scaling the sheer cliff like a fly, his bare feet adhering to the surface.

Thirteen

Life is an eclectic collection of loose ends, sacrificed and forgotten.

—Tananius-Ofo, a note left
in the Crystal Library

"There is only one true church of God," Tananius-Ofo said, "and I run it. I haven't run it very well of late, but . . ." He cleared his throat, looked away. His eyes welled with tears.

"I have an idea, sir," McMurtrey said, making himself more comfortable on his pillow. "Why don't you return to D'Urth with us? We'll nurse you back to health with the love you deserve. The whole star system will draw together to pull you through this. Let us help you as you've helped us."

"What a nice thought," God said, "but I'm afraid it's impossible." He wiped his eyes.

"But why?"

"Cease! I've made arrangements for a last party and that's it. Enough is enough! Now, decide which of you it's to be and I'll be on my way. Shusher can drop me at one of my little hidey-holes on the way to D'Urth, just a short detour. Everything is prepared and waiting for me. It can't be changed, don't you see?"

"How is your successor to be determined?" McMurtrey asked.

"I'll leave that to you," Tananius-Ofo said, with a wry smile.

"Well," McMurtrey said, "could we begin by asking you a few questions to sort our thoughts out? It's been said that the only great truth is that life is meaningless. Is this true, Lord? What is the meaning of life?"

"I can entertain only one more question from each of you," God said. "You've asked yours, McMurtrey. Mmmm. Okay: That which is most important need not be spoken about; that which is most important cannot be spoken about. There are no lines when you reach the Place of Truth, for you can count on your fingers those who have truly been there."

When it became clear that this was Tananius-Ofo's complete answer, McMurtrey thanked him, and without fully understanding the words, set to memorizing them.

"May I go next?" Orbust asked, glancing around.

They nodded and gestured him on.

"Is God allowed to get angry sometimes and swear?" Orbust asked, smiling sheepishly. "Not the deepest question, I suppose, but it seems like we spend our lives watching what we say. I know I have. Is that question too trivial?"

God laughed. "No question is too trivial, for every tiny piece in the universe fits together. As God I can do anything I want to do, for I make the rules. I curse occasionally when I'm angry, sometimes even when I'm not angry, just to hear the words. Would you like to hear some of it?"

"No, sir. I was just, uh—I wish I had asked something else."

"How would you like me to kill or maim your slimy little wimpshit ass?"

The onlookers gasped.

Orbust nearly fell off his pillow.

McMurtrey caught his breath. This wasn't God! He couldn't use language like that!

Cast out all preconceptions.

Tananius-Ofo smiled. "You're all thinking I wouldn't say that if I were really God. But I say to you, what do you know for sure? You spend a few billion years in charge and see what you have to say."

Yakkai was next, asked, "Appy said you were critical of self-serving prayer, sir. I'd like to hear more from you about that."

"I overheard your comments about organized religion," God said, "about priests using fear tactics to keep their flocks in line. Some may think it odd that I agree with an atheist, but I must tell you that all the human religions are

like unauthorized or butchered biographies of me. . . .
Here and there a few truths, but full of errors. There is,
as I said, only one true church of God. I don't believe in
priests or artificial hierarchies, for such systems change my
words to suit their own power games, their own purposes.
Sometimes there are so many unauthorized religious tenets
and rites that it's nearly impossible to separate gold from
mud."

"I can't tell you how much it means to me to hear you
say that," Yakkai said.

"To help you sort some of it out, remember this: If
several religions agree on a particular doctrine, it is likely
that the doctrine is true. Cast aside minor dogmatic differences, lay one major doctrine over another and find the
commonality. Many faiths believe in God, for example,
but disagree over trivial points, over picayune religious
stories. Cast aside the trivial points, and what do you
have?"

"Truth," Yakkai said grudgingly.

"Quite often. Many religious disputes, even wars, are
attributable to conflicting religious stories. Certain prophets are said to have done this or that, and an elaborate
framework and power structure is hinged upon their words
and deeds. I won't say which prophets I actually contacted
and which were frauds, for you didn't ask that, did you?"

"No, Your Reverence, I didn't." Yakkai bowed his
head.

"There should be an organized religion," God said, "but
only one."

"Is this the center of the universe?" Feek the Afsornian
asked.

"Mmmm. I sense that we are on the point of singularity,
the place where the Big Bang originated. It's not coinci-
dental that I'm here where it all started. Oh, it's different
now than when I arrived. . . . I shaped this planet to my
wishes and tastes. I won't go into all the clues that tell me
everything must have started here, for that's quite a complex matter. Everything in the universe is expanding outward from this planet's center of mass, but not
symmetrically, not identically sized pieces traveling at
identical speeds at perfect angles. Yes, this is the 'center,'
but one would have to know what he was looking for to

find it. This is the point in the universe where all parallel lines intersect."

"Thank you," the black man said.

"Can a female god do as good a job as a male god?" Corona asked. "Can a female god do a better job?"

"Tsk, tsk," God said. "Two questions! This universe has had female gods, somewhat as described in ancient human mythology. You could have this job, Corona, and so could you, Zatima—if that is determined. And I'm sure either of you would do a better job than I've done."

Very diplomatic, McMurtrey thought.

"My religion has long scoffed at the Wessornian deity concept of an old man in the sky," Makanji said. "Thankfully you do not have a beard, and do not reside in the Wessornian concept of Heaven. My question has been answered, sir, for I wondered what you looked like. As you suggested, you don't have to look like this; it was a choice you made."

"I trust my appearance does not displease you?"

"Oh, no," Makanji said. He and God exchanged excellent smiles.

"Here's a little secret," Tananius-Ofo said. "In appearance I have two principal differences from D'Urth humans. My skin is gray, and there's a little something about my tongue."

A slender white thread emerged from God's mouth, and this thread expanded into a net that spun in the air and ensnared Corona. Quickly the net slipped off the startled woman, became a thread once more and returned to God's mouth.

"My angels used to call me 'Netman,'" Tananius-Ofo said, with a smile. "Just a little something I set up for amusement. Great fun at parties. Think I'll use it to catch a little lady at my last wingding."

"Very impressive," Corona said.

"A few men and women in history have had tongues like mine," God said, "but not for centuries. I discontinued the accessory, as people were constantly tripping over their own tongues."

"Seriously?" McMurtrey asked.

God's eyes twinkled.

Now Taam the Hoddhist priest spoke, to ask, "I've been

wondering lately if we were brought here to remove the religious battles from D'Urth, if we were supposed to fight it out in deep space and get it over with once and for all. I didn't bring any weapons for such an occasion, but I couldn't help noticing that others did."

God shook his head. "I did consider a Great Debate, one *without* Orbustian Snapcards! The winner would have become God. That might have worked if all the ships had made it, and I suppose you could debate it out now anyway and I could judge the proceeding. But that would be time- and energy-consuming, so I'd prefer another way. Why don't you all draw lots?"

"To become God?" McMurtrey said incredulously. From the expressions of others in the room, he saw that they shared his disbelief.

"Sure, why not?" Tananius-Ofo said. "How do you think I got here?"

"That explains a lot," Yakkai said.

God heard this, and looked at Yakkai ferociously, causing the atheist to tremble.

"You're referring to certain . . . glitches?" God said.

"Why lie?" Yakkai said. "Yes, I was. Primarily to the 'glitches' that allow human and animal suffering to continue. Those communication breakdowns you've had are unfortunate, too, where your messages are either lost in translation or changed intentionally after you have passed them on to prophets."

"You're either a brave man or a foolish one," Tananius-Ofo said.

Yakkai couldn't control his muscles, became a mass of trembling flesh. Curiously, his face did not betray fear. It was angry, defiant.

"You know I'm doing that to you, don't you?" God said.

"Yes!" Yakkai shouted. "I'm not afraid of you!"

The Lord's stern face broke into a wide, gummy smile, and Yakkai's trembling went away. "I was just kidding," God said. "We didn't draw lots. We drew laser pistols! Naw, none of that happened. Without regard to the past—for this a different situation—what do you think should be done here to select a new God? It's up to you to decide."

"I didn't get my question," Zatima said timidly.

"And so you didn't!" God said, with surprising cheer. "Well, let's have it!"

"Why does Appy laugh like that? I mean, he sounds insane, and it's been very disquieting on the journey here."

"Appy laughs at the utter folly of humankind. Every once in a while it just strikes his funnycircuits and he has to let fly a good one. That's all there is to it."

"Not quite," Yakkai said impertinently, "for humans are reflections of their God."

God scowled, but for only a moment before the gummy smile returned. "In my younger years, when I was hot-headed, I would have skewered you for that. I've mellowed out, luckily for you."

"No matter whom we select," Yakkai said, "that person will likely continue much of the same foibles, for we have only humans in the running."

"Ah!" God said. "That is correct, but it is not correct! Remember I said I selected this form for humans and for myself? Without going into all the trade secrets involved with being God, I assure you there are options."

Yakkai rubbed his chin, said, "In the beginning, I presume this new God will be human. Other choices of form will be less familiar to him, and he's likely to continue in the form he is most familiar with, the most comfortable form."

"Perhaps." God looked at Gutan, who had not yet asked his question.

Gutan appeared to be in some pain, was rubbing the knuckle above his severed finger. "I'll pass," he said.

"Come now," God said. "Surely there must be something you'd like to know, something to help you decide whether or not you want the Big Job? That pain in your missing finger, for example. Wouldn't you like to know how to end it?"

"I wouldn't ask such a question. I deserve whatever pain I have."

"Penance, eh? Mmmm. As God, you could end your own pain."

"I wouldn't want to, unless I could end everyone's. If I were God, this pain would be my reminder."

"Bravo," Yakkai said.

"Sort of like a string around your finger," Tananius-Ofo remarked.

"When I entered Mnemo," Gutan said, "I suppose I was searching for a purpose to my life. I felt terrible about what I was, wanted to recapture old events and make them right where they had been wrong. Silly thoughts, for the events had already occurred and couldn't be changed—"

"Do you want to ask that question?" God asked. "You don't sound very certain."

"—No. I definitely wanted to go back, back, and back some more in memory, all the way to the beginning of everything, back to the Mother or Father of It All. Back to the primal memory of God, I suppose. I've always understood death more than life. It was like . . ." He sighed. "I embalmed people at first, later executed them, and all the while I made love to the dead—I inseminated the dead! My whole life surrounded death. I didn't want to die in the machine. I wanted to live, and live differently. It was a continuum I wanted to reverse, I suppose. From an emphasis on death and after-death, I wanted to find life. But I couldn't go directly to life. I had to skip to birth, even to pre-birth, and that was available only through the machine. I'm not making a lot of sense, and there isn't much time. I'm sorry."

"You wanted to find the Creator," God said. "And the Creator was supposed to provide you with all the answers. I'm supposed to be your guru."

"Something like that."

"Man needs to learn by experience," God said. "Primarily his own experience. That's one of the great successes in the processes I set in motion: seeing a person advance through his own efforts, seeing him overcome adversity, often rising from his own bile . . . seeing him succeed when the odds were heavily against him. You've reached me, Gutan, through a somewhat circuitous route, but you're here. And I don't have all the answers you need. There is no pot of gold at the end of the rainbow, no crutch with a capital C for you to lean on. You've got to do it yourself. The few words of wisdom I could offer you aren't going to turn things around. You've got to *want* to turn things around, and you've got to do it for yourself. No God could do it for you."

"I find myself able to think a long way back in time," Gutan said. "For the first time I'm wondering how future generations will view me, what the judgment of history will be about Harley Gutan. Every instant of my life is a focal point, I suppose, where I'm delicately balanced between my ancestors and my grandchildren. I pray for the wisdom of the ancients and the forgiveness of generations yet unborn. I don't want to be God. I don't qualify, for the things I need to do are on D'Urth. I need to go back and see if I can find some normalcy. I want to have grandchildren. I want normal relationships."

Gutan paused, smiled. "Sounds pretty dull, huh?"

"Some of the best things are dull," Tananius-Ofo said.

Gutan spoke briskly, nervously: "Is it possible for me, with all the terrible things I've done in my life, to find God?"

"You're here, aren't you?" God said.

"What do you mean? Oh! But can't you—"

"Only one question per person," God said. "Next!"

"That's everyone," McMurtrey said.

"When you asked your question about the meaning of life," Tananius-Ofo said, looking at McMurtrey, "you didn't know I would only allow one more question per person. Had you known, I sense you might have asked another. I'm not checking your thoughts now, just using rather normal senses. If this is the case, I should allow you another question. I mention this because I don't want it said that in the end I wasn't fair."

Surprised at this, McMurtrey thought for a moment. "I have many questions," he said after a time. "I don't know if I would have asked another first. I too wish to be fair. If I'm the one who becomes God, I don't want it said about me that in the beginning I wasn't fair."

Tananius-Ofo laughed.

"It is laudable of you to say that," God said. "But I insist, and I'm still the boss. Go ahead with one more, and that will be the last."

McMurtrey glanced at Corona, as if to ask her permission for this holy favor. Her expression urged him on.

"What are the duties and obligations of God?" McMurtrey asked.

Tananius-Ofo smiled. "Gods should behave in certain

predictable ways, to avoid chaos. Periods of chaos occur
when the wrong God or gods take power, or when humans
do not understand the nature of these deities. I must reveal
to you that my illness has been causing me to lose more
and more ground in this universe. As I said, there is no
Satan throwing his weight around, leading the forces of
darkness. I wasn't entirely candid, however. Other gods,
good and bad—entities from within this universe and outside it—have been trying to extend their domains. Power
is never a static thing. It increases, decreases and changes
in scope all the time. This is an unchanging rule of the
universe.

"Each universe can have one or several gods. All of you
or only one of you could do it. At various times in history
there have been single gods and multiple gods. Look at
ancient D'Urthian mythology and the multiple gods of
some of your religions—most of those recorded events
never occurred. But some of them did. The whole history
has been confused pretty badly."

From a reservoir of McMurtrey's soul, Tananius-Ofo's
words echoed through his brain.

"Some of the god entities still live in varying degrees,"
God said, "and a number of them want their old jobs back.
I took power from a pantheon of gods. They asked me to
take charge, transferred their powers to me. But not all
of the gods agreed with this majority opinion. Some were
tossed out."

"Fired?" Yakkai asked.

God nodded. "Power, once achieved, is difficult to relinquish. I've wrestled with the subject for millenia, since
realizing I wanted out. The gods who were forced out have
been discovering methods of restoring their powers. Even
now they are mounting an assault against me."

"A physical assault?" Corona asked.

"I'll put it this way. They would if they could."

"You haven't made this sound very attractive," Zatima
said.

"The truth rarely is," God said. "Reality is a splash of
cold water, a harsh awakening. Well, ladies and gentlemen, who's it going to be?"

A very long period of silence followed, lasting at least
five D'Urth minutes.

"What about your famous prophets?" Orbust asked. "Wouldn't one of them have been a better choice?"

"You've run out of questions," Tananius-Ofo answered. "We really must move along. I'm sorry."

"You asked for volunteers," McMurtrey said. "I'd like to volunteer."

"Are you sure?" Corona whispered to him.

McMurtrey didn't look at her, felt sad for not doing so. But he had made his decision, didn't want to look back. There would be no temptations. But God spoke of women. Did that mean . . .

God can set up anything, McMurtrey thought. *I could have a harem here. Or just Kelly. But Kelly is strong, maybe too strong. It wouldn't work out. . . .*

God smiled upon McMurtrey, asked, "Are there any others?"

None spoke up.

"Then it's settled," Tananius-Ofo said, looking at Corona. "You folks can drop me off at my party and that'll be it."

"I'm—I'm God now?" McMurtrey asked. "I don't feel any different."

"There are a few formalities," Tananius-Ofo said. "And you won't simply be 'God.' I'll dub thee 'McGod.' "

McMurtrey smiled, stiffly. He still didn't feel any different.

"I'm glad you're the one, McMurtrey. You've been my first choice since I decided to transfer power."

"Could I still back out?" McMurtrey felt railroaded, as if the people in the room with him had been conscripted by God to deceive him. Were they all conspirators? Kelly too? At least one or two others should have wanted to become God! But no matter the answer to any of this, McMurtrey had no real thought of reversing his decision. He needed a challenge like this, felt he could handle it as well as anyone else.

"No way out now," God said tersely. "That's it. You have to do it. Just kidding. Sure, you can change your mind any time you feel like it. But I don't think you will. If I thought you would, if I thought you weren't qualified for the position, I wouldn't tell you the trade secrets I'm about to reveal to you. After I take a little rest, for this

has been most wearisome, you and I will enter the Crystal
Library for the Power Transfer Ceremony."

When God awoke from a brief nap, he took McMurtrey
aside, into a very large side-chamber. Behind them, the
way they had entered closed noiselessly, into apparently
solid rock. This left no visible way out, which McMurtrey
found unsettling.

"You'll have to reopen it yourself," God said. "You'd
better hope I show you how before I drop dead!" He
chuckled.

The chamber was lined floor to ceiling with shelved
books, of a most unusual variety. They appeared to be of
clear prismatic glass and were very large, with pages of
black print visible through crystal covers that threw lovely
spectrums of blue light around the room. The spine of
each book was at least the height of McMurtrey, and he
struggled to read the titles. They appeared to be in Unglish, but he was too flustered to focus. One volume lay
open on a whiterock table at the center of the room.

"You've come a long way for a guy who used to run
around with a chicken on your shoulder," God said.

McMurtrey smiled.

"These are the greatest books in the universe," God
explained, "culled from the minds of men and gods to
form my incomparable Crystal Library. These are composite God- and human-channeled editions, created in
much the same way that I assisted you to create the fleet
of ships. Throughout my career I channeled the thoughts
of the greatest minds, bringing their words to these volumes—as ideas change, words and pages change. Sometimes I do it with the consent of the contributor and
sometimes I just do it. Whatever it takes to get the information."

"Are Gluons involved here?" McMurtrey asked. "I
mean, didn't we channel images onto the Gluon Shusher,
impregnating the Gluon with matter?"

"The book materials are impregnated onto cousins of
the Gluons," God said, "known as Sools. Unfortunately,
Gluons like to travel too much, and that would never do
here. They're inveterate tourists, so library books would

forever be missing, off in some distant quadrant of the universe!"

"I can understand how you'd feel that way."

"I know you're afraid of what's about to happen, Evander, but wash away your fear and accept this. It is said that we fear most what we least understand. Come forth, understand and fear no more."

McMurtrey was told to stand over the table and read the first chapter of the book there. He did this, while Tananius-Ofo climbed a librarian's ladder slowly, sat at the top and looked on. The black-etched words on each page should have been difficult to read, since the pages were clear and vitreous, but a foggy haze appeared beneath the top page's words the moment McMurtrey began reading, a haziness that made the proper words stand out in clear relief.

He felt like a trainee assigned to read a training manual, but did not complain.

As he reached the end of each right-hand page, the page turned automatically, and as he became immersed in the contents of the volume, the pages turned faster and faster.

"This is incredible," McMurtrey kept saying. "Absolutely incredible. I can't believe this! Wow!"

In a very short time he completed the chapter and gazed up at Tananius-Ofo.

The old man sitting atop the ladder had his chin resting on his hands, and looked impish. He beamed at McMurtrey. "Now you understand the basics of godmanship," he said. "The way of miracles, transmitting voice across the universe, how to defend against attack, how to attack if necessary, how to shape-shift planetary materials. None of it is that complicated, and I believe you are a quick study. Of course you'll need to practice the techniques, for every god soon learns that 'practice makes better.'"

"I'd like to try something simple to begin with," McMurtrey said, "but I didn't see how to do it. If I wanted to bring something here from across the universe—nothing large or complex—uhh, say my pet chicken from D'Urth—how would I do that?"

"Chapter Three," God said. "For a cargo that small,

may I recommend a tiny oxygen-saturated bubble impregnated on a baby Gluon?"

"There are other ways of doing it?"

"Countless ways! Permit me to demonstrate this one?"

"Please do," McMurtrey said.

"I only wish I had the time or energy to demonstrate every technique for you, but I'm not up to it. Don't worry, you'll pick it up anyway."

Tananius-Ofo climbed down the ladder arthritically, and when he reached the floor he began turning his body around and around. Faster and faster he went, spinning until his features could no longer be seen and he was a beautiful, whirling blue groundflower, flashing white and silver.

Like a spinning top, he spun around the room, circled McMurtrey and then zeroed in on McMurtrey and spun wildly toward him. McMurtrey tried to get out of the way, but God's mellifluous voice called to Him, "Fear not, McGod! Come forth, understand and fear no more!"

Now McMurtrey went awhirling in the blue ball, and he learned the arcane way of transporting No Name across the universe. For an instant McMurtrey expanded in a brilliant supernova and became all living things that had ever existed or ever would exist. One cell from the Organism of Mankind—a boy living in St. Charles Beach—took No Name to the bubble and placed the chicken inside.

"Life is not composed of segments, as seen by the parochial observer," McGod said, his first pronouncement: "All life, all time and all events comprise a single unfolding day."

"It is so," Tananius-Ofo said.

"I see that life forms are not what they appear to be," McGod said, to God emeritus. "They are not sacks of skin. The multidimensional sensory images transmitted from one to another are false, and this is a problem I must face one day."

"High energy," Tananius-Ofo said, "that is the key to survival and is, as well, the means of destruction. High energy created the first elements of life, the inchoate god-forms."

"And that first spark, was it caused by an excess of matter over antimatter?" McGod asked.

"Perhaps you will discover the secret one day. I never did. Funny, it's like the war-mobilized nations of old D'Urth. No matter how technologically advanced a nation became, there always seemed to emerge a nation with something new, something more deadly. So it is in the cosmos. No matter how much a god knows, there is always the unknown, inevitably a god or other life form out there that knows more. Thus you must remain on constant vigil, never letting your defenses down, always searching for the newest, latest piece of knowledge. Nothing is final."

"Continuing education?"

"You expected easy?"

"No, but it makes me tired just thinking about it," McGod said.

"You ain't seen nothin' yet," Tananius-Ofo replied. His voice betrayed great relief.

When Tananius-Ofo and McGod emerged from the spinning groundflower, McGod smelled sweetness, as though a spring D'Urth breeze were blowing across flower blossoms. He breathed deeply, felt the calmness of eternity.

McGod felt perfect. Ahead lay a long, long lifetime of work, of learning, of teaching, and he felt equal to the challenge.

Just imagine how good this job will look on my resume, he thought. *Prior employment: God of the Universe. Yeah*!

"I don't know how to read your mind yet," McGod said. "Even if I did, I don't know that I'd presume to do so. Tell me, please, did you put the idea of a Cosmic Chicken in my mind? Did you pull a little prank on me with that?" One edge of his mouth curled up, the precursor of a smile.

"With all due respect, I've answered all the questions I agreed to. Life is the sorting of priorities and acting upon those decisions. I have something to say that is more important than the answer to your question. Forgive the impertinence of an old man. It is this: Even in the midst of contentious gods and other life forms that you will learn about, beware most the D'Urthian Bureau of Loyalty. One day you may have to do something about them."

"I will study the matter."

"As my successor, McGod, I hope you'll keep what I

started essentially in place, that you'll promote my programs."

"I assume I'll develop plenty of my own programs too."

Tananius-Ofo appeared dismayed. "Yes, such is your right. But before you toss out anything I've done, study it in detail. All my reasons are documented in the crystal volumes. My thoughts are here beside those of the greatest minds who ever lived, for I was one of the great thinkers. Don't listen to my enemies, for their motives are impure! Even the form of man and the modified net-tongue form I selected were carefully thought out decisions."

"I won't do anything hastily," McGod assured him.

"An associated caveat: The longer you remain in the first godform chosen after assuming the mantle of godship, the more difficult it will be for you to change to anything else. So if you select a nonhuman form for yourself, or even a modified human form, be prepared to stick with that decision. It is called the Persistence of Godform, and is one of the Lost Secrets held by rival gods. They may try to use it against you as they tried against me, offering to allow you to change form in exchange for some or all of your god powers."

"How long do I have before I must decide?"

Tananius-Ofo touched the open volume on the table. "Read Chapter Two," he said.

In his reading of the first chapter, McGod learned the secret of planetary shape-shifting, and he employed this technique to reopen the doorway of the chamber.

"Nicely done," Tananius-Ofo said.

They emerged from the chamber arm-in-arm, approached the waiting D'Urthians.

"It's done," McGod said. He told them his new name, and they smiled with him, ever so gently so as not to offend.

"You look the same," Corona said. "I expected you to glow or something. Your skin is even peach-pink, not the gray of Tananius-Ofo."

"He's much younger," Tananius-Ofo said, with a broad, gummy smile. "Now into the ship and let's—"

Tananius-Ofo slumped, and McGod held him up for a moment before lowering him gently to the floor. The old man's eyes flashed in twin white sparks, then became blue and dead, staring into eternity.

"T.O.!" McGod exclaimed. "Oh, no, I don't know how to save him! I must learn, I must learn!"

He ran back to the Crystal Library, flipped wildly through the pages of the volume on the table. It was all a blur. He couldn't focus, couldn't see anything he needed. "Was it in one of the other volumes? Might it be one of the Lost Secrets, in enemy hands?"

Corona was at his side, and she placed an arm over his shoulder. "He wouldn't want you to bring him back," she said.

"Long live McGod," Harley Gutan said, from the other chamber.

McGod sat on the floor and wept openly. "I'm terrified," he said. "I have so much to learn."

Fourteen

People see what they want to see, just as they believe
what they want to believe, no matter the mountains of
contradictory evidence before them.

—From The Autobiography
of Tananius-Ofo

At McGod's instruction, Yakkai and Gutan carried Tananius-Ofo to the Empire couch, where the body was laid down gently and covered with the royal blue robe. There Tananius-Ofo would repose until the new Leader of the Universe determined how best to dispose of his predecessor's remains.

"Now I must ask you to leave for D'Urth," McGod said. "There is much work for me to do in the Crystal Library."

All bade goodbye and good will to McGod, and he wished them a safe journey. "I'm going to find the section on Omniscience," McGod said, "and after that will come Omnipotence. Thus will I watch over you and care for you on your return flight."

"You're starting to sound godly," Corona remarked, with a caring smile. "I can tell you have a sense about yourself now, a new feeling of confidence. I'm proud of you!"

"Thank you, Kelly."

McGod felt himself detaching from Corona, as if he were cloistering himself. It didn't have to be that way, for Tananius-Ofo had mentioned his own weakness for women, albeit without telling whether he had acted upon such urgings. The information might be in the great library, in journal or diary form. McGod envisioned himself creating copious files on himself, for he was an important person now and there would be all the time in the universe to make it just right.

McGod wouldn't lie, wouldn't gloss over the historical documentation, for that would be a most unseemly thing to do. But he didn't think he wanted to be perfect, either. Tananius-Ofo hadn't made himself flawless, and somewhere in the library were the reasons for this.

If I'm to be imperfect, in what way should it be? A tiny lie here and there in the Journal of McGod? What about that idea of a harem? Maybe wanting to be perfect, and the very act of becoming perfect, are imperfections per se. What curious thoughts!

"May I kiss you goodbye?" Corona asked. She was near him, having approached while he was deep in thought. The old proclivity for daydreaming hadn't changed yet.

"What? Oh, yes, go ahead." He leaned down, allowed her to peck him on the cheek.

McGod felt like hugging her, felt like telling her how much he still loved her, that he would give all this up instantly in favor of her. But he couldn't do that, couldn't leave the shop empty. Never again could he concern himself with personal happiness.

But hadn't he chosen this position in order to be happy? Why had he volunteered? It had been an impulsive decision, he realized, and in the wake of it McGod didn't know the answers to his own questions. This struck him as simultaneously frightening and funny. He still had questions to ask of God.

Corona and the others were entering the passageway to leave, waving, and part of McGod wanted to run after them, to be just like them. He turned away, and when he looked back they were gone.

The small party of travelers stood at the entrance to the caverns, with Makanji in the lead, surveying the ledge.

"It's impassable," he said. "A section of ledge has fallen away—must be where Jin fell."

They took turns surveying the ledge, and all agreed that they could not reach the ship. Just as they were about to return to McGod for help, the ship came to life, and in a smooth whir of noise it extricated itself from the cliff face where it had been perched. It flew the short distance to

Corona and the others, secured itself to a new spot on the ledge, and positioned its ramp for easy access.

All passed over the ramp into the ship, except Corona, who lingered at the cavern entrance.

"Let's go!" Appy's voice blared, across the ship's P.A. system. "No way to recover lost time!"

"I'm staying!" Corona shouted. She swept one arm across her body, indicating they should take off.

With hardly a moment's hesitation, Shusher's ramp was withdrawn and the pomegranate-shaped ship rose toward the white sky, bouncing a high-pitched whine off the cliff walls. There were faces in the windows, and waving hands.

She found him in the Crystal Library, leaning over a huge crystal book spread open upon the table.

"We've some redecorating to do on this planet," Corona said.

The startled look on McGod's face indicated he hadn't yet learned the secret of Omniscience.

"You're not supposed to be here!" he said, in a scolding tone. But she could tell he was glad to see her.

"Neither are you!" she retorted.

They laughed, the first good laugh of McGod's new reign, and McGod heard the laughter carry through the caverns of his domain. It was a good thing, laughter, cutting as it did through the colorlessness of the place. But Tananius-Ofo had a reason for making his planet this way. Somewhere in the library . . .

"Are you going to declare Cosmic Chickenhood the official, one and only religion?" she asked.

"I'll have to think about that."

Corona glided effortlessly across the floor, as if in a magical dream, and they embraced.

"I have some rough thoughts, a radical concept," he said. "Tons of details to work out. I'd like to reprogram mankind to nonviolence. I think the answer may be tied in with biocomputers, with Gutan's experiences and with the work of Professor Pelter on Mnemo. It's linked as well with D'Urth's BOL and their work on cyberoos. Somehow I've got to break through the BOL cloak and find good people in that organization who will help me. There must be some good ones there, and if there are, I'll find them."

"Maybe it's like a computer programming problem," Corona said. "I have some experience with that. The human brain needs to be erased or deprogrammed. . . . Maybe we could come up with new pathways for electrochemical impulses to follow."

"Just think of it, Kelly! A new and wonderful human being, one who acts lovingly to everyone. Humanity becomes a beautiful collective life force that enhances all living things around it. For the first time, harmony between man and environment."

"We'll figure it out, darling."

He looked at her, smiled. "*We* will, eh?"

"Sure. I want to help."

"As for the ICCC, I don't know. A new religion is coming into perspective—one that will end all the foolish clashes of ideology. I think I'll call it . . . Novarianism. It's a cosmic church that builds no edifices to itself, a church without a priesthood, without a power structure. It's full of the new humans I want to create, the ones who are pure of heart. They don't need buildings to pray in, don't believe in pouring money into structures and then sitting at services once a week. This is money and time misspent, and they should spend each Sabbath doing community work for the poor . . . painting houses and improving structural safety, helping anyone who needs it. Novarians will pray outside, staring into the evening sky. And when they do that, when they do it right, I'll see to it that one of my biggest stars goes nova in a brilliant burst of color to fill their minds with wonder. It will be a faith these humans have never before imagined! I see a new Heaven and a new D'Urth. . . . The old images will pass away!"

Corona giggled. "A question for McGod, please."

"Call me Ev. On second thought, better not. McGod is best."

"I was just thinking of a star I had named after me when I was a little girl. For a fee, my name was printed in the Star Registry. But the damned—uh, sorry—the star went nova. It blew up and I cried for days. I wondered after I grew up, should I have asked for a refund?"

"You're suggesting I should concern myself with correcting the smallest of wrongs?"

"I don't know. But if you're going to blow up a lot of stars, just think of the problems it could cause."

"I'll have to think that through," McGod said. "I know! I'll create a new star and blow it up within moments, before anyone can name it, before the life forms of planets can grow to depend on it. I'm sure all the instructions are somewhere in the crystal books Tananius-Ofo left me."

Corona smiled. "Don't forget communication, darling, for that seems to have been a principal failing of dear old Tananius-Ofo. He passed his messages on to prophets, and in the dissemination process important details were lost in translation or intentionally distorted. At the end, his only hope was probably to combine the various religious stories and try to 'sell' them as a new Great Story that included many parts. It would have been a formidable task."

"You're right."

"Don't forget the Apostles, either—those seven who knew you are heading back to D'Urth at this very moment. But they have no message from on high; you've told them virtually nothing. Mark my words, they'll talk anyway. Some will claim to have been closest to you, and volumes of your pronouncements will be published. They'll dredge up things you said on D'Urth and aboard Shusher. There will be distortions no matter your efforts."

"Well, we've got some new technological gadgets that old Tananius didn't have when he started out. He could always use the Big Voice on one or two people at a time, or even a few thousand, but apparently he never had the power or the energy required to speak to trillions simultaneously. Maybe a simple radio or televid in every house, connected to me, and the folks will get straight-skinny from me every morning."

"Put your hands on the radio," Corona intoned, "and say I believe, I believe!"

"Smart aleck. Maybe I'll use a radio receiver that's implanted in their brains shortly after birth."

"Sounds like a police state to me. And what about Free Will? You could crush that with your new and improved human. Maybe you'd be intruding too much with those ideas—pardon me for saying so."

"I'm going to reshape mankind!" McGod exclaimed. "There are tradeoffs!"

"I don't know," she said, with a great sigh. "We'll talk about it, darling."

McGod thought for a long while, after which he said, "I only want to know one thing, Kelly. Are you after my job?"

Corona smiled sweetly, did not reply.

MULTI-MILLION COPY
BESTSELLING AUTHOR OF DUNE!

FRANK
HERBERT

___ THE ASCENSION FACTOR* 0-441-03127-7/$4.50
___ THE LAZARUS EFFECT*   0-441-47521-3/$4.50
___ THE JESUS INCIDENT*   0-441-38539-7/$4.95
___ MAN OF TWO WORLDS*   0-441-51857-5/$4.50
___ DESTINATION: VOID   0-441-14302-4/$3.95
___ THE DOSADI EXPERIMENT 0-441-16027-1/$3.95
___ THE WHITE PLAGUE   0-441-88569-1/$4.95
___ EYE   0-441-22374-5/$3.95

*By Frank Herbert and Bill Ransom

For Visa and MasterCard orders call: 1-800-631-8571

FOR MAIL ORDERS: CHECK BOOK(S). FILL
OUT COUPON. SEND TO:

BERKLEY PUBLISHING GROUP
390 Murray Hill Pkwy., Dept. B
East Rutherford, NJ 07073

NAME_____

ADDRESS _____

CITY_____

STATE_____ZIP_____

PLEASE ALLOW 6 WEEKS FOR DELIVERY.
PRICES ARE SUBJECT TO CHANGE

POSTAGE AND HANDLING:
$1.00 for one book, 25¢ for each ad-
ditional. Do not exceed $3.50.

BOOK TOTAL $ _____

POSTAGE & HANDLING $ _____

APPLICABLE SALES TAX $ _____
(CA, NJ, NY, PA)

TOTAL AMOUNT DUE $ _____

PAYABLE IN US FUNDS.
(No cash orders accepted.)

275

Frank Herbert

The All-time Bestselling
DUNE
MASTERWORKS

__DUNE	0-441-17266-0/$4.95
__DUNE MESSIAH	0-441-17269-5/$4.95
__CHILDREN OF DUNE	0-441-10402-9/$4.95
__GOD EMPEROR OF DUNE	0-441-29467-7/$4.95
__HERETICS OF DUNE	0-441-32800-8/$4.95
__CHAPTERHOUSE DUNE	0-441-10267-0/$4.95

For Visa and MasterCard orders call: 1-800-631-8571

FOR MAIL ORDERS: CHECK BOOK(S). FILL
OUT COUPON. SEND TO:

BERKLEY PUBLISHING GROUP
390 Murray Hill Pkwy., Dept. B
East Rutherford, NJ 07073

NAME_____

ADDRESS_____

CITY_____

STATE_____ZIP_____

PLEASE ALLOW 6 WEEKS FOR DELIVERY.
PRICES ARE SUBJECT TO CHANGE WITHOUT NOTICE.

POSTAGE AND HANDLING:
$1.00 for one book, 25¢ for each ad-
ditional. Do not exceed $3.50.

BOOK TOTAL	$ _____
POSTAGE & HANDLING	$ _____
APPLICABLE SALES TAX	$ _____
(CA, NJ, NY, PA)	
TOTAL AMOUNT DUE	$ _____

PAYABLE IN US FUNDS.
(No cash orders accepted.)

253